7/17
Rep. copy

D0394482

T F

THE MESSENGER

STEPHEN MILLER

DELACORTE PRESS / NEW YORK

THE MESSENGER

A NOVEL

The Messenger is a work of fiction. Names, characters, places, and incidents either are the products of the author's imagination or are used fictitiously. Any resemblance to actual persons, living or dead, events, or locales is entirely coincidental.

Copyright © 2012 by Stephen Miller

Published in the United States by Delacorte Press, an imprint of The Random House Publishing Group, a division of Random House, Inc., New York.

DELACORTE PRESS is a registered trademark of Random House, Inc., and the colophon is a trademark of Random House, Inc.

ISBN 978-0-345-52847-6
eBook ISBN 978-0-345-52848-3

Printed in the United States of America on acid-free paper

www.bantamdell.com

2 4 6 8 9 7 5 3 1

First Edition

Book design by Susan Turner

For my brother

*The highest form of triumph is the victory of soul over matter,
the victory of belief over pain, and the victory of faith over persecution.*

Sayyid Qutb

THE MESSENGER

PROLOGUE

If they were to make a feature film of her life, the script would always be trying to map the source of her flawed personality. The premise would be "How could she do such a thing?" The entire story would essentially be an examination, an *artistic* interrogation, not one rendered from her by a paid torturer in an unnamed client state.

In a situation like this the audience is always promised an answer; after all, they have tickets and are entitled to satisfaction. Surely in her backstory there has been a problem, an inciting incident: What exactly was her root grievance? Was there just one? How far do you go back? After a frustrating period of research, this is the way the screenwriters would try to explain it:

She was nothing.

True.

She came from nowhere.

True.

She grew up in a war zone.

Sometimes it was like that, yes. In the camps. You can't call them camps anymore. They are cities where people live and die.

Was she was abused as a child?

Abuse, it all depends on what you mean.

Abuse. Trauma . . .

I was not raped, or . . . molested, if that is what you mean. I was one of the lucky ones. Three of my closest friends were raped by soldiers and police.

The lives of women in many fundamentalist communities are difficult. Power groups embed themselves within ideology that mirrors a construct of local law and tradition that is all about defining the woman's place.

Yes, the place of women is very important.

But within these theocratic communities, aren't there built-in limitations, strict prohibitions on a woman's ability to obtain a divorce, or an education, or the possibility of choosing a career?

Everyone's education is different, and a career is not the most important thing for many people.

You had brothers and sisters?

Yes.

Yes, how many?

I had two brothers. Both were killed and then my father was taken away, but he returned. We were moved back and forth many times. We had no other family and often not so much food. I was shot at the first time when I was a child. My cousin was killed when he was nine, killed in the street by soldiers driving by. I saw soldiers playing with the heads, playing football with the heads of people killed in my village. I was standing in the street and a boy was run over by a personnel carrier in front of me. This was on the edge of the village many years ago. Now there is no edge. It's a camp. We lived there for our protection, we were told. This is more the sort of thing you meant when you were talking about abuse?

Yes. And you wanted to fight too?

I wanted to fight, yes. I do. Very much.

With all your heart, with your soul?

Yes, of course. What else can I do? Work within the system? I loved my family. Loved them with all my heart . . .

And now you are . . . taking the ultimate step.

I give my life. It is my sacrifice.

For God.

For God. Yes. I fight all the time.

And would you be a martyr?

I would be proud to be.

And that last is the kind of thing they would use in the scene. It takes place at a table in a gallery that surrounds a garden beside a mosque, a quiet place, and her eyes alternate between the flowers and the grizzled face of the actor playing Mansur al Brazi.

Filmed, this scene would not display as many bullet holes, and the windows would be more artfully smashed. The garden would be watered and distant noises would not intrude, but most unrealistically there would be no smells. No burning rubber or rotting flesh. No spoiled food or sewage. No sound of flies, no body odor. Nothing on fire.

At the end of this foundational scene, her character would realize the consequences of her contract with Mansur al Brazi. There would be a moment of understanding; the actor might look out toward the flowers as if seeing the world for the very first time.

So, what did she glimpse in that precisely crafted dramatic pause?

Many things. Unending poverty, the broken cities, the villages crumbling, no schools, no hospitals, closed borders, humiliation, decaying teeth, the empty bellies, the ignorance, the despair. Like any other girl in the camp, if she stayed and kept living there she would grow old in a hurry.

Could anything be said for that?

Yes, it wasn't all bad. There was beauty—the snow on distant mountains, the magnificent skies, the stars. If she stayed, there would undoubtedly be sublime moments, times when she could take a deep breath, or even sing. In the daytime she could go walking; she would have plenty of friends. The women helped each other. It took more than flakes of white phosphorus to extinguish an entire culture. Life in the camp was a soap opera told in multiple voices—relatives, enemies, grievances, fears, corrupt officials, small-business failures, and petty triumphs, punctuated by explosions and gunfire.

She had survived this far, had she not? She might continue un-scathed? So, why was she even *talking* to someone like Mansur al Brazi?

Because . . . she was not strong enough. Because of the way they murdered her brothers, Amir and Ra'id, gunned down first and then mutilated; at least they were together. Because of the way their deaths killed her mother. And, yes, fine—because she was afraid, terrified of having to go on living that life; her family stripped of its men and with no protection, only one step away from starvation, decades of suffering followed by death after years of . . . nothing. She was smart enough that she could tell her own future. There was no choice.

Her father was mixed race, gone for six years now. Supposedly he was living with a cousin in another "village" a hundred kilome-ters away, but there had been no word. After her uncle died, her mother's family had nothing, everything had been taken. How to survive? Marry, be a mother and start agonizing about her own children being killed? That would be the rhythm of a "peaceful" life.

The problem of growing into that peaceful life had dominated her childhood in one way or another. All the other children wanted to be space cadets or musicians. There was no one to talk to. Only the dry slopes, the clouds, the torment of the wind in the dirt streets, these were her only friends. Everywhere else she looked she saw only fear.

And the fear would be unending. Both choices were death. One just came faster. Everyone knew what someone like Mansur al Brazi did. The details were secret and dangerous and thus he was respected in a world where danger was constant. His choice meant money for the family. It meant striking back. She was quick-witted enough to know that.

She imagined her death in the greatest of detail, had already ac-cepted it as the price, long before she spoke to al Brazi. She could see the flash of the detonator, the jerk of the cord, the final digit entered on a cell phone, a switch connecting, a timer ticking down to zero—

white heat. Flesh blown into a mist like one of the Black Widows. Gone.

In that heartrending dramatic pause she would appear so young. Only a child. Honestly, how could she know what she was getting into?

But then she would turn to the waiting face of Mansur al Brazi. And her gaze would be steady, almost challenging, as she said the lines where she agreed to die.

"For God. Yes . . ."

It would be best if she were played by someone young, dark, and beautiful—Natalie Portman. Yes. That would be the scene.

But what was the truth of it?

Well, after that, after the big scene—she was gone. Taken by two men she had never met before, and a woman, riding in the backseat of a Land Rover. Her first terrifying airplane trip in a six-seater, a night on a passenger ferry. Different vehicles, houses, and hotels that she was assured were safe. Then by ferry to Malta. To Tunis, and then to Cairo. It took almost six months. The woman was very sweet; large almond eyes and a lilt in her voice. Penelope, she called herself. "Or just Penny," she explained.

Cairo was the real start of the transformation. Clothes that she had to be taught to wear properly. At first she cowered in the bathroom, a fantastic tiled chamber of wonders. But she heard the woman—Penny—laughing outside, and came out to applause and praise for her beauty.

To put her on the right track, Mansur al Brazi visits. Behind him is another man. Younger. Handsome. She will come to know him as Cousin Ali. He looks at her with narrow sly eyes, as if they both share some private joke, and she cannot help but smile. He becomes a friend. Yes. Just like a cousin.

Her immediate purpose was to attend school, they explained. When she asked the woman about "when it would happen," she was kissed on the cheek and told "to forget about all that . . ." As far as any sort of imagined training—learning how to fieldstrip an AK-47 blindfolded or throw grenades—no. She is to apply herself, do well, and learn to talk to the other children.

"Don't rush. When the time comes, God will call you. For now you get an education and build yourself into a new person. You are no longer who you were. From now on, you are *Daria,*" Mansur al Brazi says. He shows her a photograph.

It is a snapshot the size of a playing card. Creased and stained from being pried in and out of a wallet. A girl's face, heart-shaped, beautiful eyes and a level brow. A girl who could have been her a few years ago. A child with a child's steady innocence, gazing at the lens, open to interpretation.

"From now on, Daria, you are to be just like the others. Get rid of your *hijab.* Imitate the Western girls. Dress like them, learn to be one of them. Have fun!" Penny says, and they all laugh.

It has been explained to her that the money is already going to what's left of her family and she must now forget about them. It is unfortunate, but no contact with home can be allowed. It is for her own protection, and for her family's safety. The government is riddled with spies and no one can keep a secret. Only when it's absolutely safe will she be able to see them again.

"They know you love them, little one," Ali tells her. "Don't worry."

It was easy after that. It was like a wave. A wave of discovery and pleasure.

After Cairo they took a tourist cruise to Palermo. They stayed in a hotel, and then later at a villa. Everywhere, she attended schools or was supplied with a tutor.

There was the luxury of having the television on at all times. And food, wonderful foods, fantastic smells. And out the windows were other young people. Boys and girls together. By the end of the summer, she could even get along in Italian, and they moved once again.

It hurt to say goodbye to Penny, but one thing they are in her new family is brave. There were no tears. Neither of them would allow it. Penny left, going to wherever people like her go, while Daria began her next academic adventure.

School in Florence that first year begins miserably. There are four girls in each room, and they all have decided to hate her. With good reason, she supposes, since the distance from Palermo to Florence is farther than the moon. She is intimidated by the older students and their brazen attitudes. She is a clown, none of her clothes are fashionable, and she comes to the crushing realization that she is truly ignorant and guileless, an embarrassment, and therefore everyone's enemy.

She takes refuge in her books, listens, learns, and practices her accent. Survival means not only learning Italian and English but also diving into a series of survey courses in the liberal arts. Aware that she has gotten off to a late start, she has to work at her lessons and concentrate. Florence being what it used to be, there are regular field trips—to museums, galleries, concerts, ruins. It's Michelangelo and the Medici, and the rise of Europe and the Holy Roman Empire, and everything is paid for in euros.

As much as possible the students shy away from the prefects and try to make a life for themselves in the streets and clubs. Now she can revel in her permission to be like the others.

She smokes a cigarette, she rides on the back of a motorcycle. She falls in love for the first time with Tété, who is from Dubai and talks with a drawl that makes her heart quicken, and when he dances likes to glide like Michael Jackson. Anytime they can find a dark corner, he wants to kiss, and they begin their love affair in a rush. She puts him off for weeks, but after a pause for sulking he always returns with cheerful persistence.

When they do it, it is in an apartment that one of the boys from the American school uses as a pad on the weekends. It's raining and dank and the city is chilled and stinking. Tété has made some deal or promise with his Western friend, and they pick up the key and, hand in hand, rush over there and turn on the heater.

It is over . . . far too soon, she thinks. Tété with his head col-lapsed on her shoulder. Wet kisses of thanks. He jumps right off her, mindful of the condom and its dangerous contents. She watches him walk in and out of the bathroom, his long bones, still feeling the scratch of his beard on her breast. He makes jokes, does odd little jerky dances to keep her laughing. They become lovers all through the spring and summer and it is . . . an unexpected heaven.

She is one of them now, she decides.

No one teases her now. The other girls look at her with some-thing like respect. She enjoys learning the Euro slang and hanging out. She likes the courses and most of her teachers. The school is a sort of finishing school, a rich person's solution to the problem of child rearing. There are summer programs designed to prepare the students for entry into university. The teachers are of the highest quality, well paid. Boys and girls from all over the world board there, and everyone has money.

Freedom. The memory of it brings a tear. Her final year has won her the most freedom of all. It's meant to be occupational, a series of apprenticeships. Other schools in the city send their students to do the same. In addition to being a debut into the ranks of the executive class, it's party central.

Be like the others, Daria has been told, and she does so. As part of her protective Italian coloration, she masquerades as a Catholic but finds it like a gaudy zombie movie, all the ritual and the lore and the . . . fetish of it. The fragments of bone and hair, a withered finger, wine changing into blood, and crackers standing in for the body of the Messiah. How stupid can people be! And the statues that are everywhere; the bleeding, flaming hearts, Jesus with his eyes rolled up to heaven. Stab wounds between the ribs, nails through the palms. Garish ecstasy—the gaping mouths, the sunken cheeks, the nonstop blood, the white skin and supermodel-vacant stare of the Virgin. Of course, she feels like screaming—it is as logical as Kris Kringle, and nothing more than plaster idolatry that will crumble with the first artillery shell.

The Pope? A ridiculous old pervert, and an ex-Nazi at that. And everyone is supposed to ignore it? She would happily be a suicide bomber if they would let her pick the Vatican. She would be disguised as a nun . . . and can see herself kneeling, kissing the old man's ring. The mere touch of a button, hidden in her clothing . . . She would do it.

The nuns. They are the worst, she decides. Horrible winged creatures, with dumb faces, recruited from the ranks of retarded children and delivered to the Church from failing farms, ugly girls who will never get a husband. Well, a convent is the best place for them, probably. They should all die.

But by now she has become almost a complete Italian. She knows how to genuflect, she thinks Ferraris are the fastest cars in the world, and she craves her espresso in the morning.

As a student she's not the best, nor the worst. She finds English easier than Italian, which is too bad, since she's supposed to be an adopted child of Turin. In a perverse way, her accent makes her more popular. Exotic. Her skin a little darker, her jet-black hair a little more curly than the Italian girls'. From the south for sure, and you know what those girls are like. All sin.

She is called out of class early one day for one of Cousin Ali's visits. She spends an hour on her hair, another on deciding what to wear. She has a crush on Ali now, and tries to hide it by being cool and aloof, and putting him down whenever she can. He takes her to dinner at a grown-up restaurant. The men look at her now. Italian men will whistle at anything, but she is not unattractive, she realizes.

"Enjoy it," says Ali over *una tagliata di manzo,* his napkin tucked into the front of his fine suit. "Enjoy it, but remember who you are."

"I will," she says.

He wants to know how she's getting along, so she talks about the school and her friends. The pranks, the absurdities, the unreasonable demands that are made on them by the administration. Ali listens and smiles and encourages her, but always reminds her that her family and a great many others are depending on her.

"Yes, Daria. Have a good time, but you must be hardworking and not fail." He stops for a moment. Looks severely at her, cocks his head to one side as if he has suddenly discovered something worrisome. "Tell me truthfully, do you want to stop?" he asks.

When they make the movie, this is the part where Natalie will have a hesitation. But then she will recover and assure Ali that no, no . . . she's still ready. Willing. Eager to give her life for God.

"It's completely normal to enjoy all this," Ali says. He looks around at the posh restaurant. "It's made to be enjoyed. Rich food. Nice clothes. Everything is comfortable. Who wouldn't like to live like this?" They laugh.

"It's decadent. It's wasteful. Every morsel is made off the sweat of some peasant's slave labor. It's destroying the earth, the atmosphere. It is powered by money. Money going up, up, up into the pockets of Jews and Americans. It looks like heaven, but really it's hell."

At this point Natalie will look around, not quite understanding.

"They have manufactured a complete illusion. All the unpleasantness, all the bad parts have been bleached out of it. Very good," Ali says, appraising the restaurant. "Bravo. Very good indeed."

Ali has explained that on paper she is an orphan, adopted by the Vermiglios, an Italian family *simpatica*. He even takes her to meet them in Turin, cautioning her beforehand to say nothing unless she is asked by Signor Vermiglio directly.

Their house is ancient and moss covered. Signor Vermiglio is old and walks with the aid of a silver cane, beautiful, but marred by the addition of a neon-blue plastic boot on its end. He invites Ali inside, but leaves her on the porch. It hasn't been swept in some time and there are leaves rotting in the corners of the balcony. When they come out, the old man is laughing, but Ali is very serious. Tired of him already, she decides.

"Signor Vermiglio wants to get to know you a little better, Daria," Ali tells her.

The old man stands there, then reaches out and grasps her shoulder with his bony hands. "Beautiful," he says.

"*Grazie . . . Papa,*" she replies, and they all smile. He asks questions but doesn't seem to be able to hear her answers. Ali has to re-peat everything. By the end of it, they are almost laughing at the old man. Altogether the interview with her paper guardian lasts a mere fifteen minutes.

They drive back into the city, joking about him. They have been able to make the deal with the old Italian because he is dying, Ali explains. "He has nothing to lose . . ."

Ali drops her at the hotel and abandons her to room service and television, only returning at midnight to check if she's sneaked out and gone clubbing. She pretends to wake up when he opens the door. A little moan as she turns over.

"Go to sleep, little one," she hears him whisper at the door.

"Is that you?"

"Yes, go to sleep."

"Did you have fun? Did you go out?"

"Go to sleep."

"Was I good today?"

"You were very good, Daria." It's his voice she loves. He talks like a big cat purring. Like a leopard. "The Vermiglio family is very happy to have you with them."

"Do you have a cigarette?" she asks, propping herself up on one elbow, the sheets held chastely across her breasts. Ali comes in and sits on the edge of the bed. Lights it for her. "You should go to sleep now," he says.

She lets the silence build, the coal on the end of her cigarette glowing, dimming, glowing again.

"I'm not sleepy, Ali . . ." she says, and reaches up to touch his cheek.

Ali is different. A man. He knows how to do things and she gives herself completely to him. It is like being whisked into the heart of a thunderstorm. The power of her own body, the energy it contains. This is really her first time, she thinks, and when it is over she sinks into a dreamless sleep.

At breakfast, he looks steadily at her. Is there a smile? He touches her hand. In the elevator, he leans against her and kisses her hair. They make love again after breakfast, and lie there talking. She tells him all about school, about Tété. He listens and when she asks, "Where were you born?" he only shakes his head.

"This is very dangerous . . ." he warns her. One hand follows the long curve of her hip. "This is very dangerous . . . it has to end." His eyes are appropriately sad. "You understand, don't you?"

She kisses him and they make love again, and when they are done, lying there listening to the scooters buzzing up and down the street, she turns and pushes her lips into his shoulder. Whispers what he needs to hear: "Yes . . . I understand."

Back at school for the final term, she breaks all the rules. She can't have Ali, and Tété has moved on. It hurts because he truly was a sweet boy and they laughed. She falls into a depression, scratches her brothers' names in the stone wall of her bedroom. Has conversations, imaginary debates with her father, where she screams at him to fight back. Fight back once in your life.

In her clearer moments she flagellates herself with guilt and does penance by throwing herself into her role. So what if Tété has gone? There are plenty of other boys. They all think she is pretty, or . . . pretty enough. Enjoy it, then.

She drinks a little. More than a little. Too much. Gets sick. Learns how to cure a hangover. Learns how to dance dirty and learns how to tell the boys no. Everything is available—makeup, cigarettes, and hashish that arrives at odd times, always the result of some conspiracy by boys, and shared out with the girls around candlelit circles, accompanied by coughing fits and laughter.

It's all permitted if you're a tool of God. It's not sin if you are doing it for a reason. In your hidden heart you are simply abasing yourself for the greater glory of the Creator. At night, in the privacy of her own bed—and always alone now, because she is not really a slut, really she is a good girl—in the darkness she asks herself: Do you have any doubts?

No.

Are you sure? It's normal to have doubts.

Well . . .

Well, what? Aren't you normal? Aren't you scared?

No.

You're sure?

No.

Aha . . . Maybe you are normal after all. Well, we'll see. . . .

DAY I

D aria pays the taxi and walks into Berlin's sparkling new
Brandenburg International Airport.

The ticket they've booked for her is with Air France, a
flight that will get her to New York in the afternoon, but she has
always been fast, always rushed ahead with things. It's a little touch
of panic, she thinks and takes a deep breath. She could change the
ticket, get into JFK earlier. There is a Lufthansa flight. She could
gain some hours. It would be more effective.

So she moves the ticket, even though it means a two-hour wait.
It's also one less airport through which she will have to pass. There's
a two-hundred-euro penalty, but since she's swapping two first-class
tickets, it gets waived. *Macht nichts.* Nobody has to know. There's
no one who's meeting her on the other side, so everything's cool, as
they say in America.

She endures the lines, the security procedures, the metal detectors, pat-downs, body scans, and repeated requests to discard all her
liquids. She has displayed her passport; she has checked her baggage, and having complied with all requests and requirements, gets
to the gate with plenty of time to kill.

Her choices—her hair, clothes, and makeup—have not been entirely her own and have been made quickly, but she is satisfied with the overall presentation.

"Dress like everyone else, Daria," she has been instructed. "Wear something comfortable, and"—this last she thinks is almost funny—"remember to take good care of your health."

The whole morning has been like one extended shock treatment, everything moving fast, and having exchanged the ticket, she feels like she's a little more in control.

Giving in to her nervousness, she ambles around, from gift shop to newsstand. Stares at rows of candy bars, memorabilia, T-shirts with German colors. Not really seeing anything, but turning her face away, still looking for a place to hide. She is still doing that, she thinks.

She is still a child, deep down. Too easily lulled by novelties. Still realizing the meaning of things long after they've occurred. Distracted sometimes like any young person, and missing clues that should have been obvious. She had been telephoned for a medical interview, given instructions to taxi halfway across Rome to have a little place scratched on her shoulder and a droplet of vaccine placed on it. An *inoculazione,* the nurse called it. It was the woman's first in twenty years of nursing. An older nurse was helping her by looking in on the procedure. "You're traveling soon?" she asked Daria.

"To Brazil. To visit my fiancé," she says without hesitation, and the two women laugh. She leaves with instructions not to scratch or pick at the scab that forms. Afterwards there will be a scar, like actors had in the old movies. And the older nurse laughs.

At the time it all went right over her head. It was a strange afternoon, and this is what it meant, and she hadn't even noticed because of course she was going out and was already planning her night.

But everything is different now. Everything happening suddenly, and now she's . . . scared. Of course she is. And ashamed of her fear. Trying to turn her back on everything. She wills herself to calm down. Takes long, slow deep breaths as she scans the newspapers and magazine racks looking for a clue—*Why now?*

Why is she preparing to board this plane, on this particular day?

It's late in September, there's no special anniversary to celebrate. No great atrocity, assassination, or coup d'état that must be avenged *today*. There are governments on the verge of chaos all over the world, too many places where the armies have come into the streets.

So . . . why is today the day she must go?

She cannot figure it out. Finds her way back to a mostly empty section of seats, an island of solitude where she can close her eyes. She gets the iPod Nano out of her bag, plugs in some long trance that reduces the world to a windy silence, and transforms her into a tired passenger at the start of a long day. Like everyone else.

She may have slept. She can't tell. Everything seems so artificial around her. None of it is helped by the architecture, which can best be described as space-colony. On the television above her head, a racing car is pinwheeling off the track until it splinters against a wall of tires. Announcements are made in a quartet of languages. When it's time, she is allowed to board early because of her class, and finds 4A, on the right side of the aircraft.

Lufthansa Flight 7416 is everything their marketing department promises. Daria is not quite petite, but she knows that swaddled in a Lufthansa blanket, fully reclined, wearing a set of noise-cancelling headphones, and resting on a puffy antibacterial pillow, she'll look as comfortable as a sleeping kitten.

She buckles in, presses her skull back against the headrest, and lets her eyes roam the indecipherable controls arrayed around her seat. She can't focus on anything. When will the police suddenly appear in the aisle? She's suddenly nervous. She can't take her eyes off the floor and stares at her fingernails, the carpet, afraid to make eye contact with the passengers taking their seats around her.

The safety information is explained. She gazes at the card as if it matters. There are awkward-sounding bumps and collisions in the cargo bay of the plane. The air is chilled, then suddenly turns stuffy. She tries to catch her breath, but she can't. Her hands are clammy when she presses them to her cheeks.

The doors are closed.

The airplane begins to slowly taxi away from the gate. The pilots make their announcements. She is sweating. For a moment she feels sick and checks to make sure there's a paper bag in the seat in front of her. The attendants make one last voyage down the aisle, then buckle in.

She presses her hot cheek to the window. Slashes of gray pavement and artificial turf. Engines screaming, the gigantic airplane rolls down the runway. Now it's too late for her to get off; strapped in, she's a prisoner as they bump along. Then, as if the pilots have gathered their courage, they rush forward and, somehow defying the laws of nature, lift into German airspace.

Across from her a woman, very stylish, opens the Lufthansa magazine and looks over with a smile to acknowledge their mutual brownness. Daria nods, and fans herself. The woman's smile broadens. *"Sie bringen uns gleich Champagner. Alles wird gut."* A lilt to the voice, the curve of the vowels. Her earrings alone are worth ten thousand euros, Daria suspects.

"Grazie," she replies. The woman smiles and returns to her magazine.

For a moment she watches the glamorous woman paging through the magazine, evaluating, rejecting, considering, judging. Exercising her taste.

She realizes that for a few moments the shock has vanished. Is it just human contact? She breathes. Just as predicted, the champagne arrives, served to her by a dark-haired German boy.

Lufthansa Flight 7416 with its 372 passengers has departed in the morning. From Berlin it is direct and expensive. First class, very much more so. There will be a meal coming, but the boy hands her a blanket in case she might want to turn in early or if the air-conditioning is too much. He's very handsome and eager to please. Maybe he's new to the job and, like her, a little awkward; trying to cover by acting cool, his smile coming and going as he works the aisle.

Once up in the air, everything is okay, everything is fine. You can see it in the weary, relaxed gait of the flight attendants as they go up and down the aisles taking drink orders. When the boy serves them champagne, the stylish woman looks over. Raises her glass. *"Cin cin,"* she says. *"Salute,"* Daria murmurs. They both take discreet sips. The champagne is cold, refreshing. Perfect. Just what she needs.

The climb has been straight and powerful and now they are comfortably near the stratosphere. So far it's been just what you would want in air travel—uneventful. She takes another fizzy sip. But only moments after she has started to relax, a long series of tremors ripple beneath the wings and unsettle the plane.

On the screen in front of her, there is an animated silhouette of an airliner describing a yellow arc across a leaf-green Europe. These days the volcano is quiet, and now the jet is above Norway, almost at the coast. Soon they will break away and Lufthansa 7416 will find herself crossing an expanse of deep blue with only sprawling Greenland to look forward to. . . .

The spells of turbulence, like Daria's panic, come and go. Sometimes the stillness is worse.

She should be riding in the back like a refugee or a soldier. Well, she has been a refugee, but now she is a soldier first of all. Yes, a soldier fighting a war. And at the moment she is fighting it quietly. Nervously. Yes, okay . . . all that's admitted. Her excuse for the nerves is that it's the flying, simply the flying. Those unanticipated bumps one encounters at five hundred miles an hour.

She is Signorina Daria Hirsi Vermiglio, but that too is a lie.

She's supposed to be invisible, but now she is fanning herself, enjoying the champagne and a laugh with her anonymous friend across the way. There are movies on the screen that she quickly learns to access, and between pauses in their conversation, both of them touch their way through the menus. Most of the films she's seen, but there is always something interesting. Her eye falls on a documentary about Le Corbusier . . . but she doesn't want to think. Not now.

And wouldn't it be more normal to chat with the woman, to become her companion for the trip? If her strategy is to be invisible, shouldn't the best tactic be to act in an ordinary way? Go ahead, have a conversation with a stranger, why not? It will only look natural.

It turns out that the handsome woman is Sinhalese, born in Goa but raised in Sri Lanka and married to a German for many years. "Travel is hard," the woman says, "and the only tolerable thing is to go first-class. We are slaves. We chase money, we chase money all over the world. Poof!" She makes a grabbing motion with one hand at the invisible money and raises her glass.

"Do you fly a lot?" Daria asks.

"No, not really. Only a few times a year. Every time the airlines say that it is all new. Everything new and supposedly better." They have switched to English. The woman has lived in London for thirty years and is fluent. "But really it's the same, and now I hate everything about it. They cut costs and it's more and more dangerous every day—oh, I'm sorry." The woman reaches across the aisle and, before Daria can react, pats her arm—the fingers gentle against the fabric of her jacket. It's a touch that will kill her.

They both laugh at Daria's apparent nervousness, and after a few minutes, when their conversation takes a lull, Daria curls up in her blanket with the champagne flute. She is just not ready, she thinks. Everything is happening too fast.

Shock. Looking at the little cartoon airplane lost out there in the wide blue.

She watches one of the in-flight movies; produced in Hollywood, but carefully designed to appeal to all the major markets. It's the kind of movie she's seen a hundred times, the same story but with minor variations. It is violent but no one bleeds. There are no curses, or rather none you couldn't hear in any school yard. It is realistic, but everyone is beautiful. It is relevant, but there is not a word about Israel. Or Chechnya. Or Algeria. Never anything about Algeria. Or the camps. Or Sudan. Somalia. Nothing really about them. Indonesia? Jordan, Lebanon? Might as well not exist, she thinks. Gone. Vaporized. First you are erased from their culture, and then you're erased from their maps, then finally you're just erased. Isn't that what they are doing? Isn't that what they are always boasting? *We'll pave your fucking country.*

She's heard that.

And she's carefully learned the definition of "jihad": struggle, striving. And when they are trying to kill you, you fight back. That's the progression, the ramping up of an individual's commitment. Common to all of humanity, why is it so hard to understand?

The beautiful boy comes around with her meal. The Germans are noted for their breakfasts; there are eggs, potatoes, some kind of sausage, a twist of orange and some bits of melon. A packet of brittle toast, a tiny cup of yogurt. The coffee is poured from an elegant silver service. She eats and watches the movie. The two stars are trying to decide if they love each other enough to go through with the rest of the plot. She thinks she knows the answer.

Quietly she smiles and eats, listens to the ridiculous dialogue. She cannot stop thinking about simulations, about the masks behind the masks. It is the shock. The mental shock. Jangled, people would say—"You were shaken up by events, jangled." Sometimes the jangling lasted the rest of your life. But now she feels as if life *is* a movie, planned out, edited, and prescreened in the eye of God. Looking around the huge airliner, her certainty grows. She can feel it in her bones. It is the physics of life, a ball running down a board of pegs toward its ultimate hole, the destination decided just as surely as God knows she will eat the last of her scrambled eggs. It has all been written long ago.

The leading man reminds her a little of Tété, and that is maybe her one regret. Even as she lets herself float back to those sunlit happy hours, she realizes that she is just giving in to . . . what? Juvenile nostalgia. Romance. That's the fun of it, she supposes. An imam would say that the fun of it was exactly what was wrong. Men and Women were not intended to have fun, but to mirror the creative act of God. To work and have children, to further God's plans. Fun has no place in it. Fun, flirting, romance, it is all based on the attraction of the illicit. She knows that.

Still, he was so sweet.

There is an announcement that punctuates the soundtrack. The pilot repeats it twice, once in German, again in accented English. They are climbing to avoid the turbulence.

It is time to work. She goes to the little galley where the first-class attendant is brewing up more coffee. She asks for water and is given a plastic cup. Affecting to help out, she pours the water herself. It comes from an ice-cold plastic bottle. She runs her hand across the top of the cart where the drinks are prepared, leans against the counter and searches for a napkin, touches the attendant on her shoulder by way of thanks. Steps into a vacant washroom, and touches everything. Runs her fingers through her hair, stares at her reflection in the mirror.

There is no tear in her eye. The wide unlined brow, her nose small and straight, but mostly it is her eyes—dark and dancing. She half-turns and looks at herself over her shoulder. Yes, she can dazzle with that smile, and her eyes seem to gleam. A small mouth but full lips. The face of death, they will call it, she thinks.

Ostensibly to get some exercise, she walks the length of Lufthansa 7416. Her hands travel from seat back to seat back as she keeps balance. This is for you, Amir, this is for you, Ra'id, this is for Mother, for my lost childhood, this is for all the people in my building, on my street . . . for the ones living in tents, for the times of starving, and all the ones who were killed or will be.

At the rear of the plane, she steps into another washroom and runs her hands over everything; she flushes, fondles a paper towel but doesn't use it, grasps the faucets, inspects every surface, every knob, bends down and breathes on the door latch as she opens it, and then strolls through the aft galley and asks for another glass of water.

The flight attendants mostly ignore her while they continue chatting in feathery, accented German. They are her opposite in every way. Golden-haired wraiths, hyper-conscious of maintaining their thinness. The German phrases elude her, but in her new state of heightened shock she has the gift of fully imagining their conversations. There is no glamour anymore in flying. The wages are getting lower as too many airlines compete. Safety standards are eroding, and the union has no clout. These girls will get out of the racket as soon as they snag a husband.

One of the attendants has her back turned and Daria touches

her on the shoulder, and returns the cup for the recycling. Then she brushes close by the other, rounds the corner and begins the long trek toward first class, careful to touch each seat back as she goes.

At the end of her lap around the cabin, Daria arrives back at her seat to see that her fashionable neighbor is awake and reading, a pair of elegant gold-rimmed glasses perched on her nose. "It's a long flight," she says.

"Yes, very."

"It's good to move around."

"Yes, it is. I get uncomfortable," Daria says, stretching theatrically.

"Your muscles cramp."

"Yes. Exactly."

"My husband sometimes works with the air force and they have to fly terribly long missions. They have rules that they have to move around so the blood in their legs won't pool, but it's impossible in those little planes."

"I would think so." Daria looks at the woman for a moment. "Is that a good book?"

The woman makes a face. "It's okay. They're always the same," she says with a shrug. Perhaps embarrassed to be caught reading something so insubstantial.

Daria puts one hand over her mouth, as if to stifle a yawn, stretches her back from side to side. "Do you have family waiting for you?" the woman asks. The question is hesitant. Almost as if she were afraid to ask something so intimate.

"No. I'm on business."

"Really?"

"Yes. Writing an article. A travel article."

"Oh, really. A writer!"

"It's my first assignment."

"Well, you must do a good job. That's exciting. It's good to travel, especially when you're young."

"I know. I'm lucky."

"And plus they pay you for it!" The woman laughs. It is a beautiful laugh. Infectious.

Across the aisle, someone in a blanket rolls over; the woman goes back to her book, and Daria goes back to her movie. The action hero and the ingénue have been separated. The villains are all ugly, sexually predatory, dark skinned and have scraggly beards. Just more of the same Hollywood propaganda.

Berlin. Only last night—a lifetime ago, Daria thinks.

The message from Ali was that she should come there for a job interview while on leave from her publisher. *Klic!* is a weekly magazine based in Rome, and she is a "sponsored intern." Not quite a job, it is a way for corporations to kick-start a reporter who might later do them favors. There are girls and boys who do this all the time, she has learned. You just have to be halfway attractive, able to use a digital camera, and prepared to cough up two hundred words on the latest celebrity scandal. She was hired at the magazine for her final summer at the school. And that meant it was goodbye to Leonardo, whom she had only just met.

But it was a job, the first step on the career ladder. She was moving up, and, since she had been ordered to, still enjoying the ride.

It wasn't hard. It wasn't really work. Mostly it was fun. She had met Roberto Benigni, and Mariacarla Boscono, which was great because she said they could have been twin sisters, footballer Francesco Totti, who was posing for a fashion shoot and was a complete dream, and Camilla Ferranti, who was famous because Berlusconi called the head of RAI to get her a part in a TV series. The worst part of the job amounted to standing around outside some fabulous club, because reporters were hardly ever allowed in. The internship was set to run out after Christmas, and she was already wondering what she was going to do, when the message came that her cousin had bought her a ticket to Berlin.

It was nothing special, nothing cinematic. Just a pink message slip. *Please call the personnel manager. Everything has been arranged.* All she had to do was get to the airport on time. She arrived yesterday afternoon. At the Regent there was a note waiting in her room. No signature. The company was called Seyylol AG and was

interviewing applicants to join their public relations department.
They had a suite at the Adlon and she was to be there at 9:00 p.m.

She knew immediately what it was really about.

For the rest of the day, she tried to be like the Berliners. It was
cool and windy, the leaves of the lindens starting to turn. The end of
a hot summer. She walked around the inner city, avoiding the fabled
shopping opportunities on the Ku-damm, and instead heading up to
Friedrichstrasse and losing herself in the maze of streets around
Hackescher Markt.

Germany was like everywhere else, she decided. Maybe more
ironic, but they had earned that the hard way. Riding on the S-Bahn,
she saw the colors of skins and fabrics running the full range. There
were women in saris and women in headscarves. They all avoided
one another's eyes. There were artists who'd just gotten out of bed.
Retired couples returning from their visit to the doctor. There were
the gray-faced ones who were still trying to adjust to the fall of the
Wall, and then there were the invisible ones, the students and slack-
ers and the lost, who sat in the corners, grabbed a smoke on the
platform and were happy just to get through the moment. Always
there were tourists—obese, obsessed with their waterproofed sun
hats and digital cameras, maps bristling from every pocket.

The German language was insane; she could catch only a few
words. Uppermost in the news on this particular day was a financial
scandal—photos of middle-aged politicians and energy magnates
captured in casual conversation while walking across a busy street.
Whatever they'd done didn't translate, but it seemed more incriminating seen through a telephoto lens.

She went into an Internet café and bought an excellent espresso
and spent two euros to surf for a half hour, hoping to find a clue for
her sudden mobilization. But beyond the latest environmental crisis
and the continuing deterioration of the capitalist economies . . .
there was nothing.

She thought the choice of the Adlon odd. It was a famous hotel,
certainly not the most invisible place. She had imagined a creaking
walk-up in an immigrant ghetto. Maybe it was a real job interview?
They could have decided she needed to acquire more cover.

She ate street food and did everything with plenty of time to spare; showed up on time, dressed just as she would for a day at *Klic!* Hip but quality. A short skirt with black tights. Boots that looked strong and scuffed. A peacoat-inspired jacket, and an expensive blood-red top for the only touch of color.

At the desk, they directed her to the suites Seyylol AG had booked for the interviews. When she knocked, the door was opened by a young man she had never met before. Very thin and yellow skinned. There was a sliver of chrome clamped to his ear and maybe he was listening to someone, but whatever, he couldn't meet her eye. Or maybe it was the tights.

"If you have a mobile?" He held out his hand, and she dropped her backpack down on a chair instead of giving it to him, draped the jacket over it.

The young man walked away a few steps. "If you require tea," he said, pointing to a table across the room. Then he went out of the room and down a short hallway. Across from her was a window, from which she could see the blocks of the Holocaust Memorial, a few lonely Jews wandering in and out of the labyrinth, indulging their grief over man's inhumanity to man.

A moment later and the young man was back. "This way," he said.

The man in the bedroom was a stranger. Over fifty, she would have guessed. A high crown of graying hair, white on the sides, barbered carefully around the ears. This was it, she realized.

"Hello, Daria," the man said. "I am honored to meet you."

"Hello." She waited to see if he would take her hand. He didn't.

"Please sit. We do not have a lot of time. Your cousin tells me you are still committed?"

"Yes," she said. "I am."

"We have changed our tactics." As he speaks to her he looks beyond her to the television, where a documentary about lions and water buffalo is playing.

"You are intelligent and I'm certain you can see what's happening. If the timing was better, if it were not so important, we could have allowed you to make a farewell message. But, unfortunately . . ." For a moment she sees her mother, her face laced with wrinkles, eyes always on the floor, never talking, lost inside herself after her sons had been murdered. Her husband gone somewhere, and her never knowing . . .

"It doesn't matter. They know I love them."

"I'm sure." He looks at her for a long moment. "Daria, no one is forcing you, but our friend has told me that you are very strong and true to your word. You volunteered, yes? Of your own free will?"

"Yes."

"You are a beautiful young woman. Any man would be proud to make you his wife. You have your whole life before you."

"I know what I am doing."

"Fine. Good." He nods. For a moment his gray eyes stare at her. "Then . . . this is how we do it now. We try to make our effectiveness last. This is why we are using germs. Not bombs."

"Germs?"

He takes a breath, almost a sigh. Glances toward the television. Is it to see the time? "You understand, Daria, that it is better if you don't know some things?"

"Yes. Yes, of course," she says, a little embarrassed. "How it happens, it doesn't matter to me," she says, but actually she has never imagined anything other than an explosive ending to her life. Never.

"It is a very special pathogen we have made. It is an old disease, Daria. A disease that everyone thinks has gone away. They used to immunize everyone for this disease . . . myself as a child, but now, not for many years. It is smallpox, have you heard of it?"

"Yes . . ." Now the taxi across Rome makes sense. She remembers the word "smallpox" in the same way she remembers "chlorophyll." It's just a science term. It has no relevance to her life.

"Smallpox comes in different varieties. The old kind could kill one in three, eh?" He holds up fingers for her to count. "The only samples of smallpox in existence are hidden away in very secret government laboratories. Obtaining a sample was extremely expensive. And then we had to modify it, we had to make it into a weapon, something we could use, you see?"

He sits back against the headboard, adjusts the pillows piled behind the small of his back. "It was easily done, once we had the equipment." He shrugs.

"Now the virus is . . ." He searches the television again. ". . . like an athlete on steroids, a technological feat we can be proud of. That *you* can be proud of," he tells her.

She nods her head. "Fine, then."

He reaches out as if to pat her on the shoulder, but stops himself at the last second. "To take this step . . . it has always been a problem. After all, to spread a plague, something that could even come back and hurt your own people, this always has been a last resort, otherwise someone would have already used it, yes?"

"I would think so, yes."

"So, the time has come. This is the last resort." The man stops. Waits. Seems to be getting his breath. Is he sick?

"You are to be a carrier, Daria. You are an arrow. You are going straight to the heart." He uses his fist to rap at his own chest.

Almost without her noticing, the young man crouches beside her, a syringe in his hands. He swabs her shoulder and gives her an injection. Painless.

"Without this you would surely die and then your usefulness would be over. Everything, of course, is untested. We are not a drug company." The older man smiles at his little joke. "All I can guarantee is that this will slow it down. You may have a few more weeks, or you may live to be a grandmother," he says. He's not smiling now. Looking at her sadly, she thinks.

After that it is simple. Go into the adjoining room. There is luggage and new clothing for you. Take off everything you are wearing and put it in the garbage bag. On the table there is a bottle; it contains the virus. It is just like a bottle of cough medicine. Go into the bathroom and wash your hands with it. Close the drain so you don't lose any. Run your fingers through your hair, it lasts longer that way; when you dry your hands, wipe them on your skin. Leave the empty bottle in the wastebasket in the bathroom. Later, for when you bathe, there's a shower cap and a pair of rubber gloves in your luggage. Get dressed in the clothes on the bed. Everything should fit.

"If there's a problem, tell Youssef," the older man says. "When you are ready you will be taken to your hotel. Stay alone in your room, if you are hungry order whatever food you require. In the morning, retrieve your papers. The bill has been paid. You don't need to worry. A cab will take you to the airport. All you have to do is follow your itinerary, don't wash your hands for a few days, touch everything you can. You're going as a journalist and a travel writer. But you know all about that, yes?"

"Yes."

"Instructions will be sent to you by email. As a draft, do you understand?"

"Yes."

"You are very brave," the man says. He is wearing a blue shirt with a white T-shirt beneath it. Newspapers are spread out across the bed and kept in place with two cell phones. Across the room an opened briefcase is on the writing table.

In the next room she does exactly what she's been told—strips down and even throws in her underwear like a good girl. The clothes they've picked out are conservative—a pantsuit, a white fitted office-girl shirt. Shoes with good soles for walking.

In the spotless bathroom she plugs the sink and then pours a dollop from the bottle into her hand. It is a thin oil of some kind. There is no smell. She looks at it pooled in her hand, pokes her finger in and swirls it around.

Smallpox.

Really the name of the disease doesn't matter. It could be anything, anything they could buy and turn into a weapon. Typhoid. Plague. Ebola.

In the mirror—the face of death. She rubs until her hands are dry, then pours another puddle into her hands and runs it through her hair, massaging her scalp. And then again. Like a vain woman, she takes too much time, apparently, because Youssef comes knocking at the door.

"*Un momento . . .*" she calls, and finishes the last of the liquid in a hurry, using the last on her face, neck, up the forearms.

When she opens the door, Youssef is right there. She makes him wait while she puts on lipstick. He's almost trembling, looking at her in the mirror. She finishes and pouts. Digs in the little bag, looking for perfume, and gives herself a little spritz.

"Don't waste it," he says severely.

Only now does she realize that he too has volunteered to die. For a moment she thinks about kissing him, but he is so prim that it would probably give him a heart seizure, so she only smiles. All the bridges have been crossed now. All the decisions have been made.

"I'm ready," she says, and the shock begins.

The flight attendant wakes her with the present of a hot towel, which she pretends to use, just dabbing it on her eyes. On-screen the little airplane is still over the blue but getting closer . . . closer.

The second meal service comes with complimentary wine, even a selection of varietals. A pasta dish for the vegetarians, a fish choice, or the inevitable beef.

Outside is an iron-gray sea with wispy clouds. Thousands of feet below, a great cargo tanker is just a tiny gash in the water.

Everything is still moving too quickly. Almost as soon as the meal has arrived, the dinner things are cleared away. Somewhere in the back a baby is crying on and on. There are chimes over the intercom and a request for everyone to fold their tables away and raise their seats to the standard height.

"This is the part I hate." The Sinhalese woman looks across at her and smiles. As they get lower, Lufthansa 7416 seems to go faster. The air thickens. The great plane tips from side to side as if suddenly discovering its weight.

Her ears swell shut with the pressure and there is a sharp pain that flicks across the bridge of her nose. She swallows and opens her mouth, trying to clear her sinuses. Through her window, far away, is a coastline; a ragged road around an undulating bay. Then the pilot banks, and she is given her first glimpse of the city.

A tremor runs through the great airliner. The fuselage is shivering, like a huge animal suddenly excited as it approaches the stables. Go with God, she has been instructed. An arrow. Straight to the heart.

Below her, millions wait for death.

DAY 2

Night. Rain. A storm system coming up from the Gulf. Joyce, the last of the season's hurricanes. Spawning tar balls and tornadoes.

But more than the wind is knocking at his front door.

Sam Watterman pads downstairs, snaps on the light, peers out on the porch to see a female Decatur police officer and a man in a suit. It's nothing good. Never anything good at this hour.

"Hold on a second." He shudders. Then he turns off the alarm and undoes the deadbolt.

"Yes?"

"Dr. Samuel Watterman?"

"That's right. What's the problem?"

He can hear the tremble in his own voice as his brain parses the possible tragedies. Should he invite them in? Do they have a warrant?

The man in the suit raises his hand—a clip-on badge and photo ID in a plastic protector. "I'm Special Agent Michael Lansing, Federal Bureau of Investigation. We'd like you to come to the field office with us."

"It's pretty late. Can't I come by in the morning? No, no . . . that's not very realistic. Well, I can't leave tonight anyway. Who's going to take care of my wife? She has a medical condition." The tremble has gone and he's whining now, standing up for his constitutional rights on his own two spindly legs. The rain is spraying on them all, blowing under the little porch overhang.

"Do you have an alternate caregiver you can call?"

"No."

"The officer can stay here. We'll send a nurse out."

"Is this really an emergency?" he challenges. "It's three in the morning."

"I'll be glad to stay with her, sir," volunteers the Decatur officer.

"Okay. Okay. Okay . . . Hold on . . ." Watterman says, turning back toward the stairs.

"One of us has to go with you, sir."

He stops. "Oh . . . right. You think I'm going to kill myself. This is bullshit, you realize, don't you? Come on." They go up the stairs to the bedroom.

"What is it?" Maggie says from the bed.

"I've got to go downtown. They think I'm going to kill myself. They want to leave Officer . . . um?"

"Payne, ma'am. I'm sorry for the intrusion—"

"Officer Payne is going to stay here with you while I go. Is that okay?"

"No, it's not okay." Maggie's face has gone white. "What do they want?"

What can he say to that? He's been through it all before, and she has too. For a moment they just look at each other. He finally shrugs, and she looks down at the duvet, then at him. For better, or for worse, or for really, really bad, her eyes tell him.

"Do you know first aid?" he asks the cop.

"Yes, sir, I'm trained in that."

"Good. She uses these tanks to augment her respiration. They pop on and off. Beyond that she can take care of all her own needs, can't you, hon?"

"Anything special you need to show me, that will be fine, sir."

"Okay . . . You're going to watch while I get dressed?"

"No, I will," says the FBI agent.

He puts on his pants, then reaches for the chair at the corner of the bed. His hand stops, poised above yesterday's shirt, a little lost. "How long am I going to be gone?"

"I really have—"

"Right . . . right. Okay. Be on the safe side, right." He takes a fresh shirt out of the plastic, unfolds it. It's distracting with Lansing standing there watching, and, out of his rhythm, he ends up leaving the shirt cardboard on the blanket at Maggie's feet. Thinking, It's stupid, a fresh shirt. The first thing they'll do is take his clothes and put him in a jumpsuit. He turns the shirt around in his hands for a moment and then pulls the little purple dry cleaner's tag out of the bottom buttonhole. He has no choice anyway. Not about the shirt. Not about anything. It's happening again. A burst of radio static from out in the hallway where Officer Payne is calling in.

"What exactly is wrong?" Maggie asks.

"I really can't say, ma'am."

"Same old, same old. Crap and bullshit allegations. Just crap . . ." Sam says and then shuts up, trying to curb his tendency to rant at the slightest provocation.

"Unless you know what's happening, Sam, just don't go."

He has always been able to count on Maggie to push the envelope. There is a pause, Lansing waiting for him do the negotiating.

"I don't think I have a lot of options, hon."

"Don't we at least get an explanation?" Maggie says. She's getting angry, which is wrong, almost rising off her pillow and waving her hand at Lansing.

"No, no, don't worry, just keep calm," he tells Maggie. "She's supposed to stay calm," Watterman says to the agent.

"Make sure the officer has her medications," the agent says.

"Right . . ." No choice involved, just obey orders while they take you to the wall, while they shovel you into the ovens, just do what they say. He pulls a sweater on.

"I'm retired, you know. I've been completely out of work for a decade except a couple of times here and there. This is bullshit. Reopening something like this? The man in question is dead. *Dead.* Did you know that?"

"I don't know anything about it, sir. I'm just the messenger boy."

"Right, right . . ." It's that old feeling starting to overwhelm him, being under someone's thumb, the loss of control. A prisoner all over again.

"Oh, God . . . these people . . ." Maggie says.

"I'll get a chair and sit out in the hall. If you need anything, ma'am, just call me," the officer says.

"I'll take care of this and be right back. You're going to be all right, hon," Watterman promises, kisses her goodbye, shoots a meaningful look at Officer Payne, and follows the FBI agent out into the rain.

The car is a slate-gray sedan. If you looked closely, you could see the antennas. Lansing lets him ride up front. They head into the storm, out of Decatur, toward Memorial Drive, making for the Federal Building in downtown Atlanta, he guesses.

"They're going to send out a nurse for your wife. She'll be here within the hour."

"Right," Watterman says. And then, a moment later, he suddenly shifts in the seat. "Goddamn it," he spits.

"You all right, sir?" Which Watterman translates as, *Do you want me to cuff you?*

"No, no, I'm fine. Yeah, I'm fine. Absolutely terrific."

He looks out at the rainy street. They're at the intersection of Memorial Drive. He'd hoped all this shit was over and done, and now . . . up from the bloody grave it comes again. He'll never be able to shake it. Never. They've been going the wrong way for several miles and now Lansing ramps onto the beltway. "Where the hell are you taking me?"

"Out to the field office, it's up off of 85 there," Lansing says.

"I know what's happened," he says. "People have small minds. They have their crappy little reputations to protect . . ." That's what it is, that's what it must be, he thinks. "I've got enemies, okay?" he says to the young FBI agent. "It could be Dean Stansbrey, or maybe even Reilly, somebody at Georgetown. And I can tell you, plenty of people have built healthy careers blaming me for their screwups. Or maybe you geniuses at the FBI or the CIA want me to go over my testimony again and catch me lying."

"Don't give me a hard time, sir."

"Tell me, have you ever been in court? I don't mean in your capacity as a willing tool of the state, or everyday shit like being sued for a car accident, but real court? Serious court? That ever happened to you?"

"No, sir. I haven't."

"Well, you don't need to murder people in this country. You can do it completely legally. That's when you discover who your real friends are. It's a transformative experience. I still haven't paid off my legal bills. May you be so lucky something like that never happens to you."

"This is a Homeland Security matter, Doctor," Lansing says, keeping his eyes on the road.

Daria cannot keep from looking out the window. Landing at JFK, the heart of Manhattan settling in the distance, the plane touches down.

They exit the mammoth aircraft, *danke, danke* to the pretty women and the dark-haired boy, and are channeled through Jetways and glassed-in corridors. *Welcome to the United States of America* is everywhere, along with some artful shots of the president looking all-knowing. But the building is cold, there are no amenities, surveillance cameras are bolted to every post and pillar, and policemen and soldiers are on patrol carrying M16s. Once again air travel has ceased to be glamorous, and they find themselves herded about like animals in some vast slaughterhouse. Great attitudinal African American women with holsters and pepper spray canisters snapped onto their belts shoo them from phase to phase. They are separated and separated again by the storm. . . .

  ". . . unless you are a member of the armed services, anyone who is arriving in New York after having visited Cuba, Sudan, Syria, or Iran . . ."

Some of the barriers are temporary. People are required to divide themselves based on the first letter of their last name, which of course means however it is written on the passport, nothing at all to do with a "last" name.

". . . Afghanistan, Algeria, Iraq, Lebanon, Libya, Nigeria, Pakistan, Saudi Arabia, Somalia, or Yemen, please use the green lane . . ."

There's nothing hidden about the security procedures. It is open, admitted. Obvious. A nation proudly guarding its border. "Give me your tired, your poor" . . . wasn't that the famous poem on the Statue of Liberty?

". . . If you are a citizen of Mexico, please wait behind the red line, right here . . . Muchas gracias . . ."

In the varied colors of the security workers' skins, she sees revealed the United States' much vaunted commitment to equality.

". . . anyone deplaning in the United States on business purposes please proceed directly to . . ."

Her nervousness has completely disappeared due to the sheer length of the process. She smiles at all of the border guards—thank you, thank you for doing such a good job of protecting us. Since each touch of her documents is a death sentence, she gladly hands over her passport and customs declaration. By the time they deal with her individually, she is ready.

The immigration officer sits tiredly at his kiosk; she approaches, smiles, hands him the passport. He takes it and looks away. Camera, she is thinking. As instructed, she places her thumb on a digital reader. Now Daria Vermiglio is in the system. The officer flips through her passport.

"Italiano . . ." he says.

"Yes," she says, smiling. A visitor proud of her English.

"You're here on business?"

"Yes, I am a reporter."

"You're working? You're on an assignment?"

"From *Klic!* magazine." The officer looks at her blankly. "It's for teenagers . . ."

"Okay. How long are you going to be in the United States of America?"

"Only two weeks, maybe one week longer, if they will fly me to Hollywood."

He doesn't even look at her standing there, still smiling.

"Well, what you've got is a thirty-day visa. If your publisher wants you to stay longer, you have to reapply at any U.S. consular office. Have a nice stay." He uses his stamp to validate her passport.

Customs, immigration, Homeland Security—it passes like some dream. Once again she encounters the well-dressed woman as they exit with their baggage. "Do you know the city?" the woman asks.

"Not really."

"Your first time?"

"Yes."

"Oh, you're going to have fun. Where are you staying?"

"At the Grand International? It is supposed to be charming."

"Your magazine must really love you. You will definitely enjoy it. And if you get into any trouble, you must call me. It always helps to have a friend." She passes her a card.

"Thank you, I will."

"And there is my email on there too. I don't do the, uh . . . Twitter."

"Yes. Tweet."

"Like birds. Tweet-tweet, yes. I don't do that. It has been very nice meeting you, signorina."

"*Arrivederci e grazie . . .*"

"*Niente, nessun . . . è stato un piacere incontrarla.* You know, I am at the Pierre, it is only just on the other side of the park. We could share a cab. It's better that way in New York, if you've never

been . . ." the Sinhalese woman says with a little shrug. It is a gesture
that says that although she may have been rich for these last few
decades, she still remembers how to pinch a rupee or two. Daria
knows instantly it will look better that way.

"Yes, let's share."

The Sinhalese woman, long ago consigned to death by her own
friendly impulses and Daria's requirement to fit in, has now become
her angel and guide. Once in their cab, the woman points out things,
recommends restaurants and galleries. Money is never mentioned,
since having flown first-class, Daria is obviously on an expense account. They are riding across a famous bridge into Manhattan; the
afternoon light is hard and the shadows flit rhythmically across the
windshield.

Her name is Sally, the woman says. Actually it is Saloni. Her
father sold and repaired refrigerators in a town near Goa. He was
successful and this ensured that she made a good marriage, to a
husband who inherited a quartet of farms when his uncle died.
"Back when it was Ceylon," she adds.

"Omar immediately began buying and selling. I left home and
didn't come back for fifteen years," she says.

"I'm sure it's very painful to be away for so long," Daria replies,
looking out the window, and—still in shock, naturally—only thinks
of her mother for a moment, and has to turn her face away to the
looming city. "I hope to see my mother for Christmas," she finally
says.

"You must. I'm sure she misses you."

"My father is dead. Or missing." The softness in her voice surprises her. Shock or not, the need to talk has won her over, and . . .
it feels good to talk. Why be so secretive? There's nothing this
woman can do with any information she might confide. Sally will be
dead soon anyway.

"He was taken away by soldiers," Daria says. "Two times, and
then it was decided that he should leave, he was going to live with
relatives, and my mother is still waiting for him."

"Oh, my . . . dear . . ." Sally touches her heart and then reaches over and clasps Daria's hand. After a moment she digs in her purse and comes out with a tissue. "I'm so sorry."

"Everyone has something . . . it's okay." Daria looks up at her. "There's nothing I can do about it, is there?" she says, forcing a smile, looking away from Sally to the back of the cabdriver, safe behind his protected barrier, ignoring them completely.

They slip into the purple gloom beneath huge buildings that flank the gigantic street—the widest and straightest she has ever seen—seemingly heading straight across America.

Ahead of her there is something blocking the street, and the taxi abruptly slows.

A policeman.

Standing there in his safety vest, his hand raised to stop them. There is a great tremor in her chest, and she sits up straight.

"There are always traffic problems," Sally says as they stop.

Now a trio of policemen are walking back and forth, all glued to their radios. They don't look her way. They don't seem to be interested in her cab at all.

"I was here when the Pope visited. It was true insanity, I assure you . . ." Sally laughs beside her.

The delay is all the more nerve-racking because there seems to be no reason for it. No cops are taking cover and drawing their guns and screaming for her to get out of the car. They just sit there, all traffic stopped. Waiting.

Then, crossing fast, a quartet of motorcycles followed by a half dozen black limousines. "It could be anybody, who knows?" Sally says. "Something at the UN . . . or maybe Sarkozy is in town . . ."

Once the VIP convoy has passed, they are released and the cab picks up speed as they race up the avenue. Daria is glued to the window now, craning her neck to stare up at the towering buildings . . . and when she turns back Sally is watching her, smiling.

"New York is a fantastic place, Daria. You're going to have a good time."

Only moments later the cab swerves to a stop in front of the white and gold awnings outside the Pierre. Except for these ostentatious awnings, they could be in Europe, in Berlin, outside the historic Hotel Adlon. The dark face of the driver says something to them, and he pops the trunk.

"I wish you the utmost success," Sally says, and they share a little hug.

She knew this would happen. She knew she would look into someone's eyes. From the moment she unscrewed the little bottle and poured the fluid over her hands, inside herself she *knew*. She had let her guard down, but what was the difference? Deaths had to be accepted. The method didn't matter, didn't affect the principles of her actions. A suicide bomb would maim and kill plenty of so-called innocents. She was doing the same. That was the point. That was the definition of terror.

So, there is no tear she has to wipe away, and, shivering, she waves goodbye to Sally as her cab pulls into the traffic stream and turns toward the glittering Grand International Hotel, just across the park.

He has been deposited in an interviewing room up on the sixth floor of a glass-walled building. It is the FBI's Atlanta field office, but it looks like any other anonymous suburban office building.

The interviewing room is not much different from other similar rooms he has visited: A table and three chairs placed in contravention of every dictate of feng shui. A camera lens poking through the top corner of the wall opposite. Others almost certainly. Assuming he takes the single chair, facing him is a large mirrored window that provides a good view for the evaluators next door. He walks right up to it, shades his eyes and tries to peer through. More cameras in there, probably. He takes a step back and raises his right hand.

"Hi. Nice to be back." Then he goes back around the table, sits and waits.

Lansing brings in a female agent to help with his interrogation.

"Aren't you going to read me my rights?" he can't help but snap.

"Not at the moment," the female agent answers. "I think they just want to ask you some questions." Playing the good cop, intro-

ducing herself, a soft handshake. Martine Grimaldi is her name.
Lansing leaves them, probably to make a beeline into the next room
to watch.

"Do you want a lawyer? We can assign someone . . ." Grimaldi
almost smiles.

"That's the last thing I want."

"I just need to clear up the basics, okay?" She has a folder to
consult.

"Fine. Sure. Go right ahead. Ask away." At least he's not cuffed
to the table.

"You're the same Dr. Samuel S. Watterman who authored the
report of the Committee for Biowarfare Preparedness in the Fall
2001 issue of the *Journal of the Federation of Amer—*"

"Yes, yes. I'm the guy. I did it. I was the evil genius who gave us
biowarfare. Amerithrax was my creation, if not my idea. It's all in
the court records, despite the fact that the whole point of everything
we did was to warn our superiors, and the government at large. . . ."

Grimaldi looks at him with her big eyes. "Why don't we just go
through the background one step at a time, okay?" She turns a page
to start again.

"Okay . . . I'll confess," he says. That brings her head up. "How
old were you when 9/11 happened?"

"Old enough."

"You remember the anthrax letters?"

"I learned about it later."

"Okay. Right after 9/11, seven letters were mailed. One to a
newspaper editor in Florida, then three to the major networks, then
another to the *New York Post*. Then two more were sent to politicians. All of them had anthrax spores in them . . ."

Grimaldi sits back, gripping her pen with both hands. No doubt
some kind of interrogator's neutral pose she's been taught at one of
Quantico's finishing schools.

"Anthrax looks like powder, just like white dust, but it's lethal.
The politicians escaped, as always, but in the end it killed a woman
in New Jersey, another woman in the Bronx, the editor in Florida,
and postal workers who worked in the sorting rooms."

"Yes, that's right," she murmurs.

"So . . . five homicides, okay? And then they had to completely decontaminate the buildings. Just the postal buildings cost forty-two million dollars, and at the time that was serious money."

"Right . . . We've got all that."

"Well, you can forget all that," he says. "Ancient history. All that stuff is completely out of date, I hope everyone realizes that. Please get it in the record"—a nod at the mirrored window—"please pass that up the line . . . it's completely out of date." He says this with certainty, even though his security clearances have been re-voked for so long that he's an ignoramus in the field. Of course the dark sciences haven't just stopped. Everything has kept on moving behind a cloak of secrecy. Except him.

"I had a good life, okay? A *real* good life. I was working with USAMRIID *and* I was working with the CDC. I was at the peak of my career. Right at the peak, you know?"

"Okay . . ."

"I was looking at early retirement, a place at the lake, maybe some consulting at Johns Hopkins or Princeton. I was up for *awards,* part of a team that even had an outside chance of a Lasker Prize. If things had worked out we might have even moved back to New York, which Maggie would have loved. Right at the peak . . ."

"Yes . . ."

"Then, bang—this stuff emerges out of my lab, the lab I ran, the lab I *signed* for. Suddenly I'm not a genius anymore, I'm a *suspect.* Investigations out the yin-yang. They came and searched the house in biohazard suits . . ."

"Yes," she repeats, just watching him.

"Legal bills? Hemorrhaging money. Overnight, I'm a traitor, I'm a terrorist. Didn't matter there was no evidence. Retired! Retired at the age of fifty-four. Pension is just about enough to buy dog food. I'm on everybody's blacklist. Very few Christmas cards coming through the slot. Evidence? No. No evidence. Until Bruce Ivins kills himself, okay? You've got that in your archives, right?" he says, tap-ping the folder with his finger.

"I've got that. Yes," Grimaldi says. Her face is frowning now.

She'd be a great elementary school teacher. Every kid would fall in love with her.

"So, one day Ivins pulls the plug on himself. Now things start coming to light. Oh! Big discovery—Ivins was *unstable*! Crazy, alcoholic, drug addicted, marital problems, you name it. Now they're claiming they'd been watching him all along. Wow! Case closed. The Justice Department makes their half-ass statement, but by that point I'm a little out of the professional loop, you know?"

"That sounds pretty rough," Grimaldi says.

"*Rough?* Yes, you could say it was rough. And then there's the medical with Maggie. Insurance says it's preexisting. Everything goes for that. You guys trashed my life, young lady, and now—"

A little tap at the door. Lansing comes in. A few whispers and he pulls her out of the room before she's even got started on her backgrounders. Is it Sam's imagination or does she suddenly stiffen? Does the blood run out of her cheeks? They leave.

And then nothing. Nothing at all.

Nothing for a half hour, maybe longer, until they come back and move him down the hall.

"What about my wife? Am I under arrest?" he asks Lansing as they walk along.

"As soon as I can better inform you, I will, but you're staying here with us for a while."

"What? *No!* I can't stay here! Wait a minute—"

"They're sending someone to get your clothes."

"Clothes? What do I need clothes for?"

Lansing says nothing. His lips are pressed together in a tight crease. He probably *can't* say anything. He probably isn't even allowed to *think* anything.

"Man, this is the most anal situation in the world . . ." But by then they have reached his new room, where Lansing lets him in and leaves—locking the door behind him.

Her room is actually a suite; very modern and, by European standards, as large as a football field. It smells of "new." No expense spared. Her poisoned luggage has been rolled in and set upon a rack in the clothes closet. The operation of the television cupboard with its enormous screen has been demonstrated. On the writing desk there are all sorts of guidebooks for her to peruse. The menu for room service comes with a fourteen-page wine list. If she needs a taxi, she can call the front desk and they will have one waiting for her. There are two restaurants and a very good bar. Anything, anything at all, just call. The boy practically has his hand out.

"Tell me, what is the name of that street?"

"That street, running like that?" The boy goes over to the window and points. "That's Broadway, and at the end of the block there is Fifty-sixth. This your first time in the city?"

"It's a very big street."

"Yes, I guess it is." He's not that cute. A little embarrassed, perhaps, to be in the room with her. Alone. They are close enough in age.

"Are you staying long?" he asks.

"Just a few nights."

"Whatever you need, ma'am." He makes a little bowing motion with his body and starts to leave.

"Yes, thank you—" Back in shiny new Brandenburg Airport she had gone to a kiosk and cashed five hundred U.S. dollars in twenties and fifties on the credit card. She peels one out of her billfold. "Thank you," she says again. *"Grazie . . ."*

And then she is finally alone, and in less than the time it takes to kick off her shoes, the shakes come.

She begins to tremble uncontrollably, and when she breathes it is in short gasping yelps. She rolls back onto the bed and presses her face into the pillow and tries to control her breathing. The pillow smells of disinfecting detergent. Unbelievably fresh. Like being smothered with a pine forest. When she dares to let in some air, it is frigid. She pushes her feet down under the covers, and puts her hands over her face.

Each time she thinks she can breathe naturally, it starts all over again. All she can do is wait it out, coming down from the panic in slow stages until finally, mercifully, it stops.

From where she has fallen on the bed, she can see one side of a gigantic building, rows of concrete, steel, glass. All parallelograms. Unending geometry. Glass that is meant to reflect the sky, the architects would have claimed. Artifice. Purposeless, grandiose, humanless construction. Buildings designed by machines. She stands and walks across the carpet and looks out the window at the angled streets.

She supposes it is the fear of getting caught. And the fact that she has passed through the most important barrier—the border of the United States.

She has done it!

Yes, it is true—to a certain degree she has already completed her mission. Perhaps her shaking is only relief at having not been caught. It catches in her throat for a moment, and she laughs. Below her a steady stream of cars surge up . . . *Broadway.*

The hotel boy is dead now too, she realizes. Between her shoulders there is a chill and she goes back to the bed and tries not to think of him. Or the nice woman . . . Sally.

All soldiers get like this, she reminds herself. Anyone when they go into combat. The young recruit has his first taste of war, his first sight of the gore . . . In the movies they always throw up. But no, that's not it, she thinks, because she's seen gore, she's seen people killed. Seen her brothers' bodies after they left them to rot in the street.

She sets up her laptop, registers on the hotel's wireless, goes online and searches "smallpox." There is a lot on the Web about the disease, and even more on biological warfare. Indeed, everything is as she has been told in Berlin.

Smallpox—so dangerous that it became the first disease ever totally eradicated by humans, finally conquered in 1979.

> . . . *best defended by vaccination. To combat such an emergency, the WHO has millions of doses stockpiled should there ever be a reemergence of the disease.* . . .

Apparently "eradication" must have meant different things to different people. The superpowers held back samples for research purposes in secret laboratories. A defector from the Soviet Biopreparat blew the whistle on extensive manufacturing operations, which revealed twenty tons of smallpox stored in Zagorsk.

The disease was ancient and terrifying. It had been used as a weapon ever since men discovered that it could be spread from person to person. It was called a pox because of the pustules that erupted on the skin of the patient.

> Variola major: *The name given to the smallpox disease around* A.D. *580 by Swiss bishop Marius of Avenches. The basic forms of the disease were codified by English doctor Gilbertus Anglicus in the year 1240. . . .*

The symptoms were, in the beginning, similar to an ordinary flu—fatigue leading to a fever. The patient would have vivid dreams that verged on hallucinations. A sore throat might or might not lead to a cough, but from that point, the virus was easily spread.

> *. . . and being exclusive to* Homo sapiens, *it can only infect humans. Mortality rates vary with the individual strain, but classic variola major kills upward of a third of those infected. . . .*

She searches until she comes up with a full description of the way she will die. Once again she is given an account of the symptoms: the bad cold, fever, nausea, vivid dreams, and a spreading rash . . . There are archival photographs of long-dead victims sitting up in bed with pustules crowding across their faces like a swarm of bees.

There is more, but she stops.

So . . . these invisible things, these creatures on her skin, in her hair, in her blood and breath—they are her bomb, her exploding vest. They are her box cutter and the poisoned tip of her arrow. Something special has been made, some technological feat that she can be proud of. Weaponized and put in a bottle like cough syrup.

She looks around the room, walks over to the windows.

Is this terror? she asks herself. Is she not terrified? Her palms are cold. She has a slight headache; looking down onto the street, she feels dizzy. Is she getting sick?

She presses her hands to the glass and tries to see down over the edge of the building. Some people fall to their deaths. Others jump. Either way, it would be terrible, she thinks—eyes open, screaming, watching the street rising up to you.

It is like that for her now. Nothing more to lose.

Is she just simply afraid of dying?

She clicks open her email . . . and sure enough there is a draft of a supposedly unfinished message waiting. When she opens it there are no instructions, only a long list of targets. Everything in alphabetical order, which is to say, no order at all. Hospitals, banks, police stations. Centers of command and control. She scrolls all the way to the bottom. At least ten pages' worth if she was insane enough to print it out.

She finds a phone book in the desk, it's four inches thick and weighs ten pounds. At the back are sections on Government Services, Medical Services. She goes back to the top of the email list and reads down again. Nothing there that she can't find in the phone book.

She erases the draft. No evidence unless they seize her hard drive.

Daria sits there for a moment. Takes a deep breath. Her heart is racing and she decides that the thing to do is get right to work while whatever she's poured over her hands, massaged through her hair, or had impregnated in the fabric of her clothes still lives.

Down in the restaurant she leafs through the tourist guide and works out her own list of targets. It's not exactly confidence inspiring that Berlin has given her the absolute minimum: plane tickets, credit cards, and a list that includes everything under the sun. Okay, she'll have to make it up as she goes along, and right now her idea is to spread the germs to every high-trafficked place in the city.

To be honest, she is a little worried about playing on the details about *Klic!* magazine. She can pass out business cards all she wants, and there's even a website with a *Contact Us* button in four languages. Let's imagine that someone might eventually answer the phone: Would they back her up? How is she to know? What would Ali do?

While waiting for her espresso, she looks at her hands, turning them over. The skin is just as before, no rash or tenderness she can feel. The toiletry kit survived riding in her checked luggage—toothpaste, moisturizer, lipsticks. Undoubtedly they have been augmented with the virus. She's not to waste it.

Sooner or later she'll need to take a shower. But right now, the important thing to do is to mingle. To be the arrow she was designed to be: a trendy young journalist from abroad, newly arrived on a mission to pump up the glamour of the Big Apple and sell to teens the indescribable thrill of being anywhere else other than at home with your parents.

She's allowed the smiling young men and women who staff the front desk to advise her with directions. She tips generously to everyone, *ciao* this and *grazie* that.

She walks out the doors.

The weather is fine this late September afternoon, the air clean, a breeze that comes and goes, smelling of oak leaves and soggy grass, and she decides to begin her campaign of destruction with a stroll through Central Park.

If they made the movie of her life, it would have to include this triumphant sequence—Natalie Portman walking along, staring at the cliff faces of the huge buildings, a stainless-steel sculpture of the globe, a bronze of a long-dead explorer. Natalie waiting to cross the river of traffic . . . then finally breaking away from the crowd and into the great park, smiling at the babies, giving way to the joggers. Her passionate movie-star heart thrilling to the beauty of the landscape, swept across it, drawn like an arrow to the Guggenheim Museum.

She recognizes it from art books. Yes, the swirling white Guggenheim Museum, designed by Frank Lloyd Wright. She pays, checks her jacket and bag, and strolls up the endless ramp that winds ever higher through the gallery, musing on where she should be going next. Her hands linger on the railings. The muted sounds and fantastic art wash over her. She visits the bathrooms. There's something thrilling about knowing that by tomorrow the process by which she infects a building will be second nature.

She gets to the top of the spiral, then takes the elevator back down, reclaims her jacket and bag, and gets a cab. The driver is pitch-black. America has the largest number of black people she has ever seen. "I'd like to visit the site of the Twin Towers," she says.

"Ground Zero? Of course, ma'am," the man says, and she recognizes his accent as from somewhere in the Caribbean.

"If I go there, is it far to get to the Underground?"

"You mean the subway? No, ma'am. There are many stops. Very easy."

"I'm a reporter and I'm writing about what people do in New York City," she says, taking the opportunity to practice her story.

"I see, I see," the man says. He steps on the brakes abruptly and she sits back and looks for the seat belt. "These people are crazy," the driver mutters.

They duck and weave through the lanes of traffic. It is an odd sensation to simply trust the cabdriver as the city rushes by. Infinite, anonymous, gargantuan. There are flashes of recognition, landmarks she's seen many times via film and television. It takes at least a half hour to make the trip through the gridlocked streets.

And then . . . the sky seems to open up and she is stunned at how big the site is. . . . The scale is gigantic. Acres and acres of destruction. She had no idea. She only knows the images she has seen of the collapse, and no television can really convey the scale of it.

Except for the historical significance, it's a boring neighborhood, mostly bankers and lawyers and a steady swarm of pilgrims—tourists who come in all sizes, students, singletons, the elderly with their canes, chairs, scooters, and walkers, all paying homage to the great strike against Satan that occurred on this spot on the eleventh of September, 2001.

The site itself is fenced off with blue plastic billboards covered with Web addresses. An expanse of ruined earth better left to weeds, but now crammed with pipes and tunnels, cement mixers and cranes, men and women toiling in reflective vests and hard hats around the red steel skeleton of the promised replacement: an even more iconic twisting glass icicle called One World Trade Center. She walks until she comes upon the memorial park that has been built on the footprint of the original two towers. Bronze barricades inscribed with the names of the dead. A great many newly planted trees with reflecting pools and waterfalls to generate white noise that will soothe visitors and help them forget what they have come there to remember.

It's all she can do to keep from shouting. She catches herself grinning and tries to put on a serious expression, but it's almost impossible. Oh! What an extraordinary accomplishment: dedicated martyrs, language training, a few weeks of flying lessons, and some box cutters. What did 9/11 do to the United States? To the whole world! Now the fear is palpable, written in full-body scanners and concrete barriers. Any time an American has to endure the security searches at an airport, or go through a metal detector at a sporting event, city hall, or federal building, they know who is really winning the battle. The Americans and their allies could send their commandos to kill Bin Laden, orbit their drones over the mountains of Afghanistan for a full eon and the righteous would still rise up to oppose them.

Above her the skeleton rises. Birds wheel. White clouds form and re-form in a blue sky. Music, the sound of the traffic, horns blaring, brakes squealing, engines roaring. She looks up and turns on the sidewalk. It all circles above her.

Smiling, tears in her dark eyes. Surrounded by the clanking monster; the snapping of the welders, the generators, the cement pumpers and dump trucks as they climb the dusty ramps in and out of the sprawling building site—

Are they thinking of this rebuilding as a symbol of defiance? Of victory? Getting on top again? Celebrating their indomitability as they reclaim their hallowed ground?

It is nothing. It is less than nothing.

✳ ✳ ✳

From her handy tourist map she has discovered that she is near Wall Street. Logically, most of the lesser demons who maintain the devil's heartbeat make their living inside these surrounding offices, but there are couriers, deliverymen, clients, and functionaries coming and going, everyone constrained by the vehicles whizzing by.

It is a cool autumn day. She'll walk.

The Twin Towers are more than just symbolic, but striking at Wall Street means driving her arrow into the heart of the capitalist system that powers all of godless America. There are many great financial temples on this street. All she has to do is visit them one at a time.

Playing her part, she arrives at the Exchange and seeks out a publicist. She is directed to an obviously gay man, somewhat over forty, who is empowered to deal with inquiries from the media. She assures him that she is harmless, explains the rather insubstantial publishing philosophy of *Klic!*, and after a few laughs is shuffled off to Candace and Sharee, two admin assistants.

"You know, it's silly, really, but it's good publicity. We are a magazine primarily for teenage girls and maybe a few boys. It's about the reader going to New York City and meeting someone, an ordinary guy, cute, attractive, but one who is part of the workforce, you know?" she explains, smiling all the time.

"Sure. Certainly. Romance." Candace and Sharee exchange a look.

"That's right. For young people. I need an interview, just a very little interview. It's only a hundred words. It's nothing. One of the boys who works here, who he is, what special music he likes. He is single, we hope, but is he seeing anyone? Does he like European girls? That would be a plus."

"Mmmm . . ."

"You know, a cute guy."

"Sure. We have some of them," Candace says. She shrugs and looks over to Sharee, who agrees.

"One of those ones who waves his arms around all the time, all excited. You see them, you know . . . *bidding.*"

"A floor trader."

"They have jackets on, and it's obviously hard work, I know."

"Oh, those guys, yeah. They have a lot of stress."

"And so they need a girlfriend . . ." They all laugh. Candace and Sharee take her out on the floor and point out two or three young men. She takes her time, deciding.

"Interview?" one of the traders asks Candace as he passes by.

"That's right. *Sports Illustrated* for women—swimsuit issue."

"Not me," he says. "Don't wanna scare my daughter . . ."

Daria takes a minute or two before picking one out. Candace and Sharee set her up in the coffee room, where he comes to meet her once he's on his break. She gets his name, gets his vitals, a little background about how he got into the business. What's his favorite movie? Hobbies, sports? Does he have a girlfriend? Who is his biggest hero?

"Nelson Mandela," the young man says straightaway.

"Really?"

"That's right, Mandela . . ." Some of the other guys come by and knock on the glass and laugh at him. After a dozen stupid questions it's over and he puts his arm around her and smiles while Sharee takes their picture with Daria's camera. Then he ducks back out to make some serious money, his real hobby.

"That was good," says Sharee.

"He's going to get a lot of Italian girlfriends emailing him now," Daria says. "Okay, so . . . what about an eligible bachelor who is maybe just a little bit older? You know, we give these girls hope. You might marry the first one, and if you do he'll turn out like this second guy. He's going to be successful, be a good father, make lots of money, still hot . . ."

"The whole fantasy, huh?" says Sharee.

"It's exciting, but it's a happy life."

"We should hook her up with Maliya over at NASDAQ," says Candace.

"Yeah, she knows all the business news people."

"I don't want to impose, but it's only five minutes. It might be fun?"

"Oh, they'd be happy for the break. And you could interview some women too, show them some positive role models," Sharee says, as if she were the first person on the globe to think of such a thing.

"That's a very good idea," Daria says, and squeezes her arm.

"We do all the work anyway. . . ."

His name is Burke, and he's in his thirties. Used to women, you can tell. Confident and dark. Good hair, in shape, but maybe wound a little tightly, like some soldiers she has seen.

He likes to laugh over dinner, a kind of a happy-hour meal—burgers and nachos and beer. There are three or four others from NASDAQ, all friends, and they tease her about Italy and tell her all about MSNBC and various celebrities from business television they have met. Mixed in are behind-the-scenes horror stories meant to impress her, a foreigner, not even a business reporter, who doesn't understand the first thing about the exchanges. She's totally safe and they have fun showing off for her. One of Maliya's friends is Urjal, who's a media specialist and prods her for more information on *Klic!*'s corporate parentage. Does he suspect something or is he just researching? She shrugs and laughs, spreads out her vowels, talks faster than anyone else, becomes the life of the party, and can't help but notice that everybody is happy to see her getting along so well with Burke.

Will alcohol help or hurt the antidote she has been given? she wonders.

Later, in the cab back to the hotel, Burke is happy with what is shaping up to be an easy conquest. He sees her craning her neck at the window. "It's fantastic, isn't it?" he says, looking into her eyes.

All she has to do is smile, she is thinking.

A few more blocks and they are at the Grand International. In the elevator she lets him kiss her, and he is fumbling at her dress by the time they get through the door into her room. He is laughing and joking about how fast everything is going. She doesn't even pull the curtains, pushes his head down between her legs and lets him work for it. He doesn't mind at all, and as he is climbing up atop of her he gentlemanly asks about a condom.

"Don't worry," she says. "Don't worry about anything."

It is over soon, too soon really, for her to relax and remember Ali, and beautiful Tété, and Leonardo's laugh. . . . Those three, that's all. That's her entire database of love. Unexpected knowledge accumulated along the way as she filled out her pretend identity. With Burke it is fast and thrilling, and crazy because they are strangers, and when it's done they lie there, panting, her clothes only half off, and him still in his shirt and socks.

"I guess you have to go?" she says to him.

"No, no . . ."

"If you have to go, I'll understand. I have to work in the morning, too."

He turns and looks at her across the bed. He frowns a little, then smiles. "Okay, sure. You're probably right."

She watches him get up, find his pants, tuck himself in. The beautiful tie that gets loosely knotted around his neck. "Can I call you?" he says.

"Sure, but I'm going to be working the whole time."

"I hope I didn't disappoint you."

"Not at all," she says. "I like American men."

DAY 3

Waking up in the night, a little sweaty, a little lost, probably from the alcohol, probably from the shock of being somewhere utterly strange and bizarre, she sees by the bedside clock that it's almost five-thirty. She orders a minimalist breakfast from room service, then waits, staring out into the foggy blue light of dawn. She feels fine more or less. Jet-lagged, a little hungover, a little sore from Burke, but she asked for it.

But something has clicked in her dreams. She realizes that she has been making bad tactical decisions, just buzzing off in the wrong direction. Yes, she could destroy America one Burke at a time, or she could try to think logically. For a moment there are tears in her eyes. Fear, she decides. She is scared. Anyone would be. Look at what she is trying to do—it's immense. Look at the finality of what she has already done. She will be dead soon herself. As dead as Burke or any of the others she's touched. The whole world, going down the toilet together, martyrs, infidels, rich, poor, black, white, and brown—all washed away.

In the mirror she examines herself for signs of disease. Nothing.

She paces out into the room, stands naked by the windows, looking down onto the empty street. Someone could see her now, if they were only watching. Someone with a sophisticated spy camera that could see in low light.

There is the sound of the room service, and she puts on her robe, much too large for her, and goes to get her breakfast. Powered up with a chocolate croissant and a double espresso, she begins to get a little clarity. From the telephone directory and by Googling, she develops today's targets.

Should she go for the FBI, for the mayor's office, for City Hall?

Go for it. And maybe go for the hospitals today too, she thinks. Nothing throws off a civilization like thousands of dying people pounding on the emergency room entrance doors. Might as well get them off to a good start.

Once outside it's the names she sees. Logos are everywhere, on walls, the sides of trucks, splayed out across the gigantic shopwindows. Of course, she's seen the garish European version, but this is . . . everywhere. So thoroughly embedded into the fabric of Manhattan daily life that for those who reside in this fantastic hellhole it has become invisible—just as a fish cannot see water. She gawks like a tourist. It is, after all, her role. Enjoy it, enjoy it . . .

She has two credit cards, one from *Klic!* and one in her own name, both handed to her by Youssef as she was leaving the Adlon. With them she withdraws a thousand dollars and begins doling out twenties to cabdrivers as she crisscrosses the city.

At each stop, the same routine. Go in, ask a question. Ask to see someone who might help her obtain . . . it can be anything, a job application, an interview, a bit more information than the receptionist can provide. If possible, shake hands politely. Hand over one of her dwindling supply of *Klic!* business cards.

The clerks and lower-level assistants that she encounters take her in their stride. "Crazy people come through here all the time," one young assistant with rebellious blue hair tells her. She gains access to waiting rooms, bathrooms, and elevators, elevators, elevators. In the city's bloodstream now, she thinks.

A great many people love Italy, it turns out. A significant percentage are descended from Italian immigrants and jump at the chance to try out some half-remembered childhood phrases on her, everyone groping for their vocabulary, and apologizing for their accents.

After only a few stops, she discovers the famous New York brusque attitude, and takes immediate pleasure in killing the grouches and gatekeepers—human T-cells, little better than slime—who run on a fuel of envy and petty jealousy, and who only exist to slow her down. She always hands them a card. When she is alone in an elevator, she takes some remainders and first breathes on them, then licks them in the hope of increasing their lethality. These cards are reserved for the worst of the species.

She makes a note to shop for better shoes, and stops for lunch at a funky, jam-packed restaurant on Forty-fourth near the Avenue of the Americas. Over a plate piled with huge portions of tasteless greasy food, she studies her handy tourist map, trying to figure out if she is anywhere close to striking the Port Authority, which sounds like the most important thing around, but she discovers that she is ten blocks from Greeley Square and thus close to Macy's.

Soon she is wandering through the gigantic store, letting her fingers trail over fabrics, plastics, and leathers. She makes a pretense of checking the prices, smiles and asks for help.

By then she's sick of the new shoes she's worn since Berlin, and lets a pair of shopgirls put them in a bag while she slips on a fabulous pair of Dr. Martens ankle boots. Deciding to abandon her assault on the Port Authority, she takes a short cab ride down to Twenty-third Street and over to Fifth Avenue near the Flatiron Building, pleasing the driver with a crisp twenty. She picks up a pair of tights, a short dark skirt, and a big loose sweater with a hood from the Gap. She decides to change, twirls in the mirror and assesses herself—a spoiled art student spending plenty of Daddy's money. She'd like a haircut, but that's against the rules. She fishes in her bag, and finds the perfume they gave her back in Berlin. . . . It is only the size of a lipstick. She turns it over and over in her hands, admires the way the light plays over the facets.

And then gives herself a spritz.

On the corner a business center is advertised, and she has them run up another five hundred *Klic!* business cards. She wanders the neighborhood until she can pick up the cards, pile into a cab, and drop everything off back at the Grand. Then goes out and does it all over again.

By using her time profitably in the waiting rooms of the corporate headquarters, she has learned many things about the way the American capitalist monster functions. At this moment she is sitting in the offices of McCann Worldgroup, looking around, marveling at the way her mind is changing after only two days in America. Liberating.

Maybe it is a land of liberty, of free thinking. Or maybe she's just growing up. First of all, she has ceased to blame it all on the Jews—the Jakob Schiffs, and the Rothschilds, the Loebs, the Kleins . . . Greed is universal, and times have changed. After all, the richest man in the world is a Mexican. No, she has discovered the new truth about capitalism—it does not discriminate, except against the poor. Race and nationality mean nothing—all it takes to get in the door is cash, whether from Bahrain or Buenos Aires.

So, it's not the Jews, or more correctly, not *only* the Jews. Neither is it the gangsters, or the robber barons like Rockefeller, Vanderbilt, and J. P. Morgan. They've been left in the dust by vast corporations with no seeming purpose at all, conglomerates who have their filthy fingers in every imaginable pie. The police, the teachers, and the armies of entire governments are in their thrall. Still, her more liberal thinking hasn't stopped her from visiting Proskauer Rose, the United Jewish Communities, and the World Bank offices—little whirlwind assaults on old dragons in their lairs.

She is starting to understand the allure of the American dream—it's the idea of a supposedly level playing field. Once seen, it's everywhere. Peddled at every opportunity. It's what they recruit you with; black, white, brown, gay, or straight, you can do it too! It's the carrot on the stick dragging second-generation immigrants into business schools and chaining them to decades of debt. But even the business magazines admit that with the high cost of education, the promise of success is being denied to a growing percentile of the lower class.

Of course, facts don't really get in the way; with so few dreams in its arsenal, this particular capitalist whimsy lives on—anyone with grit, determination, and a willingness to get their hands dirty can pull themselves up from the very bottom of the pyramid. And then, once you've gotten to the top, it's time to give back. This scenario is worshiped in thousands of ways, commemorated in Rockefeller Center, in the Guggenheim, in the Brill Building, the Stephen A. Schwarzman Building, the Koch Theater, the Ronald McDonald House, and the Harvey Milk High School. *This bench is dedicated in memory of our loving mother, from Grace, Billy, and Chad.* The dead determine where you sit.

She plays anthropologist as she wanders along, trying to find any remnant of the original island of Manhattan. Of course there is nothing left of the indigenous peoples . . . tricked, starved, or murdered off their land by the tightfisted Dutch in the middle of their turn as masters of the earth. Then, as European fortunes went, so went the Neue World. The Dutch gave way to the English, and the English fell to their rebellious offspring. Colonizers giving way to robber barons, captains of industry giving way to international capital. Money flying through the air at light speed. The belly of the beast.

She works her way down her list, visiting offices, asking if there are any cute guys she can talk to, being told to wait, or bounced to whoever handles their marketing. By the afternoon she has reduced it to a formula. She grabs an espresso at the Cinema Brasserie and then walks up to Forty-sixth Street into the Barnes & Noble store and wanders through the sections, admiring the universe of books they have there.

It's easy, being an arrow.

Even in New York, Americans are too polite, she thinks. She asks to use restrooms, she fills out forms, she shakes hands. She checks her balance at the ATM. She shops. She runs her hands down the banisters, inquires of the security personnel if there is a place to smoke. She touches all the faucets in the restroom, the toilet paper, all the latches on all the doors, the lever on the soap machine.

A helpful janitor tells her where the closest fire station is. He even stands out in front of the consulate of the Philippines and points it out for her.

It's like that everywhere she goes. She just takes people's suggestions as she goes about killing them.

The members of the FDNY are used to the celebrity treatment by now. Even in Italy she had been deluged by photographs of ghostly firefighters staggering through the toxic rubble of the Twin Towers. There have been statues cast of them, and you can still see movie stars wearing their T-shirts and caps. Their heroism is taken for granted worldwide.

So she knows it is not suspicious when she walks up and asks if she can interview a strapping young rookie for the benefit of European teenagers. Josh and Tanis come out. She takes them one at a time, happy to explain that Tanis will be good for the boys. To raise the temperature and give the department a little more publicity, Tanis unbuttons the top button of her uniform shirt and exposes a few square centimeters of chest. They are cheerful, competent wisecrackers who pose leaning against their beloved pumper truck.

As usual, Daria asks to use the washroom, and Tanis points out the women's. She is inside when the sirens start up and the station erupts with the sound of the trucks' engines.

She gets out just in time to see them roaring away down the street. One of the older firemen, his hair frizzed white at the temples against his blotchy dark skin, follows their progress out on the sidewalk, his hands at his hips.

"It's very exciting," she says. The man has turned and is frowning at her.

"Can I help you?" he says.

"I was just in the washroom. I'm a reporter." She lifts her digital camera.

"Okay . . . did you get your picture?" he asks.

"Yes, it's good. I got everything and then, boom—whoosh!"

"Yes, it can be like that around here."

"Do they go to the fires often?"

"Nooo . . . it's all sorts of things. Hell, it can be somebody leaving their stove on about half the time." He laughs and rubs one of the toes of his shoes against the pavement, gives it a little tap like a dancer would. "It can be anything. Hazardous materials, bomb threat . . ." He turns and looks at her meaningfully. "We are the first responders, you see."

"Yes?"

"Police, fire, doctors on the emergency ward. Something bad happens and we are going to get to it first. That's what I mean."

"Sure, that makes sense. You have to be prepared," she agrees. "Can I take your picture?"

"Aw, now . . . you don't want some old fart like me . . ."

"No, it's good. It might help these teenage girls think about something other than getting a date with the latest football player . . ." She raises the camera. He takes off his glasses, goes serious, and looks directly into the lens.

"We lost six men from this engine company when the Towers went down," he says while she frames him. "I lost two of my best friends. I was in the hospital for four months straight. My wife divorced me," he says, shaking his head. "So, if anything bad happens like that again, we have special training, we know how to deal with toxic waste, and we're all vaccinated," he says, pointing to his arm.

"Really?" It only makes sense, she thinks.

"In case there's some outbreak of plague, or some . . . unknown big event."

She looks at him for a moment. "Is it dangerous, being a fireman?"

"No, ma'am, not most of the time, no. But when it *is* dangerous, it's *extremely* bad," he says, and laughs. Turns, heading back inside the big doors. "I have to close this up now. You got everything you came for, didn't you?" the old man asks.

She nods and waits while he hits a switch that brings down the great doors, leaving her outside in the cool shadows.

"Here's a little breakfast for you." It's a new FBI agent, who comes and goes without giving any more information. And it's useless to ask, Watterman knows. Useless.

Coffee. A bran muffin. A metal-covered plate with eggs, sausage, a bagel with lox, an arc of Bermuda onion, and some withered-looking capers. A plastic spoon and a crescent of honeydew melon.

The single bed has been unexpectedly comfortable. There is a bathroom for him to do his business. The room is Spartan enough, but boasts a real table that isn't bolted down. A lamp. Writing paper and some pencil stubs, the standard camera placed obviously in the top corner of the room. Everything wired for sound, of course. On an end table there is a selection of magazines, but the newest is from the previous summer. They must be the kind of things FBI agents read in their downtime. *Golf, GQ, Sports Illustrated.* A crinkly *Vanity Fair.* Half-naked fashion models and celebrity scandal. In the night-table drawer a Gideon Bible, a copy of the Book of Mormon, and an English translation of the Quran; not much solace for a fallen Jew. No television. No windows. Ventilation provided by a grate in the ceiling.

He waits. Men can wait for years, he reminds himself.

After breakfast another hour goes by while he reads *Road & Track* and ponders why anyone, ever, would want to restore a muscle car, then Lansing pokes his head in.

"There's been a change in priorities and personnel. They are going to continue with your interview as soon as possible."

"Yeah, hey, can I get a telephone?"

"I doubt it, but I'll boot it up the line."

"It's been an entire day. Am I under arrest? If I am, I'll break down and pay to see a lawyer. And if I'm not, I still want to see a lawyer."

"Things are changing fast, sir." And then, when Lansing goes—he leaves the door open.

Something about the casualness of it makes Watterman angry. Is it by accident or design? Is it some test? Is he going to be lured out to the office corridor and thus qualify as an escapee? Everything is a mindfuck with these guys. The youngest ones are the worst. Dirty tricks, cheap psych jobs. Leaving the door open like that is the most juvenile idea, and it makes him angry at Lansing for even trying something so stupid.

Crazy. Watterman jerks his head, trying to limber up the crick in his neck. There is the perpetual headache. It's probably the progressive lenses in his glasses. Over the years he's learned to compensate by lifting his head. Sitting in front of the computer or driving for any distance makes it worse. He shakes his head back and forth and slowly tries to free his shoulders. Way too much stress. And why not? Now he's back, folks! Back in the vortex where tax dollars are sucked down the drain into the War on Terror, the War on Drugs, the War on Poverty. Endless, fruitless war.

But there's something else. He can feel it. It's a disturbance in the goddamn force. Things are changing, moving too fast. First they drag him out of bed at three in the morning, he's swept into the fray, and now . . .

The door is wide open. People coming and going. He sees Agent Grimaldi striding through the office with a full cup of tea, dodging coworkers. A pause to exchange a few words with an older man, then they both go their own way.

By now he has come to love the open door, but he's afraid that if he goes and stands there, they'll notice and lock him up again. He could complain. He wants to complain, but he's like a dog that's been beaten. Better to wait them out, play nice. Give them what they want and then maybe he can get his cell phone back.

But the door beckons and he can't fight the temptation. He stands, and as if bored, ambles over to the opening, one arm resting against the jamb, letting his neck roll around. Letting whoever is on the other end of the camera see that he's stopped right there on the prisoner's side of the threshold. He's not going anywhere, he's a good boy.

Through the fourth-floor windows, he can see a gray sky and a piney-fringed view of Atlanta. It's still early on a school morning, but already the whole place is swarming with agents.

"We should go to the lab," he says to the first agent who comes along—the man just nods and keeps going. The CDC labs are not that far from his house, down by Emory University, and if there's anything in his cloud of expertise going on, they'll know all about it there. A few seconds later he buttonholes two more agents passing his open door.

"Look, I need to talk to Special Agent Lansing, all right? It's important." From a cubicle an even more lowly agent looks up and sees him causing a problem. She stands. "Dr. Wasserman?"

"Watterman, Watterman with two *t*'s. Wasserman was my grandfather. He changed it because he wanted to assimilate."

"You should wait back inside, sir."

"No, I shouldn't. I should go out to the CDC. Look, I *know* what's going on."

"Sir, just wait in here." Iron in her voice.

He takes a step back, hands up in the universal defensive gesture. "*Please* tell Agent Lansing we should go to the CDC labs. It's an emergency."

"You're still in custody until they finish your interview, sir."

And this time she closes the door.

He curses, he paces, he shoots the bird to the camera. He fumes. He has saved *Golf* for last because it will cause the most pain, and perversely he decides to make this the worst experience of his entire life, and begins turning through the pages with relish. All golf courses look alike, he thinks. You'd have to be obsessive-compulsive to tell them apart; bizarre landscapes. Titanium technology will conquer all. Will the first space colony have a golf course? Probably.

Lansing comes back in, sits. "Lunch is coming." He looks like he's been up all night. Staring a hole through the table, and then snapping out of it. "Do you want anything?" he says.

"Sure. I want to go home and see my wife. And I'm ready to make a statement. I've repeatedly agreed to cooperate, but what you and I actually should do is get over to the lab."

"What about the lawyer? You still want one?"

"No . . . no . . ." He actually sees a mental picture of dollar bills flying through the air. "The nurse got out to my place eventually, correct?"

"I'm sure she did. I'll double-check for you, Doctor." Lansing wearily gets up from the chair.

"No. Don't go. Why don't I just make the statement for the cameras and finish up?"

"Don't push it," Lansing says, and shuts the door.

Eons pass. He takes off his jacket, starts inventing ways to kill himself with it. He could eat it, rip it apart with his teeth, make a noose and strangle himself with it. Set it on fire somehow and escape when they came running . . .

The door finally opens and an older, presumably more senior FBI agent comes in. He has the suit and a fresh shave, and smells of mint. A tight smile. Barrigar is his name. Little American flag pin in his lapel. More agents come in and find places for themselves in the corners. Everybody is quiet now, looking from one to another, and then back to him. Grimaldi comes in. Now there're six of them crammed in there.

"There's been a . . . release, Doctor. Anthrax, both at the CDC and at the hospital. Perhaps elsewhere," Barrigar says.

"Not an accident?" Watterman can't hide the tremble in his voice.

"We don't think so," Barrigar answers.

"An attack. Anthrax. Was it letters, like last time?"

"No."

"So, of course they're testing at the lab and the hospital. What about here? Have they tested here?" he asks, working to keep the fear out of his voice. The agents all try not to react, but he can feel everybody tightening up.

"We're being tested right now."

"Good, good . . . Forget what I said about going to the lab."

"The CDC labs are under quarantine at the moment."

"Yes, right. Good. Of course. Well . . ." He looks up at them. There's nothing really to say. "Spores *inside* the labs?"

"No."

"Outside. In the offices?"

"That's right. And also other locations."

"Right." That only makes sense. "Okay. Well, what do you want with me? I suppose you think I did it?"

Barrigar stares at him. All the FBI agents hold their breath.

"You know none of this surprises me. Not one bit. I've written paper after paper on this exact situation. Well, I'm not staying here. I'm a consultant. You've got to pay my fee if you want to pull me out of bed and waste my working hours. I already told Havercamp—"

"Who's Havercamp?"

"The director—god*damn* it. *Shit!*" He's losing his mind, going senile. Havercamp has been retired from the directorship of the CDC for a decade at least. Christ . . . falling apart . . . "Look, I can't stay here. I have to get back. My wife has a very serious condition and she depends on me for . . . for emotional support. That's extremely important for her health—"

"We have some questions for you . . ."

"This has nothing to do with me!" Adrenaline is pumping through his system and he is starting to lose it. "Nothing," he repeats.

"There's still some basic questions we have to ask, Doctor. I need you to account for your movements over the last two years."

"That's easy. I haven't been anywhere."

"Nowhere?"

"Stayed right here in Atlanta. Look, suppose I just go home? Just put one of those damn ankle things on me. Call it house arrest. It would save the taxpayers my upkeep—"

"Dr. Watterman, you're going to be part of a conference call. Five minutes from now. We'll get a phone in here, and a monitor.

You take the call and then we'll go from there. We can't keep you against your will."

"Actually, I think you can."

"We'll talk after the call," Barrigar says. That tight little smile, and then he gets up and leaves along with his posse.

Daria goes for something to eat at a cafeteria across from City Hall, and takes her time with the menu, lingering in the line, leaning close to the glass, peering at the entire range of food selections. Going all around the salad bar, leaning close in and inspecting every radish.

In the end she sits at a small table and consumes about a tenth of a plate of mushed chicken—too salty—and some spinach wilted to the consistency of algae. She wipes her mouth and moves the napkin all over the table. Does it another half dozen times. Goes over and borrows parts of a newspaper from the table of a young guy. Cute enough. He looks like a student.

She ends up with a business section and part of the entertainment section. The economy continues to repair itself slowly; some oddball markets are doing better than older, traditional repositories for investments; costs have to come down, and jobs have to go up—that's what passes for wisdom on the business pages.

The front of the entertainment section is gone, so she reads what's left—the continuation of an article about an experimental theater company's production of a show on Eadweard Muybridge, an analysis of how Broadway's recruitment of Hollywood "stars" has become the default business plan on the Great White Way—

"Here you go, I'm done with this . . ." It is the cute guy. He hands her the sports section, which boasts a half-page photograph of a gap-toothed hockey player.

"Thank you," she says.

He nods and smiles.

And it would be so easy, she thinks.

And she could make him stay.

She could make him talk to her for a little longer.

He has gone now, that smile like smoke.

A big event.

That night she returns to the Grand International, puts her camera battery in the recharger, and holes up with room service calamari and a bottle of red wine. The movie is an old one, *Giant*, with Rock Hudson, Elizabeth Taylor, and James Dean in a triangle. It's one of those movies that is a lot like the city, she thinks. She's never seen the whole thing, just little snippets of it, and she marvels at Dean's twitches and his sloppy voice and the way Hudson and Taylor are consumed by greed, love, and ambition.

Inexplicably, she bursts into tears, her chest hurts, and she coughs several times.

. . . *symptoms begin much like an ordinary influenza* . . . Perhaps this is it, she thinks.

Once Rock Hudson gets old, he gets real, and he and Taylor continue their epic tiff while Daria sits there, dabbing at her face with a wet washcloth. She is too tired, she realizes. She is doing too much. She has to take care of herself. She has to be prudent. She has to hold on. She takes the wine, turns the cork over and wedges it back down into the bottle, puts everything over on the night table.

And at that moment she notices the message light on the telephone.

She hadn't seen it before. Has it been on since she came in? She had ordered room service and then stepped into the shower, her hair capped, washing with rubber gloves. She'd only been in there long enough to shower and towel herself dry—two or three minutes. She hadn't heard anything.

Then she'd come out and clicked through the channels until she'd landed on *Giant*. There hadn't been any calls.

She picks up and gets the switchboard, and is instructed to hold for her message. After a pop and a whirr of static, a robotized woman's voice comes on.

"*Your message at 8:42 p.m., from Mr. Creighton. Please return call to: area code seven-seven* . . ." Daria scrambles for a pen and rushes to take down the number, is so flustered that she thanks the nonhuman operator, and hangs up.

She boots up the laptop, opens her email, and looks in Drafts. Nothing.

Outside it has grown windy; she can feel the force of the gusts against the tall windows of the hotel.

She has no idea who Mr. Creighton might be.

DAY 4

Mr. Creighton gets in her head and will not let her sleep. They could take her now, she thinks, tossing and turning in the immense bed in her hotel room. She's got her clothes laid out because she is going to get a very early start, prodded by the advent of Mr. Creighton on the line. Maybe they'll take her in the morning at the front desk, but wouldn't it be easier just to come up in the wee hours? They might pick the lock, jam a needle into her arm and smother her like they did Mahmoud al-Mabhouh in Dubai.

Okay. So why not? What's stopping them? There's been no bust, so Creighton has to be Ali. And he's calling because something is wrong. Whatever it is, it's too important to leave in a hotel message.

Unable to let it go, she falls asleep, wakes up, rolls over. Not quite like sleep, more like an enforced rest. She gets out of bed, boots up the laptop and checks the drafts of her email—

Nothing there, nothing on Facebook, nothing tweeted to her at *Klic!*, nothing texted to her phone. Nothing. She paces around the room until she gets chilled and then goes back to bed. Sleep. That's all she wants. Oblivion.

The thing to do is to get out in the morning and return the call to Creighton when she can. Then work her way down the list of targets. Stay on schedule, right? The thing to do is work harder. If she is going to be caught, then she should make it as inconvenient as possible for her pursuers. Work it, as they say.

She finally does fall asleep and then awakes with a start, having left the curtains open. The sound of distant honking, the occasional siren. Below her is Broadway.

It's showtime, she thinks.

Back in his tenure, there used to be several ways to get into the Centers for Disease Control and Prevention complex, but today there is only one, guarded by a platoon of black-clad emergency response police.

Lansing drives, with Barrigar in the front. Watterman sits in the back and waits while they pass through security and park beside what looks like a construction contractor's mobile office. It has been elevated on railroad ties to allow for plumbing, and along one side is a ramp to comply with the disability laws. The ramp intersects with a set of plywood stairs at an Astroturfed landing in front of an orange door. Duct-taped to the door is a sheet of paper with a single word—DIRECTOR—printed across it.

Inside, taking up one end of the trailer, is a shabby foyer with two desks, a landline, a laser printer, and a door that a nervous aide opens for them.

Joe Norment, the current director of the CDC, is on the telephone, he waves at them to take a seat while he finishes his conversation. There are two good chairs, which Watterman and Barrigar take, and Lansing decides to stand.

"Green grows the grass, Teddy, just remember that." Norment laughs and hangs up, extends his hand. It's been about eight years since Watterman has laid eyes on the man. They shake.

"How are you, Sam?"

"Not that good, actually. Maggie's sick, and I want to get back to the house."

"Give her my best and tell her that I'm still pulling for the Mets," he says. That pinched mouth, watery little eyes. A true devious mouse. Some stupid joke from the era of Mookie Wilson.

"I hope they give you the resources you're going to need, Joe," Sam says.

"What the hell are you doing here?" Norment asks him.

"I've risen from the dead."

"Dr. Watterman is consulting for us," Barrigar says.

"More taxpayers' money going down the drain, because there's nothing for you to do, Sam. It's under control."

"Well, that's great," Watterman says, turning to Barrigar. "Maybe I could go back home now. It's not that far."

"We're here to coordinate and liaise, Dr. Norment." Barrigar says it flatly.

"Sure. Sam and I know each other from way back, don't we, Sam?"

"Yep, from way back." Norment is short, fair, and more bald now than Sam remembers. The kind of man who uses what little friendliness he can manufacture only if he wants something. An animal of the bureaucracy. It's been so long since Sam's hung out with any of these people that he's forgotten what they are like. It's almost a shock to see Norment still alive. Still working away. Well, it's the run-up to flu season. The CDC is probably busy.

"Okay, Sam, I'll give you and the FBI my report. But weren't you in on the conference call last night?"

"Oh, yes." He'd waited all night for the conference call, and then it was just like it had always been, layers of obfuscation and bullshit. No one speaking directly. Not that he had much choice about it—in the end he'd agreed to consult for the FBI because he needed the job—but listening to the voices over the line he was secretly glad he'd been out of the hurly-burly for all those years. Maybe Amerithrax was the best thing that ever happened to him.

"Well, there's no news since then. Yes, we've detected anthrax spores in three locations here at the CDC and at one location at DeKalb General Hospital." Norment sat back in his chair, shrugged and turned his hands up to the sky as if to say *That's it.*

"Right. That's what you said last night. How come they've got you in the portable, Joe?"

"My building is under quarantine. Look, if you're a consultant, maybe you should consult."

"Sure. Have you got a look at it yet?"

"No. Not personally." It figured, Sam realized. Absurd as it was, Norment was never a microscope guy.

"So, not having looked at it, you don't know if . . ."

"If it's weaponized? Something as exotic as Bruce Ivins could have made? Something imported from *Russia*? I rather doubt that, Sam."

"What about samples stored here?"

"All accounted for."

"No information on any likely suspects? Anybody get fired, or book off work and not sign in the last couple of days?"

"No," Barrigar says quietly.

"Come on, Sam. This is your specialty, isn't it?" Norment is smiling.

"Have you started checking all the other vectors?"

"Such as?"

"There's a university right across the street. Some international students over there, I'd guess. That's worth a test. Maybe the airport—gee, where else? Maybe the federal buildings, the draft board, the nearest synagogue . . ."

"Sure you would, Sam. The draft board? Yeah, sure, that's exactly what you'd do. And you'd start a panic. Blow things out of proportion. We've got three *little* sites. My boys and girls tell me these are minimal. And we've managed to handle things quietly."

"So, somebody walked in, dumped some spores on the floor . . ."

"Yes. That's exactly what happened. All our people have been vaccinated already—that's new since your day—we're already cleaning up, and I'll be back in my office by the first of the week." Norment smiles.

"There's a list of vectors. For the Atlanta area, for DeKalb County. It might be out of date, but it's a start. You can look it up. It might give you something to do, Joe."

"I've got plenty to do, Sam. Thanks, it's been fun chatting. Love to Maggie." Barrigar has been in enough pissing contests to know when it's time to leave, and he finally stands. Sam is already at the door when he hears the agent's voice behind him.

"Dr. Norment, we're sending out an investigation team today. We'll be wanting to interview your staff."

"This hasn't got anything to do with my staff! This is from outside, definitely. *Interview my staff?* That's absurd," Norment says, his voice rising.

Watterman turns and watches him. It is really weird. Like déjà vu all over again. *Absurd.* A decade earlier, he had said almost exactly the same thing. Almost the same thing.

Word for word.

Most of the morning talk shows have audiences. She lines up for standby tickets for *The View* and gets in. Smiles, applauds, waits as the room heats up. Whoopi and Joy are professional and engaging and Whoopi makes a few jokes during the commercials. Daria takes the opportunity to leave, visit the bathrooms, shake people's hands. She texts Creighton, gets nothing back and as she walks across the city tries calling, but the number just rings a dozen times and goes dead.

She works her way from *Good Morning America* and over to NBC for the *Today* show. Eventually she washes up at Fox and has to wait for almost a half hour before being shuffled off to Kyle, who is gay—outrageous with orange streaks in his hair and wearing some kind of shiny lotion for his skin.

He tells her that there aren't any jobs at all, but "You speak languages, so that's good." He leans back in his chair, eyes her narrowly. "And you're hot enough. I mean that in a good way."

They laugh. He takes her information and an infected *Klic!* card and walks her back to the lobby.

She uses her cell to try Creighton again, with no result, and decides to try for *Martha Stewart.* Now she cannot help looking around to see if she is being followed, but the city is so busy they could be anywhere. She has grown used to the gusting winds down the canyons of buildings, but now there is a change. The weather has turned, perhaps for the first time of the season. It's going to rain, she decides.

Martha's show starts at two; she pays to get into the studio audience and repeats her tactics there, and is out by midafternoon.

She takes on all the great networks one by one. Visits their stages if she can get in, or calls on corporate offices and sets up ad hoc job interviews. They all love the languages, and she's obviously vivacious enough to do PR, so she gets good penetration. She's in her good clothes—the tight little suit and the big lethal hair. Killer fragrance and the smile nailed on, and off she goes.

She infects everyone at MTV, but gets nervous when one of their marketing clones decides to do a search on *Klic!* She smiles and steps out of his office to take a call, puts the phone to her ear and just keeps going out onto the street.

It feels good. It feels wonderful. She's on top and if the germs on her hands are still good, she's taking God's revenge with every breath she takes, every taxicab, every elevator button pushed, every handshake. She runs on espresso and chocolate, and is not shy about taking on targets of opportunity. She goes into the *New York Times* offices and asks to put in an ad, then stops the whole process to think about maybe buying a bigger one, or maybe she should talk to someone else about proposals for *Klic!*'s upcoming U.S. market launch. With newspapers tanking and ad revenues sinking, they bend over backwards to accommodate her.

Elevators rising, falling.

At one point she catches sight of herself in a mirror—a buzzing Italian diva, bursting out of her fitted power shirt, heels drilling all the way down into the diseased psyche of the Americans. Like a leper hiding under layers of theatrical makeup. Shameful, decaying, and broken. She glimpses herself in the reflections on windows, on polished granite, in the facets of revolving doors, lenses of security cameras . . . Now she is a brain virus, she thinks. Some germ that divides and divides, leaving the victim berserk, memories lost, perceptions gone awry. She will spark nightmares, hallucinations, delusions. Now they will talk in tongues and flay themselves as they are driven mad.

And nothing shows on her face. Nothing at all.

When entertainment and information merchants are proud of a show, there are always posters, shrines to promote the current hits produced or picked up by whatever corporation she's visiting. Walls of smiling or smoldering young actors—boys still in the throes of puberty, girls waiting for the right guy.

Then there are the so-called reality shows, the business shows. Celebrity gossip and game shows. As one penetrates deeper into the well-appointed offices of the studios, the décor shifts, displaying memorabilia from more-venerable hits. Often she will recognize an actor's face from a familiar role—Eva Longoria in *I segreti di Wisteria Lane*—but there are plenty of icons from television shows so ancient they are unintelligible, cultural artifacts that should be in a museum: *The Lone Ranger, I Love Lucy, Mork & Mindy.*

By late afternoon, she is dazed and needs to sit down somewhere to rest her feet and eyes.

It's insane. Everywhere there is advertising. Where she looks, or where she chooses *not* to look—pays off for these people. Oh, it's not much, but later, statistically, when she thinks of spending some money, she'll make a decision. Usually that decision will be made in ignorance, with no hands-on knowledge. At that point she will pick a brand—maybe the last one she's seen, or the first one that comes to mind, but always one that she *trusts* or *likes*. Those feelings can be measured, those feelings can be evoked with images. And it's everywhere.

You can't look away. They won't let you.

America is the site of a good idea gone insane, she thinks. Its fragile psyche is propped up by a few precarious narratives. A hero will come along into the executive office. America is the biggest, the best, the most successful. She wins the most gold medals, has the meanest army, the highest tech. Americans are proud to respond should they be called upon to make the ultimate sacrifice. Good-looking and rich is nice, but ideally one should be intelligent and hardworking. Being a schoolteacher is a lousy job. Management is what everyone should aspire to, even the workers; however, everyone knows that financial matters are complicated. Naturally this requires legions of specialists who actually run the economy, and that's probably best—that the actual running of things should be left to the experts. Mathematically challenged need not apply.

America's ego was protected by a shell of case-hardened bullshit. The myths and the propaganda were its armor. Here was the battle for the hearts and minds—in these towers above her. Up there, ambitious boys and girls her age stoked the fires of the mythmaking apparatus. Here the news was spun, stars were born, deals were cut, reputations were polished, and America tended her face. Once it was all gone her citizenry would be revealed for the cowering, naked dogs they were.

She finds herself standing at a corner, lost amid the rush of the city.

Suddenly . . . she needs to hide, to get away. Her stomach swirls. She changes course and abruptly goes into Macy's, forces herself to walk along the aisles.

Panic, that's what it is. Sudden, irrational panic. She is convinced that somebody is watching via the cameras in the ceiling, somebody is following her on a parallel aisle. She is careful not to break into a run, keeps to an easy stride, pretends to look at the merchandise as she goes, and once she gets across the great floor she pushes her way outside again and discovers she is next to the entrance to the subway. She turns, walking back the way she's come, searching for the face of her pursuer . . .

But there is no one. Is it an omen, this unheard message from Creighton? At the very least she will have to change hotels. How long will her identity hold? She has no security. How long before the virus is discovered? Soon in Berlin, surely. The computer says a classic case of smallpox has a seven-day incubation period, but what if it's "on steroids"? A few days? A few days at most. By then people will start to sicken and CIA agents will be searching for Patient Zero from among recent arrivals.

She goes down to the subway, puzzles out the fare machines, buys a MetroCard and pushes her way through the turnstiles. The subway map confronts her—looking like nothing so much as one of those diagrams of the reproductive system. She finds her place on a mustard-colored vein.

As in any big city, it helps if you know where you're going. New York has managed to confuse her. She is running out of time, and realizes that she will never be able to visit all the high-priority targets.

She edits her list down to a handful, but right away, at the Israeli consulate, she strikes out and is reduced to breathing on the glass that separates her from a stiff-faced guard. She attempts to give him a *Klic!* card but he waves it away and all she can do is lamely agree that, yes, it's reasonable enough that people should phone for an appointment if they hope to book a publicity interview with the consular office. She offers to come back. Is there a more convenient time?

"This is not a tourist stop," the guard says, stone-faced.

She smiles and promises she will do as he has suggested, then leaves, thinking that even if she were to follow the procedures, it would be just like the Israelis to run some kind of a computerized check on her and, upon turning up a big fat zero at *Klic!*'s offices in Rome, arrest her as she waits in the embassy foyer.

She walks down Second Avenue, frustrated, head down to avoid the hidden cameras on the roofs, thinking that it was probably stupid to even dream of taking on the hyper-paranoid Israelis, and that she's moving way too fast and overreaching whatever plans her handlers had made for her.

But . . . that's part of the problem. It's something she should have at least asked about in Berlin. They never gave her any . . . any training, or any specifics, or even any advice. No time for the farewell message. Obviously the situations that are cropping up for her hourly were never anticipated.

The United Nations building is eerie because, for all its modernism, now it seems so old, everything a little shabby and out of style.

She takes a brief guided tour, asks if there might be any cute Italian boys that she can soul-capture for team *Klic!* By the time she's finished, it is after five and men and women are leaving in ones and twos. Should she trust her cell phone? Everybody knows they can be traced, the drones can track their signals. She's been paranoid all day, and she knows she's being paranoid now, but at the same moment, across the foyer, she spies what she thinks is probably the last bank of pay telephones in the city.

"May I speak to Mr. Creighton? I'm returning his call."

"*Your name, please?*"

"Signorina Vermiglio."

There is a beat.

"*One moment,*" says the same voice. There is an accent, but it could be anyone, anywhere in the world.

She waits. Looks out on the street; smatterings of rain, fluttering flags from all the nations one can imagine.

She is waiting. Waiting for a long time.

Too long.

She hangs up and is out onto the plaza in a New York moment. She lines up behind three cabs' worth of diplomats who have decided to knock off from solving the world's problems. Others are arriving right behind her, all sorts of people—diplomats, translators, tourists. A welter of languages surrounds her. There are women in saris, men with strange braided hats; a troika of Africans moves to the head of the line just in front of her. She glances back to the entrance. A security guard has come out and is looking over at them.

She turns back, waiting while the Africans wedge themselves into the cab ahead of her. Finally it tears away from the curb and it's her turn. "Pennsylvania Station," she tells the cabdriver. As they leave, she looks again through the back window. Now there are two guards standing there.

Just standing there.

When they get to Penn Station, she walks all the way through and right out the other side and grabs another cab back to the hotel. The whole time she is thinking furiously.

If they know where she is already, they could have gotten her at the hotel, could have followed her all day long and arrested her with ease. But they didn't.

So, it's definitely not the FBI or the CIA.

It has to be Ali, she thinks. It has to be.

She does not need or want another Burke, so she spends the evening alone, purchasing a rush ticket to the theater to see Helen Mirren in *The Glass Menagerie*. Her ticket to this decadent event costs a hundred and twenty dollars. The conceit is that a mother cannot allow her daughter any kind of adult independence. The men show no spine at all and are essentially cowardly. She doesn't know the play and has never heard of Tennessee Williams. It is the movie star Helen Mirren that has attracted her, but in this production she speaks strangely and poses against the furniture. The set is meant to evoke a nightmare of deteriorating wooden houses, but looks only half built.

She watches as the daughter, played by a waiflike blonde, costumed like Alice in Wonderland, stumbles through the play and unrealistically falls for the man procured for her.

This is their art, she is thinking. This is the high art of the Christian conquerors, the race that extinguished its nomadic native peoples and laid waste, first to their own continent, and now the world. Still the same myths, she thinks. Reduced to its essence, it's the same idiotic delusions that govern everything. All around her: retired people and greed, punctuated by the occasional starstruck teenager. The fine fabrics of the audience's evening wear, everything rich and understated, even the designer blue jeans worn by the grad student who's come to smirk at the very people he aspires to work with.

At the intermission she goes to the restroom, touches everything, reclaims her coat from the booth, tips lavishly and leaves.

It has rained during the first act, and now she walks through the wet streets surrounding Times Square. She is angry, perhaps feverish. Her brain fizzing. Thinking that this is truly *it* . . . she has shot herself into the pituitary of the United States, the center of its terrible urges and repressions. If the SUV with the amateur bomb had gone off a few years back, there would be a curfew here now. But instead New York still flaunts its hedonism amid dazzling lights, barely concealed pornography, conspicuous consumption, and the promise of unbridled wish fulfillment.

But she has won. The arrow has struck home.

All around her the digital whirlwind grows, changes, refreshes. This is what it feels like, she thinks—the fabled Big Apple buzz. In the distance are the omnipresent sirens. But the people continue their laughing, their faces contorted like denizens of hell. There is music playing from some boom box, and a group of boys in fat pants are dancing on flattened refrigerator boxes and passing a wool cap around. She tries to imagine an explosion—the shattered glass, the choking smoke, the screams . . .

She looks up into the beginnings of a new rain. Above her is a huge flashing sign, a billion LED pixels all to display a movie star promising beauty that will last forever.

It will not happen.

Back at the Grand, a man gets in the elevator with her. He smiles. He is white, young, and fit. He could be a cop, or a CIA agent, or . . . just a guy. For a moment she thinks about letting him have the car to himself, or pushing the button for a lower floor and getting out. But he stares straight ahead and, when she gets off, stays behind. "Good night . . ." he says quietly as the doors slide shut.

She walks down the carpeted hallway. It's empty. Somewhere she can hear a muffled television from one of the rooms. At the end of the hall, someone has a tray out for room service to pick up.

Another two paces and behind her she hears a door being unlatched.

She keeps on going. Waiting for something, listening for steps on the carpet. She tries to pick up reflections from the glass in the framed art on the walls, but can't. Has to walk on. Hearing nothing, when she turns the corner she takes an opportunity to look back.

Nothing. Whoever it was has disappeared.

Her skin has gone clammy. Her face, drained of blood. Her heart is rippling like a scared bird.

The keycard in the lock. The light turns green. She pushes open the door.

Nothing. Everything's normal. She stops at the threshold and looks back down the hall. Nothing.

A maid has come in and turned down the bed. There is a cluster of chocolates waiting on her pillow.

No message light. She exhales, sits on the bed and rubs her face. There is a headache that is lurking back behind her eyes.

Less than thirty seconds later, after she has kicked off her shoes and pulled the cork out of the wine bottle, the room telephone rings.

"Yes?"

"*Good evening, Ms. Vermiglio. Front desk—*"

"Yes?"

"*In preparation for checkout, would you like us to have your bill sent up, then all you have to do is sign it in the morning?*"

"My checkout?"

"*Yes, ma'am, we have you checking out tomorrow? Checkout is at eleven, and this way it speeds it up for you.*"

"My checkout?"

"*I'm sorry, just let me look at . . . Yes, ma'am, that's what I've got here . . .*"

"Yes," she says. "I see."

In the night, anthrax spores are found at four additional Atlanta area locations—two new ones at the CDC (underground parking lot, main complex bathrooms) and two more across the street at Emory University (student union washroom and Biology Department offices). Back at the field office Sam Watterman puts in a call to Norment, and is informed that the director is busy and cannot be reached at the moment, but will return his call.

An hour later more white powder is discovered in the waiting room at the headquarters of the Atlanta Police Department, and over the next half hour come reports of spilled powder on the floor at St. Joseph's Hospital and inside the Atlanta Medical Center.

Well, for the CDC it's no longer being handled quietly, Sam thinks, and he is not surprised when no call comes in from Norment, who actually is busy right now.

Sam Watterman makes himself available to the FBI, which amounts to giving his Biological Warfare 101 speech to any agents who ask. It must be good, because they keep asking. The rest of the time he hovers over shoulders and puts in his opinion if he thinks it might do some good. The response, so far as he can see, seems to be basically on track; biohazard manuals have been brought out and dusted off, the Marine Corps's Chemical Biological Incident Response Force has been contacted, elite decontamination teams are en route. The finding of spores at the university's Biology Department spurs a search for a disgruntled student or faculty member, and that's where the local detectives begin to focus their investigation. Across the city, buildings where the suspicious powder has been found have been quarantined, and employees are being rounded up, questioned, vaccinated, and started on an intense course of antibiotics.

He should feel shocked, but he's not. He should feel energized or angry, but he's not. He doesn't know what he feels. Not detached. No, not detached at all.

In search of what's bothering him, he paces. Past the windows, staring out into the night. It's late and there's hardly any traffic on the foggy highway. Walking. Down the field office corridors, through the aisles separating the cubicles; restless, aware that . . . *something is wrong*. None of it looks quite right, even though it all matches scenarios he and his teams built and ran back in the Dark Ages before the turn of the century.

And it is while he is pacing, fretting and mulling things over, that he happens to be standing next to Lansing's desk when the call comes in.

"Roger that . . ." Lansing says. He is writing as he talks and does not even notice Watterman standing there.

". . . in Washington . . ."

Watterman takes a huge breath, almost a gasp. He knew it. He'd suppressed it, but all night he's been subconsciously waiting for this moment. Really, for years he's been anticipating it. Years. And now it's here.

"And when did they arrest him?"

He moves into the cubicle. Lansing looks up at him. He shakes his head dazedly, a dark expression creasing his tired young face.

"And . . . how many targets?"

And a moment later, "Unconfirmed. Roger . . ." Looking at Sam as he says it. "Okay. Testing now . . . roger . . ."

Sam feels the prickles of sweat standing out on his forehead.

"No, he's right here. He's right beside me," Lansing says and looks over to him.

"Yes, I've got it . . ." Lansing says, and begins writing again. "Library of Congress . . . Washington Monument . . . Smithsonian . . . National Cathedral . . ."

And for Sam there is nothing to say, because he already knows what's happened.

DAY 5

Since Mr. Creighton (she guesses) says leave in the morning, she leaves. Early. She makes excuses to linger in the lobby, but there's no one waiting. No one in the restaurant, no one in the bars. She drops the keycard at the front desk and heads for the street.

Out front—nobody.

Thinking, All right, what now? No direction. No planning, no advice. No backup. Nothing in her email. Just meaningless telephone calls. She looks around for fit young men with close-cropped hair talking into their collars. Nothing, nothing, nothing.

She's angry now. Angry and a little scared, a little thrown off, but, yes, it's better to be out of the hotel. She feels like she's free.

Free . . . looking up at the gigantic buildings . . . the park. The absurd rectangular park. Like a memory of nature, so big that there is an illusion of freedom while walking through it. Walled off by a city that stretches forever, distant horizons barely glimpsed beyond the infinite grid of streets. Anyone can get lost there; no one really can fully understand such a place.

The important thing is to keep playing her part. Whatever message is being implied via Creighton's calls, it can't be good. Someone informed the front desk she was checking out. Okay. Now, if anyone is watching, they'll get what they wanted. If they're not going to come up and introduce themselves, they'll follow the cab if they can, or at least trace her movements. Maybe they haven't arrested her because they think she is part of a team and are waiting for her to lead them to the others? If so, the game has changed.

With luggage and a laptop, she needs to give the cabbie a plausible destination, so she tells him to take her to LaGuardia. Spends the ride chatting with the man about what she should expect on her Mexican holiday. He has to reach for an opinion, since he's never been there himself, but has heard it can be dangerous. He is originally from Fiji. On the dashboard there is a plastic saint. Around her base he has twisted a pink lei.

"Is that the Virgin?" she asks.

"No, no, that's Santa Clara," the man says. "She's the patron saint of television."

"Really?"

"Yes. My wife is on the television. She does the weather."

Cash, a big smile, and a twenty-dollar tip to help him remember her. "*Adios,*" she says just to put a button on it.

She ducks inside the departures lounge and follows the signs, dodging the long waggling trains of luggage carts, goes back outside and takes a shuttle to the arrivals lounge, pops out just in time to catch another shuttle to a Budget car rental agency. When she gets there, it is manned by one hefty-looking black woman and a tall young man with acne.

She tries to rent a Mustang, but they don't have any and she has to settle for a Dodge. She asks if it is fast enough, because she is going to be on the highway a lot.

When they ask where she wants to drop off, she says at the airport in Miami, Florida. An extra charge? No problem. She doesn't need any insurance, but she buys a tank of gas so she can bring it back empty.

She puts everything on her own card, slams on her sunglasses, heads for their lot, and is led to the car by a guy they've got working there. He is on a cell phone and makes her wait, finishing the call before he starts processing her rental. She stands there for a full minute and then digs out her perfume. When he finally gets done with his call, they walk around checking the car for scratches and dings.

"How long does it take to get to Boston?" she asks him.

"Depends on the time of day—sometimes four hours, sometimes a long time."

"If there's a lot of traffic?"

"That's right."

The two of them have made little dashes and circles wherever they have found a flaw. She makes her initials on the diagram of the exploded car. Now he's noticed her and tries to show what a gentleman he is by putting her bag in the trunk, and then opens the door for her.

She shakes his hand and kills him one more time, just for the cell phone delay if nothing else.

Outside, the streets leading away from LaGuardia are crowded. She has no idea where she is going, and follows any sign that takes her back to Manhattan. Eventually she comes out on Columbus Avenue, recognizing it from the endless cab rides she's been on over the last few days. She turns and heads uptown until she finds a parking lot. The traffic is clogged, and horns are blaring when she attempts to change lanes. Three lots later she finds one where they sell parking by the week. She buys two weeks on her card, dumps the Dodge, entrusts the keys to the man in the kiosk, and rolls her bag down to the corner, where she waits a long two minutes before she can pick up another cab.

She gets dropped off at Penn Station, finds her way to the ticketing area, and tries to puzzle out the routes. There are trains running all the time. Short commuter trips that won't require her to show identification.

She lines up and asks if it's possible to purchase tickets in her mother's name. "Or perhaps a book of passes? If I were using it every few days . . . she lives in Atlantic City," she explains.

"Yes, ma'am, you want a multiple ticket pass. You and your

mother can go back and forth from here to Philadelphia and continue on to Atlantic City. That's the cheapest and most flexible way to go. . . ."

Daria buys her multiple passes, walks until she finds a coffee bar where she can get an espresso, and then parks herself and thinks about the whole thing for a while. She could wait there in semi-anonymity forever. She scans her end of the lobby. There are policemen and private security guards and she pretends to check the pictures on her camera so that she won't make eye contact.

No one knows where she is.

Maybe she has attained freedom? Unless there's some sort of tracking device in her luggage, which would be easy enough. Mossad could have come into the hotel room a dozen times and bugged her bag. They probably have GPS devices smaller than a pinhead.

Ali. Ali, Ali, Ali.

And then she starts thinking that maybe a major railway station is not the best place to be lurking . . .

Back at ticketing she lays down a false trail by buying a ticket to Niagara Falls that will be leaving at three forty-five that afternoon. That gives her almost an hour and a half where she can grab a commuter train to somewhere else, anywhere. There's the Acela Express, advertised as the green, progressive future of rail travel in America. It will get her to Philadelphia in one hour, Baltimore in two.

And . . . why not continue on from there? Why not? It's easy to go right into Washington. Why not? The virus that she poured over herself in Berlin can't be effective for much longer. The perfume is half gone and soon she will be too sick to travel. So she should go. Go now . . . go to D.C., visit Congress, take in all the coffee shops around Langley.

In the washroom she changes into her most nondescript outfit. The last thing she wants now are the Burkes of the world ogling her. There are jeans, just tight enough to be attractive, the kind of thing that any young woman with a shred of vanity would wear, the hoodie to shelter her face. She rubs off all her makeup, pushes her hair around. Different, or different enough? She stands there in the washroom doing a complete makeover. Other women come and go. No one notices her or cares.

She eyes her rolling luggage and decides that she'll pick up something else down the railroad line. A backpack. Something that a university student might use. She delays before ditching the *Klic!* cards, trying to decide if she'll only be leaving them more clues in the garbage. Does she need a new identity? It's cold in the cavernous restroom.

"The face of death is scared now, isn't she," she says to the mirror.

Staring at herself for a long moment. Crazy, crazy, crazy.

"No . . ." she says to her image. "No, I'm not. I'm not scared at all." She almost believes it.

She checks the suitcase into a short-term baggage locker, walks around and down, takes the tunnel to the subway, gets on a 1 train and heads uptown. The car is only half full and her cell phone works just fine.

"Hello, Mr. Creighton?" she says when they pick up.

"*Whom may I say is calling?*" A different voice this time.

"Ms. Vermiglio. I'm in a hurry."

"*One moment, please.*"

"I'm in a *hurry,*" she says. Waits. Waits again like last time. "Hello?" she says. There is no answer. Something is wrong. They know she's already tried. They should be right there, waiting. Ready to go. Assholes . . .

Still nothing.

She snaps the cell phone shut and sits there while the train roars along under the city. There is a newspaper folded up on the seat, but someone will eventually unfold and read it. Having no better idea, she cleans her fingerprints from the cell by wiping it on her hoodie and lets it slip to the floor under her seat, the first step in a long journey northward. At 103rd she gets out, crosses over, and takes the next train back the way she came, to Penn Station, where she has time to reclaim her luggage, buy an American-sized burger, and climb aboard the Acela Express just as the conductors are closing up the cars.

It is a little early and the train is maybe two-thirds full. Every fourth person is on a smart phone. She goes as far away from people as she can, which isn't far, sits down, plugs into her music, eats half of her burger and throws the rest away.

Once it wobbles out of the yards, the Acela is reasonably smooth. She watches backstreet New Jersey rush by. Gray wasteland and the remains of chemical plants. Scrub growing along the right-of-way punctuated with neon blue and orange tarpaulins and an occasional tent made of sheets of clear plastic strung to the branches and then abandoned. Buildings that are black with grime dating back a century.

Through the music—something blissful she downloaded eons ago in Cairo—she hears happy voices. There are two students dressed as Civil War soldiers, one blue and one gray, coming through the car and giving a spiel about touring the battlefields. The shorter is a girl with a painted-on mustache. They have been delayed by a retiree, a rickety veteran, who nevertheless is neat as a pin, sideburns trimmed, the memory of a flat stomach, a steadfast set to the jaw. There are thousands and thousands of these men, and already, for Daria, they are becoming a type. The veteran's wife sits there enjoying the fun while the students regurgitate what they know about geography and military strategy.

"You can head west up to Antietam and see that. You can see the bridge and that was very bad," the boy says.

"Bloody work," says the vet.

Daria looks away and slides up the volume and waits for them to finish discussing the stats of historic American death, but they don't leave. In fact, the clowns attract another mythologizing necrophilic ghoul, this time a little round balding man, a history buff who enthusiastically joins their conversation.

To get away, Daria walks along until she finds what passes for a lounge car. There is a stainless steel bar being tended by a tandem of middle-aged Amtrak staffers. There are meal selections, mostly sandwiches that are wrapped in plastic. Neither of the two staffers seem to care about their job, the food they serve, or the people who are buying it. From their body language and attitude, it's obvious that they are overworked, underpaid, bored, and/or eternally pissed off, and would rather be doing anything else but. She waits her turn, asks for some potato chips, and then inspects the package carefully.

"Do these have oil? Maybe I should take some of the others—" she says to the man, who efficiently grabs back the chips and waits for her to make up her mind. She opts for a nuked slice of pizza and a Coke and, by the time she has done so, has spread everything she can to his hands: carefully counted out her change, looked away and politely blocked a cough with her palm, and actually touched his finger when he reached forward with her coins. Smiling the whole time. "You're so kind," she says to him.

She is not really hungry, and when the pizza is ready, she finds a seat in the corner of the car and picks at it while paging through a not-too-badly crumpled *USA Today*. The newspaper is mostly concerned with sports and scandals, but her eye is attracted by a report on the arrest in Israel of a man distributing letters laced with a white powder. Analysis is being done, but it is feared the man was acting as part of a terrorist organization.

She carefully reads the article again. It has the dry feel of something taken off a wire service and actually says very little. Because its subject is foreign it occupies a bare two inches in the overall universe of *USA Today*.

The hour has passed too quickly. The sordid little snack bar is closed in advance of their arrival in Philadelphia. She goes back to her seat and, when they coast into the station, takes her bag and the laptop and climbs down from the train. Inside, she watches while the Acela heads away without her, and then lines up to buy a ticket on the next train that will take her to D.C.

She has fifteen minutes, and she does her regular routine there in the station, going to the bathrooms, paging through the magazines in the little bookstore. Buying some gum, holding up a sweatshirt to see if it will fit. In the process she learns that Philadelphia occupies a place of mythical importance to the United States of America; this is obvious from the posters and souvenirs on sale, which prominently feature the damaged Liberty Bell. The motif is everywhere, ultimately reduced to a silk-screened graphic that adorns T-shirts and snowglobes. If it's not the Liberty Bell that's being hawked, it's the paraphernalia of one of the several sports teams who are resident in the city.

The train glides in and she rushes along the platform to the cars. This is a much simpler, tawdrier train than the Acela. Just ahead of her, an elderly woman is helping her forty-something child up the stairs onto the train. At the top they turn together and, with the aid of a porter, begin to navigate to a seat. She sees the daughter's face— the features appear squeezed, and the expression is flat, but the close-set eyes are restless, roaming across everything in their path. They settle on Daria and she looks away, embarrassed to be caught staring.

"You can sit anywhere, ma'am," the porter says once he has got the mother and daughter into their seats. The mother looks up as Daria passes by. A beautiful woman once, Daria realizes. Lovely bones, and a fine spray of gray hair that frames her face. Good eyes and a lot of tiredness.

She walks past them, holding her breath and being careful not to touch their seats, and moves all the way through and behind into another car, hoping that somehow her deadly aura won't carry to the two women. She aims for a seat in the back of the car, but just before she gets there, an elderly couple comes through and takes it, and she has to go one more car to find some space.

It is a warm day in September and the light streams in the window. She stares out across the narrow station yard. There is a fringe of rough grass beside the tracks, and bees are combing the blossoms, their darting movements faster than a human can see, picking, choosing, gathering.

She'd helped her uncle and brothers tend hives one summer. As long as Amir or Ra'id was with her, it was permitted. She was the youngest and a girl, and after she'd helped her mother, nothing more was expected of her, so she got to watch the fantastic creatures come and go while her brothers stripped the hives of honey.

In those short days she had fallen in love with the honeybees, with their intricacy and their obsessive will to survive. The sweetness of their product was truly a gift from God. Seemingly out of

nothingness they built their waxen labyrinths. They created a special jelly that they used to transform an egg from a common worker
into a queen. If you ate it, it could cure wounds.

Once, Amir had come to her, a swarm of bees draped across his
shoulder and neck. He walked stiff legged and was trying not to
laugh and startle them. So many stings would be fatal. She put her
hand out and in a moment one of the insects landed on her finger
and began crawling along, then another and another until a little
bridge had been formed between her and her brother.

He just stood there and smiled at her. She let her hand move an
inch or two away, and slowly they all returned to Amir's shoulder.

"Magic . . ." her brother said to her.

At night her mother told stories and they sat with the cousins
and sang. But mostly she was outside from dawn until darkness.
Sleeping under the trees, fig trees and a lonely pear that were protected with nets. At the end of the summer, all the children helped
her uncle put out sticks with glue to trap the birds. They had food
then and her father was near enough to visit. It was the last good
summer. With her brothers and the hives. Everything got worse after
that.

She watches a lonely bee foraging on the vegetation that grows
beside the tracks. Is her future written? Will she just finally run out
of flowers, be forced to travel so far from home that she loses her
way?

An announcement is made that she dimly hears above the Nano;
a shiver creaks through the car. They slip forward; the bee, the grass,
the flickering ties of the tracks, the trees, the streets, blur into nothingness.

Now everything has been zapped up into emergency mode.

Suicidally, and in disregard of his warnings that Washington
was poisoned and therefore they should be holing up in the nearest
bunker as per the most recent Continuity of Government plan, the
FBI decided that Dr. Samuel Watterman's presence was required at
the White House. There was a flight in a very fast, very maneuver-

able FBI business jet to Andrews AFB, where he was bundled into an SUV with blacked-out windows and sped across town. The whole process made him aware of how out-of-date and ineffectual he was, and left him paralyzed and pissed off.

Once they got to the West Wing, of course, there was a wait, and the FBI contingent had to mill around, shuffling back and forth in the breezeway before being ushered down the hall to the Roosevelt Room.

"You okay, Doc?" Lansing whispered to him.

"I could use a bathroom."

"Better just suck it up for now."

The Roosevelt Room was decorated differently than when he had first been there, long ago and far away in the Reagan administration.

Back then it was a great cast of characters in an administration riding high. Ed Meese. What's his face, Stockman . . . the monetary wunderkind who was going to save the world. Oliver North, who was always up for a good time; the kind of guy who liked to pull frat house pranks and painful practical jokes. His big thing was Rex 84, an emergency management plan the government could use to legally incarcerate dissenters. There was a certain kind of terrible logic about it, Sam had to admit. The details all came out later. At the time he'd known nothing about it.

Yes, those were the top-secret days. Back when the designation meant something. Fun times with the monsters. Lots of compartments. Lots of high-octane secrets. Reagan was a movie star and was enjoying life that summer of '81; it had been only a couple of months since the shooting, and they dressed him up like a cowboy and got Nancy out with him, smiling, and shaking hands so that people would forget all about Hinckley.

Sam had been thirty-three at the time, working at keeping his Democrat's head down and burnishing his reputation as a biowarrior with one foot in public health. They sat him in the back row of chairs that had been set up around the rim of the Roosevelt Room. Since it was a Republican administration, the equestrian portrait of

Teddy Roosevelt was over the mantelpiece. All the biggies spoke in turn. Havercamp droned on and on. The Secretary of Health and Human Services laughed and nodded. Reagan's people, despite their commitment to trim the fat from the budget, were committed to the best biowarfare defense systems money could buy. So was Caspar Weinberger.

There were plenty of obstacles, not the least of which were non-proliferation treaties that had been signed. Regarding the whole field of biowarfare, there were two types of reactions, Sam thought. The Denial crowd, who were ignorant of basic epidemiology, and the Avengers. Both sides needed the Poisoners, and he was eager to make a career at the interface. In any government, in any epoch, there had always been scientists ready to work on the most secret of arts, and, yes, back in the day he'd been one of the best.

The Denial crowd really didn't want to parse it too finely, but what they truly longed for was the perfect defense, a biologically impenetrable membrane. Making the germs was comparatively easy; it was much harder to come up with a defense against them over, say, the next century. Weinberger and his friends were more than ready to throw money at the problem. Little wars were breaking out everywhere, and they wanted it confirmed that bioweapons were too sophisticated and expensive to be developed by terrorists.

But Watterman refused to give them that.

BACCHUS had been one of the experiments he had designed to demonstrate the case. As far as the treaties went, the program was right on the edge, and therefore a carefully guarded secret. Watterman, the good administrator, knew all their funds were drawn from the blackest of the black budgets, and since he was a rising star, and biowarfare was a "sexy threat," he was confident when he predicted that BACCHUS would be funded within a month. He hadn't even been thinking about it very much; BACCHUS was only one of the programs he had administered.

The point of Bacchus was to see how cheap it would be to produce a credible biological weapon. It was his baby from the beginning and he brought it in ahead of time and way under budget. He'd been very proud of it: a lab the size of a mobile home or shipping container, equipment bought off the shelf. Germs? You could get botulinum out of your garden. The weaponizing was the greater engineering challenge, and let's say you wanted to do some tweaking; that took time, money, and big brains, but he demonstrated that even an inefficient bioweapon was disproportionately dangerous, and cheap.

Yes, those were the days. Ed Meese loved him. They talked about scotch. When the meeting broke up, he met James Baker, who said he was "interested and concerned."

But that was three decades ago. The cocaine years. Big hair, *Raging Bull*, Kenny Loggins, and Pat Benatar.

The Democrats were in the White House now. FDR's portrait hung over the mantelpiece and Teddy was on the west wall. The décor had changed, but everything else was the same. He made for a seat at the back, but Barrigar took him by the elbow and led him to the long table. "Right here next to me, Sam . . ." he said. In seconds the room had filled up.

"I'm Tom Roycroft, I'm the Secretary of Homeland Security, and I hereby direct that recordings and minutes taken from this meeting are restricted. This is no media, secure and secret . . ."

Roycroft. Watterman recognized the face of the Secretary of Homeland Security, but had forgotten his name. It was obvious that he was in charge, because of the body language of everyone around him. It might have been respect or loathing, but a bubble surrounded Roycroft that kept human contact to a minimum.

". . . purpose of this meeting is to assess the nature and dimensions of the threat, to ensure our coordination is at optimum efficiency, and to ascertain the identity of the perpetrators and their sponsors, and to apprehend and bring them to justice. We have a huge public health emergency and we will be covering that as well. . . ."

They dimmed the lights and Major General Gordon "Gordo" Walthaer, the commanding officer in charge of USAMRIID, began his report. Beside him, a colonel operated the laptop for Walthaer's point-by-point, displayed on a screen that emerged from a sideboard at the end of the room.

Maps with yellow flags showed where anthrax samples had been found—seven locations in Atlanta and twenty-four in Washington, D.C. Samples had been taken, sealed in crash-tested, fireproof boxes, and were being delivered to USAMRIID labs by helicopter.

Sitting beside Roycroft was J. Benton Davies, the Director of the FBI. When the lights faded back up, he began the FBI report.

Davies said the FBI had learned that there were at least two anthrax attackers. The first had entered the United States on a flight originating in Vienna five days earlier. He was Tariq Sawalha, and his target had been Washington, D.C. Sawalha was twenty-one and held Italian citizenship but had been born in Dubai. He had offered no resistance when he was captured. He was suffering from inhalation anthrax, but was medically stable and talking freely. Helpful and cooperative. The Atlanta terrorist who had targeted the CDC headquarters was unknown and still at large.

While it was clear from Sawalha's interrogations that he believed he was alone, and that he had no knowledge of the CDC attacker, nevertheless the FBI was assuming the strains of anthrax used in both cities were identical, and that the terrorists had been trained, supplied, and financed by a common source. As Davies spoke, he couldn't help but glance down toward Evan Kubica, Director of the CIA.

The Secretary of State weighed in.

". . . do any of us have anything like a signature that would indicate a national program in Iran, or any other client state . . ."

General Walthaer shook his head and said the anthrax was still being analyzed in his labs.

". . . what would be a best estimate of the probability of additional attacks?"

All eyes turned to Kubica, who could only try to restrain himself from shrugging. "There's a significant probability, but no certainty," he finally said.

"... in addition to your long experience immersed in these issues, given the availability of technology, what is the feasibility that a small player could accomplish the technological feat of ..."

There was a silence around the table. Suddenly Watterman realized that everyone was staring and he had been spoken to.

"... how much could a terror program like what we're witnessing be downsized ... maybe be deliverable by something located in a garage, or a container, or ..." Roycroft was trying to clarify things.

"Well, uh, Mr. Secretary ... if you're asking what are we in for, I honestly don't know, but as far as feasibility goes, it's not hard at all." Across the table Joe Norment from the CDC pursed his lips and rocked back in his seat. In the alcove nearest the door to the colonnade, he saw Reilly standing there with his arms crossed, shaking his head.

"Sam's long background is in exactly this kind of thing ..." Barrigar was saying.

"Whoa ..." he interrupted. "That's true, but I'm not up to speed on any of this. There's lots of phases, there's manufacture and then there's delivery. It sounds weaponized to me from what I've heard so far, but I haven't looked through a microscope myself. Was it active?" He looked down the table to Walthaer.

"Yes. Active."

"All right, it's active. What that means is that it's small particles, one or two spores, not heavy clumps. That means it can float easily through the air. It's like having a cigarette with you that's burning all the time. According to the briefing paper, Sawalha admitted he carried it in a bottle of talcum powder in his luggage. He'd sealed it in a plastic bag and didn't open it until he got to Washington, but it would leak right around the threads in the cap anyway."

"But in your opinion, does that prove the involvement of a state? Is there an organizational signature?" the Secretary of State asked again, the strain beginning to tell in her voice.

"It's *hard* to make anthrax active. It's hard to weaponize in that manner, but there have been a lot of advances since ..." And for a moment he fell silent, a little hiccup. "—since the Amerithrax situation, and besides . . ." And then he did fall silent.

"Besides, what, Doctor?" Walthaer prompted, a little impatiently.

"Besides, it was our conclusion that anthrax would best work as part of something bigger."

"I think it's important that we have seen nothing to indicate that there is a second pathogen." Norment was frowning.

"What do you mean 'something bigger,' Dr. Watterman?" said Roycroft.

"We discussed this in detail, you see?" Watterman said. "That's what BACCHUS was all about." He actually wasn't supposed to say the name. He didn't know if BACCHUS was still a top-secret program or not, but it probably didn't matter anymore. "We tried to think like an attacker would think. We tried to war-game it. Anthrax worked best if it could be used in a blitz, to gum up the works, slow down the CDC and local health authorities from dealing with the real demon."

"Smallpox," Walthaer picked up, saying it to the entire room.

"Or something else, maybe," Watterman said. "Anything else. Ebola. Swine flu. Spanish flu, dengue fever, Lassa fever, SARS, Marburg. There's lots, you name it. Did you see bricks?" he asked Walthaer. Through a microscope, smallpox virus would look like clusters of bricks surrounding the much larger anthrax spores.

"No bricks. Nothing."

Norment grimaced and raised his hand. "I wasn't around back when Dr. Watterman's team made its predictions, but I want to emphasize again that we have no other indications . . ."

It went around the table a couple of times after that. Watterman didn't speak again. No one asked him. Maybe it was too much. The realities were shocking. They were staring one of the Four Horsemen right in the eye and they were scared, and what they wanted was reassurance. He wouldn't give them reassurance. That was just as much a crime as making the stuff in the first place.

The rest of the meeting was devoted to the possibility of finding evidence that might link to Iran as instigator of the attacks. It was sort of like moving on to the meat course. The stealth bombers were all gassed up and ready to go. He caught Norment looking at him a few times. Reilly was gone to work his evil somewhere else. He must be just about ready to retire too. Forty years in the darkest bowels of the CIA probably would generate a pretty hefty pension, Watterman calculated.

The meeting broke up with a fresh reminder that everything that had been said in the room was top secret.

Roycroft came over. "We want you to stay in the loop this time," he said, as if being in purgatory for ten years had been Sam's idea all along. "The general says you've agreed to come back on board?"

"Sure, that's no problem. I'll do everything I can."

"We don't pay as well as academia or Big Pharma. I know out there you'd pull down high six figures. We can't match that and we're in an emergency."

"What about the medical? My wife is—"

"I'm sure we could get you on a plan, Doctor. Don't worry."

"Okay. What do you think, Lansing?"

"I'm not your booking agent, sir."

"Look," he said to Roycroft. "I need the money. I work on a fee-and-expenses basis. It's three grand a day, not a penny less. That's a good deal, a lot less than some lawyers I know. And I work from home. That's in Atlanta. If you take me out of the region, there's travel time and per diem on top of that . . ."

"Don't worry about the money, Doctor. We can print as much as you need." Roycroft laughed and walked away, heading for his first press conference of the day.

Somehow the sight of the woman and her broken daughter has affected Daria, and she cannot just sit there and listen to music on the Nano, no matter how anonymous she would like to be. There is a bar in the next car back, actually nicer than the one on the Acela, and she sits with a couple of alcoholic businessmen who are knocking back early vodkas to ease the commute. She thinks about a beer, but instead buys a carafe of sour red wine for fifteen dollars and sits down to nurse it. She needs a book to deflect the attentions of the men, but it is too late and the nearest, red-faced and happy, leans over to comment that they're lucky that the train is running on time. She smiles but turns her attention to the Nano earbuds, plugs them in and begins scrolling through her playlist, looking for something, anything that will just transport her . . . away.

The man, seeing that she's not available, goes back to his friend, who is making a show of looking out the window. He shakes his leg like a man suffering from a heat rash, and tugs at his belt, trying to loosen the fabric around his middle. "I'm going to start wearing kilts," he says.

An Amtrak attendant comes into the bar car and goes behind the bar and begins talking into his walkie-talkie. A third man suddenly walks in and slides in beside the two drinkers. "Better whoa up on the sauce . . ." he says. "We might be driving, Big Bear."

"No . . . What the hellizat about?" says the happy man.

The window gazer turns around. "Don't lie to me . . . I don't deserve any more pain," he groans.

"What's up, Ned?" the happy man calls out to the attendant.

"Don't know nothing, yet," the attendant says. He clips his microphone back on his sweater and heads back up the train. The happy man looks over at her and raises his eyebrows. "You ready to be snowed in, sweetheart?" He winks, and raises his glass.

She pours another glass of wine just as an announcement comes over the intercom.

". . . inform all passengers that we will be disembarking at Baltimore station. This will be the last stop of the day. We'd like to apologize for any inconvenience, but it's out of our hands and we have regulations we have to follow, ladies and gentlemen. So, we're sorry but this will be the end of the line and we will not be continuing through to Washington. . . ."

"Oh, what a crap fest . . ." says the window gazer.

Ned returns and the three men begin to question him around the bar. She can hear his voice—defensive: ". . . No, we don't have any notification about it, and I don't know anything except it's some kind of emergency . . ."

"These things are always late," says the happy man to her.

The train has slowed noticeably and she realizes that they are clanking over the switches at the edge of the Baltimore yards.

". . . and gentlemen, welcome to Baltimore. The train will be stopping at this station and we will be ending our trip. Repeat. There are shuttles available to our downtown station. Welcome to Baltimore; unfortunately, this is our final stop for the day. . . ."

She gets off along with everyone else and hikes down the platform and into the station. There is a coffee bar and a television showing CNN. The sound is too distant for her to hear, and she doesn't want to press herself up to the counter and watch. But most of the customers are looking at the set, and the barista has stopped. That's how Daria can tell it is a genuine emergency instead of the normal "breaking" news.

She's been watching BBC and RAI for the last few years, but after only a few days in America she can recognize the jovial young host; he shuffles his notes back and forth and glares into the camera as he talks. Across a corner of the screen is a red banner:

ANTHRAX TERROR STRIKE

Over his shoulder a graphic comes up—a passport photograph or something taken for an identity card—

Below is his full name—*Tariq Abdel Sawalha.*

Tété . . .

Her heart stops. She steps back.

Her first instinct is to be sick, then it's to run. Her knees are weak, and she turns, looking for a way out of the station. She begins to walk toward the exit, rolling her luggage behind her, starting to sweat. She pushes her way through the doors, and right outside in the parking lot is a police car with its flashers on. Milling on the sidewalk, other marooned passengers are on cell phones, calling taxicabs, coworkers, spouses . . .

Look normal, she tells herself. Look normal, *be* normal. She takes a shaky breath, goes out, waits by the curb and in a few minutes is able to share a cab to downtown Baltimore with Gillian, who works for the city and was going to have to come back to the city later tonight anyway. The bus station is on the way. She suffers through the ride and invents a story about going to see her mother, who lives in Richmond.

"Just wait until tomorrow. There are good hotels. You'll get out in the morning. They'll probably be up and running by then," Gillian tells her.

"I have to get there tonight."

"Well, if you've got enough money you could take a taxi, but don't go by way of D.C. . . . or just go around it. It's starting to sound scary down there." Gillian laughs and shakes her head.

So . . . Tété too, she thinks as they ride along. That means there were—that there probably still are . . . *more*. She has not been alone. There are many arrows flying. Now Creighton's warning makes more sense.

Tété! How long have they had him? Did he leave on the same day she did? But how could they have caught him so quickly? Could he have been . . . was he . . . a double agent?

She tries to think back to every conversation she ever had with him. They never, ever talked about politics or anything remotely serious. It was all silliness and football and movie stars and fast cars. She never kept a diary, or wrote anything that might . . . They used to dream about crazy things, childish things, streets of gold in the clouds, fabulous dream houses they could live in. He was a little boy, really. That was why he was so charming.

She starts to cry, but wipes the tears and gets back her control. Tété . . . did he, could he ever suspect that she too was part of a . . . well . . . of something that was obviously a larger operation . . . ?

Tété caught spreading anthrax . . .

Anthrax . . .

She remembers the *USA Today* article about the arrest in Israel. How big is this? she wonders.

"Here you go . . ." says Gillian as they swoop into the bus station parking lot to drop her off; she pays with a twenty and leaves with a polite "Thank you."

Her cover has to be blown. It's only a matter of time now before they trace her. If Tété hasn't given her up already, they'll just rake through his background. Italian secret police and CIA agents will surf through all his records. They'll vacuum up her name along with everyone else's. And then they'll get a match when they look at arrivals into the U.S. over the last two weeks.

The hotel will gladly tell them all about her. That will get them her *Klic!* credit card number, so her cards are no good anymore. If she uses them, they'll be on her instantly.

Tété can't last. He'll tell them everything that comes to mind. She knows him. He's not hard enough. And she knows all about enhanced interrogation techniques. She knows about waterboarding and stress positions, sleep deprivation, truth drugs, and techniques of humiliation. She knows enough. No one can stand it. Sooner or later Tété will fall apart and tell them. She, Tété . . . and if there are others, probably none of them have had any training, the kind of training that you would need to resist. Just like her, none of them have any fallback plans. Now they are all fugitives.

Across the lobby of the bus station, there is a large timetable that refreshes via a series of flapping letters as each bus moves higher in the queue. There is only one open ticket window. The next bus displayed is heading for FREDERICK.

She goes right up and buys a ticket. She's on the edge of panic. When she talks to the woman at the window, her voice comes out raspy and she has to cough and clear her throat. She has no idea where Frederick is or how long it will take to get there. She's just running now.

And less than fifteen minutes later, she is seated halfway back in an air-conditioned Greyhound, leaning through the corners as the bus navigates in lurches to get into the supposedly "fast" lane of rush-hour-clotted I-70. Below her the Americans are choking on their own vomit, she thinks, looking down at the rivers of cars.

It is amazing how people can individualize their vehicles. Loving care and twenty coats of paint lavished on a pickup truck that gets ten miles to the gallon and will never actually carry a load of gravel. There are a great many gun racks. Bumper stickers abound. There are Democrats, Republicans, people who attend Tea Parties, and people who are boycotting oil. None of them are shy about loudly proclaiming their politics to whoever is behind them.

In the rear windows float the names of universities: Duke, Harvard, Tech, each with its attendant symbol. A blue devil, a demon deacon . . . a snapping turtle. The specialty license plates are a crowd of political statements as well. There are veterans, of course, veterans everywhere, young ones and ancient ones who should not even be on the road. There are people who believe passionately in the beauty of their state, the virginity of Virginia, the willingness of North Carolinians to take up flying. There are fish and Darwinian amphibians, and fish eating smaller fish. Twisted magnetic ribbons of various colors adorn the tailgates and trunk lids of many of these cars—more advocacy. All these people choosing sides and making alliances so frenetically, and yet there they are, stuck in traffic going slower than a tired dog can walk.

She plugs in, turns up the volume, and tries to sink deeper into her role. She will get rid of the huge rolling suitcase, take a change of clothes and her toothbrush and stuff it all into the first backpack she can find. She's going to look like a young American, not a tourist. She won't have much money, and she's going to travel light.

An hour later the bus turns off the crowded superhighway at a town called Mount Airy and half the passengers get out while only two get on. One is a young soldier, all his hair shaved off on the sides and only fractionally longer on top, a fully stuffed backpack on his shoulder, dressed in sagebrush-colored fatigues that have some sort of dazzling pattern printed on the fabric. From a distance he probably thinks he looks like the desert floor, she imagines. Still, he is smiling and, seeing her, wedges his gear into the seats behind him and then takes up the row across from her.

She thinks that she should kill him. Be friends and kill him. If she were thinking clearly, wasn't terrified and on the run, she could do it. All it would take is a smile. She looks over at him, his face sunburned from the training, new muscles bulging beneath his shirt.

"How far is it to Frederick, do you know?" she asks.

"Hell, with the traffic like this here and with everything that's goin' down, it'll take at least another hour. Everybody's been called in . . ."

"Is it very big?"

"Frederick? Nah, it's not that big. It's pretty small really, just a medium-sized place."

"Can I get a room there?" she asks. The boy looks at her for a moment and then out to the highway as once again they grind to a halt.

"I guess . . . you oughta be able. Sure." Then, after referring to the outside again—"But I don't know . . . everything's real crazy right now."

"But I could find a hotel, or . . ."

"Oh, yeah. Sure, you can find *something* . . . You oughta be able to . . ."

"I just need to stay one night."

"Well, one of my buds has a girlfriend and she's up in Chicago right now, so he could maybe fix you up at her place . . ."

"I should try the hotel first . . ."

"Nah, come on, save your cash. When we get there I'll . . . hold on." The young man pulls out his cell phone and punches in a number. "Hey-oh . . ." he says a few seconds later.

They are going through a long stretch of fields and distant developments of huge houses, almost identical, set into rows that drape across the recently cleared hills. All around the new houses are scars of fresh orange soil; elsewhere these have been patched over with fresh ribbons of turf. The houses are, like the cars, variations on the same theme, all the same palette of colors—beige, white, or, on rare occasions, leaf green.

"Beam me up, Mr. Scott. Airborne . . ." the soldier says, snaps the phone shut, and winks at her. "He'll get back to me, no sweat."

His name is Aaron and he is a skateboarder who wasn't good at school and enlisted for the occupational training. It's pretty good. Now he has money for the first time in his life, and the Army will let him go to college if he gets accepted. The way he talks it sounds like a good business proposition. He has been in for nine months.

A few minutes later his cell rings and he exchanges cryptic comments, looks over and makes the "okay" sign, smilingly describes her as a "close friend," and then snaps the phone shut.

His moods seem to alternate between hyperaggressive and scared child, and all she has to do is listen to him. Sooner or later he will make, or feel that he has to make, a move on her. The apartment has been arranged. Scott is going to meet them with the key, and Daria can stay there all weekend if she wants.

"I don't know," she says. "Maybe this is a bad idea . . ." She doesn't actually calculate before she says it. It just comes out. Maybe she doesn't want to kill him; he's such a child.

"Hey, look . . . I'll let you in, and maybe I'll come by in the morning and we can have breakfast or something, but I'm not going to be around, so . . . there's not a . . . not a . . ."

"Okay. If you're sure."

"Everybody's coming in. I was sitting there with my aunt Neenee and the phone rang, and that's it for this po' boy . . ." When he says that "everybody is coming in," she learns that his unit has been called to duty. "Because of the terrorist thing . . ." he says. And she realizes that he means Tété.

"If we run up on anything like that, if the FBI finds something that they think is a biological agent or a chemical agent, that's when the alert goes." He works at Fort Detrick, he tells her. Security and administration at ". . . You-sam-rid," he says.

"What? What is that?" she says, even as she starts to remember it from her research.

"Fort Detrick's the home base for USAMRIID." He spells it out for her. "The United States Army's Medical Research Institute for Infectious Diseases—the government's medical labs. It's sorta like the Centers for Disease Control down in Atlanta, except we're military. Chemical warfare branch, germ warfare, biological warfare countermeasures, all that kinda stuff. It's a spooky place. Scientists doing experiments. Very scary, you know?"

"I guess . . ." she says, amazed at the coincidence, and continuing to listen. She can tell he's impressed by the place.

"Oh, yeah, it's nervous-making shit, girl. You don't know what's going to come outta them chimneys. And something goes into effect, like this goof down in D.C., we go operational. So . . . I'm not going to be bothering you very much, okay? What's your name, little sister?" He smiles at her.

"Maria . . ."

"Where are you from?"

"Hollywood," she says.

"I guess so. How come you're going to Frederick?"

"I just had to get out of Baltimore." She shrugs. "There was this guy . . ."

"Sure. Yeah. Okay . . ."

"So, I just up and left. Thanks for the loan of the apartment . . ."

"Nah, hey. It's nothing . . . You take your time."

When they get there, Scott turns out to be a ferret-faced fellow soldier whose girlfriend, Tina, is coming back after the weekend. She's been contacted, and said it's okay, on the condition that "Maria" keeps the place clean, pays for anything she breaks, keeps the noise down, and replaces the groceries. He looks over at Aaron. "There's a gas station that sells sandwiches and stuff over there, and a KFC down at the mall; I guess that's about it."

"It's good enough," she says.

Scott heads back to his car and rumbles out of the parking lot.

Aaron unlocks the door and they wander through the stale-smelling rooms. The apartment is actually more like a townhouse, with a kitchen that opens onto a living room and a single bedroom upstairs. Aaron gives her the tour. It all smells of cigarettes and stale beer, and if she weren't already infected, she'd be afraid to touch the linen or step in the shower. Maybe it was a mistake to have taken up Aaron on his charity.

"Is this going to be okay for you?" he asks. Great big scared eyes, like a kitten.

"It's really great. Thank you," she says, blowing him a little kiss from the top of the stairs.

"Hey, Maria, I might get off tonight, who knows?" he says as he heads out, slinging the heavy pack over his shoulder.

"You can come back, if you want." It's actually beautiful to see how happy he is when she offers.

He raises his hand in a little salute. " 'Re-viderchi," he says, still smiling.

DAY 6

She did the sheets in hot and hot, ran them through the dryer, and tried to decide if she should use Tina's bed or make a place for herself on the sofa.

At nine the telephone rang; Aaron calling to say that, because of the emergency, he wouldn't be able to make it over, but that he would try to come by in the morning. Also there was some bad news, he said. Scott wanted her gone tomorrow. It didn't matter that he had vouched for her. Scott claimed Tina was pissed off about the arrangement, but Aaron didn't believe him.

She cleaned up the apartment as she went. It wasn't really dirty, but it looked like Tina had left in a rush. Things undone, clothes still in the dryer. Food left in the fridge while she was in Chicago doing whatever she was doing.

Tina's real name was Celestina Pedroza. Scott, in his role as caretaker, had managed to pick up the mail and dump it in a cardboard box next to the sink. There was a sheaf of unpaid bills, photographs magnetized to the refrigerator door. Several were of children, and a woman she decided was Tina holding babies. A thin, dark woman, long brunette hair, and a look in her eye that said she might have a taste for the wild side. Bottles in the garbage, a bong hidden in a drawer beneath the TV, and in the night table two boxes of condoms, lube, and a vibrator zipped inside a white nylon pouch. On the bedroom windowsill was a shoe box half full of letters to Tina. In Spanish with stamps from Honduras.

She unpacked and weeded out her clothes. Maybe Tina could do something with them. Supposedly they were loaded with whatever germ she was carrying. Where would be the best place to leave them? For now they got laid out on the recliner facing the television.

While she was waiting for the laundry and cleaning up a place for herself to sleep, she plugged in her laptop on the kitchen counter. There was a weak unsecured connection in the building—someone called Zappz—but she connected and found Baltimore on a map, and then discovered Frederick to the west. By increasing the scale of the map, she zoomed down to where she thought the apartments were . . . on the northwest side of town.

And there she was. Just down the road from USAMRIID—the United States Army Medical Research Institute of Infectious Diseases.

Amazing, she thought. Amazing coincidence. The opportunity made her dizzy as between Wikipedia and the "you-sam-rid" website she learned more about Fort Detrick. As a target, it was too important to pass up, but the problem, especially now that Tété had been caught, was how to get inside.

She found the television remote under a throw pillow on the sofa, flipped through channels to the news, and waited through a commercial for the latest disinfecting mop, and a preview for a television series about cops pushed beyond the edge. An animated vortex dissolved to reveal the genial host who promised—

"*. . . an examination of the anthrax terror that has paralyzed the nation's capital—is this the new Black Death?*"

Almost immediately there was a fresh set of commercials, for chocolates, for absorbent towels, for more-fuel-efficient vehicles not yet built, for Viagra, for health insurance no matter how unhealthy

you might be, a promotional clip for an upcoming football game . . .
Then Tété's mug shot filled the screen. A caption across his neck
read, THE FACE OF TERROR.

Tariq Abdel Sawalha had been captured after acting suspiciously
in the corridors beneath the Library of Congress, where someone
noticed him sprinkling "a white powder" near a heating vent.

> "... spokesperson from the CIA reporting to us, saying that
> they are tracing 'persons of interest' and analyzing 'several
> credible sources' that might shed light on the possibility that
> Sawalha and the Atlanta attacker were acting as part of a
> larger cell . . ."

The sheets and pillowcases ended their cycle in the dryer, and
she went upstairs and made the bed. There was a great woolen blanket, and a sleeping bag on top of that, and she took them out to the
front steps and shook them out.

When she came back to the television, there was an older man
in a policeman's uniform talking at a press conference. Under his
voice she could hear the spasms of the flash cameras.

> "... want to emphasize that every possible precaution is
> being taken; we have isolated the buildings Mr. Sawalha vis-
> ited.
>
> "We have one hundred percent confirmation that all
> agency employees in those buildings have been contacted
> and are being treated at this moment.
>
> "Mr. Sawalha has already provided us with information
> enabling us to reconstruct his route over the four days he
> was in the capital. All those locations are quarantined and
> are being tested. . . ."

She returned the blanket to the bed and then watched more of
the news. Now a man in a suit, younger, his face a serious mask, had
taken the podium and was briefing the press on the effort to undo

Tété's work. She could tell by the panic in the reporters' voices how scared they were.

Good.

She went out to find the "KFC," which, after a glimpse of its towering illuminated sign picturing a smiling old man in a strange tie, she realized was the famous fast-food franchise. There was one in Rome that was always full of tourists. Outside, while she was waiting for her order, there was a loud rumble of exhaust.

A car was driving up. It was wide and low, painted orange with black flames, and when the motor was switched off, a series of tiny black lights winked out in sequence under the wheel wells and behind the grille.

Four soldiers came in and placed an order. They were dressed in fatigues, like Aaron's, and their shoulders bore the same insignia. They looked at her while they were ordering, and one actually smiled. When her number was called, she paid for her box of chicken, biscuit, and something called "coleslaw," and took it across the parking lot and back up the sidewalk to the apartment.

In the fridge door was half a bottle of chardonnay, and she sat in the recliner, ate her KFC meal and flipped through the channels.

Tina only got basic television, so Daria got a good dose of community news. There were photographs of fatigue-clad members of the Twenty-first Signal Brigade arriving at Fort Detrick for security. A roadblock had been thrown up on both ends of Military Road.

When she landed back on the national news, she saw similar precautions were being taken all over Washington, D.C. There was footage—she had seen it three or four times already—of an out-of-focus Tété, a black bag over his head, revealed through the smoked glass of an SUV as it bounced down into a basement garage. Poor beautiful Tété.

She started crying and put the wine back in the refrigerator because now it was too dangerous to get hammered. The stakes were too great and she had big decisions to make.

She looked over at the laptop. They would be looking at everyone Tété ever had known. They'd be onto her, probably were onto her now, right now. Could they trace her computer somehow, even going through Zappz's router?

She got up, went over to the kitchen counter, and shut down.

Maybe she could sell it.

She examined Tina's bills and unopened mail, looking for something she could use. For starters she had the address and telephone number. A little more digging got her Tina's date of birth and a credit card number. She copied it all down on the back of a bank statement. Judging by Tina's clothes they were almost the same size.

She started pulling out anything else she thought she could use. From the shoe box in the bedroom she copied the addresses of Tina's Honduran family. She looked for but could not find an address book.

The problem was figuring out how to strike at Fort Detrick and then get out of town somehow, but it was like being in a cage. The more she learned, the worse her situation was getting.

On the eleven o'clock local news, she learned that enhanced security procedures had been put in place around the perimeter of the base. Traffic was restricted. The campus of Frederick Community College out on Opossumtown Pike was completely closed to students, because the school was adjacent to the boundary of Fort Detrick.

She was right at the center of Tété's anthrax swarm.

Too dangerous.

She found an alarm clock and checked the time against the television.

"... not only in Atlanta, but startling new developments regarding a previous anthrax attack in Israel and why, when we heard about it, our government did nothing. All that plus an interview with a Georgetown University medical expert who has been warning the Department of Homeland Security for years that something like this might happen. ..."

* * *

Lansing ferries Sam Watterman through his life, which has devolved into a double helix of meetings he is forced to attend even if they are irrelevant to his expertise. He really does try to think before he speaks, keeps a pretty good lid on his temper, and resolves to do everything he can to erase his reputation as an irascible retread brought in from the Cold War. He hopes it works, because he secretly is enjoying being back in harness, and is even getting used to falling asleep in armored SUVs.

He jots his reminders and ideas alongside his hours in a White House notebook he lifted from the West Wing, and has been surprised to notice his fortunes rising in tandem with the crisis.

He is the beneficiary of the inevitable equation: There is an emergency, someone has decided that he is part of the solution, therefore he attracts resources. In its role as catalyst, the FBI has provided him with Agent Aldo Chamai, who looks sixteen, but is already showing signs of obesity. It turns out he is part Filipino, blessed with an uneven tuft of dark hair that sprouts from the crown of his head, and wears glasses carefully designed to hide their thickness. A wisp of a mustache and a spritz of acne across his cheeks. Chamai is huge, at least six-two. He was probably a great center on his high school football team.

"The other thing I did wrong was to be a hippie," Sam says to Lansing. "I did my undergraduate at Berkeley. From '64 to '68 and then postgrad until '72. They see that on the résumé and it's a dead giveaway. Career dive. You get involved in protests, you go to meetings. It's an interesting time to be living. And God forbid you should ever inhale . . ."

"That's not such a big deal anymore, Doc."

"Nevertheless, if you stand up and call out the criminals, well . . . You can subtract thousands of bucks per year over the course of your career because you did something idealistic in your youth. Lab work? You're on your own cloud, dreaming up stuff. You're a hermit and people don't come into it, but if you get into administration? It's savage. They eat each other's children once you get into the office."

"Politics is everywhere, Doc."

"Vietnam, the civil rights movement . . . feminism. I guess it was worth it."

"Human progress," Lansing says. The J. Edgar Hoover Building floats by. Surrounded by concrete barriers, metal detectors. Burly policemen wearing masks. Not that any of it would keep anthrax out.

"Did we get an update on Sawalha?"

"He's pretty sick. But that's not going to stop them scheduling as many interviews as they can before he dies," Lansing says.

"He doesn't know anything. They just gave him a plane ticket and a tourist map," Watterman says.

"Doesn't matter, Doc. They're going to drain him like a prune."

"The guy they want is the creator, the god, the guy that made it in the lab. You need somebody with a certain amount of skill to weaponize anthrax, even a little bit. It's a problem of size, and static energy. The goal is to armor the spores so you keep them alive, and at the same time get them to float."

Lansing navigates the closed-off streets of the capital. As they approach the roadblocks, he flicks on his siren. There are soldiers at the bridge, managing traffic.

"The talcum powder bottle Sawalha carried holds 325 grams of anthrax. He said it was full when they gave it to him in Vienna. He used almost all of it around Washington. With the kind of dispersant qualities it has, particles with such low mass—and I'm basing this on what Walthaer said in the meeting—from the second they gave it to him, Sawalha was doomed. It only takes twelve spores; you breathe in twelve spores and you're dead. He was breathing them in all day, every day."

"Carrying it in his pockets . . ."

"Sure, just put it in your pockets. Take your hands in and out. You'd have to refresh it. It would go pretty quick, just float right through the fabric. Fine. Bravo, good job, yes, they quarantined all the locations, but we need to get his exact route, where he walked. Buses he took. Cabs. If he took the subway . . ."

"Homeland Security's all over that, Doc. The Metro is shut

down. They tested at the airport in Vienna. They didn't find anything."

"Oh, right, I really believe that."

When they arrive at Justice, Grimaldi comes into the parking lot
and waves them back into the car. They simply spin around and
drive out in silence. Seven minutes later he's at the Washington field
office, sitting across the desk from a very grim Special Agent Barrigar.

"We've been putting pictures in front of Sawalha. He didn't recognize anyone. Except this guy . . ." Barrigar opens an envelope and
spills out a sheaf of photographs.

The images are from diverse sources—open source and archival,
but also recent surveillance photographs. Wide angles and flat light.

A man.

Brown skin mottled with age. Dark hair graying and thinning
over time. Included in the package are a half dozen older pictures:
yearbook portraits, smiling faces cropped out of group shots, something from this decade, something from that. Barrigar arrays them
across the desk in a cloud.

"Do you know this man, Doctor?"

"Sure," Sam says, gazing at the face oldest in years—something
probably taken only a few weeks ago. A senior citizen not unlike
himself.

"That's Saleem Khan. That's 'Dr. Death.'"

She sleeps only a few hours. During the night she has been startled
awake several times, sometimes by her dreams, but earlier there was
noise from the apartment next door—heavy boots walking in. A
door closing, then someone clumping out and down the steps again.

Jumpy, she tells herself. Scared. What is she afraid of, dying? She
gets up and looks through all the drawers to see if Tina has a gun. It
would be in the bedroom, where most Americans keep their guns,
maybe on a shelf? But there is nothing. She gives up and falls back
into the bed. Her throat is raw and dry.

Is this the start of the flulike symptoms? Remembering Youssef crouched beside her, the needle sliding into her arm—could she have been given a combination of the two—anthrax and smallpox? For a moment she feels nauseous. What has she let them do to her?

From television she knows that anthrax spores are tiny—two hundred make up the width of a human hair—and are lethal unless treated immediately. But she hadn't been given a wispy powder that would carry on the wind, she'd been given a *liquid* that was supposed to be smallpox.

But that didn't have to be the truth, did it? Maybe when the fluid evaporated, anthrax spores suspended in the solution would dry and become transmissible. What if the injection was one virus, and the liquid another? The oily feeling was long since gone from her fingers. She had dutifully covered her hair and used rubber gloves in the shower in New York, and she had been running her hands over everything in sight. Could her touch still kill?

Finally acknowledging that she is unable to sleep, she gets up in the dark room and feels her way into the bathroom and pees. Finds herself ritualistically touching everything. By the time Tina returns, the apartment will be a stew of microbes. Daria has already made her decision to keep running. The terror threat is bright red and there is no more likely place in the world to get picked up than Frederick, Maryland.

She carefully hangs her business suit in Tina's closet. Takes her other clothes and tucks them into a pillowcase. Makes up the bed, spritzes the pillows with her little vial of perfume, and then leaves it with Tina's toiletries as a gift for the next time she goes out with Scott and friends.

Tina has a backpack . . . almost new, a blue duffel bag that can be configured to be worn over the shoulders. Daria stuffs the laptop in it, puts on her street-urchin outfit, takes the envelope with Tina's numbers and stuffs it in her pocket, pulls the hoodie over her hair, locks up, drops the key through the slot, and plugs in the Nano as she crosses the parking lot in the predawn.

She walks for about a half hour. There is a strip mall near the highway and she stops there to call for a taxi.

It's only three dollars to get into the heart of the little city. With so many soldiers around, and in the middle of heightened security, the town is restless. The coffee shops always are the first to open and she goes in, has her starter espresso, and watches CNN. It might be theoretically possible for her to get into Washington, but certainly impossible to get near any of the government agency buildings, or close to the Capitol or White House.

". . . and now more evidence that there have been multiple international bioterror attacks. In addition to reports from Israel, there are new accusations against Pakistan by the government of India over what they claim is the release of biological warfare agents in three cities. . . ."

She walks along the historic brick sidewalks of Frederick. The town is appropriately quaint and obsessively preserved. Charming antiques shops, huge churches, and plenty of places to spend money when you come up from Washington or Baltimore on a day trip.

As she walks she works out a plan. It's pretty simple; she'll head for the bus station and take the first bus to anywhere. She has to ask directions because she has somehow gotten turned around in all the historical architecture. In a parking lot beside a Catholic church, she stuffs the pillowcase full of infected clothes into a donation bin, a good choice, she thinks.

On the way to the bus station, she passes a car lot. There are hundreds of them, it seems. All the young soldiers have money for the first time, and immediately rush out and buy a car. Car lots, fast food, and pawnshops.

But this is not a car dealer's lot. It's called Rick's Wrecks-4-Rent. It's closed, but she takes a few steps onto the lot to check out the cars. They seem sound enough, a year or two out of date, dented fenders here and there, nothing serious.

She finds a restaurant, goes in and orders a giant-sized American breakfast. Sugary pancakes, and bacon. Eggs. She is surprisingly hungry for someone who is near death. She finishes off with a sour black coffee, but the rental car lot is still not open. She stuffs the backpack in a locker at the bus station and wanders around the surrounding blocks admiring the little brick buildings, all kept in perfect trim, the better to evoke the region's heritage—Hessian farmers who settled the area in the mid-1700s. Just yesterday in Muslim time.

She circles around and comes back to the rental car lot. A young man is inside and more than happy to rent her something to use while she visits her sister. She uses Tina's address, and shows reluctance when he asks for her credit card.

"This is for her, my sister. She's renting it, not me. Can I pay cash when I bring it back?"

"Sure. We just need the card number for a security. We don't even run it. Tear it up when you bring the car back."

She uses Tina's card number and books the car for two weeks, gives the man Tina's name and her driver's license number. "Can I get unlimited kilometers?" she says.

"Well, its unlimited *miles* in Maryland and Virginia."

"We don't need that much really. We're just going to be right around here in . . . Frederick."

"No problemo . . ." says the young guy. He makes an imprint with Tina's number written in, laughingly accepts Daria's international driver's license, and in five minutes she's on her way to get her stuff out of the bus station locker, and getting used to driving a totally nondescript white Nissan Sentra.

Navigating around the roadblocks, she circles Fort Detrick. It's divided into two vast tracts of land, and except for the olive drab vehicles, and signs that are untranslatable acronyms, it looks like an agricultural college surrounded by razor wire.

Naturally, there is no way in except by a truck rigged with plastic explosives, and really, there is no time to waste. Plus the danger is off the scale. She is on the run now and the smart thing to do is give up on Fort Detrick.

Scott will come by later to make sure she's gone. He'll see the thank-you note she left. He might wonder about it, but he will discover and accept the twenty-dollar bill, and the big rolling suitcase she has so generously left for Tina. The place will be neat and clean.

When she returns, Tina will marvel at how responsible he's been and forgive him for all his sins. He'll put today's junk mail in the box, and when he sees Aaron again he'll really give it to him about missing out on that foxy girl because of Uncle Sam.

Driving out of town she pulls off at the Frederick Towne Mall, which, she learns, is proudly situated on something called the Golden Mile. It is, in essence, a parking lot surrounded by stores the size of airplane hangars. She is nerved up and trying to make a getaway, but this might be her last good chance to strike at Satan . . .

So she makes herself walk through the huge displays, fondling everything, refusing the assistance of the clerks, and passes right through to the next store in line. If she is still infectious it will eventually get to the soldiers, their wives, their families.

Using Tina's name and address, she applies for a discount card at something called the Bon-Ton, goes into a changing room, tries on and rejects a few little tops, and then leaves. She's calmer now, just walking.

She discovers an Internet café in a run-down little muffin bar with a cowboy theme. They claim to sell espresso there, and there are two computers she can buy time on.

On the *New York Times* site there's more about the lockdown of both Atlanta and Washington, D.C., and a list of high-profile government officials who have been taken to Walter Reed Army Medical Center for treatment against the anthrax spores they have inhaled. There is a photograph of blue-plastic-suited technicians carrying what looks like a vacuum cleaner up the steps of the Capitol building.

Maybe she has a fever or maybe she's paranoid, but it seems the clerk is looking at her suspiciously—well, it's a little early for shoppers. She shuts down her account. She's not worried about someone tracing the search. "Anthrax" is probably getting ten million hits per minute right now.

The corridor opens out onto a mostly deserted food court. She finds the bathroom and goes in. Her face is hot. She splashes water on her face over and over again, and then looks at her hands. It is as if she can see the bones right through her flesh.

The door behind her opens. Two women in green smocks come in. One has a spray bottle that she uses to clean the door handles, while the other uses the last stall. Daria is too nervous to stay there washing her face and looking at herself, so she leaves. She finds an exit and pushes her way out the big glass doors and onto the mammoth sheet of asphalt.

She has to search for the unfamiliar Nissan—practically invisible since it looks like every other car in the lot—finally finds it, and drives away thinking she has done as much as she can. Now it's time to put some distance between her and the security forces ruthlessly locking down Fort Detrick, because Tété is talking, and if they don't have her name already, soon they will. And soon her photograph will be retrieved from every surveillance camera from Baltimore to Berlin.

And soon that will be it.

But she will not just roll over and surrender. She might be a woman, but she is also a warrior. She has pledged her life to God, indeed she has already given it, and regardless of what happens to her, regardless of her skin falling off . . . she will fight. She will resist them. With the last drop of her diseased blood. Forever.

Shaken, absorbed in her thoughts, her mouth hardened in a tight line, she grips the steering wheel and drives along the so-called Golden Mile (the pathetic delusions of these Americans will never cease to amaze . . .), and when she gets to the junction of the highway, she makes a decision and swerves onto I-70.

West.

The biggest thing wrong with FBI agents, Sam Watterman thinks, is that they seem to be constitutionally unable to hold the slightest conversation without making it seem like a grilling. Behind the smiles and the offered bottles of water and cups of coffee, what they really want is an exact account of every moment he had ever spent with Khan. Where did you meet? Where did you stay? Any correspondence? Phone calls? Exchange of bodily fluids?

"I told you. It's all on the record. I saw him, I *glimpsed* him across a crowded room, maybe . . . four or five times. Said hello, shook his hand a time or two. I met him lots of times, but I spent time with him only once. A conference in São Paulo. He wasn't giving a paper. In fact I don't think he ever gave more than one or two. You could check it. He was born in Egypt, but his parents immigrated to Cairo during the Second World War. Maybe they were Lebanese? You'll have to look it up. He was, even then, one of the guys on the horizon. We all keep track of them, you know."

"Actually, we keep track of them . . ."

"Then you should be able to follow his movements better than I." Sam Watterman feels a flicker of pride in his grammar.

"Just take us through it, Doc."

For a moment he looks around at their young faces. Everybody in the room has crossed the line. They are all riding the thrill-wave of biowarfare. He's seen that look before and it doesn't get any prettier.

"You have to remember, a guy like Saleem Khan, he's a manipulator. Guys like that don't play by your rules. He wants what he wants because he wants it. I don't think you would describe Saleem as 'motivated by feelings of patriotism.' "

"You said he worked for Iraq."

"Sure, the UN published that. Lots of people worked for Iraq at one time or another. And he worked for Pakistan. *You* told me that. I know he consulted . . . to lots of places. He's got to make a living, after all."

"He's a freelancer. Have syringe, will travel."

"Yeah, he is, essentially. And a guy like Saleem, he's slick. You must be following the money, right?"

"We have some financials. He has a lot of accounts."

"I'm sure he's got a lot of everything. So, what does he care? A few million nameless people here or there . . . for an asshole like Khan . . ." For a moment the man's youthful face floated in front of him. Always smiling, always laughing. Always dressed to the nines. Hollow.

Yes, of course, they had known each other by reputation. As for their dramatic meeting in São Paulo, there was precisely one round of drinks in the hotel bar before Khan dashed off to a dinner date with a handsome couple who'd come to pick him up.

"What did you talk about, Sam?"

"Retroviruses. We talked about retroviruses," he says quietly, remembering. "That's what everybody was talking about."

HIV was brand-new then. No one knew how to stop it and everyone was afraid of it mutating. Its stealthy approach and its dramatic fatality were attention grabbers. That night, among the revolving knot of microbiologists, epidemiologists, and bio-spooks at their table, speculation began that HIV had been manufactured. That it was tweaked and targeted. Could such a thing be done? The South Africans had a prolific biowarfare program; were they behind it?

But, no . . . it was foolish. Crazy. And you couldn't really use a weapon like that unless you had a defense in place. So, did the South Africans have a cure for AIDS that they were keeping secret? That was a defining precondition; there was no utility in having a biowarfare capability unless there was a way to immunize your high command, your military, and ideally your whole population. It was the classic problem of targeting—stopping the germs from blowing back and killing your own people.

Khan's friends had come in to get him. A young couple. Nice clothes. The woman quite attractive and wearing jewels.

Khan had stood up, lifted his farewell glass. "It's like drinking," he'd told them. "The strength of a bioweapon cocktail is undeniable." (*Sip.*) "But the hangover is hell." (*Another sip.*) "The only thing that will save you is the vaccine." (*Drain glass, exit to applause.*)

"He was very charming . . ." Watterman says. "But you have to remember that ultimately, biowarfare is unthinkable. Actually . . . it's a fascination. Like how some little boys are in love with cars or airplanes, or the uniforms of football players, or their mother's lingerie . . . it's a fetish. The devil's dream."

"Okay." Barrigar nods.

"When we set up our projects, maybe something like BACCHUS, the whole purpose of that was—"

"This is not about your involvement in BACCHUS, Doctor."

"Oh, yes it is! That's exactly what it's about. It's about discerning the absolute boundaries of the threat. How cheap could someone build a credible biological weapon? Could you make it using off-the-shelf components? Could you put it in a trailer, could you put it in a toaster oven? So, *we did it.* We wanted to measure it. If we could measure it, then we could budget for it. Administration. Administration of death. You tell yourself you're being realistic, that you're fighting fire with fire. You give yourself permission and now it's gloves off. No rules in this kind of fight. You know what I mean, don't you? Black ops, wet work. I'm not ashamed of it. I was a patriot. I did it. I got paid. It's what we do. It's who we are."

"If it's so unthinkable, why is Khan involved?"

"Because it's not unthinkable if you have a cure."

Barrigar had been doing the questioning, and Chamai was keeping notes. The door opened and Lansing came in. Barrigar got up and they took it out into the corridor.

When they closed the door, Chamai put down his notebook. "Say, Doc, were you around when Kennedy got shot?"

"Yeah."

"Do you remember it?"

"Sure. I was in high school. We were rehearsing for the talent show. There were some girls down by the piano listening to a . . . to a transistor radio?" Watterman held his hand up to represent the size of the antiquated device to Chamai, who was a total digital geek and the slobbiest FBI agent he'd ever seen.

"We could see the girls were crying, and everybody went down to the lip of the stage. They shot him in Dallas. Sure. I remember that. I remember every detail. Cuban missile crisis. I remember that. We went home from school that weekend not knowing if we'd ever come back, yeah."

"Whoa," Chamai said. "Did you know David Kelly, head of the British germ warfare thing?"

"Of course. It's a small world."

"You think he was murdered?"

"I have absolutely no comment."

"What about the thing in South Africa, PROJECT COAST?"

"It's all in the record."

"Did you know Frank Olson?"

"I was six years old when he fell. Or was pushed. He was on LSD, right?"

"That's the story. What about the mysterious deaths of government-employed microbiologists over the last forty years?"

"Whatever you've been smoking, please, I'd like to buy some off you."

"I'm just asking, Doc."

"Look . . ." Watterman said, leaning closer to the young man. Their voices had fallen to whispers. "There's not always fire wherever there's smoke, okay? Not *everything* is a conspiracy. People just fuck up. Shit happens."

"A lot of shit in a perfectly straight line, I don't know, Doc."

"This is what's wrong with the Internet. Sloppy verification."

Lansing and Barrigar came back. The door was open. Barrigar didn't bother to sit down. Behind him, a Marine captain waited in the hall. Barrigar stood at the end of the table, stared down at it, shook his head. He looked gray. He took a sudden breath, and tapped the top of the table with his fingertips like a pianist testing the action.

"Just got a report of a *smallpox* case," he said.

Sam realized he was holding his breath.

"Just one case. But . . . probably more. In Germany. A hotel worker in Berlin." Barrigar's voice sounded tired, papery. "We're going to be moving."

Barrigar helped Watterman up and Lansing took him by the elbow as they left the room and headed out of the building. There's a list of vectors, Sam remembered. *His* list. *Schools, hospitals, subways, theaters, sports venues, airplanes, business hotels . . .*

Walking, trying not to break into a run as they headed en masse down the corridor. When they got to the elevators, there were too many of them to get into the same car. Lansing held him back and Sam stared into Barrigar's stricken eyes as the doors closed him in.

This is the DWIGHT D. EISENHOWER HIGHWAY, signs proclaim every few miles. Stretches of it have been adopted by various civic groups or corporations. There are regularly spaced green and white signs spanning the highway, but she does not recognize the names— HAGERSTOWN, CHAMBERSBURG, MARTINSBURG—they mean nothing to Daria.

"For the second day, Wall Street has had a fever, then a violent coughing session, a sudden head cold, and now extreme nausea is taking billions out of the market. . . ."

There is something peaceful in the endless hay farms, poultry farms, and even the great depots for the long-haul trailers that are planted around the landscape. Incongruous housing tracts drape themselves across the foothills, edging right up to swatches of preserved woodland as the highway curves across the low mountains. A river loops along below, keeping her company.

". . . with only pharmaceuticals showing gains, but investors were hesitant, undecided about what this would mean for the more volatile health care sector. . . ."

She is traveling along a great artery; the highway is not unlike similar *autostrade* in Italy, or the great banked autobahns in Germany, only not as smooth and with much reduced speeds. Even the little Nissan is easily capable of doing the speed limit.

It wouldn't do to get stopped and have to hand over her identification, so she lets other motorists pass. Commuters who ply the highway daily, gigantic tanker trailers carrying canola oil, hoppers full of oats, stacks of caged chickens, rolls of steel, new automobiles— everything imaginable.

She makes her first mistake where I-70 divides into another

great artery. There is a swirl of concrete ramps, too many decisions to make at too high a speed, and she opts to go straight, staying with EISENHOWER. A few miles later she sees a large sign welcoming her to Pennsylvania.

That's wrong, she thinks, and having no desire to end up back in Philadelphia, she drives on, looking for a place to turn around. It takes forever until she reaches a little place called Pigeon Cove Road, where she can ramp off.

At the top of the ramp, she turns right and idles down the asphalt, but there is very little on the road: a long red barn with dozens of huge rolls of hay stacked along one side, a gravel business with a trailer for an office. She reverses and goes back over the highway, and turns again, pointing the Nissan back the way she's come. But after a few miles of low hills and endless fields, she realizes she's stuck on some side road with no way back onto the interstate.

She turns around yet again and drives right past the overpass at Pigeon Cove Road, and keeps on going until a few miles later she sees a red, white, and blue I-70 sign.

At the intersection there is a garage and used-car dealership, and she pulls over. Inside, a large man named Ed informs her that if she wants to go west to Cumberland, what she should do is get back on the highway and head back to the intersection and take the ramp off onto I-68.

"I don't want to go to Cumberland, I want to go to . . . Las Vegas. Can I buy a map here?" she asks, looking as helpless as she can.

"Get you a road atlas out of that display by the door. Cover the entire You-nine-id States. Get you wherever you want to go."

There are several maps in a large display rack beside the door. She rejects the local and state maps and spends twelve dollars on the road atlas, a large spiral-bound book containing maps of the United States, Canada, and Mexico. On the cover is a photo of a highway rimming the coast and a distant green farm that slopes down to the sea. There are no cars, people, or animals in the picture, but a banner below promises "pages of fabulous drives and adventures."

"That good enough for you?" Ed asks.

"Fabulous adventures? I guess so," Daria says, giving him her money.

"You want a big Coke with that?" he asks.

Outside, she sips her Coke, studies the maps, turns the ignition key of the Nissan, and tries to plan her getaway. That's the most important thing, just to get away . . . lead a trail away and help protect the others, whoever they are.

In America, the way they do it, the east-west superhighways are even numbered, and the odds are north and south. If she had stayed on I-70, she would have driven into Pittsburgh. What's wrong with that? It's a famous place. Is she missing something by not going there? She finds a map of the city and looks to see if there is anything of value there. She has heard of the city. They have a famous football team . . . if she could log on to a computer, she could learn all about it.

As she sits paging through the maps, a pair of thickset Maryland state troopers pull up and get out of their car, adjusting their strange peaked hats—wide brims with little pyramids on top. Cowboy hats are what they are supposed to be, she supposes. Cowboy hats with crowns, like mounted policemen or light cavalry. As silly as the *carabinieri,* she thinks. More myth. More lies. What kind of country is it whose greatest lies are told to her own people?

She pulls back out onto the highway and heads west . . . into the afternoon sun. She's lost her dark glasses, probably left them back at Tina's. Now she'll have the sun in her eyes until she can stop and buy a new pair.

A few miles down the road the state troopers blow past her, steady and sure and their speed up above eighty, she guesses. She has no clear idea how fast that actually might be, since she is still unused to the foreign measurements. She watches them vanish into the distance, stays at the limit, and cautiously tries to figure out how to work the cruise control on the Nissan as she curves and curves and curves through the undulating scenery of western Maryland.

"*. . . with the jitters in the credit markets, we're seeing all the classic symptoms . . .*"

It has been a long day already and by Cumberland she is tired. She crosses the border into West Virginia, and keeps on going until Morgantown, where there is another great joining of arteries. She takes I-79 South, heading for CHARLESTON 142; it's just a name on a colossal green sign, she knows nothing about the place and doesn't really care.

The sun is slanting low through her passenger window now, warming the seats and putting her to sleep, and she slows and ramps off; she has learned to recognize the true exits from the false ones like Pigeon Cove Road, and brakes to a stop in an attempt to get an espresso at an IHOP.

It turns out they don't sell espresso at this IHOP and she has to settle for a horrid, acidic concoction poured out of a huge glass urn right there at her booth.

She is early for dinner and late for lunch. The IHOP, its mission to satisfy American appetites notwithstanding, is nearly empty and she can see and hear the television that hangs above a nearby counter.

". . . that the care for this young man is the finest in the world, and they are being as transparent as possible, at least as far as his medical condition is concerned. What we're going to see is Mr. Tariq Sawalha standing up and walking, moving his limbs, and answering simple questions about his health. We're going to get medical updates, but any more than that, it's a stretch . . ."

There is the too-familiar clip of Tariq's entry into the garage, then Tété's face flashes up, followed by a series of portraits; among them she recognizes the man she'd met at the Adlon. Dressed differently, a little younger, but it's him. *Saleem Khan,* the caption says. Surrounding him are two other sudden demons—*Bahar Wahid,* and *Colonel Jamal Ulov.*

The head shots vanish to reveal the genial, gray-haired host. Beside him is a digital map of Washington, D.C.'s inner city. He waves his hands across its surface and with deft touches zooms in on

famous landmarks. As he speaks, the photographs turn red to indicate that they have tested positive for anthrax spores. She knows
some of the monuments: the Lincoln Memorial and the tall obelisk,
the Washington Monument, rimmed with flags in case you didn't
get the point.

Everybody in the dining area, she sees, is watching the television. The waitress comes to take her order. "How are you today?"
she says, not looking at Daria. She wears no makeup at all, and her
hair is pulled back in an efficient ponytail. She is going on forty,
Daria decides.

"I'm okay. Tired, that's why I wanted the espresso."

"Get down into Charleston around the college area and you can
find it. What'll you have today?" she asks, topping up the coffee.
Daria orders a chicken salad and sits there sipping at the coffee and
watching the television.

The news has shifted topics to the growing crisis along the India-
Pakistan border. Footage of rioting crowds from the vantage point
of what looks like a third-floor balcony. The scene changes: a crowd
of boys, with balaclavas and scarves pulled over their faces to hide
their identities from the police cameras. They hold all sorts of mismatched weapons—butcher's knives, staves, machetes—and one
boy, pushed to the front, hefts an automatic rifle. They are chanting
and dancing, taunting the camera. They are happy, she realizes.

"There you go . . ." the waitress says, centering the chicken
salad in front of her. She sees the direction of Daria's gaze.

"Isn't it just awful? My sister and her family are down in Atlanta. They spread it there too . . ."

"Atlanta?" Daria asks, not quite knowing where it is.

"Down at the Center of Diseases," the waitress says. Her voice
is warm. Southern and musical, everything said with a sigh. Tired,
but friendly. Suddenly Daria does not want to touch her, does not
want to infect this woman.

"Now . . . everything all right?" the waitress asks, and when
Daria, unable to speak, simply nods, she turns and heads back to the
counter.

The scene on the television has changed yet again. A different correspondent stands in front of a white façade . . . a government building of some kind. Behind him, a ring of soldiers have barred entry into the facility.

She picks up the fork and pushes her salad around. She has opted for something called "ranch" dressing. The chicken looks like putrid white flakes drizzled over the leaves.

She takes a couple of mouthfuls, the food like paste on her tongue. On the television they are talking about the hospitals, and the strain of coping with the anthrax attack. The number of cases is building far beyond expectations.

". . . There was a lot of chatter—and we know there was 'significant travel activity' starting in the first weeks of September. And I might add, Brian—something they are emphasizing to the press—Roycroft said it this morning— America is not the only target. And the working premise is that this is a coalition of some sort."

"So, it might get worse?"

"I hate to say it, but I think that might be a definite possibility. . . ."

Suddenly she feels nauseous, something about the smell of the salad, about her fatigue. She gets halfway to her feet and then vomits across the table. "Oh, my God . . ." she hears someone say. She is trembling. She collapses back into the seat, grabbing for a napkin.

"Here you go, ma'am. You want to come with me?" It is the nice waitress again, her voice like honey. She is helping her to her feet. Helping her. Daria pulls away, but it is too late now. They have been too close. They are not friends, but you don't have to be someone's friend to infect them.

"I'm sorry, I'm sorry . . ." she says, and allows the poor doomed woman to help her find the ladies' room. She takes some paper towels and scrubs her face, blows her nose. Stands there for a moment and looks at herself. Her hair is wild, her face pale, yellowish. Her eyes rimmed with red.

She is sick, she thinks. She is going to die. She stands there just staring at herself, then cups her hands under the faucet and washes out her mouth once more. The water tastes brassy and has a smell as if it were laced with chemical purifiers. The aroma brings fresh tears to her eyes. All she can do is lean on the sink and try to get her breath under control. She rips a paper towel out of the dispenser and dries her face, then uses another towel to clean off the counter.

She is sick. Really sick. She is going to die.

She turns away from the mirror, walks back out to the counter. Magically the mess has all been cleaned away by the nice waitress. She has spread enough germs in this restaurant, enough for one too-short life.

"I'm sorry," she says to the woman again.

"It's all right, honey. You take care now . . ." she says, absolving Daria of what little guilt she knows about.

The parking lot is hot. The air is hotter than in the restaurant, which Daria now realizes was air-conditioned. The air is clean, despite being adjacent to the wide superhighway. She breathes deeply. Climbs into the Nissan and makes her way back down to the interstate.

"I'm sorry," she says to the restaurant, wiping the tears from her eyes.

She drives . . . the movement of the car, the slow curves through the mountainous poverty of West Virginia lulling her. Staring out at the highway, the cars and trucks that pass her, and that she in turn passes. Ordinary people. Just ordinary people.

Somewhere down the road she sees a line of military vehicles, great lumbering trucks with camouflaged canvas coverings sheltering dozens of young boys in uniforms. She follows behind them for a mile or so and then passes slowly, gets in front of the convoy and lowers her windows. Maybe her spores will be carried back to the soldiers, maybe one soldier will catch whatever she has and spread it to his brothers. She has begun to cry again, and she raises the windows back up, her hands shaking on the steering wheel.

If everything is written, why is she so miserable? It must be the disease. She is an arrow; the moment she was loosed from the bow her future was determined. She drives and drives through the remainder of the day toward a blood-red sunset, driving until she can outrun her thoughts. She should be acting differently; while there is time she should take the opportunity to come back to God. She can pray now, she can become a practicing Muslim again, can't she? Her mind is in torment, a thousand questions crowding in on her. She ought to be able to answer them, to open her heart to God and put her mind at ease. It's normal to be frightened, especially of the unknown. It's normal to want to cling to life, especially when you are young. It won't be much longer and everything will be answered. She has to have faith. She has to be strong.

But she is exhausted now, and pulls off in the darkness down the entrance to a rest stop somewhere beyond CHARLESTON, locks the doors, cracks her window, lowers the seat back, and closes her eyes.

She is sick. She is going to die.

DAY 7

There is a distant tapping, like a carpenter or a woodpecker. And then Daria wakes up to see a West Virginia state trooper using his ring finger to tap on the car window right next to her head. There are raindrops on the glass; it must have rained during the night. She blinks in the sun and tries to lower the window, but the ignition key has to be turned to do it.

"How are you doing in there?" the trooper asks as she reaches toward the ignition. The key sticks and then turns and she fumbles with the controls until the window slides down, and she can talk to the cop.

"Good morning . . ." she says. Her voice is raspy. She needs water. "Is everything okay?"

"You all right in there?"

"I . . . got tired driving."

"Where you headed?"

"Uh . . . I'm going to . . . Texas."

"That's a long way."

"I know."

"Just for your information, you're not allowed to sleep overnight at a rest area."

"Oh, I'm sorry, I didn't know."

"It's for your own protection. We patrol the rest areas regularly, but it can be dangerous for a woman traveling alone." As he lectures her, all she can see is his silhouette. The wide-brimmed hat against the sun, the blocky outline, the belt with all its paraphernalia. She raises her hand to shield her eyes from the sun and get a look at his face.

"There's predators out here. You know what I mean?" he says.

"I guess. Sure."

"All kinds of people running around."

Yes, there are, she thinks.

"Where you from in Maryland?"

"Uh . . . Frederick."

"This your car?"

"No . . . my sister rented it."

"Rented it . . . okay." He walks a few steps to the front of the car; mouth turned down, critically scanning the front end, as if he is going to kick the tires. She can see that before tapping her awake he has unsnapped the clasp on his holster.

She feels intensely uncomfortable. Her bladder is full and she has broken out in a sweat. Her skin feels raw. She has a sudden urge to take off all her clothes, and would if the trooper weren't right in front of her. He's just standing there, glaring at her, undressing her in his imagination, like all men. Behind her, she hears a blast of radio static. She looks in the rearview mirror and sees that he has parked his patrol car right behind her, blocking her in. She opens the door and starts to get out.

"Just wait inside, ma'am."

She settles back into the seat. Scared now. Worried. "I was tired," she says out the window.

"Sure." Now the trooper walks back to his car and consults his radio. She hears the answering crackle of the radio but none of the conversation is intelligible. They go back and forth three or four times. At the end he comes back to her side of the car.

"So, you're heading down to Texas? Business? Pleasure?" She can see his face now. He's dark, the kind of man who could shave all day long and still have a shadow on his cheeks.

"My sister has a job set up down there."

"Oh, yeah?"

"And she needs some help with her little boy," she says. He is a first responder, she thinks. "Is it okay if I go use the bathroom?"

"Sure . . . be my guest." She gets out and starts up the sidewalk to the low building that houses the toilets. "You better lock up. Somebody'll come along and steal this thing."

"Oh," she says. "I'm not quite awake . . ." She tries to laugh, but his voice has stopped her there on the concrete walk. She tries to control her shaking hands as she turns and climbs in, inserts the key, raises the windows, and locks up. He just watches her the whole time. She gives him a little smile before she heads back for the toilets. Without the stupid uniform he would be kind of cute. He returns the smile.

Cops. They are all used to women trying to work them for favors. Men in uniform, they know they can get anything they want. If he decided to write a ticket, she would have no choice but to pay or go with him. He could bargain for whatever he wanted from her. That's the power equation and both of them know it.

The bathroom is huge, dark, and smells like concrete that has been marinated in lemon disinfectant. There are no locks on the doors to the stalls, but the seats are clean enough.

After she flushes she stands there at the sink and takes a series of deep breaths until she can go back outside. She looks okay, but cannot stop her hands from shaking.

When she pushes open the door she sees that he is facing away from her, talking on his radio again. She has a moment—just a flash of panic—where she almost starts running around the building and into the woods. It's stupid, a stupid idea. She has to get control. She has to calm down. Behind her, the door squeaks on its hinges as she starts back down the walk to the parking lot. He must hear it because he looks back and stops in mid-sentence. It might just be her imagination but he suddenly looks more serious. Something is happening, something has gone wrong.

"Can I see your driver's license?"

"Sure . . . it's inside," she says, gesturing toward the automobile.

He steps back away from the car, hand on his holster, watching while she unlocks the car, gets in, and digs through her duffel bag until she comes up with her license.

"I thought you were from Maryland?" he says, looking at the big paper international driver's license. It's like a booklet in different languages.

"I am now. Originally I'm from Italy."

"That's what this is? Some kind of Italian license?"

"Yes. When I get to Texas, then . . . I'll get a new one."

He studies the license for a few minutes, opens the pages one by one. "You have some other ID?"

"I have my passport."

"Passport. Okay, let's see that."

Daria groans inwardly at having to find the passport, angry that she's being manipulated by this stupid cop into leaving a trail. She finds the passport and hands it over to him. Each exchange is another transfer of virus, she hopes. That's what he gets for slowing her down, for looking at her, for *inspecting* her.

He is frowning now as he leafs through the passport. Of course it's in a foreign language and he can't understand anything except the entry stamp from JFK that will alert him to the fact that she's only been in the country a single week.

There is another blast of static from his car. *"Four-nine, four-nine . . ."* she hears the dispatcher say. The trooper shakes his head, scowls, and goes back to his car.

She can't tell if he hears when she starts the engine. Maybe he's been lulled since she's been so cooperative, but when she lets off the hand brake, that gets his attention and he half-turns.

When she jams her foot down, the little Nissan rushes backwards and crushes him against the side of his patrol car. He goes down somewhere back where she can't see, and she slams the car into drive, crashes up over the curb onto the grass of the rest area. Slewing around, the wheels slipping in the wet earth . . . slowing, slowing. She knows she should let off the gas, that trying to go faster is just making the tires spin uselessly, but she can't help it—

Now she can see him. The officer is crawling forward. He's managed somehow to get his gun out of his holster and has propped himself up with one arm, while she is just sitting there skidding around, the Nissan floundering in the grass. This is it, she thinks. This is where she is going to die—by a bullet, not a germ—shot down in a rest area in West Virginia.

An explosion. A gunshot, she realizes, an old familiar sound—and something instantly penetrating the car, something that takes her breath away. The shock of it lifts her foot off the accelerator, the tires dig in, and the car crunches over the curb down onto the pavement. She cranes her head to see the trooper fallen over on his side, the automatic dangling from his fingers.

Still she can't get her breath, even as she scrambles out of the car and runs over to where he has collapsed. The side door of the patrol car is crumpled where she jammed him into it, and he has coughed . . . something up. It looks like blood and water and vomit, and below there is a wet stain spreading across his pants. He is making strangling sounds and his fingers twitch. She reaches down and pulls the gun out of his hand and he doesn't even resist. PRESTON is etched into a gold plastic name tag pinned above his shirt pocket. His wallet is a big lump in his damp back pocket and she unbuttons it and yanks it out. Maybe seventy-five dollars in cash. A pair of credit cards. She takes the cash and the cards, dumps the wallet on the pavement, takes a step backwards, ready to bolt, but then remembers—the passport.

Where is it? She can't see it, and she drops to her knees. It must have fallen under him, and she gropes around for it beneath his urine-soaked hips—nothing, nothing. She gave it to him. He had it in his hands. *But where is it?*

She stands, looking around frantically, and then, on the seat, sees the passport—through the window of the crushed door where he dropped it.

"*. . . four-nine . . . four-nine . . .*"

There are no other cars in the rest area; she's just lucky, she thinks. She grabs the passport and turns, only to see the Nissan, driver's door flapping, as it slowly rolls across the pavement and up onto the grass, crunching into one of the pine trees planted there as shelter for the picnic tables.

She runs to the car and throws herself into the front seat. There is a hole there, punched all the way through the door, and now she can feel the throbbing in her side. She pulls up the edge of the hoodie—a red splotch of blood.

With her fingertips, she feels. Something just under the surface, and a searing pain where the lump has lodged against her rib, just below the band of her bra. She can't stay there to tend her injury; her heart is tripping along like a snare drum as she jerks the car into reverse, spinning the wheels again, skidding backwards onto the pavement, and then speeding away. . . .

Flooring it. All the way down the ramp and onto the interstate. Something must have happened to the muffler when she crashed over the curb, because the Nissan now sounds like a racer, a low growl that changes as the transmission cycles up the gears. She only slows down when she hits eighty, and then forces herself to back off down to the speed limit, the automatic and passport on the seat beside her.

Everything has changed.

He has undoubtedly run her plates, and the make and model of the car, probably even reported her name. She is now an identified fugitive bleeding from a half-spent bullet in her side. She has killed a cop, and she's seen enough American movies to know what that means.

She is almost to Huntington when she sees a pair of state patrol cars barreling down the other side of the interstate, flashers on and sirens wailing as they speed toward their man down. What's happened is . . . someone has stopped, stopped to go to the bathroom, maybe stopped because they have had their breakfast and have to pee, because the kids are complaining. But they've stopped, and someone has seen him, someone has called 911 . . . And she pushes the growling little car faster until she is welcomed into Kentucky.

She ramps off the highway, continues along a smaller road for a mile or two until she finds a place where she can pull off and get herself together.

A quick walk around shows her that the Nissan is damaged, a dented front bumper from the pine tree, a broken taillight, and a dent across the trunk, plus the single ragged hole in the side of the driver's door. She hides behind the open door and checks her side.

The bleeding has stopped all on its own, but there is a stain the size of a saucer there on the hoodie, so it will have to go. Every time she breathes it hurts, and if she tries to lean to her left, she sees spots and almost blacks out. She takes off her T-shirt and wads it under the bra so that it makes a bandage, roots around in the duffel bag and comes out with a sweater that is bulky enough to cover everything up. She holds her breath and kneels behind the car and tries to pry the license plate off, but it is bolted on too tightly for her fingers.

From the road atlas she sees that she can keep going on this road and will arrive at a larger town . . . Flemingsburg, in only a few miles, and that this will in turn lead her to a larger highway by which she can reenter the interstate.

There is the inevitable strip mall near Flemingsburg, and she parks around the side of a drugstore, goes in, and, as casually as she can, buys a large roll of adhesive tape, some gauze bandages, rubbing alcohol, and a bottle of Tylenol Extra Strength. At the register she pays with some of Officer Preston's cash, and then, crouching behind the door of the Nissan, makes a bandage and tapes it over the hole in her side. The bullet is still in there, she can feel it, a hard little egg there against what she has decided is a broken rib. Now she's glad she ran him over.

She tosses her bloody clothes into a dumpster. Then, holding her breath because every time she bends she wants to scream, she gets back in and drives away down the narrow state road. She slows to look for fishermen below, then tosses the stolen credit cards over a bridge railing. This part of the highway is brand-new, an attempt by the state of Kentucky with the aid of the federal government to upgrade its tattered infrastructure, but the houses and farms she sees are either hovels or the outlying fields of what she suspects are incredibly wealthy estates.

Horse country. Kentucky is *horse country,* she remembers
that . . . the Kentucky Derby. Now she passes one of these ranches;
white board fences, endless, unearthly lush pasture upon which the
absurdly inbred colts can practice their running. Horse racing is a
big thing, even with the Arabs. It's just mindless brutality as far as
she's concerned. Like caged birds. Terrible. How can a horse's life be
worth ten thousand humans?

In the tiny town of Sharpsburg, she approaches an obviously
abandoned house. Now she is thinking like an animal and by reflex
she taps the brake—she could pull over, move in and nobody would
know. It is a stupid idea that she rejects almost immediately, but she
stops the car.

There is a FOR SALE BY OWNER sign that she uproots from the
rutted dirt track that leads up to the house. The plastic sign pops out
of the metal frame, and she drops the frame in the ditch. She drives
on, maybe another mile or two until she finds an intersection, pulls
over and backs the car onto the grass, props the sign on the dashboard, jams all her stuff into the duffel pack, and—trying to move
without groaning—walks carefully onto Route 11 with her thumb
out.

"Where did you say you're going to college?"

"San Francisco . . . San Francisco . . . University," Daria says.

"That's good, that's good. It's good to get an education. I should
have done that myself . . ."

The man who has picked her up is in his forties, maybe in his
fifties. It's hard to tell. He has a round face, and is going bald in
patches. He wears a starched white shirt and a black nylon windbreaker that says DIGICON on the pocket. He does something with
networks and smells of peppermint and keeps looking at her instead
of the road while he tells his life story. His name is Dean, or Duane,
or Daryll. She forgets immediately.

She doesn't have to listen. It's not expected of her. It's easy for a
pretty girl to get a ride. The men are bored and horny, and will

gladly carry her a few miles in the hope of some kind of romantic liaison. They have been rejected so many times that they really don't expect anything to happen. If they hit on her all she has to do is glare, or mention that she has a virus. Sometimes telling the truth is the best way to chase these sex fantasies back into the dark. Outside of Lexington he drops her off, all smiles, ultra-polite and too afraid to make a pass. She waits at the entrance ramp to the highway for about a half an hour until she gets another lift further toward the city.

She's in pain, but she's moving. Almost a third of the way across the long state of Kentucky, she calculates.

She gets lunch at a Waffle House at the off ramp closer to the center of Lexington.

"... *what is now being called the Berlin Plague. And it's a disease that was supposed to be extinct. Smallpox rears its deadly head once again....*"

She sits at the counter and eats a burger and fries and stays riveted to the television set. When the commercials are done, a report is presented, an interview with a German bureaucrat; the man is in his sixties, and the crawl beneath his name identifies him as a high-level representative of the World Health Organization. There is a slight delay, and when he answers, his speech is heavily accented.

"... *Yes, it started with one case that was a worker at the Hotel Adlon Kempinski.*"
"*And that's in Berlin?*"
"*In Berlin. Yes—*"
"*The Adlon, that's the hotel where Michael Jackson dangled the baby out the window ...*"
"*The same, yes ...*"
"*And, Doctor, isn't what makes this so dangerous is that smallpox was eradicated from the globe, we never thought we'd see another case of smallpox again, right?*"

"Yes, that is correct. Since 1980 we have been working under the assumption that the pathogens were completely eliminated."

"Wouldn't that indicate it's not a naturally occurring outbreak? We know that the Soviets, and perhaps others, Saddam Hussein and maybe even al-Qaeda, had clandestine programs to weaponize these germs and viruses . . ."

"Well, as far as the Soviets go, that is true. When it was discovered initially that the Soviet government had stocks of smallpox, there was an international effort to disarm—"

"Our president Nixon was very much involved in that."

"Yes, that is—"

"But clearly, something slipped through the cracks."

The German expert puts his hand up to his ear, frowns . . .

"By that, I mean it's obvious that someone must have had access to these germs."

"Well, yes. It seems so."

"Are there any other cases?"

"There may be other cases, but there is a delay—"

"Yes, it takes time, several days for the disease to incubate. Thank you, Doctor. We're going to turn right now to our panel to see how this is playing out, not just in Berlin, but here at home. . . ."

The smallpox is already being analyzed, the host reports, in an effort to decode its DNA and discover the exact strain and thereby the lab from which it was presumably stolen. It's all about finding someone to blame.

". . . and we're being told this strain is from India itself."

"No, no, not quite. There were samples collected in India in 1967—hence the name, India-1—originally by Russian scientists, but where it went after that . . . frankly, it could be anywhere. We have some of the India-1 smallpox

*in our own labs as well as several other strains. We won't
know if this is India-1 or an older strain, or a new strain
until it's decoded—"*

"Or a hot strain . . ."

*"That's right, a hot strain, which means it's highly trans-
missible, highly lethal—"*

*"But doesn't that confirm exactly what some of our
members of Congress are saying? This theory that India is
the one behind all this, the anthrax, the smallpox—that all
of that is simply a ruse."*

*"I've heard that. It's needless, inflammatory specula-
tion. Completely irresponsible."*

*"Where can we find the truth in all of this, that's my real
question. . . ."*

Apparently the truth may be found in the next spate of commercials; for whitening strips, for lower prices on mattresses, for something you can plug into your phone line and escape paying for calls
to anywhere for as long as you want, for a superknife that can cut
vegetables or tin cans thin as paper and never wear out.

She stares at her plate and heaves a painful sigh. It all begins to
run together. She killed a man this morning. She's been shot.

Shock.

She stares around the restaurant. It's like being in a zoo where
they've misassigned you to a cage with the wrong species. She marvels at how completely dysfunctional all these people are. Primates,
crazy baboons. And the women. The women on the television, the
women in real life. Breasts are very big for Americans . . . well, they
are very big for Italians too . . . but every woman displayed has
prominent breasts. What does that say about them? Does America
need to be comforted, to be loved? To be nurtured and fed on demand?

Daria breathes again. She is hot. She has a fever. Suddenly her
skin is so itchy. She is desperate to take off her clothes.

She looks around. The television news is back on. There is a clip
of the American president making a speech. He says nothing new or

different. He's confident that the agencies, the scientists, the hospital workers, all the machinery of this vast, glorious nation will continue to answer the call. . . . It's all platitudes. Internationally, he is going to meet with both sides in an effort to arrive at a peaceful solution.

"You want me to top that up for you?" The waitress refills her glass without waiting for an answer. This is a new discovery, iced tea. Sweet and spiked with lemon. She drinks off half the glass at once. She still feels hot.

She has to get out of the Waffle House. Get away from the memory of the officer in the pool of his own blood and urine, the way his fingers were still moving. Like he was trying to scratch the neck of a cat . . .

She can't think about it, it's too much. And she will have to do something about the bullet, and the throbbing pain every time she takes a breath. She just wants to lie down and cry herself to sleep, but she can't. No . . . no, she tells herself.

She can't surrender to these monsters. She won't give in. She will keep going. She has set her course and she will kill, kill, and kill some more. But somehow she has to find a way to bring this wrecked plan to a pause, and get her head together. She volunteered, she *wanted* to be blown to bits, she wanted to have a fiery instantaneous death, to go out violently and have it over with. Not like this.

She drinks more of the tea, turns away from the television, and fumbles out some of her cash—it's starting to run low now . . . a good terrorist should be able to manage her money better and die with a final two pennies to close her eyes.

Daria leaves a tip for the waitress—unfortunately it won't immunize her—gently shoulders her pack, and heads out to the ramp that will take her away. Anywhere will do. Just away from what she has gone through this morning. And it isn't long—only a few minutes later and she gets a ride, his name is irrelevant, she forgets his occupation instantly. He asks how far she will go, and she says Denver. She falls asleep leaning against the cool window, and dreams of when she was a little girl and none of this mattered.

When she wakes he has his hand on her thigh, and she slaps it away and screams at him. It comes out in her childhood dialect and he looks confused. It's wrong, the wrong thing to do. She doesn't want to be memorable, doesn't want to stick out at all. She is careful to stay in the car, pull the seat forward and get her pack before the car stops. For an instant, her hand on the automatic, she thinks about blowing Mr. No-Name into the next world, but instead jumps out onto the grassy shoulder while he gives her the finger and burns rubber down some unknown Kentucky side road.

There is a long stretch where no cars come, and she ends up waiting by the on ramp for a sympathetic or horny soul to finally take her into Louisville. She sits in the grass and tries to count out her money, dividing it into two piles, one to hide in the backpack, another to carry with her. She is dizzy and spots are forming on her field of vision like spitting raindrops. It's not really raining, but the hallucinations pucker everything she looks at. In the afternoon she finally scores a ride. At first she thinks it's a school bus, but then realizes that it's a family of hippies.

She has never actually met any real hippies; a man and woman, both with long hair tied back in ponytails, and two children who are, they brag proudly, homeschooled. They are in the process of blowing this pop stand, fleeing . . . going back to the farm in the light of all that is happening in the world today. The man has a weathered face, with smile-wrinkles, and a missing bottom tooth that mars his appearance. He smells like wood.

The bus has been converted and has a sleeping loft for the children cut into its roof, and a second bedroom down below. There is a sound system, and Daria is given a seat on a low sofa halfway down the bus, and tries to will the children not to play with her but, starved for human companionship, of course they do.

They have renamed themselves the Trulite family; he is Happy Trulite, or "Hap," and the wife has kept her original name, Matilda—now shortened to Mattie. The boy is Cosmic (Mick), and Fern, the youngest, is the daughter.

It's all smiles on their journey off the grid. They don't try to hit her up for gas money, and gladly share their sunflower seeds and raisins. She can sit there without moving too much and listen as the children show off, singing nursery rhymes and drawing, producing fantastical pictures of chimeras—spacemen with wings, dogs with three tails in multiple colors, a sky full of whirling stars, fish, and blocky letters of the alphabet. She watches them sadly. It's too late now. Too late.

She falls asleep with an empty cup of comfrey tea clasped in her lap.

It is late afternoon by the time the Trulites drop Daria off on the outskirts of the city. She walks slowly, painfully, through the sprawl until she discovers a beauty parlor in one of the strip malls and goes in. It's called Ellevate and the hairdressers are all young, beautiful, and pierced. There is tinkly music playing, and the whole place smells like a mixture of a florist's and an estrogen factory.

One of the girls looks up. "Hey, how are you today?"

"Can you squeeze me in? It's a big job, but I've had it . . ." she says.

"In about a half hour we've got a space. What were you thinking?"

"Everything off. And I want to go lighter. A lot lighter."

Emily, the hairdresser, has her doubts about whether going blonde is such a good idea with hair as dark and as thick as hers, so they compromise on red. Tilted backwards, she is shampooed and it feels wonderful—warm, soothing, and completely rejuvenating. Time passes in a blur. It seems like only moments and the floor is littered with her dark curls, and by then she is floating, just listening to the spaced-out music while Emily does the color.

"Let me know if this irritates at all. It looks like you have a little sensitivity . . ." she says, her soft fingers riffling through the newly shorn hairs at the back of Daria's neck.

She closes her eyes and lets the morning's murder dissolve away. With the soft fingers massaging her skull and the ethereal music, she almost achieves something like nirvana. It's too late now. Too late for feelings or for regrets. What good will it do? Choices? She decided a long, long time ago. Her course was set.

An arrow in flight.

When the job is done, Daria stares at herself in the mirror. She is totally transformed, sassy and hip, and looks more her age as calculated in American years. Bending is hard, but she manages to get up from the chair without groaning out loud; she adds a tip and pays with most of her remaining cash, smiles all around. She walks out of Ellevate and along the walkway that winds through the mall. Counts her money and decides to splurge on a pair of fashionable sunglasses that work with her new hair.

Then . . .

Walking along, seeing her reflection in the store windows . . . it's not Daria Vermiglio anymore. It's a stranger.

Someone she does not know.

Watterman is insufficiently important to rate evacuation to the underground bunkers at Mount Weather. That's for the upper crust like the President and the First Family, the congressional leadership, cabinet secretaries, people with serious clout. Other extremely important persons are being evacuated for temporary residence at Site R in Pennsylvania, or Cheyenne Mountain way out west.

No, for ordinary *apparatchiks* like Watterman there is a chicken farm. Or at least it looks like one from the road. A long steel building nestled among several others spread out across a broad sloping field in what he thinks is Tennessee.

Or it might not be Tennessee. He doesn't know, because from where he was sitting there was no view out the windows of the helicopter. They land in a pad that's been cut in the woods. You could get four helicopters in there at a time, Watterman figures. A minivan and a dilapidated school bus are waiting. They drive out of the woods and onto a two-lane highway for a few minutes. It's like going on a field trip in high school except everyone is texting on secure cell phones.

The cool of the day has made the surrounding fields foggy, the colors are muted, the leaves have started to change.

They turn off the blacktop, go through a cattle-guarded gate and into a huge field upon which have been built a series of . . . chicken farms. They park around behind so that they will be out of sight of the road.

The doors have seals on them and the whole place is under positive pressure to blow the germs back outside, a comparatively cost-effective place of refuge. Inside, there's everything you need to sit out the end of the world. Food, clothing. Laundry. A bar with satellite TV. At one end are the sleeping cubicles.

His cell phone is taken away and encased in a Ziploc bag; he gets an orange cuff fastened around his wrist—it's a cross between a bicycle lock and a house-arrest collar. Then Lansing escorts him down to an open area. It's industrial seating grouped around coffee tables. Walled off with dividers, bulletin boards on wheels, and portable lighting units. There's activity all around and Lansing and Chamai drop him to go take care of FBI business. He finds a place to sit and lets his gaze sweep around the great booming shed that looks like it's going to be home for a while. He wonders how Maggie is, when he'll be allowed to talk to her again.

When Lansing comes back he sits and brings him up to date: "The Germans have tracked Khan through Berlin. Also we know that two men met him in Vienna, but he was ticketed to travel alone. That suggests he met accomplices in each city."

"That all sounds reasonable, Mike, but I'm not really law enforcement . . ."

"Sure, I'm just informing you, Doc. So, they are producing a database, everybody who flew in and out of Berlin, right? Everybody in the Adlon. Hotels in Europe make you surrender your passports. We've got Khan in Vienna to distribute the anthrax to Sawalha plus one more; after that he goes to Berlin and starts spreading out this Berlin pox. Did anybody brief you about the anthrax that was released in Israel last week?"

"That's news to me."

"Okay. Supposedly it's chemically different or something, so says NIH."

"Well . . . that just implies a level of cooperation, coordination."

"Yes, it does. Arrangements, alliances, that's conspiracy. Could Khan pull this kind of thing off?"

"He's a germ guy, not an administrator."

For a moment Lansing looks disappointed. "Well, we know that

Khan is just one part of it. You said we should go for the creator, and he's admittedly the kind of guy who could develop the stuff, but if there's two varieties of anthrax samples, that would indicate at least one other source, a different scientist who also developed his own batch of anthrax. The labs supposedly say they can back that up."

"Nightmare," Watterman says.

"But, okay. Here's the big news for today. When they coordinated the Berlin database with INS and airport arrivals, they came up with two names. People in school with Sawalha. Plus three more who attended other language schools in Florence, Italy."

"I know where Florence is."

"So, that means possibly eight, nine, let's say maybe ten that Khan kicked off just by himself. Could he administer something like that?"

"All to the United States?"

"No. I don't know. This is all happening right now, Doc. Not just here, probably in other places too."

"Right, right . . ."

Watterman stands up from the seat. His back is stiff. Everything hurts. Anthrax starts off feeling like a flu. Maybe he's allergic to the Cipro he's been gulping every four hours. India, London, Beijing, he is thinking.

"Go get me a line into Joe Norment and people from NIH right away. We've got to get some real hard focus on this Berlin strain of smallpox variola. If I'm going to be any good, I need that as fast as possible. What's happening there? They must be on that already—"

"Smallpox samples are supposedly en route."

"Well, look, make sure that Joe gets his share. It doesn't matter about identifying the strains or finding the source, all the cop shit can come after. It doesn't matter what everybody else is doing, okay? We're looking for a tweak. It's the DNA structure of the Berlin smallpox strain we need to focus on, okay? You're going to get that rolling for me?"

"Sure, okay."

"Genie is out of the bottle now. . . ."

* * *

Louisville isn't much. An old city walled off from an older river by a network of awkwardly placed highways. She has ridden this last part of her voyage by city bus, almost empty except for members of what Americans call their "underclass"—bulging black women with shopping bags and sore ankles, undocumented refugees, and rickety old men wearing embroidered baseball caps with cryptic names of ships now in mothballs.

It is the America you never see on television, the drab part with termites and a bad smell coming from the dumpster. Nothing funky or cool. No beatbox or wah-wah pedal, only the bottom of the pyramid—the place where America eats her own, the fuel the leviathan must consume to keep going.

Daria gets off the bus when she sees a group of poverty-stricken wretches lined up around a church. It is a food bank, and, not having a place to live or cook, she really doesn't need their particular type of charity. But spending a few minutes in the line gets her directed to the Salvation Army's women's shelter just around the block, and she hefts the pack over her shoulder and walks along, past the soot-encrusted bricks of the old city.

She is lucky, she is told. There are remaining beds, and she is read the rules—no drugs, no weapons, no alcohol. One of the black-clad "nuns" that officiate in the building gives her permission to check her pack into a locker.

She discovers additional rules—everyone must share in the task of keeping the shelter clean while they are in residence. Two meals are served, at times posted on the dining room wall. There is a curfew of 11:00 p.m. Smoking is allowed only on the patio deck.

She hides in a bathroom cubicle and changes her bandage. The flesh around the shallow bullet hole has swollen and is tender. When she pushes on it a clear liquid oozes from the wound. She will have to wait to dig out the bullet, wait until there is somewhere she can scream in private. She tapes herself back up, and when the announcement is made, she goes out to the grotty dining room for her evening meal.

It is like dining in a prison, she supposes—a glop of creamed ground beef with noodles and a cheese sauce, a few leaves of lettuce, and a puddle of peas and carrots. Sweetened iced tea to wash it all down. It is a diet that would lead you straight into addiction if you were not there already.

There is a common area, and she sits in an overstuffed donated armchair, tries to stop scratching at her skin, takes shallow breaths, and watches while the other women flip around the channels. Sooner or later they land on the news. When it's too depressing they flip away, but it only comes up again.

"... attacks in at least three locations, in New York, in Washington, and in Atlanta, specifically at the Centers for Disease Control. Just over an hour ago we learned that there is a suspected case in the Los Angeles area ..."

"... multiple attacks ..."

"... don't forget that this is all having a huge effect on the airline industry ..."

"... everyone living in the area is being advised not to travel, it's that simple ..."

Someone has flipped until the channel ends up on a war documentary. The black-and-white footage of American soldiers is plentiful: young men laboring in the hot Pacific sun passing ammunition boxes up a sandbank, young men cleaning their ancient weapons, young men being carried back on improvised stretchers. The then-president, a grim face Daria remembers but cannot name, makes a terrible announcement. A day of infamy. American historic trauma, relived over and over . . . Geriatric survivors remembering how the kamikaze was the terror weapon of the day. Someone changes the channel.

Daria looks around the room. Here too most of the women are black; it's no surprise to her now, this flip side of the land of opportunity. The women are "Black" in the same way that she is an "Arab," which is to say not black or Arabian at all, but simply non-white. The ultimate sin. All sinners—all ages, from girls barely emerging from their teenage years, to women who are pregnant, to the old and infirm. Beaten and abused, addicts and alcoholics who lost hope long ago and who have given up on finding it again.

> "... and breaking news just coming in to our headquarters here in Atlanta—more cases of the so-called Berlin Pox and how it is spreading, not only to the U.S.A., but perhaps as many as a dozen other cities around the world. . . ."

It is race, yes, but it is also class that brings these women to the shelter. They have no money, few skills, little motivation, a long history of defeat, and a dearth of expectations. All that waits for them on the streets is exploitation, poverty, and violence. They huddle over their cups of stale coffee, fortify their soup with crackers, and scuttle out to the patio to smoke their cigarettes. They are scarred and tattooed, outside and in. Some talk like men, and some don't talk at all. All they want is to get through the night.

> "... we emphasize to our viewers that panic is not an option. We have an adequate stockpile of vaccine and have ordered additional production. . . ."

Each day these women are confronted by alternative visions of what they ought to have been, compared and contrasted with their present degradation. There is no shortage of encouragement that only drives the depression in deeper. Advice. Programs. Abstinence. Empowerment. All delivered as if they are sparkling brand-new ideas. All they have to do is look around! There are plenty of models out there—not just fashion models—whose presence serves to remind them of the intelligent choices they missed. Even if they turn away they are rewarded with advertisements—fabulous Amanda Seyfried wearing mascara to make her eyes look even better. Charlize Theron selling perfume. Could these women afford that? Will they ever attain even a fraction of that white perfection? Smell better for whom? To what end?

". . . of course it was by design. It's a terror attack. It's a direct attack on Washington using anthrax, plus on the Centers for Disease Control, and the National Institutes of Health. . . ."

Down a hellish catwalk the women of the shelter flounce, failing once more to put their not-so-dainty feet right in front of each other, failing to display the designer's clothing at its best, failing to have good hair, smooth skin, to purse their lips just so. Failing, failing, always failing.

". . . which means hospital workers, our military, police, and emergency medical personnel are vaccinated first. We're doing this very quickly because unlike the anthrax, which simply floats on the wind, the Berlin Pox virus is spread in several different ways. We've all heard the old stories about how our native people were tricked into receiving infected blankets. . . ."

These women are victims, and she, Daria, has no business being there. Why pass along her germs to these poor sisters? She should be at Fort Knox, just down the street; she should invent some way to crash the gates, shoot her way into the bullion room and die in a hail of gunfire. Would they get the message then? Would they understand that the enforced blessings that the nuns require before serving them the god-awful evening meal are only an additional indignity, a mere distraction from the cruelest of jokes?

Because no Jesus is coming to save these women.

When Watterman finally gets permission to call home, it's too late and Maggie is "resting comfortably," a nurse's voice assures him. He is using Chamai's secure cell, stumbling along a few paces behind him down a wet path that extends along the outside of the long steel wall, while the young man struggles with the zipper of his tent-like FBI windbreaker. They are taking the opportunity because the building is going to be locked down soon and access to the outside will be forbidden.

The wind is up, rushing down the valleys between the wooded hills. Far across the factory roofs, he can see the trees bending as a weakening hurricane Joyce tries to spawn tornadoes in her wake. Crappy weather. The cold would help preserve the disease and the wind would spread it, but then again, the rain might help wash it out of the air . . .

"*. . . and she's got plenty of spare tanks for now anyways . . .*"

"You sound different. Which one are you?" he asks the nurse.

"*I'm Alice. I've been here twice now.*"

"What happened to Irene?"

"*Irene got sick and had to stop.*"

It causes him to stop on the wet path. "*Goddamn it . . .*" Chamai's voice floats back to him on the wind; he's still trying to fix his jacket.

"You're okay, though? Was Irene *quarantined,* do you know?" Sam's voice quavers.

"*No, sir. She really does only have the flu.*"

"Okay, okay. And everything is fine? What about her eating? She doesn't eat that well at the best of times."

"*She's eating everything.*"

"She is?"

"*She did at dinner. I don't think you have to worry about that.*"

For some reason he doesn't want to hang up, even on this distant voice, so courteous that it will tell him anything he wants to hear. "And is she sleeping? Her sleep can get thrown off easy, you know?"

"*She's sleeping okay. If she watches her show, she watched* Dances with the Stars *tonight. She likes Edgar, he's the one from Brazil.*"

"Right, right . . ."

"*And we talked about your daughter, and she showed me the pictures. You know, I lost a child myself.*"

"Oh . . ." His heart stops. His tongue feels like lead. "I'm so sorry," he manages to reply.

"Yes, I did, Dr. Watterman, so I sympathize, because I know how hard it can be."

"Yes. Yes, it is. Yes. Thank you," he says to . . . Alice. Chamai has kept on walking, leaving him . . . *immobile* there on the path. Finally the boy has zipped his windbreaker up, and now is patting his pockets looking for a cigarette. Sam sags back against the steel wall, bends over staring at the grass path. Yes, he thinks, yes, how hard it can be.

"But, to tell the truth, I think she liked speaking about her, you know? Remembering the good times?"

"Yes . . ." Watterman says, his voice almost a whisper. He has never, will never like talking about it. Never. What can you say about a drunk driver that hasn't already been said? What can you say about a beautiful girl eradicated just as she was becoming a woman? Nothing. Nothing at all. So why do it? Why go there? Why try to revive her, preserve her? It's unrealistic. His beautiful Amy. He could love her until the day he died, but she wasn't coming back.

". . . and then she had a cookie and her tea and she watched her show and now she's sleeping like a baby."

"Good," he says. "Thank you, Alice," he says.

So . . . in the end there are no real problems. Even in the middle of an apocalypse, everything is fine.

He and Chamai stand there in the windy silence and watch the dark hills, the low clouds speeding over the obscene buildings. The boy likes to talk, and Watterman has learned from him that there are tunnels that are being opened so that a second of the adjacent chicken-farm buildings can be used. Everyone seems to feel good about it. Energized. The Department of Homeland Security is throwing resources at them, so they must be doing something right.

Chamai has found his cigarette and lit it. He is one of a crew of geeks who are just now coming to maturity amid the chaos of the chicken factory. It's a transformative time for him too, Watterman sees. He's avidly following the game, as badges chase terrorists across the continent. It's something they can all root for, something they can accomplish, he thinks. Light at the end of the tunnel.

". . . and so they have all the credit card numbers, they've got names off of that. Deeper down is your corporate records, but they can get all that . . . Banks, telephones, that shit's coming out of the system all the time. Canada's on it, Mexico is on it."

"Forensic accounting," Watterman says.

"Oh, yeah. Wireless communications, the NSA—just them alone, they suck up a tremendous amount. You know what fucks things up worst of all?" He doesn't wait for an answer. "Spelling mistakes. Number out of place, picky little shit like that."

"Right, 'smart but dumb.' "

"Yes, sir. That's what I'm talkin' about."

Watterman hands the phone back to the boy, and they turn around and head back to the sealed doors. "I ever tell you about when we used to use punch cards?"

Chamai laughs. "No, sir, you didn't. That's crazy . . ."

Inside the chicken factory there is constant repurposing as space and furniture are configured to respond to the attacks. A long room on one side has been carved out, wired, and screened. Altogether it produces a deluge of information. All those billions of dollars of counterterror infrastructure spending coming back to haunt him. Apparently Watterman, Lansing, and Chamai are now part of ART—the Anthrax/smallpox Response Task Force. Watterman finds it profoundly depressing. Huge screens display their lack of progress so far.

Banks are vectors. ATMs are vectors. Banking and credit card information plays a crucial part in chasing down the villains, and Watterman remembers Robert Redford's admonition in *All the President's Men*—follow the money. Pay phones. Grocery stores. The produce section is great for spreading certain kinds of pathogens. All the places people go. All vectors.

In the middle of the broad central street a meeting place has spontaneously grown up; it reminds Watterman of the gloriettas in Mexico City, traffic circles where people can congregate. He has found a personal sanctuary on one of the modernist bench seats that rim the outside of the circle. It's quiet enough to work and he's close enough to the FBI cubicles that he can be found when they need him. If he has to be in the chicken factory, at least he'll make an effort. He pushes for information, and Lansing agrees, making sure that Grimaldi and Chamai keep him up to speed by providing him with the relevant bulletins, updates, and revisions.

In the "bar," he meets other consultants. Deke Foreham, who has come over from the Defense Intelligence Agency. His pet theory requires him to liaise with the Border Patrol, because he thinks separate teams of terrorists have entered from Ciudad Juarez.

"It's the softest way in we've got. Just walk along, find a low spot, cross the mudhole . . . no trace. No credit card, no pictures. Hour later you're in El Paso." Sam shrugs and orders another double scotch. It's his last for the evening. This is war and the FBI bartender has informed them that there are limits.

Vectors. He spends his time trying to decipher Khan's game. There are plenty of office supplies: He's liberated a legal tablet and dug up a box of pencils, then stalked through the chicken factory until he found a sharpener. Now he starts doodling out a solution. There's only a few ways it can work, he thinks. . . . Time slips away on him. He takes breaks and ambles around. Skylights. The place needs skylights. The bar has closed down. It must be night, because everyone else is sleeping.

There is a flurry of activity and he watches two agents conferring over a photograph that has just come out of the printer. They begin making copies. He walks over and stands at the end of the paper feed.

Khan, Khan, Khan . . . by the dozen. Older, still well dressed as ever in this JPG captured by some government's border security camera. At first glance you wouldn't take him for the devil.

His game has to be a version of the purloined antidote strategy. It has to be. First you develop a high-lethality bioweapon. Once you develop a cure you restrict doses of the precious vaccine to your loyal friends and associates. On the day of the attack, you release the germs and hide out. Have a glass of wine while simmering. When it's all over you come out of your sealed bunker and take over the earth. Free love and lots of resort property. No more problem with resources. No more problem with global warming. *Lebensraum.* That's the dream. That's the nightmare.

But there is only one way it can work.

Chamai comes on shift. He brings coffee, muffins. Asks if Watterman needs anything else. Anything at all.

"Have they got the samples yet? Did you phone?"

"You know, you ought to get some sleep, Doctor. Tomorrow's going to be big, I got a feeling."

"What about the damn samples, Aldo?"

"They're crackin' 'em as we speak, Doc. Really, you should go fall over somewhere . . ."

"Yeah . . ." he says. "What time is it? Okay, don't tell me. You're right." He's gone through almost the whole legal pad, and he's been sitting on the bench seats so long he's paralyzed.

As he manipulates his joints in an attempt to stand, another agent comes by. There are gunfights in Italy, where security forces have cornered a cell of terrorists and have been forced to shoot their way into the building. Also, an updated list is passed out: IDs of suspected terrorists and associates being sought within the borders of the United States. Bulletins have gone out to every law enforcement agency in the country. The agent hands both of them copies. Watterman glances at it; it is only about a third of a page long, which is good, he thinks.

Antosio, Prand K.
Bandar, Chel
Gil, Delmos
Gil, Prana
Ismail, Abu Yassin

"We have to break out Khan's people from this list, you know that, right?" he says to Chamai.

"Working on it as we speak, Doc. Oh, and you've got a call

from a fellow named Sanjay Mijares in Mumbai. Just press star," Chamai says, and holds out his phone.

Koslova, Marina R.
Motosi, Angela
Motosi (son)
Nejia, Fidel A.

Sanjay's voice way down the line. "*. . . hell here, my friend. Absolute hell . . .*" Watterman, tired, can barely listen. Of course it's hell in India. And it's going to be hell everywhere else too, and soon, he thinks.

Sofiane, Omar
Vermiglio, Daria H.
Yaghobi, Namar

"Have you run your samples, Sanjay?" He shouts into the cell phone and waits. The encrypted telephones cause a lag. It's like talking to an astronaut on the moon.

"*Yes, Sam. It's classic variola major and the amount of penetration was extremely high. They say we have sufficient inoculations, but no one really believes it. Of course, more can be made—*"

"You're sure? It wasn't tweaked? It would be logical if it was tweaked," he insists, knowing Khan, trying to guess how he'd game it. It has to be tweaked.

"*Thank God, no, Sam. That would be a true misery. We did ours and it's a classic virus and has not been modified. I have not yet received European samples, but they should be arriving any minute. Where are you, Sam?*"

"I can't tell you."

"*How's Maggie?*"

"Maggie's fine. She said to give her love to your mother."

"*Oh, Mum's been dead for five years now.*"

"I know, but she doesn't remember."

"*I'm so sorry, Sam. Please give her a big kiss for me.*"

"I will." They both fall silent for a moment before they lurch into the business of quantifying the unfolding tragedy in India. Does Sanjay know anything about Khan or his whereabouts since the epidemics have been launched?

"The security people tell me nothing, Sam."

"Don't let them get away with anything. We need every bit of information if we are going to beat this thing."

"Yes, Sam. I won't."

"It's time to lay down in front of the bulldozer, Sandy."

"I know, Sam. I have told the Army, I have told all my contacts in security. Politicians and all those in planning for epidemics, I have told them many times. Not only myself, I'm not a hero, Sam, but many others. But they didn't listen and now they are hiding their failures. Admitting that you are wrong takes courage, Sam, and I do not think they have it."

DAY 8

The women who have been rescued overnight by the armies of salvation are expected during the day to go out and look for work, a process that begins with being herded out the front door, where they cluster to smoke and try to develop their plans. Most just start walking and Daria follows suit, her pack slung across her shoulder on her good side. For lack of a destination, she simply heads deeper into the heart of town.

Looking for a doctor is out of the question. No one gets a hole like that in their side by accident. And she can't risk showing her incriminating ID. Better to just limp along, and she heads down the sidewalk, trying to dream up a plan to actually gain access to the vaults at Fort Knox, or at least make some kind of step forward in her program to bring the Great Satan to justice.

When she thinks about her progress so far, she gets angrier and angrier at Mansur al Brazi, Saleem Atcha Khan, and dear laughing Cousin Ali, because, as an American might say, they have hung her out to dry. Given that she is on a suicide mission, this shouldn't matter, but it does. If you are going to die—and more specifically, if you are going to die for a cause, if you are at war with this enormous machine called "America"—then shouldn't you sell your life as dearly as possible? Shouldn't your handlers have planned a little more efficiently?

For instance, there is no second set of identification papers, which would come in very handy just now. For instance, the whole Mr. Creighton fiasco has demonstrated a lack of communication. For instance, there is no way of getting any money, of which she is in desperate need, and worst of all, she's being forced off target.

Specifically, what is the point in just killing the poorest of the poor? Cleansing America of the women at the homeless shelter is only helping the enemy, not hurting it. It only relieves the godless upper classes from the burden of taking care of its castoffs. Moreover, this type of action runs contrary to all Muslim teachings. A good Muslim opens his house to the stranger, a good Muslim gives alms.

No . . . they may be the bow, they may be the string, they may be the archer, but she is the sharp tip of the arrow and she knows best. The mission has been rushed, shoddily conceived, and it makes her angry.

The bullet hole—even if it's become infected, she can keep going. But her skin is killing her. It must be the smallpox, or an allergic reaction to the injection she was given in Berlin, the one that is supposed to slow down her death and give her the chance of being a grandmother. The very idea is funny, but laughing hurts, and when she does so, she gasps.

After about two blocks she becomes aware that she is being followed.

Her stalker is one of the women in the shelter. Daria had glimpsed her at the dinner. Noticed her because she was different than the others. First, she is not black or Hispanic; second, she is white-blonde and one of the few pretty girls who have required rescue.

Oh, there are a lot of girls back there who were once pretty. And almost all have been at one time pretty enough. Girls with good bones. Girls who could make someone's heart quicken. All those once-pretty girls who have been sucked dry of life. Girls who can't control their limbs, and now walk in jerky zombie steps. Girls who know too much about heroin, cocaine, or meth. Girls who blame it all on men. Girls who are killing themselves for . . . whatever reason. All these beautiful girls dying, dying . . . Even right here in Louisville, this city that is trying so hard to be elegant and historic. Dying.

But this blonde seems healthy enough, with clear, bright eyes, and she walks along purposefully, not staggering like a junkie. It doesn't compute really; a girl with her kind of looks should be able to make some money, if not on the street then at least as a waitress, or with some better clothes as a clerk. She's pretty enough to work for *Klic!,* assuming *Klic!* even exists anymore.

The girl catches Daria looking back at her and she raises one pale hand, nods, then catches up to her. "I'm not sleeping there again. That place is a living hell . . ." the girl says—the way she says "slipping" for "sleeping" and "liffing" for "living" marks her as another foreigner, a European of the eastern persuasion—". . . and I don't need them to tell me that I am a sinner, I already know that . . ."

They stand there on the grimy historic sidewalk of Louisville, Kentucky, staring at each other, eye to eye. "Hi, I'm Nadja, and I am running away too," the girl says.

"I'm not running away. Who told you that?" Daria asks.

The blonde Slav is smiling at her now. "Sure, sure. However you want to have it."

"I'm on the way to Hollywood."

Now the girl laughs. "Okay . . . that's sounds like a realistic plan. Do you have any money?"

"Some. Not much."

"So, how do you think you are going to get there? Do you have an agent?"

"I'm going to hitchhike."

"Yah, yah . . . of course. You don't mind getting raped in every province from here to California? Okay, bon voyage." The girl—Nadja—walks on ahead.

Still hurting, and still needing to make some decisions, and still basically lost, Daria follows. When they get to the intersection, they both pause and look both ways. "I don't know any of the streets here," Nadja says. "Stritts" is the way she says it. She hasn't even checked to see if Daria was following, she just assumed it. It's insulting, but now she looks around and smiles.

"I am going to help my sister in Kansas City. We might as well travel together. It would be much safer, don't you agree?"

Daria thinks about Officer Preston and the unknown content of his radio conversations back in West Virginia. Only yesterday, yet an eternity ago. They will be looking for a woman alone. "I suppose it would be."

"The first thing is to get some money, don't you agree?"

"Yes, you can't get anywhere in this country without money . . ." Daria says. It is the immutable truth, brought home in the most tactile way by the disinfected sheets at the Salvation Army shelter, by the groans of the women within their turbulent dreams, by the mirrors—not even mirrors really, but highly polished stainless steel, so that they can't smash their fists into their reflections, hurt themselves, and make a mess.

"There's an army base here," says Daria. "Soldiers always have money."

And Nadja looks at her for a long moment, and then smiles.

Instead they sell the laptop, getting a hundred and fifty dollars for it at the used-computer store. "Don't worry, I'll wipe it," the guy says.

With what Daria's got in her pockets and Nadja's share, if they pool their money they have almost five hundred dollars.

Breakfast is taken at Starbucks. She sips her way through an espresso and then another while Nadja wolfs down muffins, breaks up pieces of chocolate croissants and pushes them at her while they make their plans. This is the last big meal, a celebration of their setting sail, so it's permissible to splurge.

"I think it's more than enough to get us there."

"To Hollywood?" Daria says, remembering her cover story.

"No, to my sister's place. Paulina. She lives in Kansas City . . .

we can take a bus." The road atlas shows them the route. "You didn't want to do blow jobs with the soldiers really, did you?"

"No . . ." They both laugh. She winces from the pain. And Nadja sees it.

"Are you okay?"

"Mmmm . . . fine," she says. Looking down onto the surface of the table in Starbucks.

"You can stay at her house for a few days, if you want. Maybe find a job and make some more money, maybe enough to get to L.A.," Nadja says, waving her fine hands in circles around her head.

Daria's face is hot. When she drinks the espresso there is a thickening at the back of her throat, and she strangles a cough. Everyone knows about the epidemic and she wouldn't want to start a panic. "Here, eat this . . ." Nadja urges. It is a piece of cantaloupe on the end of her fork. "Eat . . ."

A friend, Daria thinks. Maybe that's what she needs right now, a friend. And it would be better to travel together. And "they" will be looking for just one woman traveling alone.

"Kansas City. That sounds good, I guess," she says. Glad to say it. Glad to give in to this beautiful blonde optimist. Together they could take on and poison battalions of American servicemen, but . . . with a bullet hole in her side, maybe this is not the best time.

Nadja smiles and nods. "O-kayyyy . . ." she purrs. And they laugh again.

Back at the bus station, they reject the idea of an express ticket. Nadja wants to take the local. Daria tries to breathe regularly and agrees, since she is dying, probably in at least two different ways, and guesses that by taking the slower, cheaper route, she'll be making herself more and more invisible to the searching eyes of the Great Satan. Going among the underclass is better camouflage. She'll be so poor and worthless that society will ignore her. And blow jobs with soldiers? What does it matter? She is a whore for God—she'll paint on the lipstick, become the prostitute that brings death to the enemy, that's no problem at all.

So . . . they take the slow way for forty-nine dollars per ticket. Nadja sees this as a way to economize, even though they will have to eat out of vending machines and bus station cafés as they go. Whenever they can, they will buy groceries that are easily transportable—muffins, and apples, and chocolate bars to tide them over. Bottles of water, obviously, because every living thing needs it.

But the local doesn't leave until later in the afternoon. To kill time they walk down the street and sit in a threadbare little park. The day is warm and Daria collapses on the dried-up grass.

Like everyone else living in or visiting the United States, Nadja has been captivated by the news of the bioterror strikes. She rolls up her sleeves, sits on a park bench, and reads to Daria from a newspaper she's found.

Half the front page is taken up with an illustration of a typical American family, wide-eyed, with masks covering their faces. Looming behind their image is the biohazard symbol, like some alien spider about to strike.

". . . says that 'Israel will not ignore the attack on her security. Stability in the region has now been torn to shreds . . .' Okay . . ."

Daria lies back and looks at the clouds, experimenting with her breathing to see if there is anything she can do to lessen the pain, which has now extended to her whole left side. Nadja turns the page, holds the paper out at arm's length, shakes her head.

"Look at this—picture, advertisement, picture, picture, advertisement. Where is the new information that you are paying for . . . ?" Ignoring the fact that she has reclaimed the paper from some previous reader who'd left it rolled up between the boards of the bench. A gift actually . . .

"They control all the information, they only give us what they can no longer hide, or feed us slowly what they want us to believe. Okay, 'outbreaks in—' Oh, my God . . . *six* cities in the United States. Started in Berlin, and spread . . . to . . . various cities and towns in Germany. Also in *Paris* . . ." Her brow is furrowed with concern.

What Daria would really like to know is if there is anything in the paper about a state trooper being run over in West Virginia, but there is no adroit way to find out.

"Shit . . ." says Nadja.

"What?"

"I don't have all the newspaper . . . Some asshole stole it . . ."

It's such a beautiful day for bad news. Daria's view of the clouds is bordered by the leaves of plane trees. A bird flits by. Far over in the corner of her vision are parallel lines . . . electric wires that drape between buildings. She's not cold. She's warm, and for now her itching has stopped.

". . . anthrax has to be inhaled to kill you . . ." Nadja mutters.

Daria only half listens. Closes her eyes and rubs them, marvels at the explosion of lights and colors behind her eyelids. A fever, she thinks. She has a fever.

". . . more than a dozen jihadist groups have claimed responsibility for the multiple attacks . . ."

All that is to be learned from the newspaper is that there is a race to name a central villain. Even in death Osama bin Laden is the default choice, but the gang of six, among them Tété and Muhammad Saleem Atcha Khan, are named. There are very few biographical details given. And a certain amount of confusion. Bahar Wahid is first from Yemen, then from Syria.

After name-the-villain, the rest of the space is consumed by Israel. The Israelis have gone behind the high wall. All foreigners are being sent home. Everything is quarantined. Gas masks are being passed out and rechecked.

"Well . . . that's the shit," Daria hears Nadja saying.

"What?"

"They say there's going to be a war . . . in Kashmir."

"*War* . . . ," she repeats quietly, staring up at the clouds. She imagines all the brave young men of India laboring across the snowy mountain passes. The sons and daughters of Pakistan shivering behind their rocket launchers.

"These fucking maniacs . . . who develop this shit . . ." Nadja says. "Of course there's nothing written about that in this . . . *bumaga.*" She closes the newspaper angrily.

"What about here? Or to wherever we're going?"

"That's a good idea . . . yah, yah . . ." Nadja says, and searches again through the pages. Chicago has reported cases of variola major; so have Los Angeles, San Francisco, Philadelphia, Baltimore, and Seattle. Nadja reads the names of the cities, and sits there shaking her head. "Whether they say or not, it's everywhere now." Nadja hands her the paper, gets up from the bench, and begins to do stretching exercises.

Agency Slams Pox Count

. . . complaining that data was being gathered from too many sources, that coordination was hampered because of illness among staff at the CDC itself, and that cases of smallpox were being overreported. "Nobody has seen smallpox in forty years, so hysteria has crept into the accounting. . . ."

"It's crucial not to oversell the danger," said a senior NIH source. "There's a fine line between dealing with an outbreak and taking steps that might foster ill-considered short-term effects. . . ."

Daria rolls over on her side, then on all fours, and gets to her feet, trying to move as little as possible. She eases up onto the bench and leans back and watches Nadja do her workout on the grass.

"I know all about that stuff." Nadja lifts one leg and props it up on the back of the bench, arches over and lays her cheekbone against her knee. "We developed all that. Us, the Russians. Of course, not just us, but the Americans too. Probably the Italians; why not?"

"I don't know."

"They took animals . . . germs and little bugs and put them in the laboratories until they came out with poisons. We even saw it in the news in Russia. It was worse than Chernobyl," she says, rotating her body and stretching out, laying her breastbone against her knee, reaching out and turning her wrists slowly as if conjuring a spell around her ankle.

"Why did they do it? They did it for money. Money. Greed. That's what people don't realize. They are so happy they brought capitalism into the world. They are so proud of themselves. But now they create a monster . . ." Now Nadja comes up straight, changes legs and begins again. Just looking at her makes Daria hurt.

"Of course, with money, it's a universal desire. White people, black people. Jews. It doesn't matter who. All of them will do whatever it takes if it gets them ahead. It's like a circle—" Her waving arm draws it in the air between them.

"You are here, at the center. Your children are here, right next to you; your mother is here. Maybe if you had a good father, he is here. Then brothers, cousins, all your relatives . . . then your village, just a little further away. Then the boys from the village when they play football. Your region of the country. Go, Moldova! Go, Bratislava! Then above that, your country, the flag you root for at the Olympics or the World Cup. All human persons will willingly fight and die for your own tribe, yeah?"

"Yes . . ."

"If you are afraid, if you hate, if you have a chance to make money by using someone, treating them like an animal, it's always going to begin with a person that's outside your circle. They don't look like you. Someone with eyes pointing like this, different skin, someone with big lips, someone different. And this difference is what is called ugliness. This is basic communist theory, and unfortunately it's basic capitalist theory too, by the way."

"I know, I know . . ."

"Yeah, sure. Good. Then you know that these people who created these germs, these terrorists, they will kill like blinking an eye. Without a thought." They look at each other for a moment.

"Let's hope it hasn't hit Kansas City," Daria says.

Nadja is standing now, head down, bouncing on her feet. She bends forward, arching her back, looking up to the sky. "Do you think you can make it?" Nadja asks her.

Daria looks at her as she assumes a new pose, bugging out her eyes and extending her tongue, hands twisted and locked behind her. In the distance there is a siren that rises and falls, then stutters its way through the narrow streets of the inner city.

"I can make it," she says.

When it's time she hobbles onto the bus and they ride.

From the atlas, she knows they are crossing Indiana. A land of huge farms and pungent smells from the manure- and pesticide-laden fields that even the filtered air of the bus cannot keep out.

Above the traffic, Daria stares at the horizon. Cornfields extending to infinity. In the distance, kept separate from the highway by a strip of trees planted as a windbreak, the great feedlots process millions of drug-fattened cattle. All to satisfy the maw of America.

Indiana . . . land of the Indians. Not the same as the Indians who are now calibrating the fuses on their missiles, but ancient peoples who must have lived in this particular place. All replaced now by the unending laser-leveled fields. Here and there are the white traditional symbols of the oppressors, the steepled churches, the blue, white, and yellow troika of crosses that some fanatic has seeded about the landscape. Only in the ditches is naturalness: berries growing rampant, grasses uncontrolled, GMO seeds gone rogue.

There were buffalo here once, she imagines. And young braves on their ponies, proud with paint on their faces. Dancing their histories. Making war or making alliances with adjacent tribes. Now it's agribusiness as far as the eye can see.

Pigs and Christians. All the uncleanliness you could want. This is the earth in chains that their bus is rushing through. At the intersections, gas malls and chain restaurants with gigantic plastic signage—it all gets too confusing, a blur of fast food and food-to-be through the thick windows that don't open except in case of an emergency, and she closes her eyes. Falls asleep with a jacket and pillow wedged under her arm, and her forehead pressed cool against the glass.

Sam Watterman wakes with a definite hangover, even after having obeyed to the letter of the law the FBI bar's cutoff hours. Life, he has learned over the years, is mostly about pain management, and this morning's pain is . . . bearable. Drink plenty of water and don't mix your liquors. You're your own best doctor, and with a little training anyone can self-medicate.

Ahead of him, Chamai bounds across the wide strada that runs along the spine of the factory. Every few hundred feet at the intersections the Gen X, Y, and Zs hang out on their breaks. He has never thought of sixty-four as very old. But his age brands him as a Boomer and slowly he has become aware of being one of the few elders allowed on the voyage.

At the circle Chamai accosts him. He is with a quartet of agents. They have all adopted increasingly casual attitudes over the hours. Ties have come adrift. Chamai is cursed with being a Mr. Big and Tall who will never be able buy clothes that fit, and now his shirttail balloons out. In old age, he might look best in sweatpants and a monster Hawaiian shirt. "We're on a break because they're really pushing on the pursuit," he explains.

"Right," Watterman says. "So, do we have a line on any of Khan's people?"

"Oh, yeah. Names and photographs. It went out last night. Should be on CNN in minutes."

"Okay. I told them already, but do they know all about the precautions?"

"What precautions are you talking about, sir?" one of the agents asks him. She looks like a fourteen-year-old, with long eyelashes. The logo on her T-shirt marks her as FEMA.

"We have to round up those people and take them alive if possible. Okay? Everybody knows that, right?" he asks, but even before he does, the young agents are all shifting uncomfortably.

"These are suicide terrorists, Doc. They're not—"

"They're not going to go easy," a second agent interrupts. He has red hair and a frown. Freckles strewn across his cheeks. "Everybody's in on this—Delta Force, the Navy SEALs, every SWAT team in the country, every member of the National Guard. You don't pull that shit and get away with it." He stares at Watterman the way a bouncer at a nightclub informs you that it's time to go home.

Watterman, to his great credit, keeps his voice even. "We need them alive to interrogate them, right? But infinitely more important than that, we need to examine their blood. There's a high probability they have been immunized. If so, we want them alive, before they're dead and their cells start to break down—"

"Nobody does what these assholes did and gets away with it—"

"You need to think," Watterman cuts in. "You're not thinking. You're reacting." He stands back from them, looks over at Chamai to see if at least he gets it. "Right now it's about us finding a therapy. A cure. A remedy, an antidote to the poison, a course of treatment, a drug or a cocktail of drugs, maybe a patch . . ."

"Right, instead of growing it in eggs," Chamai says.

"That's right. Antisense—it's a technique of genetic modifications that we build antivirals out of. That's the current state of the art and how we will eventually do it, but in the interim, while we build whatever it takes, this pox could rip around the world several times. It might mutate. There's a good chance that it has been genetically tweaked. As patients enter the system, the CDC may get lucky and quickly find a cohort that has natural immunity, okay? Great, then we can build something out of their blood. But all that takes time," he says, looking around at the young people grown suddenly serious. "And more time means very many more deaths, so . . . We need to take them *alive*. Healthy. Cooperative. The deader they are, the less valuable they are. And when they are found they get isolated at Level 4, right?"

"Hot zone," provides Chamai.

"Learn to think like a virus. Revenge can come later," Sam tells the redheaded agent, and walks away.

Across the building is what everyone calls the situation room, but in reality it's a central communications center and case offices for the task force.

Roycroft is on the monitor reporting from Homeland Security, and it is here that Watterman first hears the names of the two persons linked to Khan in Berlin—a man and a woman, still at large. *Yaghobi* and *Vermiglio;* both names are presumed false.

Yaghobi traveled from Berlin to Toronto, and then changed flights and continued on to LAX. Both of those aircraft have been quarantined and are being tested. The Vermiglio woman flew Lufthansa to JFK. That plane has also been quarantined and is undergoing tests in Frankfurt. Both terrorists are presumed fleeing in the wake of the Sawalha arrest. Vermiglio may have escaped across the Canadian border, and the RCMP and CSIS are on that. Yaghobi is being traced on the Pacific coast.

The number of cases has grown to an estimated total of between fifty and seventy-five thousand.

Norment's face hangs above them on the monitors as he describes the herculean efforts of the CDC's continent-wide inoculation program. Much is made of international cooperation. Abroad, the WHO has revved up their immunization machinery, and it appears as if all the highly funded preparedness rehearsals and simulations are paying off.

While Norment waxes enthusiastic over the mass inoculations, General Walthaer sits and stares. He must be locked down at Fort Detrick, Watterman thinks. Walthaer could use an acting coach; staring down at the floor like that only makes him look depressed; he needs to keep his chin up. Of course, like everyone at the top, he's not getting enough sleep.

Yes, everybody looks like hell, so that's not it. Watterman studies the general all through Norment's report. His spider sense for official BS is tingling. Maybe there's something Walthaer knows but hasn't reported.

Roycroft is winding things up. Flawless in a perfectly tailored suit, great hair. That's what has got him this far. Good looks and no sense of humor.

"Mr. Secretary?" Watterman half stands, but Roycroft is already doing the same. "There are potential benefits that can be derived from the plasma of any of the terrorists linked to Dr. Khan, and perhaps others who . . ." Others are stirring in their chairs. "We have to emphasize that it is crucial to apprehend the suspects alive, if only as a matter of public health. . . ."

He glances over toward Walthaer's monitor. The general is looking up now. Yes. He knows something.

"General, you know as well as I do that Khan is not the kind of guy who would do anything without a back door . . ."

Walthaer almost winces, looks away, stands, and steps off-camera. Norment's is the only face left, still looming down on him from the monitor. There is a camera up there somewhere and Watterman turns and scans the ceiling for it.

"Relax. We're on it already, Sam," Joe Norment says, and then he too stands up out of frame. A moment later the image on his monitor blinks out. It is replaced with a Centers for Disease Control and Prevention shield.

Watterman stands there. The room is emptying out. "It's not a goddamn chess match!" he shouts to the vacant screens. "It's not a fucking round of golf, or betting on the goddamn game," he spits. They're all gone. He's shouting to a bunch of logos.

Grimaldi is there with one rock climber's hand grasping his elbow. "They don't get it," Watterman says to her. "They think it's something they can *win* . . ." For a moment he falls silent and looks at her. Beautiful, clean skin. Dark eyes, like Amy if she had lived.

"Viruses don't behave like we do. They don't *care* about us or our war games. The predictability of a hazardous biological event has fluid parameters, and to make the hubristic decision that it's adaptable for use as a weapon, that you can just hire the so-called experts—"

"Doctor. Sam . . ."

"—that's the real terror."

"Fine. But it's gone beyond that now."

"No, no, darling. No, it hasn't. No, no. That's what they always say, but no! It's never *beyond that*."

"Look, come on. Let's go get something to eat. We're either going to catch them or we're not."

"No, I already had my pill for breakfast. First, we've got to pull Barrigar off of the Yaghobi chase for a few minutes—"

"Ha-ha. Fat chance—"

"Look, if we can find Khan, find him alive, maybe find his hard drive, we can save a week, a month. Maybe only a day. But that's a lot of lives."

She looks at him for a long moment. Nods. "I'll get Barrigar right away, Sam," she says quietly, and goes.

When Daria wakes, it is almost sunset and they have slowed. The bus rocks forward. The fields are behind them now and they are poised at an intersection. There is no traffic, but they must stop completely. After a moment the bus leans around a corner and they continue on down a wide suburban highway. On either side are the light industrial zones that keep the American economy running.

"We are coming into Indianapolis," Nadja tells her. "We have to transfer here . . ."

Minutes later they stop at the station and the passengers get out to stretch their legs.

Daria moves like a ninety-year-old granny, leaning on the seat backs, groaning in spite of her attempts to pretend that everything is normal. Any quick movement causes dizziness. Nadja walks in front of her. Impatient, reaching back to help her get down the steps when they get to the front.

She goes into the station and paces its length and then out into the parking lot. She could just keep going. Just run away from Nadja. Just keep moving, find a friendly cornfield and die, but when she looks back Nadja is there, smoking in short jerky puffs, while she finishes her invalid's walk back along the sidewalk, triggering the automatic doors. Nadja tags along beside her. She has bought a few things—candy bars and chips in a plastic bag, a bottle of water—and carries it all, kicking their luggage along to the next bus, leaving Daria free to concentrate on putting one foot in front of the other.

They hand over their tickets and climb back onto the bus. It is cool, mostly empty, and quiet, and they make their way to the next pair of seats that will become home. There is music playing from a sound system that the driver must have activated, something about a desperado coming to his senses.

She achingly slips into her seat by the window. Nadja bites on the ends of the candy bar wrappers to open them, breaks them in half and hands Daria a hunk.

"You're bleeding," Nadja says. "You say there's nothing wrong, but you're bleeding."

Waiting for Barrigar, Sam sits at one of tables at the glorietta, doodling in his legal pad and, when that doesn't work, picking up the latest *New Yorker*. Each day newspapers arrive, doused in ultraviolet light and passed through an ozone atmosphere, then doled out along the coffee tables, but he doesn't want any more news. The *New Yorker* issue must have gone to press in the week before the anthrax attacks were revealed, and it projects a kind of cheerful grouchiness, a mix of complaint and whimsy, revelations of venality, and acerbic criticisms spread through its articles and cartoons that bring unexpected tears to his eyes.

When he looks away from the magazine, his eyes fasten on Reilly walking through the situation room. Reilly. For him to be at the chicken factories means the presence of the National Clandestine Service, the blackest operational side of the NSA. It is a shock to see him, and Watterman stops actually reading, and begins faking a simulacrum of a man relaxing on a park bench while he peeks over the top of the magazine at Reilly moving through the ART offices.

A pair of physical-plant techs walk up. They are both young, enthusiastic, and going about their hands-on labor in a relaxed and confident way. They are carrying what he estimates to be a sixteen-foot ladder, which they set up right beside him.

"Am I going to have to move?" he says.

"We're putting up some sound equipment. Speakers. You might want to slip around to that side, then you can come back. Take about a half hour, I guess."

"We won't drop anything on you, sir," says her coworker.

Don't *sir* me, he thinks. He gets up and moves around the other side of the glorietta, angles his chair so he can keep spying on Reilly, who goes into one of the conference rooms with Barrigar and a quartet of backup agents. They close the door and pull the blinds.

Reilly has spent his entire working life off the books; the kind of Washington animal that only emerges when everybody else is shit-scared or when the best option is rendition or death. Laws? To Reilly and his species, these are not even speed bumps; since the Patriot Act, almost anything can be covered with false paper. You could hide a million Level 4 labs around the United States; all of them could be engaged full-time researching, devising, and engineering offensive toxins, ringed with outsourced security. No one would ever know. "Oversight" isn't in the dictionary for those guys. In the years that Sam has been out in the wilderness, Reilly and his gang could have come up with anything imaginable.

He'd only met Reilly when it was much too late, when Amer-ithrax had snapped on the bright light of media scrutiny and threat-ened to reveal what had really been going on in the closed world of the biowarriors. In a way he actually *owes* Reilly, since it was Reil-ly's claim that evidence that might have further implicated Sam back in '82 be inadmissible for reasons of national security that got him off the hook. So . . . the most evil man in the world had been his protector. Suddenly Sam desperately wants to be back in Decatur and curled up beside his warm Maggie. It's that sinking feeling of having made another big mistake in life. Home—yes, that's where he should be right now. Another tear stings his eye.

". . . sorry, sir, we have to come around this side now . . ."

He gets up, moves back across the glorietta, and sits down just in time to see the conference room blinds snap open. Reilly is done with them now and will probably be heading back to Washington, Watterman guesses. Barrigar escorts him out of the situation room en route to the air locks. As Reilly comes out onto the strada, he glances over, sees Sam sitting there, changes course and comes over to his table. Reilly doesn't raise his hand to shake.

"You know your Khan fellow?"

"Yep."

"The Germans say they have eight more who traveled from Berlin. Yaghobi and Vermiglio are our two. That's from the Bundesnachrichtendienst, the BND—that's the German CIA. In addition Khan had at least one assistant resident in each city."

Barrigar opens a folder and displays a pair of photographs. The Adlon hadn't stinted on their security cameras, and the image is crisp: a thin-faced boy, his shirt too large for his bony frame. Doing up his necktie as he rides alone in the elevator. All bushy hair and a nose that would take him a long time to grow into.

"He's the one who actually booked the suite they used, ostensibly for job interviews," Barrigar says.

"Well, great. Okay. Then you realize how critical it is to put the same protocols out on *all* these people. Tell Interpol, tell Scotland Yard, the Germans, whoever, to take them *alive* because we need their blood," Sam chants for the millionth time. "It could be the difference between a cure in six weeks or six months. It might save a life, or it might save a couple of hundred thousand lives, or millions, or even hundreds of millions."

Barrigar shifts uncomfortably, but Reilly doesn't move. "We do what we can, Sam, but other players have their own concerns. After all the blood has a value, right?"

"Value? *Value?* What do you mean?" Watterman asks, fearing the very worst. The ultimate worst.

"*Monetarily* valuable," Barrigar says helpfully.

"Ahh . . . yes. The blood is valuable. How much would it be worth to you? Save the lives of your family, your children? Sure. Value? Yes, I'll concede that."

"Well, what do you think we should say, Sam? 'Oh, hello, Germany, when you catch these guys, we want their blood, all of it, or as much as you can spare, and definitely before they're dead, please.' '*Oh, what do you want that for?*' 'Oh . . . no reason.'" Reilly looks out around the chicken factory. His lips are pressed together in what must be a smile.

"No, you tell them you need it to make a vaccine—"

"It doesn't work like that. You explained it yourself. It's the serum, right? It's like taking antibiotics. The supply is limited. You have to take it repeatedly, you have to top it up."

"I hope you guys understand the United States isn't the only one with a chemistry set. Other people have thought about this too. Serum immunology is not so ultra-sophisticated that it hasn't occurred immediately to hundreds of scientists."

"Possession is nine-tenths of the law, Sam. So, let's suppose we can get Khan for you. Interrogate him. Learn all his procedures. Copy his formulas, secure any stocks he might have, his inventory, all that shit . . ."

"Oh, brave new world! I'm sure you can see the advantages. I'm sure you remember PROJECT COAST." Something else Sam hadn't known about until it was too late—another black operation designed to circumvent the treaties: the U.S. and the Brits farming their work out to the South Africans. But then Mandela had to come along and spoil everything.

"Every major league needs a farm team, Sam."

"Sure. And a biotoxin that could be targeted racially, wow. That's something that would really play well in the Negro Leagues, I guess . . ."

"You already answered my question, Sam."

"I think you had it answered before you flew out here."

That brings a smile from Reilly, and he pivots and starts to go.

"You've got a family, don't you?" Sam insists.

"Look, Sam. You started all this. You have no one to blame but yourself. When we get Khan, we interrogate him gently and then we get the grand prize. You said it yourself, he wouldn't do it without a back door. And if anybody gets out that door, it's going to be us."

"Sure. And after that, why not recruit him? Get him to be your new drug-design genius. We did it for the Japanese. Unit 731, none of them stood trial for war crimes—"

"Sam, there is a real world, and there is the world as you would like it to be. But you don't get to pick which one you live in." And now Reilly turns to leave.

"Or die in," Sam says, loud enough for both men to hear him, but they only keep walking, leaving Watterman strangling his magazine in his hands.

"Okay, hit it, Orlando . . ." the techie is saying to her mate. From above there is a sound like a hiss, then sharper sounds. Squeaks and chirps.

". . . a little more volume, O-man . . ."

"What is that?" Sam asks.

"It's the ambient sound of the rain forest. The psychiatrists say it will make living here more like the real thing."

Chamai comes bounding out of the situation room, a sheet of pink paper in his hand. Color indicates importance. White is nothing. Purple is ultra-top-secret. Pink is all about action.

Chamai does a slide step when he sees him sitting there. "She's not in Canada!" he exclaims. He dodges around the techies as they refold their ladder, and thrusts the pink page toward him.

"She killed a cop!" Chamai takes the page back and begins to read aloud:

"From the Office of the West Virginia Highway Patrol . . . all points bulletin: '*Wanted as suspect in homicide of Trooper W. H. Preston, one Vermiglio, Daria H., Caucasian, five feet four inches tall, weight one-one-five . . .*'"

It takes four hours before their bus pulls in for another transfer in St. Louis. After they've collected their baggage, Nadja takes her into the bathroom. They pick a stall close to the sinks, and she struggles to take off her top while Nadja rummages through the backpack for her thrown-together first-aid kit. She rests her forehead against the partition and closes her eyes. There is the sound of water running in the sink, and then the first touch of Nadja's fingers causes Daria to gasp.

"Stop it," Nadja says, and continues probing, stepping around behind her and unsnapping her bra, helping her to lean over against the door so she can get a good look.

"You've broken a rib . . . You need a doctor."

"No . . ." she says. It comes out as just a negative-sounding groan.

"No? Okay." Nadja straightens quickly and Daria groans gain. "You need something for the infection. Understand?"

Daria stays silent.

"Okay. We use this—" Nadja holds up a wad of alcohol-soaked paper towels. "But we have to clean it. Clean every day. This is the only way. Still, you might die. Because you don't listen to me."

Daria says nothing.

"Okay. Inhale. And keep quiet now, I don't want the police coming in here." Nadja begins to squeeze the pus out of the hole. Daria responds with a deep groan, like a cow lowing in the moonlight.

"You're infected already. It's all red. I can tell."

Daria just shakes her head slowly.

"It's none of my business how you got this way. What happened, did you fall down?"

"Yes."

"On something sharp?"

"Yes."

"And the tip broke off . . . maybe a piece from a fence, an old iron fence, you know?"

Daria says nothing.

"Okay, hold on . . ." Nadja squeezes once more and dabs on the alcohol. Holds her around the waist as she presses wadded-up paper towels against the wound. Involuntarily Daria writhes, in turn forcing Nadja to press harder, only making it worse. She takes a great breath and manages to cling there against the door to the stall.

There is the sound of footsteps, someone in flip-flops. A woman comes in.

"It's okay, I am helping her."

The woman only hesitates a split second, and then starts walking over. She is short and nut-brown, and looks as if she has been carrying coca leaves on her head for ten or twelve centuries and then was beamed down to the St. Louis bus station.

"She's okay. We don't need—" Nadja starts to fend her off, but

the woman boldly inserts herself between them. "Her boyfriend hit
her—"

"I fell . . . on a fence," Daria says at the same time.

The woman sniffs at the alcohol, then presses her fingers against
the edges of the wound. For Daria it seems to hurt less, or maybe she
has simply learned how not to wriggle when someone is repairing an
infected bullet hole in her side. Nadja steps back while the woman
goes to work. A moment later the woman says something to Nadja
and looks back to the front.

Nadja does as directed and hangs there in the entrance while the
woman replaces the dressing with rolls of paper towels and a deft
corset of tape intended to hold Daria's rib in place.

The woman's cool birdlike hands flit around her breasts; the
tape is pulled tight. When it's over the woman mutters something
consoling, heads back to Nadja, smiling and making a universal
gesture—fingers to her lips and blowing out a breath. Nadja hauls
out her pack of cigarettes and the woman takes two and leaves.

Nadja watches Daria as she straightens, steps away from the
stalls, and, reaching out and letting the wall guide her, walks the
length of the sinks. "You can walk?"

"Mmm . . ."

"Okay. Let's go . . ."

She walks like Frankenstein at first, then gains a little confidence
when she doesn't simply fall down. Nadja takes her arm and they
shuffle across the terrazzo floor of the St. Louis bus station. A deep
breath before passing through the glass doors and then out on the
platform to flash their tickets to the driver.

His name is Carl and he's no dummy. Been with the company for six
and with Trailways for another eight back in the day, and he can
spot the addicts and the smokers and the drunks. He tolerates whatever it is the girl has got, because the tough blonde is obviously taking care of her, and she hasn't vomited all over the seats.

"Sometimes it's a good thing to be a little blind," his daddy used
to say. "And sometimes a little deaf," his mom would shoot back.

He grew up in a comedy act, but they were right enough. You see problems, you get in a huff, let your blood pressure go through the roof, and first thing you know, you've let other people's problems get into your own life. No . . . stay in your own lane, he thinks.

And even if the world is going to hell, the moon is coming up, and it's a fine night for a drive across Missouri.

DAY 9

Daria wakes, carefully slips out of her seat and tests her ability to walk, one foot at a time. Loosening up all the way up the length of the bus in the blue-gray morning light. The front row is abandoned, maybe because it's easier to sleep in back, where the lights from oncoming traffic don't shine in your eyes.

She slides into the seat and watches the Missouri highway rush toward them. A minute or two later a woman, older by two decades, with a leathery face and a thick sweater, walks up from the back and stands there supporting herself with both hands on the seat backs.

"Hey, Carl," she says to the driver.

"How're you doing?"

"Not too bad. At least it's not raining . . ." They both laugh for some reason, then fall silent. The woman looks down at Daria. "Not too long now," she says to her, and heads back.

The sun is just rising, and the bus pushes its own shadow over the pavement as they rush into the blue distance. Carl has to turn off the interstate at Marshall, and the act of stopping wakes up most of the passengers.

The sky is rosy to the east, and the new sun is blinding as the door opens with a little pneumatic hiss and they straggle forth to find the bathrooms.

The break takes five minutes and then they are moving again. She lets Nadja sleep and sets up camp right behind the driver, where she can watch the road over his shoulder. They talk in whispers and stare together out at the open highway.

"Are you all right?" Carl asks her. "You were a little rocky there for a while."

"Yeah, but I'm fine now."

"Good," Carl says, and falls silent for a half dozen miles. "I was listening to the radio, talking about all the influenza, you know?"

"Yes?"

"It's not nearly as bad as they make out on the news. A lot of people get one of these bugs and it blows right over."

"That's good," she says.

"Maybe that's what you had."

"Maybe," she says. And after a moment, "I hurt my side."

"Oh, that's it."

"Playing soccer."

"Those things, an injury like that, you gotta be careful . . ."

"I know. You can't do anything at all, you can't bend, you can't cough . . ." Daria says.

"No. Maybe you got away with one."

"I hope."

She sits in the front seat, wondering if she's gotten away with one, and if it will just blow over, and if somehow she can just keep going, just get away from the entire American government, which must be on her trail by now.

"Life and death. You know, it's an arbitrary situation," Carl says. He tells her he sees a fatal accident sometimes twice a week. Someone skids, someone else brakes too late, someone forgets to fasten their seat belt. "It's nothing to do with being ready for it," he says.

"No . . ." she agrees. "You can't be ready." She is as ready as it is humanly possible to be, and still she is trying to run away from it. Why not just take Officer Preston's gun and bring this last act to a close?

"It's the absurdity of life," Carl says. He falls silent for another long stretch. Ahead there is a great green sign spanning the road; the rosy sun behind them illuminates it so that it glows above the American West.

Independence	14
Kansas City	All Exits
Topeka	Thru Only

The Kansas City bus station is just waking up, and it is not a good time to change her bandages. People stoked with coffee and cigarettes are flocking to the washrooms and evacuating their bodies of wastes from the day before. There is no privacy. The most she and Nadja can do is lurk down at the end of the sinks and lift the edge of her top.

"That looks pretty good," Nadja says. "Okay, tell me what it feels like if I press here—" She uses her fingertips to explore the large patch of gauze.

"Just leave it. I'm okay . . ."

"Yah . . . maybe that's best. Leave it for when we get to my sister Paula's." Nadja lets her top fall back down. Daria takes a tentative breath. No tears. She got through that.

"You're a tough cookie. You're going to be okay," Nadja tells her. "Come on . . ."

They set up camp in the coffee shop and try to figure out how to navigate to Paula's from the bus station. Nadja throws herself on the kindness of strangers and inquires about Kansas City life and culture down to the tiniest detail. They are leaving a trail a mile wide, Daria thinks as she sips her coffee—there is no espresso. As long as it's black enough, she can handle it.

Someone leaves a *Kansas City Star* on the next table, and Daria picks it up and tries to find out what's happening.

. . . treating several other members of Congress. In Washington, quarantine has been tightened since Tuesday evening, but the chaos has not stopped law enforcement in its

roundup of suspects. "The fact is that there is a worldwide effort to bring these terrorists to justice," said Under Secretary of Defense Richard Balisere, adding that he was "proud of everything that's being done right now" to improve the supply of vaccine.

She reads through the paper. The hospitals in Kansas City have been operating under their own triage criteria, and suspected smallpox cases are urged to remain at home and make contact with medical authorities by telephone. To minimize the possibility of an outbreak in the Kansas City region, the safest method is to dispatch public health workers door-to-door rather than spread the virus by having people travel in to visit the clinics. "We all have to remember that we have only two verified cases here in the metropolitan area," a local politician says.

Nadja comes back from questioning everyone in the station about how to find Paula's house. "It's not good. She is living in an inconvenient area, very far away . . ." she reports, slumping back into her seat.

"Too far to take a cab?"

"A cab? No way. We don't have enough money." Nadja scans the restaurant as if looking for a job opportunity. "It's completely across the city. We take a bus. We have to change here and there. It's confusing." She has the street names scribbled on a napkin.

"It costs us two dollars and seventy-five cents. Exact change." She takes a section of the newspaper from under Daria's elbow, glares briefly at the headlines. "This is getting sick. This is horrifying . . ." she says, letting the paper fall from her fingers.

"He stole a *horse.*" It is Marty Grimaldi, managing to look perfectly starched and groomed. "They had him last night. Cornered him in Wenatchee, but he *stole a horse* and broke out."

"What?"

"That's right. They lost eight full hours because it turns out Yaghobi can ride really well. Bastard played polo when he went to boarding school."

"Holy shit . . ."

"That's right. They had two companies of Special Forces ready to take him, and he rode right through them. Now he's up on the side of that mountain and, well, you can see . . ."

She looks down to the monitors displaying live feeds bounced to them via satellite from Washington State. A row of specialists tends the screens. There are helicopter views, and pop-up menus and maps that show the terrain from any angle. It takes him some time to recognize what he's seeing—the camera is looking straight down on fir trees and a mountainside.

On the screen a movement—a moment later he sees that it is an exhausted horse, terrified by the helicopters, trying to turn and run in the thick trees.

"Shouldn't be very long now."

But it takes another hour, at least another hour. Maybe more.

Gradually the views all tighten on one small portion of the mountain, a rocky bluff that juts out, perhaps a hundred yards below the panicked horse. One by one all the cameras end up focusing there, flicking between infrared and normal imagery.

Yaghobi appears to be resting under a shelf of rocks; maybe he is sleeping, maybe he is injured. He has covered himself with branches, but they are not enough to hide his body heat.

Now the screens show additional figures, what looks like a squad of Special Forces, creeping down through the woods. *"Gun-fire,"* Sam hears a panicky voice say. There is a jerking movement from the brush-covered cave where Yaghobi hides, then—a pinprick of bright light—

"Oh, God . . ." he hears Grimaldi murmur. A flare of white light bursts out, swiftly engulfing the length of the man, who begins to twist and jerk in a savage dance, pushing himself out of the cave and leaping, one, two—three times.

"He's done it," someone says.

Behind the burning man are smaller pools of flame, as he stum-

bles and collapses near the dark base of a tree. Sam can see the soldiers making their way down the slope, drawing closer to Yaghobi's
little hiding place. They look as if they are swaying, but more likely
they are rappelling down the cliff face.

"Take his spleen," Sam says.

Grimaldi swings around to him. *"What?"*

"Operate. Take his spleen out. Get one of the medevacs. Get
someone!"

"He's burned himself to death, Sam."

"Yes, yes. I know, I know, I saw . . . Just tell them to go in and
remove his spleen. We need his B cells." Grimaldi looks at him for a
long moment.

"Get them to do it," Barrigar says to one of the techs.

There is a pause. Maybe a dozen seconds. It might as well be a
month, Sam frets.

"Negative on viability . . ." From the infrared view, Sam watches
as Yaghobi's image loses heat.

Grimaldi is looking at him, her beautiful face troubled. Someone else pats him on the back. Why? What are they consoling him
for? Are his feelings supposed to be hurt? What does it matter, it's
not like he has lost some personal victory, is it?

Cautiously, the soldiers converge on the blur. They all know
Yaghobi is hot with a Level 4 virus, but still . . .

Unless they harvest Yaghobi's spleen now, it's too late, Watterman knows. He shakes his head, bends over and shuffles from side
to side. The cells begin to break down immediately, but surely . . .
surely they can get *something* out of him? Goddamn it to hell . . .
Above on the slope, a stretcher is being lowered. It looks like the
aluminum-frame kind that ski patrols use. The soldiers unfurl a long
plastic bag. It gleams because it's made out of some kind of super
Mylar that can't be ripped or punctured.

Some miracle weave you can wrap up America's worst nightmare in.

* * *

Here is a main street and their bus whistling along.

See this city going by? See it vaporizing? See a bomb, a good bomb, or maybe a dirty bomb, see it exploding. A plume of smoke. Screams heard distantly at first, then getting closer. Closer.

See the people in the cars? The little shops with alien alphabets, Chinese characters, Spanish words. Crazy lettering and façades jam-packed with information. Above the doors and windows are advertising placards. The windows are open, many of them. The air, churned through ten thousand motors and warmed by all the concrete, blows through the bus. Daria closes her eyes against the sunlight, soaking up the heat like a cat. She's been sleeping a lot, she realizes. Maybe her death will be gentle, when it comes. Maybe she will just go to sleep, curl up in a ball and die like a bee succumbing to vampire mites. Her sisters will carry her corpse out of the hive and toss her down to the ants. Eyes closed, half dreaming, she shakes her head. She was ready to fly apart in an explosion of nails and glass shards while attacking an anonymous skyscraper, so she ought to be ready to suffer slowly, yes?

"When we get there, you have to remember to call her Paula. She hates Paulina," warns Nadja, and then falls silent, watching the signs. They are heading through the downtown core. "This is it . . . I think," she mutters, and then goes up to the front to ask about Prospect Avenue.

Somewhere in the bus someone else is laughing. It's a beautiful morning in Kansas City.

Only two cases reported.

They have found their stop on Prospect Avenue, and now they are lugging their rucksacks along the residential streets of Brush Creek.

The blocks are sun-drenched and laid out in perfect alignment over the slightly rolling land that borders the creek. Along one street there is a high dike meant to control floods. There don't seem to be too many people, and several of the houses on the long blocks appear vacant.

A car comes up behind them. It is a low car, an American car with big everything, painted midnight blue, the engine customized and growling. Two boys, one sleeping it off.

"Hey . . ." calls the driver. "Where you goin'?"

"I'm going to my sister's," says Nadja.

"Your sister don't live around here . . ."

"Yes, she does. Can you help me with the address?"

"Where is it?"

Nadja stops and gets the paper, reads it out.

"That's four blocks. You be killed before you get there." The boy's smiling. He is a teenager, with closely cut hair and a sparkling stud in his ear. "You ain't got the bug, do you?"

"We're okay," Daria says, straightening up, and slinging the bag off her shoulder so she can drop it or grab Officer Preston's gun if she has to. "Four blocks which way?"

"Just like you're going now and then right at Bellefontaine . . ."

"Okay. Thank you," she says, and the boys roar off. Maybe she and Nadja should walk a little faster before they come back with a couple of friends to rape them. At least it's daylight.

They walk through the faded neighborhood. Here was a church, here was a family. Here was a long row of apartments that once housed the elderly. Here was a store on the corner that would send out your fine cleaning.

It must have been beautiful at the end of the Second World War. Then it would have been full of life and children, and big yards with mowed grass. But that's all changed. This morning the neighborhood is starting to wake up and have its first smoke, drink, or injection. This morning nobody can afford to go to the dentist, and this morning there is no big meal to pray around.

After he's dropped off his friend the boy comes back, his engine thrumming. It's the only thing he's got, that car. He goes right past them, turns and reverses out of someone's disused driveway, then crawls idling up beside them again as they walk down the street.

"Your sister is at Monica Morton's house. She's the midwife."

"Midwife . . ."

"What that means is, she's going to have the baby at home, with Monica there. I saw her. She's pregnant as shit."

"I thought Paula was going to be in a hospital . . ."

"No, they send her back if she goes in there. Are you from Russia too . . . ?"

"How far is it?" Nadja asks.

"Not too far. I'll take you there."

"That's all right."

"Come on now, bullshit. I'll take both of you over there." Daria gets the front seat so that she doesn't have to bend as much. They rumble on down the street and around the corner.

His name is Brutus, named for a famous Roman gladiator, the boy tells them, and he leans back in his seat and drapes the wrist of one hand over the steering wheel and lazily controls the car as it glides through Brush Creek. The 3000 block of Fifty-second Street is on a little rise of ground. The numbers on the houses are hard to see. Some have been ripped off the fronts; some have been covered over with plywood and the numbers spray-painted on. You have to figure out where to look.

3050 is on a large lot, an old bungalow-style house with a wide porch, and a set of steps that has been augmented with a black wrought-iron banister.

A driveway of broken concrete climbs from the street and vanishes behind the house. There are a few low windows set in the stone walls of a half basement—granite, Daria supposes, gray and yellow in tone and rough cut. Someone has repointed the front corner, a labyrinth of white mortar that spiderwebs starkly from the rest of the wall.

Behind the house there is a dilapidated garage overhung by the thick branches of an oak. An old car is up on blocks, a chain dangling into its open hood. Something broken from before she was born.

The street is a distant memory of an American neighborhood from fifty years earlier. She has seen magazine illustrations of such places, illustrations by a famous American artist, Daria forgets his name. Portraits of scared, sunburned, baseball-playing boys being examined by dentists, of whole families praying around the Thanksgiving turkey, of blushing girls following an oblivious older male student.

The faces here are different. Everything now is different. On the 3000 block, two houses have burned to the ground. One lot has been scraped clean—ashes and stones pushed into a heap at the back of the property, already grown over with blackberries whose thorns anchor waving fronds of plastic bags. The other site is newer, a pile of charred two-by-fours, a collapsed chimney, and trampled charcoal where men have gone in to pull out all the copper.

Between the bulldozed site and the house where Paula is staying is a wide vacant lot that has become a jungle. Once, somebody must have tried to clear all the brush along the lot line of Paula's yard, but now a bamboo hedge leans into the gutters on that side of the house; a grass fire would burn the whole thing down.

The yard itself is completely bare, scabs of dried grass of different varieties. It looks more like the surface of the moon than a lawn.

Brutus's chariot idles up the driveway and stops with a lurch beside a set of steps that lead to the front door. "Do you have to stay here tonight, or you want to go out with me for a little while?" Brutus says. He's become obsessed with Nadja already.

"You're a pleasant guy, but I have the HIV," she says.

"Naw . . . bullshit. That wasn't so bad, was it?" He gestures to his dashboard as if the car itself has been doing all the driving.

Nadja just shoots him a glare. As they climb out, it is Daria who smiles. "Thanks, you're sweet . . ."

"See there, somebody knows what's right," he says to Nadja. "I'll take both of you out . . ."

They haven't even got to the front door when it opens and Nadja's sister reveals herself. She is a tiny girl, extremely pregnant, who uses an old man's four-toed cane to support herself. The two girls collapse in tears and prolonged kisses in the Russian style. For a long stretch, Daria just stands there not understanding anything, before an introduction is made. Paulina's looks make her seem younger, but she *is* young—only seventeen. She has put on weight only where the baby is, and from behind as they go down the hall, she resembles a child carrying a large yoga ball under her T-shirt. They immediately go back into her bedroom because "Monica says I'm not supposed to be up," Paula apologizes, and rubs her huge middle.

The conversation jumps immediately back into Russian, so Daria looks for a convenient place to drop her bag, and heads back into the kitchen to make tea. There is a bag of groceries on the counter that has not been put onto the shelves, so she unpacks it while she waits for the kettle to boil.

The house has seen many better days. The appliances are old; the refrigerator shakes and growls. After a few minutes of nothing, she cycles her hand over the coils of the stove and discovers they're all broken but one. Before she handles the cups, she washes her hands in dish detergent. Will it do any good? It's far too late for that, she supposes.

Back in the bedroom, the three of them sit on the floor discussing the progress of Paulina's pregnancy, and a good number of facts begin to emerge about how the sisters have come together in this unlikely place.

First, they are running from Big Niv-L. That's how he spells it: Niv-L. It has some meaning that the girls have never quite understood. His real name is Rodney. Nadja and Paulina laugh.

The pressing problem is that Big Niv-L owns them, having paid to get them into the United States as temporary workers. If they want to buy out their indenture, they owe Niv-L five thousand dollars each, plus expenses: food, board, legal fees for all the different papers, and medical costs. They began their temporary work as dancers in one of Niv-L's clubs, but were also expected to entertain his friends, or important customers Niv-L was trying to impress. They were also expected to cater to the needs of potential partners for Niv-L's schemes, various members of his retinue, and Niv-L himself. In this way Paulina Pravdina found herself with child, and when told she was going to be forced to abort, she ran away.

"Then he decided he was going to come after *me* . . ." Nadja says bitterly. So she ran too. For over two months the sisters lost touch with each other. It was only the efforts of another girl, Venerette, that saved them, when she gave Paula the lead to Monica's place in K.C., a shelter for women in trouble and on the run from the men in their lives.

It was nice of Venerette, who was there at the start, but now she's gone. Now Paula thinks coming there was the wrong thing to do; she hates Brush Creek. After Niv-L and his crew she wants nothing more to do with ghetto people. "Except for Monica, of course."

"What about the baby?" Daria asks the girl. Paula is propped up on pillows against the wall. The bed is just a big block of foam rubber covered with a motley assortment of blankets and bedspreads. "How will you take care of it? There is no husband."

Nadja gives her a frown. For a long time Paula doesn't look up, she just sits there rubbing her stomach. "I would like to keep it," she answers in a quiet voice. "But . . . yes, I may not be able. Monica said that maybe she can help me . . ."

Nadja puts her tea down on the floor and crawls onto the bed with her sister and wraps her arms around her. They cuddle like that, silently, and Daria pours the rest of the tea into Paula's cup and takes the things to the kitchen.

Wandering through the house, she discovers another bedroom, this one with bunk beds to be used by children. There are no sheets or pillows for the top bed, but someone has been sleeping in the bottom bunk.

Off the kitchen is a dining room. There are pocket doors to close it off from the living room, and one door has been pulled shut. A sort of bed has been made up there with a recliner with sheets and a quilt. It's probably for Monica. In the kitchen there is a stack of four large blue plastic bottles of water. On the stove, a kettle and a cauldron, the kind of thing you would use for cooking pasta in a restaurant.

In the living room is a television on a crate with a long black cable entering from a hole that has been punched in the plaster. She can hear the sisters talking, and even some laughter coming from the bedroom, so she finds the remote and settles down on the sofa.

The pirated cable only receives the basic package, all the local stations and the public networks. As Daria clicks through them she is startled to hear Italian. She flicks past it, and then back—one of those old classic movies. She has seen it a hundred times back in Rome. Fellini. Laughing, grotesque faces and circus music.

There is a situation comedy, something with a laugh track. The television works fine. It's at least thirty-six inches, a behemoth that maybe they could use to heat the room if required. It has been centered in front of a soot-scarred fireplace, which, from the lack of a screen, andirons, or cinders, looks like it has been plugged.

She comes upon news of a multiple car crash, news of a basketball upset, news of a school closing. She keeps going, looking for national and international news. There is a noise at the front door, a snapping of latches, and someone saying, "Don't get up, don't get up . . ."

Monica is another huge black woman, but tightly built. "I'm Monica; are you Nadja?"

"No," she says.

"Hi. Thank you," Nadja says, coming out of Paulina's room.

"It's all right. She's doing well, but she needs to stay in bed. Are you a nurse, have you ever done any of that, either one of you?" Monica unstraps a black nylon carryall she's brought in. "There's some clean linens out there in the car . . ."

Daria braces herself against the arm of the sofa, stands, and goes out for the laundry.

Monica's car is a beat-up Jeep Cherokee. The back windows are shattered and patched with plywood and duct tape. The doors have been painted white and then a city shield has been added, stenciled with black spray paint:

Brush Creek Rescue
CRISIS OUTREACH

The laundry is in two garbage bags, and she knows it will hurt too much to carry more than one, so she doesn't even try. She hugs the first one to her chest, and takes the steps slowly.

". . . and there is no cost at all unless she goes to the hospital, and I'm going to be here when any of that happens. She's got my pager. I'll show you, I'll show both of you how to work it," Monica is saying when Daria comes in the door. She puts the bag of laundry on the sofa in the living room.

Her face feels hot, and for a moment she is dizzy. On the television the announcer is pointing to a map. The United States is represented as pale blue on a deep blue background. The individual states are finely outlined in white. Where is Kansas?

". . . see if we can get a handle on this geographically: what we are seeing here are the places where there have been reported cases of smallpox variola—"

The map suddenly blossoms red—clusters around New York, Washington. Down the eastern states. Another dot where she supposes Atlanta is. Chicago maybe, she does not quite know where it is. A dot that must be right there in Kansas City. A few more oddly spaced ones . . . places she does not know. A string all down the west coast, clusters at Los Angeles and . . . Seattle, she guesses.

Spread through the airports, she thinks. How much was because of her and Lufthansa 7416? Now it's happened, now it's too late. All she can do is stand there and watch, propped up against the archway to the living room.

". . . and here are the anthrax attacks. Just in three cities . . . multiple events, but in only three places . . . and that's what you would expect, because the anthrax is not contagious and doesn't disperse in the same way as smallpox does. . . ."

She steps back from the archway, takes a deep breath, and starts back out for the second bag of laundry.

". . . So, remember, we don't want her to move around extra, because she had some spotting. I had the doctor come in and see her and he said she's fine. But she's got orders to be completely laid back, you know what I mean?" Monica says, and goes out to the kitchen.

Daria brings in the laundry and sorts it in the front room. Mostly sheets and towels. There is a stack of diapers with a paper wrapper holding them together. She takes the towels to the bathroom and stacks them on a shelf. The bathroom is clean enough. Some of the tiles in the shower have been patched with something that was slathered on the wall, then sprayed over with some kind of plastic paint. People have been born in worse places, she thinks.

Monica comes back from the kitchen. "Everybody's going to have to help here, okay? Are you girls fine with that?"

"Of course," Daria says over her shoulder.

"Are you all right? You not sick yourself, are you?"

"My boyfriend hit me . . ." she says, touching her side.

"After a soccer match," Nadja says. "With a fence . . . post."

"Lessee . . ." Monica pulls up Daria's shirt to look. "Ow . . ." Monica says, reaching out and softly touching the bandage. In the mirror, Daria can see where a brown stain has leaked through the gauze.

"I'm going to have to look at that," Monica says, dropping the edge of the T-shirt. "But did you both hear what I say? We all are here to be taking care of your sister. That's what's going on. This is work. It's good you're here," she says, "because she is going to be putting herself through a lot."

"What if you're gone?"

"That's what the pager's for. I got mine on all the time. You call me first . . . I'll be right around here somewhere. I know she doesn't want to go to the hospital, but if she has to go to the hospital, she's going to go to the hospital. That's the law. I told her that—"

"She knows."

"She better get mentally prepared on account of she's not all that big, you know?" Monica shows with her hands the circumference a proper pelvis should be.

"Let's figure out where everybody is going to sleep . . ." Monica says.

The recliner, with a tall reading light next to it, is the hot seat. It's close to the running water, and where a telephone would be if there was one connected. It can be closed off from the living room (somewhat) with the working half of the pocket door, but it is open to the kitchen. Monica uses it when she sleeps over, which she has been doing with more frequency since Paula started spotting.

Daria is relegated to the sofa in the living room. She can see the news that way, and she's not in the way of the highly traveled path between the kitchen and Paula's bedroom.

There's not really a door, but she no longer cares much about privacy. None of them do, really, except Monica, who has hung a curtain over the broken pocket door. The sofa itself is thick, bean-bag-style, brown and puffy, covered in velvety synthetic fabric. She has landed with angels, she thinks. It might be true. The house has been at one time a Christian one, she can see a shadow and a picture hook where a crucifix once hung.

Monica's voice, coming from Paula's room: "We're going to raise up that bed. I can't bend over a low bed like that and do any good with a baby. . . ." She says she has asked her cousin and his friends to come over with a bed frame and box spring to lift the mattress to a working height.

They are big boys who arrive, led by Brutus and galumphing through the house. Boys with clean T-shirts and sloppy pants that they nevertheless avoid tripping over as they load in Paula's new bedroom suite. Brutus is cheerleading the operation, making introductions. Being particularly nice to Paulina and pretending not even to notice Nadja.

"Here's the one, here's the one that knows who's right." He smiles at Daria, and reaches up to touch her cheek with two fingers, and she realizes he's hitting on her.

The bed frame goes together pretty quickly. At one point in its life, it has been through some sort of trauma, and midway through the construction one of the boys has to retrieve a screw gun from his pickup truck. His name is Xavier and he is Monica's nephew or cousin, it's not exactly clear.

Paula watches the whole drama from the safety of a rocking chair that has been placed all the way across the room by the window. She sits with a blanket across the lower half of her body and looks out at the yard. In the afternoon light the window is glowing red.

"That's good, that's all good!" says Brutus, leaping back.

"Worrrrrrrrd . . ." Xavier says, and his friend Zeno, the quiet one, laughs.

The box spring is reasonably clean and fits within the rails, then the foam mattress goes up and Monica tests the height, leaning against the frame to see if it wobbles, and then supervises the making of the bed. There is a big mattress protector, then a rubber sheet, a fabric sheet, another rubber sheet and a second fabric sheet. ". . . so you can change the bed fast and not put her in discomfort . . ."

Brutus appears over Daria's shoulder with a big bag. "Picked you up something to tide you over. . . ." Inside are bags of potato chips, a big bottle of Diet Coke, some candy bars, and peanut butter.

"Thanks, Brutus . . ."

"I know you're going to get hungry, you and Nadja . . . we'll make sure you don't starve to death."

"That's very sweet. Thank you."

"When she gets into it, you know, then you call me. We'll be here to help you if you need us to go get anything, okay? Okay, Monica?"

"That's good, Brutus. Now y'all get out of here so she can sleep a little. All this running around is stressful."

A minute later Daria sees him with Nadja out in the front yard. She is standing in the dry grass, kicking it with her heel, and smoking, listening to him as he stands there joking around.

Dinner is macaroni and cheese, with some pieces of cantaloupe and Diet Coke. They sit around Paula's room and bring her what she needs. In the higher bed the pregnant girl seems suddenly smaller, a tiny person running her fingers over the fashion magazines spread out around her on the covers.

The two sisters fall into their memories of Russia, and Daria helps by clearing the dishes and washing up. Monica finds her in the kitchen.

"Okay, let me see this place you got in your side, now," the black woman says. She has brought her big bag in and set it on the counter.

"Oh, it's okay. You don't have to—"

"Mmm-hmm, let's just see how it's doing." She has put on a pair of latex gloves. Daria sighs and turns and braces herself against the counter while Monica folds up her top and slides one blade of a scissors under the tape and clips it away from the wound. "Oh, yeah . . ." she says softly. "Get you some antibiotics for this . . ."

"It feels like the rib is—"

"I bet it does. It probably is . . . It feels like there's a piece in there. Hold on there for a second." There is a stinging pain, and a squeezing sensation that radiates through Daria's lungs, and then Monica is pressing a wad of gauze against her ribs. "Hold on to this . . ." Daria reaches around and presses the gauze into her side. She is sweating. Dizzy. The wall opposite her breaks out in little colorful raindrops.

There is a sound of running water, and then a sharp click as Monica puts something down on the counter—

"You were climbing over a fence?"

"It's complicated."

"Uh-huh, I bet it is," Monica says, moving Daria's hand aside and putting a fresh dressing on the wound, then taping it up. "That's going to weep a little but that's good. You want to keep it draining some . . ." With her fingers she feels along the great corset of tape that Nadja wrapped around her. "This isn't as tight as I'd like," she says, and in seconds wraps another four turns of tape around Daria's middle. "Don't worry, you'll just learn to breathe shallow, right?"

"I guess . . ."

"I think you have a fever; your skin is all red. Here," she says, inserting a thermometer into Daria's mouth and bracing her by putting both hands on her shoulders. "Now you listen to me, young lady. You need to get yourself straight. You know what I mean?"

"I guess," she says through closed teeth.

"Don't you *guess*. You *know*. You get yourself figured out, or get away from here, you understand? I'll throw you out of this house in one half second if you go bad on me. You don't think I can do it?"

"No . . . I'm sure . . . I know that—"

"You damn right," Monica says. She takes the thermometer out and checks it. "You got a little fever," she says, and then looks her hard in the eye. "You get in there and get to sleep and be ready so you can help out when her time comes for labor."

Daria nods and starts to go, then reaches back to touch Monica on her big shoulder. "Thank you . . ." she says.

She goes into the living room, falls onto the sofa, and must lose consciousness, because the next thing she realizes is that Monica is sitting there, giving her an injection in her arm.

"Antibiotic," Monica says quietly, "and this one is tetanus . . ."

"Thank you . . ." Daria says dreamily, and then Monica leaves to take her battered Cherokee on its rounds while she lies still on the sofa, watching the television.

Photographs of a smoking horizon, blurry pictures of cocoa-colored mountains in the distance. Afghanistan, she thinks. A huge dust cloud as seen from a helicopter's point of view. Another shot of the same.

A map of the Kashmir, where the first artillery shells have begun to explode in the undeclared war between India and Pakistan.

DAY 10

"... so who do you think made this country? It was followers of Christ! It was the founders. Who do you think went out and conquered this entire continent? It wasn't the slaves, was it?"

"No . . ."

"And it wasn't our hermanos to the south. Zorro didn't come up here and create Chicago, did he?"

"I don't think so . . ."

"Absolutamente, mi amigo. And then—how naïve is this—after laboring in the garden for a couple of centuries, what did we do, we spread our legs! Open for business! Let's sign up for NAFTA, we've got the hots for free trade, ha, ha, ha!"

"It's not exactly free . . ."

"That's right, my friend. You and your children and their children's children are going to be paying for this deliberate folly—the purposeful economic castration of the United States of America brought to you by the godless hordes who think that black is white, and up is down, and inside out is outside in. . . ."

"Leave her alone, she's still sick," she hears Nadja say from the doorway.

She wakes out of a sleep so profound that for a long moment she does not recognize who she is, where she is. Her perceptions since landing in the arms of the angels at Monica's are fractured. She gradually realizes that Brutus has shown up with more groceries.

"This is all very nice, but we need some vegetables. Is there a store that sells that, or perhaps one of the restaurants . . ." Nadja is saying to him.

"Carrots and shit, I can get that. I get you whatever you want, Naj."

"Okay. Something to eat. She can't have a baby just eating french fries."

"I gotcha . . ."

"Not yet you don't," Nadja says, and reaches up and slaps at him, just playing really. He slips back out of range. "Hey, girl, don't light some fire that you can't put out," he warns before he leaves.

Monica stops by with Xavier and his friend, both boys on bicycles. She has brought grapes and lettuce. "Always a good idea to have something cool and wet. Get some cracked ice to suck on. She's got to keep up her fluids, you remember that. . . ." She bustles back to the kitchen to check on things.

". . . and is that not the meaning of Communism? You work at your job but you don't even get to decide, or apply. You get assigned like you're just a member of the hive. . . ."

Daria becomes aware of someone above her—Monica, sitting on the edge of the sofa. "How are you this morning?" A cool hand on her brow. She's going to be killing all these people, Daria thinks. "I have to give you the shot."

"Okay . . ."

"What this is, is the shot for the smallpox . . . and all of y'all are going to be getting them." Monica rubs the muscle in her shoulder with a cold cotton ball, everything sanitary, latex gloves.

"It's not supposed to work, you know," Daria says.

"What are you talking about? Sure it works . . ." Monica slides the needle in. There's no pain. None at all.

"It only makes it last longer . . ."

Monica takes the needle out and drops it in a plastic box that has biohazard stickers all over it. Then sits back up and looks at her with a frown. "I want to take your temperature." The thermometer whips out. "Let's check that wound. . . . Do you have any allergies?"

"Hmm-mm . . . don't think so . . ."

Monica lowers the T-shirt, reaches around and takes her wrists, inspects them closely, then her ankles.

"Something might have bit you." She shakes her head. "I think you're fine, but it might be a reaction off of the shots from yesterday. Is your arm sore?"

"Everything is sore." It sounds so obvious that she laughs and instantly regrets it.

". . . so don't underestimate the importance of an education in history, my friend. You get yourself to a good library and start reading between the lines . . .

"Mustard gas, Zyklon B, and don't get me started on AIDS . . ."

Monica takes out the thermometer and reads it. "A little high, but . . . you'll get better," she says, getting up off the sofa and heading back to spend time with Paulina.

"No, I won't," Daria says to herself.

"Turn that garbage off," Daria hears Monica say in the other room, and the radio falls silent.

Daria takes her time getting back to the bathroom, has a pee that seems to take hours, and then shuffles out to the kitchen. She is about to make tea, when she stops dead in the room, and looks around.

"No, I won't get better," she says. She hears her voice. She is just speaking to an empty room. "No . . . I won't," she says, and turns back for the living room.

It only takes her a few painful minutes to get dressed. She fumbles on her boots, and reclaims the backpack from the corner where she's tossed her stuff.

Just as she is reaching for the doorknob, it suddenly opens in her face and Brutus comes in with a ten-pound bag of party ice.

"Hey, where you goin'? I'll give you a ride anywhere you want to go . . ."

"No . . . it's okay . . ." she says, but he is past her, already down at the end of the hall. Monica steps out and sees her standing there at the door.

"Where are you going? You can't go anywhere. What the hell is the matter with you?" Nadja comes out on her heels.

"I have to leave. I can't stay here anymore." She gets the door open, but has to lean against it for a moment. "I have to . . ."

"You're just about to fall down. You can't even walk. You come with me . . ." Monica and Nadja carry her back to the sofa. She begins to cry, and they try to quiet her.

She is propped on the sofa, soft pillows wedged under her arm. Someone brings her a glass of ginger ale cooled with shards of Brutus's ice. He is standing there behind the curtains watching them through the fabric. She can't stop crying.

Monica's big hand smooths her brow.

"You just breathe deep and let everything go. You're going to be just fine . . ." she says.

She falls into a deep sleep, with Nadja sitting beside her. She doesn't really wake up, only comes to the surface every so often, missing half of the television they watch. Sitcoms so old that the hairstyles are new again. Faces that she has seen all her life. Semi-famous actors that she recognizes but the names are lost. Actors. Really they are not anything special, she decides, watching them as they go through their poses. Just ordinary humans who happen to be a little funnier, scarier, or prettier than the rest.

She and Nadja watch one of the episodes of *Star Wars*, the early years when Natalie Portman is the Queen.

If Natalie were playing her part right now, they would put oil in her hair, a pale foundation on her face, and dark circles under her eyes. Just a trace of color, green or yellow under everything. A fine sheen of sweat across her collarbones. The rims of her eyes would be red from crying, and her nose runny and sore from blowing it constantly.

She fades in and out. Dreaming of Natalie, black swans, and rocket ships. In her dreams she walks on white beaches, her brown feet digging into the sand, the surf roaring.

". . . drink some of this." She hears Nadja's voice and she feels the cool glass against her lips. Drinks. And then sleeps some more.

The next time she wakes Monica has brought a tray with a bowl of chicken soup. The television is showing a documentary about sea urchins.

"Your fever is gone. You broke through, I think."

"That's good . . ."

"Uh-huh . . . And I think nobody has caught your cold." She looks deeply into her eyes. "Tell me the truth. What are you trying to kick?"

"What?"

"Are you on withdrawal from anything? You taking pills or anything like that?"

"Espresso . . ."

"Oh, yeah . . . funny. You having those little headaches?"

"All the time."

"Well, if that's all it is, I think you can stand a cup of coffee." Monica goes back out to the kitchen.

Daria reaches for the remote and cycles around looking for the news, thinking that she is beginning to understand these women, these big powerful steamrolling mothers. Able to move mountains, keep the sass down to a minimum, and bind a whole neighborhood together, as long as they have the police on their side and enough carbohydrates.

On-screen an older man in a military uniform is talking to the youthful but gray-haired host. As he talks he makes a slight chopping motion with his hand to emphasize his points.

"*. . . not worry too much because during the incubation period you're not as contagious. So, as long as we can catch the emerging cases, then we can start on eradication.*"

"*Using the ring method.*"

"*That's correct, we use the—*"

"*Some of our viewers might not understand that. It's where you literally surround the, uh . . . infectee and immunize everyone around them for a certain distance.*"

"*That's right. We isolate the carrier from everyone else and contain the spread of the virus that way.*"

"*What's your opinion of the statements we heard from earlier today that our suburban lifestyle is actually helping spread the plague?*"

"*Well, the classic response has always been to run to the hills, but the hills are full of weekend cabins now, so . . .*"

"*And tell me more about the vaccine—there's been lots of talk about shortages.*"

"*No, that's not true—*"

"It only slows it down," she says to the screen.

Monica comes through the curtain with a cup of steaming coffee. "Don't drink too much of this if you think it's going to bother your insides."

"No . . ." she says, pushing her nose over the rim of the cup and inhaling the deep inky aromas.

Monica lets her drink, then sits beside her and lifts her T-shirt and looks at the dressing. "We are going to have to change this . . ." She goes out into the hall and brings her bag back, begins snipping the gauze away. "Take a deep breath now, can you do that? How bad does that hurt?"

Tears in her eyes, Daria does everything she is told. As soon as she can, she will leave this house. Maybe after cutting her hair she's not infectious any longer; maybe the vaccination that she got from Monica will prevent it, or delay it, or weaken the virus. Perhaps she won't be killing them.

"Can I take a shower?" she asks.

"I guess. Can you stand up and not fall down in there?"

"I think so . . ."

"Put a plastic bag over the tape. We don't want to try to pull that off you just yet. I'll help."

They shuffle into the bathroom, and she takes off her T-shirt and lets Monica build a little skirt around her breasts with a garbage bag and a long strip of adhesive tape. It is finicky work.

"Do you have any skills, Daria?"

"I'm an actor. I took several acting classes. I liked the drama. The idea that you could be someone else."

"Well, you can't." Monica frowns. "You have to be yourself."

She presses the garbage bag against the center of Daria's spine. Holds it in place, takes the tape from her and tacks it across beneath her shoulder blades. "So, you say you don't have any skills. Can you drive?"

"Sure. Yeah."

"Read and write? You went to school?"

"Sure. I graduated."

"And you're a Russian too?"

"No, no . . . I'm from Florence."

"Italy. My niece is over there at school. She's an artist too." She finishes with Daria's garbage-bag halter top, steps back and points to the bullet hole.

"You can still die from that," she says, and leaves her to her shower.

Daria digs her fingernails in and scrubs and scrubs her reddened hair. Blows soapy water through her mouth and nose until she gags, and does it again. She pushes her fingers into her ears and screws them around. She scrapes behind her ears, rubs her elbows, the backs of her thighs, her feet, opens her mouth, sucks in the water and spits it out. Turns the water up until it's steaming and rubs her skin with soap all over again, moving slowly, breathing carefully, scrubbing all the orifices, creases, and folds of her flesh as far as she can reach. She does it until it hurts, turns the water hotter until it is scalding. But it is not enough.

She cannot twist herself into shapes painful enough, cannot feel the rib spreading apart for long enough. It could not be nearly enough unless she were to puncture a lung. And even that might not be sufficiently painful, she might not even feel it. She might only start coughing blood.

And it doesn't happen, anyway. She doesn't die. She only sobs in the shower and scrubs her hair again and again, and when she dries off, notices a ring of red spots on the blushing skin of her stomach. Just a ring of red spots. Only a trace of a rash on her belly. And raises her eyes to see her face, the face of death, contort in the mirror.

"I'm sorry," she says. "I'm sorry . . ."

After a sleepless night Sam Watterman has decided that he can't just sit around on his ridiculously high consultant's fee and meekly do whatever Reilly's spooks tell him to do.

He needs to spin things, spin them his way, or he'll get spun, and he doesn't want to live through that again.

Without a secure cell phone, he has to submit a list of people he intends to call. He'd make some kind of a deal with Chamai to borrow his if he weren't afraid of getting the young man in trouble. When he complains about the policy, Barrigar says to give him the list and he'll set something up. Sam puts down people he knows will get the word out: Annette Guerrier at the Institut de Veille Sanitaire in Paris; Nick Van Slyke in London, who can move mountains for British Public Health; and Bertugliati at Johns Hopkins, who twice offered him a job that he had been too arrogant to take. Sanjay in Mumbai. With any luck he'll be able to establish a channel for the scientists alone.

Blood has value, so the wording of his message has to be careful. The important thing is to open the lines of communication.

He turns in his list to Barrigar and frets while he waits for approval. Walks through the bulletin board gallery in the situation room, where someone has taken down Namar Yaghobi's photographs.

Yaghobi dead equates to one more opportunity gone. With no surgeon on the medevac team, a local veterinarian harvested Yaghobi's spleen, but not having been fully informed, he ruined it by preserving it in a pouch of formaldehyde. Blood samples were taken from the corpse, and are being analyzed in multiple Level 4 labs across the continent; Yaghobi's blood, or what's left of it, will eventually travel the world and be studied by thousands of scientists.

Maybe it will be good enough.

He goes down the aisle of photographs of the Vermiglio woman. There is a map of the rest area, a series of photographs of the chalked outline where the West Virginia trooper fell beside the crushed door of his cruiser. A dark stain on the pavement.

More photographs. Her car, found by searchers across the state line in Kentucky. A dark hole punched in the side of the thin metal of the driver's door. Spots of blood on the seats—not much. Not buckets of blood, not enough to kill her. There is, he has been told, an abundance of fingerprint evidence. The automobile itself is "hot" with smallpox virus and has been quarantined. She's been exposed for more than a week now; without immunity she would surely be ill.

She is a vector. There is a radius. Given the timeline, how far could she have gotten by now? She has the trooper's gun. Could she have hijacked another car? If she was driving straight through, she could be almost anywhere in the United States by now. Helicopters have been combing the woods and fields near the crossroads in Kentucky where the Nissan was recovered. The assumption is that she will follow Yaghobi's example and find an inconvenient place to die. In the communications center there are dozens of screens dedicated to image analysis—overhead views from the helicopters, and others rapidly culling surveillance photographs taken at Lexington's Blue Grass Airport.

"Sam . . . ?" Grimaldi looks around the corner of the aisle.

Something's wrong. Watterman can tell immediately from her

eyes. And then Barrigar. Also very serious, walking past her to put one steadying hand on his shoulder.

"Sam . . . I'm very sorry, but your wife had . . . an episode. It's the hospital on the line for you." He holds out a secure cell phone.

Everything seems to suddenly slow down. It's gotten quiet or maybe he's gone deaf. His chest feels tight and he braces himself against the edge of the bulletin board. "Hello . . ."

"*Dr. Watterman?*"

"Yes." It is Alice's voice.

"*I'm so sorry about Margaret. But I was just in there and she's resting quietly.*"

"What happened?" he asks. Grimaldi and Barrigar are watching him, and he is surprised at how calm his voice is . . . how reasonable he feels. Another setback, another bit of inconvenience, another life-altering tragedy.

"*They say it is a heart attack, but it wasn't a hard one.*"

"What? What do you mean 'not a hard one'?"

"*She just set her food down and lay back on the pillow and I couldn't wake her. That's what happened.*"

"Ahh . . ."

Barrigar squeezes his shoulder one more time and turns away. He and Grimaldi exchange glances and walk down the aisle to give him some privacy.

"What's her . . . do they have any idea of how she's . . ."

"*I've got Dr. Nakamura right here. Just a second.*"

"*Mr. Watterman?*"

"Is she conscious?"

"*No, she's not. She's stable and sleeping. I understand you are on government work and can't be reached?*" Nakamura says.

"Uh . . . yes. Yes, I am."

"*Is this a good number to reach you on?*"

"Yes. Yes it is."

"*We'll call you when she regains consciousness, and hopefully you can talk.*"

"Yes. Yes, please. Do you have any idea . . . how she is going to, how she's doing or . . ."

Does he hear Nakamura sigh before he answers? *"I really can't say. She's not in the best of health, I'm sure you realize."*

"No. Yes, I know."

"She's in a very difficult situation," Nakamura says. *"I'm sorry,"* he adds.

Alice comes back on the line. She assures him she and Irene will take turns staying at the hospital with Maggie. The idea of her being alone is too terrible for him to imagine. Stupid, he thinks. Why did he do it? No amount of money is worth getting lured back to work. It was vanity. Just vanity and avarice. He should have said no, and stayed with her. They should be in the garden, planning already for next spring. They were happy. Stupid.

"She's in the best place she can be right now," Alice tells him. *"She's not in any pain and she knows how much you care for her. I'll tell her, Dr. Watterman, I promise. . . ."*

She sits with Paulina, listening to more of the sisters' stories— tales of self-loathing, two suckers lured by free tickets and jobs as day-care workers to Canada, and then a cascade of deteriorating situations as they escaped Toronto, then were caught en route to Stockholm and sold by their Canadian owner into Niv-L's custody in fabulous Detroit.

"Detroit? Oh, compared to . . . lots of places in Russia, it was living the high life. He broke us, right away, like animals in a zoo, there is the reward and there is the whip, and always the promises. Do what I say always and you are going to have a fabulous life, be a rock star . . ."

"But now he wants to kill us," Nadja says, bringing in the tea.

"He drowned a man once. With his bare hands. They tortured and drowned him," Paula says, looking up to Nadja. "It was Richie told me that."

"Fuck . . ." Nadja says, and goes back out to the kitchen.

"It was because of a debt. Everything is business. He had signed for us, that's Niv-L's way. He likes to do things legally. Your job is to stay pretty and don't talk back, and you get three meals a day, and you get to work, and there is free drinks, and he might sell you drugs cheap if he likes you, and maybe he fucks you every now and then just to show who is boss. That's the way it was."

Their story goes on and on like that, a saga of hellish reminiscences. Daria pours tea, and covers herself with a blanket, tries not to actually touch Paula, but that plan falls apart when she has to help walk her to the toilet.

In the late afternoon there is a series of contractions.

It is a surprise at first, and Paulina falls silent abruptly and puts her hand atop the curve of her great lump. She is illuminated only by the sun that is blazing through the curtain, really a children's bedsheet that has been hung over the bedroom window.

"No . . ." Paulina says after a minute or two.

Brutus brings over barbecue, which he has decided is something that would be healthy for Paulina to eat on the brink of having a baby. Zeno, who doesn't talk, brings in a DVD player and they hook it up and sit around and watch *Avatar*.

Xavier and Brutus have brought two bottles of rosé, and they laugh at the movie and make jokes about the possibilities of linking up to animals or each other using their tails. Paula laughs too much and gets another contraction, and the room falls silent, but again it's only a false alarm.

"You better hurry up, because we only got this one movie," Brutus says to her, which starts them laughing again.

At around ten o'clock another boy comes calling. Clumping up the steps, waiting outside the door and very serious. There is a quiet discussion on the porch, and within a minute all the boys leave without saying anything. In the distance are sirens.

"They do this shit all the time. This is the tragedy of the neighborhood displayed in front of you right here tonight." Monica reaches into her pocket and brings out her cell phone. A moment later it rings.

"There you go," she says, and gets up to take the call, walking out into the kitchen so that she can be private and they can go on watching the movie.

"We're moving. We're going to get out of here, okay?" Paulina says quietly to her sister.

"As soon as you can walk . . ." Nadja raises her hand and they mime high-fiving.

Six streets over, there has been a shooting. One boy is dead and two others are wounded and may yet die. Monica has to go out in her beat-up Jeep to do what she can. It leaves the three girls alone in the house. Nadja locks the doors and peers frequently through the front windows to see if anything is going on out on Fifty-second Street. The sirens come and go in waves.

Paulina wants to go back to the bedroom, and Nadja helps her. Daria remains, watching war rage across the surface of Pandora. It is blue people against white, only in this story the blue people win. Or at least they win this battle. Will there be a part two, in which the mining-corporation police return with bigger guns and better robots, to shoot the flying dragons out of the air? Isn't the triumph of the mining corporation inevitable? Then the blue people will have to start strapping bombs on their long bodies or learn how to use box cutters.

Nadja returns just as the movie ends, and they switch back to the television.

Two middle-aged men are yelling at each other on a news program. The volume is suddenly loud once they change from the DVD player, and Nadja mutes the sound. The men are shouting and gesturing. One of the men, the one who is the host of the program, turns to the camera and makes a dismissive gesture.

The screen changes. It is more footage taken in the mountains of Kashmir. Children are wailing, the wounded are being tended on bloody concrete floors, women are keening in grief. Roads are choked with refugees fleeing the explosions. Nadja gets the volume back on just as the footage changes. There are grim Asian faces, a phalanx of spotlessly clean tanks on parade.

> "... *who said instability in the region would not be tolerated* ..."

"This is too serious," Nadja says, looking over at her.
"Yes ..."
"I was hoping for a comedy," she says, and the two of them sit on the sofa as Nadja flips through the channels, finally settling for a commercial because it's the safest thing to watch.

DAY 11

Everything is being done in shifts. Daria and Brutus follow Monica to the mall to get groceries while Monica meets with the doctor at the clinic. The office of Brush Creek Rescue is a shabby ex-retail space in one wing of the mall. It must be a better deal for the landlord to get the tax receipt from a charity like Brush Creek Rescue than to sign a real tenant.

As far as shopping goes, there is nothing any good for sale, because the people who live around there have no money and thus a small business cannot turn a profit. Ultimately the mall is owned by . . . whom? By banks? By rich investors who shuffle it around as a loss on their books, the speculative price rising ever upward? Maybe Brush Creek is supposed to function something like a human carbon offset . . . a conservation area set aside for the broken and poor, which will permit the rest of the forest to go on being burned?

Beside the doctor's office there is a café where Daria waits for Brutus to do the shopping and to pick up anything the doctor tells Monica they might need.

The headlines in the *Kansas City Star* are devoted to the president's speech and the reorganization of Homeland Security and FEMA triggered by the Berlin Plague. A pair of dueling columnists project opposing versions of American anxiety over China's declaration of vital interests in Pakistan. Will Pakistan have a big brother backing her up? Everyone has the bomb these days. With the economy still sluggish and very little leverage, what can the U.S. do? The American president is visiting Europe prior to this month's meeting of the G8. The Berlin Plague and Kashmir are the only topics on the agenda.

The front page of a *USA Today* has the inevitable graphic showing the distribution of known cases of smallpox across the nation. Simply counting the cases is proving difficult. A sidebar reminds her once again that smallpox resembles the flu or common cold. From the first cough, the patient is capable of infecting others. Initial discomfort is followed by the typical smallpox "flush," a rash that "blossoms" centrifugally to the limbs. There are "pimples" that morph into "pustules," which are highly contagious. The pustules themselves leak and flake. Bandages, garments, and clothing should be destroyed immediately. Incubation can take from seven to seventeen days, but can occur more quickly. The result is that the graph numbers have been rounded:

Infections under care	> 950
Quarantines (incl. anthrax)	> 5,700
Vaccinations distributed	> 138,400
Confirmed exposures (incubations)	> 60,000

She looks out the floor-to-ceiling glass windows of the café.

Every cup of coffee tastes different in America, she thinks. A triumph of individualism. Out the window there is a parking lot that will never be full again, if it ever was. Dotted around it are abandoned automobiles. At any given moment, some of them will have been stolen, Brutus has told her.

She could go now, she thinks. Go right now, while the rash is just an emerging storm of red clouds arrayed across her abdomen.

She can get up. Walk to the bus stop. Just go. Keep on going. Yes, she decides. She will go back with Brutus and the groceries, get her things and sneak away.

It will be fine, she tells herself. Back at Monica's they've all had injections. It will be fine.

Yes, she will go. And . . . take responsibility for what she has done. Go and turn herself in. Tell them she's sorry. Soon she will sicken and die. They will not torture her, because they will not have to—she will willingly tell them everything before she dies.

Everything that has happened. Everything she has done. About her family, and the way her brothers were destroyed. And why she thought the way she thought, and hated the way she hated. And why she still does. They will scream at her, they will imprison her. They might even torture her after all.

But she will die. And it will be over.

After her second cup of thick and bitter coffee, she puts all her dishes and utensils in the proper bins and steps out onto the sidewalk. Monica comes out of the doctor's, waves, climbs into her Cherokee and heads off on her rounds.

Brutus comes back. He's got a whole grocery cart full of stuff, vegetables this time—Daria sees the green tufts sticking out of the bags. "I got honey, I got breakfast cereal, I got apple juice . . ." It's enough for an army, and he needs her help to fit it all in his trunk.

"I've got to get glasses," he says after he's closed the lid and they are just standing there. "I've got some kind of thing going on in my vision."

"That's not good . . ."

"I only got eyes for foreign girls . . ."

"Oh . . . you are so full of shit." And they are laughing there together for a few moments.

"Those Russian girls are hot, and those Italian girls are hot too," he says under his eyelashes, not looking at her.

"You are just horny."

"Mm-hmm. I admit it. It's a sin."

"Men are always in a hurry. You see what happened to Paulina . . ."

"It doesn't have to be like that. You and me should go out sometime."

"No . . . I'm still sick."

"Well, I can fix you up. You should take the Brutus cure."

She laughs. "Look, you're a sweet guy. I'll talk to Nadja. She doesn't really have the HIV, she just says that."

"I know. But she's too busy," he says, and turns toward the driver's side of the car. "We're all too busy. Everybody in the world is too busy . . ."

Just as they are getting in the car, there is an angry barking, and two dogs roar around the corner, tumbling end over end as they flail and snap at each other's throats.

"God*damn*!" Brutus says and starts rolling his window up. Then he stops and they both watch. It's the sound—the growling and the shrieks—that is so horrible. A third dog suddenly comes sprinting around the corner of the mall and joins in the frenzy. Together they make a tangled, tumbling ball of brown, gray, and black. One is a Doberman, or something like it, fighting with the two smaller heavy-shouldered dogs.

"People ain't got the money to keep those dogs and they let 'em go and then they run loose out there," Brutus says, and starts the rumbling engine of his Pontiac. "God*damn*," he says again as they back out.

By then the dogs are gone.

They drive out of the mall and are starting down the broad street, so wide it would be considered a highway in any other culture—a sanctuary for the internal combustion engine, but a death zone for people and wildlife, and, on a day when the commute is high, completely devoid of oxygen. Mostly it's a knife stabbed into the heart of the Brush Creek neighborhood. The street ascends gradually and from its heights she can see over the guardrails the curve of the real creek, the trees that border it, their branches mostly brown now. Without the city, it would be very beautiful.

"Shit on these motherfuckers . . . Be cool," Brutus says. There is an electronic squawk from the police car that has come up behind them, and Brutus slows and lets the Pontiac drift over to the edge of the pavement.

Maybe this is it, she thinks, as she watches the police officer climb out of his cruiser. He is young, hyper-fit. A flat stomach, and she can see the muscles press out against the cloth of his shirt, into which creases have been pressed on either side, splitting the pockets perfectly.

"Good morning," the cop calls out. His voice is tight. Sharp and pitched a little high.

She looks over and sees that Brutus has placed his hands where they can be clearly seen, right up at the top of the steering wheel. "Morning . . ." he answers.

"License and registration, please," the cop says. Brutus does it all slow. The registration is in the glove compartment, and the cop crouches down so he can see across as Daria opens it, copying Brutus and moving slowly. The cop watches them, one hand on his gun the whole time. Inside the glove compartment there is a mound of paper, a spray of CDs. Brutus leans across and picks out the registration and hands it over to the cop.

"Just stay in the car," the cop says, and goes back to his cruiser.

"They do this shit all the goddamn time," Brutus mutters. "Fucking ice cream is going to be shit by the time we get back . . ."

"The police are not so bad here. Other places, it can be much worse," she says, looking out the window. The cop has parked behind them in the right-hand lane, and all the traffic is now constricted into a slow parade of vehicles idling past, people shaking their heads and glaring at them. "Police are like that everywhere someone is different."

"Italian cops are tough, huh?"

She settles back in his wide front seat. There is a breeze coming through the window and it seems that for once all the exhaust is blowing some other direction. The sun is boiling down through the windshield onto her sore chest, and she closes her eyes.

"There was a place . . . it was near the place where I grew up. Not where I was born, but close by. We knew people who still lived there. It was close to where there was always fighting."

"Okay . . ." says Brutus.

"The police were having trouble there. People went back and forth that way, along that road, and they were having to pay to do it."

"Sure they were."

"So, the government put more police in that district. The first day, to let people know that they were on the job, the captain arrested six men. They said they were trying to escape, and they shot them all. Dead. Right in the street. So . . . it can get worse."

"They do that shit in Italy?"

She shrugs. "In lots of places . . ."

"You're some kind of refugee?"

"No . . . I'm supposed to be a journalist."

She hears Brutus draw a breath, and opens her eyes enough to see the cop returning.

"Where are you headed today, Mr. Farnsworth?"

"We're shopping for groceries. I got some frozen items in the trunk, Officer."

"You do, huh?"

"I got some ice cream in there. It's for a pregnant lady, to calm her down."

"Well, let's you and I take a look. It might not have melted all that bad. Young lady, why don't you step out and wait up front of the car."

She pulls herself out of the front seat and does as she's been told; it's the only way for prisoners or oppressed persons to get through such things. Simply do what you are told. You have to try and remember that they actually want you to get angry. That's why they do it, so that you'll attempt to hold on to your dignity and end up giving them the excuse they need to smack you down. That's what makes them happy and proves their manhood.

She leans back against the hot metal hood of the huge car. The nose of the car cuts into her back right across where she's been wrapped with tape. It's soothing in a masochistic way, like a painful massage on her spine. She closes her eyes and turns her face up to the sun while Brutus undergoes his trials. There could be anything back there in the trunk. She doesn't really know Brutus. This could be it. Any moment she could hear the cop asking to see her ID. What a coup it would be for him; he'd be a superstar. The famous terrorist caught at a simple traffic stop. It is almost, but not quite, funny.

If it is, it is, she thinks.

She looks out at Kansas City sprawling all around her. From the road atlas she knows it's a fractured place, with many municipalities. A node, a distribution hub and communications center. She is right in the heart of the heartland, in the core of the beast she has sworn to eradicate. But now . . . she is weakening. Since she has started to question, she has started to lose her focus, and to repudiate her commitment.

Now she is failing.

How much power does she still have? Can her touch still kill? Or is she merely a seed? Drifting. A germ. She had never wanted to be a germ, she wanted something else . . . something that seems absurd and out of reach now. Romantic, her childhood dream of an avenging sword . . . She was thrilled at Ra'id's anger, his fatalism, thrilled that Amir would back him up and protect him. She'd believed in all of it. She should have been a boy. She'd wanted to be a boy, to go with them. You had to strike back, you had to fight. Jihad was the only way out.

What was it that they had been taught? Survival of the fittest. That was it. Darwin. Evolution. If the theory was real, now she was one of those "incidents"—a grain of sand, an accident, just a blip in the chronicle of a great epochal change. History from this point on would be written by different hands. The great American cities would die; either the Indians or the Pakistanis would triumph. Israel would fall or unleash a global war. China and Europe, the Russians and the Americans, might ally themselves and try to contain things, but it was equally possible that each would elect to join one side or the other.

Within days the hospitals will be overwhelmed. She has just happened to be in Saleem Atcha Khan's first cohort of plague carriers. There will be others playing terrible parts, more direct and bloodstained, and far more important than hers.

The trunk lid closes with a low bass clump and she turns to see

Brutus heading back. They get in and he starts the engine and they roll slowly off ahead of the cop, careful to signal as they enter the traffic.

"Another day in paradise . . ." says Brutus as they get back on the road.

When they reach 3050, Brutus slams the ice cream into the freezer to try to reharden it, then they all congregate in Paula's room to check up on her, with Daria hovering as far as possible in the background.

Nadja is upset about something, and she takes the conversation out into the kitchen, where they can talk privately and not trouble her sister: While they've been gone she's seen someone outside.

"There's people come around to all of these houses, there's all kinds of desperate people out there looking for shit. Y'all need a gun around here. Who was it?" Brutus asks her.

"I don't know, I told you," Nadja spits. Daria goes to the sink and busies herself making another pot of tea, which the Russian girls drink by the gallon.

"What kind of car were they in?"

"No car." Nadja looks up at him. "I was on the porch and I saw a guy over there, over there where they did the digging. Maybe he saw me, I don't know, but then he walked away, back around. So I came back here and looked out through this window, and I saw him again. Going all the way in a circle, behind the yard, and then he kept on going. All the way. I couldn't see him anymore through all the jungle, but then a minute later this van came by."

"That's crazy."

"It was a white man too . . ."

"White man? And all he did was just walk around?" Brutus is standing there with one hand on his hip, frowning.

"All around. Then drove away . . ."

"That don't make no sense. This property ain't worth shit. You can't even sell it if you wanted to."

"I thought it was very suspicious," Nadja says stubbornly, and stares out the kitchen window.

"It's probably nothing. Some inspector from the city, some shit like that," says Brutus, and he steps forward and gives Nadja a hug. To comfort her.

There is nothing Daria can do about getting out of helping with dinner. Every half hour or so, Paula begins having contractions, only one or two each time, and each time they fade away. She begins to complain about sitting down, that her back hurts. Monica comes rushing over to the house for the first false alarm, and then has to leave. There are two other women she is also taking care of, she explains.

Dinner is something digestible and nourishing that will pass right through Paula if it comes to that—chicken soup, a bean salad, bread and butter, and the inevitable tea. Daria washes her hands frequently, and ties a bandanna over her hair. Still, she worries if it is enough.

For television they watch a DVD of *Toy Story* that Brutus has brought. She begins to quietly assemble her duffel bag. She will escape in the night; she just can't face them with the truth. They will beat her to death, she thinks. Brutus and his friends . . .

When the story of the toys reaches its emotional climax, she cries, and so does Nadja.

The idea is for everyone to get some rest, but Paula still doesn't want to lie down, and instead begins to pace up and down the hall. The two Russians talk in little short sentences.

The DVD ends and Brutus packs it up. Nadja takes Paula back into her bedroom, where she has finally agreed to get in bed and get some rest. Brutus says he is going to walk around the house and just check on things. Still thinking about the white guy that Nadja saw traipsing through the vacant lots.

It is probably the CIA, Daria thinks . . . the FBI, some unit of Navy SEALs, or maybe the Kansas City PD, who have staked out the house and are now silently surrounding them. Even as she goes about the living room, gathering her things, they are watching.

Scanning her heat signature through these thin wooden walls, judging exactly where to punch a .50-caliber sniper's bullet through the soft bricks of the chimney to kill only her, leaving everyone else in the house unscathed.

Without the DVD playing, the television has reverted to the news. It is all more of the same. The crisis has enveloped the world. Numbers grow larger by the minute: seventy-three cases in Kansas City, over two thousand in New York, two thousand in Los Angeles, nine hundred each in Seattle and Chicago. Another estimated fifteen hundred in Washington. Senator Frances Cheselso has succumbed to anthrax. So has the Secretary of the Treasury, M. Randolph Dodd. The fighting in India threatens to spread. China is sending armored troops to the border to ensure Pakistan's territorial integrity. The president is returning from Brussels. Israel is angry and poised for one of its neighbors to do something foolish, its jets on constant alert.

There is nothing about the continued hunt for terrorists still at large. Nothing that might explain a white man walking around the house.

She goes out into the kitchen, and flips off the light, and looks out the back to see if she can see Brutus. In the darkness of the garage she thinks she sees a little spark, just a smoldering red dot. It flares up and then fades away. She watches for one more breath. This time it moves up, flares, and then is whisked away.

She leaves the kitchen light off and starts down the hall, turning off lights as she goes. At Paula's door, she taps quietly, waits, then goes in.

"This hurts . . ." she hears Paula say from the bed.

"Is Nadja here?" Daria asks.

"She went to the bathroom," Paula says with a groan. "This fucking *hurts* . . ."

Daria goes to the front window and looks out. There is a single streetlight whose glow is obscured by the blackberries and bamboo growing along the property line next door. The dried-up front yard is a lighter-toned plain extending down to the sidewalk in front of the house. No one on the street. The tail of Brutus's Pontiac in the driveway. Distant sirens heard through the glass. She steps back and pulls the curtain.

No, Nadja is not in the bathroom, and she goes back out to the kitchen and looks for the cigarette in the garage again. Nothing.

She tries the back door. It opens quietly enough and she puts her ear to the crack and listens.

Ah . . . she thinks.

Brutus has got his wish.

Daria is half asleep on the sofa when Nadja comes in to tell her that Paulina is having real contractions now and the baby is starting to come. Paulina is right behind her, hands on her hips, striding through the room, blowing out through her cheeks. "It hurts," she says.

Daria gets up and heads for the kitchen. She has planned to leave via the back door. She's stashed a big bottle of water back there. It's the way she can most easily make her exit when the time comes. She's all ready to go, she *should* go. This is her chance . . . but now she only puts on the kettle.

A few minutes later, Monica drives up and takes charge of the bed, making sure there are new sheets, nice soft lighting in the room. Fresh air. Everything prepped and ready.

Brutus has gone home to clean up; when he comes back he brings a two-pound bag of sugar the girls require for their tea. Daria has not seen him since the little lights in the garage. "Did you discover anything out there? Any white men in vans?"

He turns down the corners of his mouth, frowns. "No . . . ain't nobody around here now, if there ever was." Maybe it's something funny in her expression, because he just stares at her for a long second and then steps back as if wounded. "Hey, what's the matter with you?"

"Nothing," she answers. "Nothing . . ." Thinking that she's missed it now. That she should have gone earlier. She should have gone.

"Aw, come on . . ." he says, and turns back to his business.

Paulina rounds the doorway. Her face is slack, but she is still blowing like a locomotive. She sags against the archway, and Nadja walks behind her, rubbing her spine while she groans.

It hurts.

At the end of the day, Sam Watterman sits at the table alone. All the way across the "terrace" of the FBI bar, or "Fubar" as it has become known to the regulars. He follows Maggie's progress three times a day courtesy of Barrigar, who lets him talk to the caregivers for as long as he needs.

When Barrigar sees he's put the cell down and is simply sitting there staring off into space, he joins him for a nightcap. Like most of the men, he's wearing a golf shirt—dark blue in his case, with a yellow FBI across its back. The various agencies have different shirts, all color-coded with acronyms printed on the back. It's helpful if you happen to be looking for someone from Agriculture (USDA) or the National Institutes of Health (NIH), one of the members of the liaison team loaned from the National Biodefense Analysis and Countermeasures Center (NBACC), or a consultant from the National Science Advisory Board for Biosecurity (NSABB), which, it turns out, has officially hired him.

They clink glasses and Barrigar cuts right to the bad news. No more international calls allowed. "We're under a complete lockdown since Yaghobi. The people that you've put on your list . . ." Barrigar winces. "It's every biowarfare expert in the world."

"Okay, so they are very successful at what they do, so . . ."

"No." He shakes his head, handing him the paper. "Write an email. I'll push it up the line." Barrigar sounds a little distracted. As if he's half asleep, or is on meds.

"You realize how . . . absurd this is?"

"I'm sorry, Doctor. There is a greater war."

"Oh, really?"

"Definitely. In the greater war, we not only follow one or more of our National Incident Management plans to deal with the attack, but we also have to be able to initiate offensive action. We have to be able to turn off their lights. Khan, as far as we know, only sent four people to the U.S. And we have accounted for three and are chasing the last one right now."

"Sure, sure. I don't doubt it. Great job." Because of the acoustics, everything has a kind of muffled booming echo to it. Talking intimately is a little harder to do. You have to lean closer or talk louder to hear your neighbor.

"Doc, the fact is we're in a world war right now. Each nation is out for themselves. The blood of these terrorists has value—you're the one that alerted us to that fact. Fine. Okay. The top of the food chain is going to take your advice into consideration. But what happens after that? Some technologies aren't ever going to be shared. This is the big shakeout. Governments are going to fall, some countries are going to go under. We have to accept that. Did you see the Africa stuff?"

"It was too depressing, so I stopped looking." Riots are being reported, more and more each day as several countries start to implode. A bombing in Pretoria. Another in Khartoum.

"No . . ." Barrigar stops. Looks over to him. "Shit . . . I'm sorry, Sam. I'm sorry. That's very inconsiderate of me. How's everything, uh . . . going?" He is a handsome man, well groomed. The kind of man who can model a shirt at any age. Not a hair out of place. Ex-Marine, Watterman remembers someone has told him.

"Oh . . . she's sleeping. No change. 'No change' is good, I guess."

"Well . . . I don't mean to cram work down your throat."

"We're all going crazy in here, I guess," Watterman says.

"Life in a submarine," Barrigar agrees, nodding.

"We gamed all this, but it's not the same as living through it."

"No, Doc. No, it isn't. Not the same at all." Barrigar suddenly sits back and taps his half-touched glass down on the table. "I can't do this . . . you want another?"

Sam looks at the glass for a long moment. "I haven't decided how far off the wagon I want to fall."

" 'Night, Doc . . . Big day tomorrow." Barrigar sighs and heads out of the patio.

"... *with disastrous effects on the entertainment industry. Senator Aikins claimed that FEMA funds should be distributed to not only the NFL but also the NBA and the National Hockey League, which have now abandoned their seasons due to quarantine laws.*

"*More on what this means for you and your family, and some tips from our panel on alternate trick-or-treating plans for Halloween, right after this. . . .*"

DAY 12

For a tiny girl, Paulina Pravdina is surprisingly strong. She has endurance in those thin little muscles. In the old system she could have been a gymnast, or a flyweight kickboxer. Instead she had been lured to the West and ruined. Beaten and raped by men who regarded her as livestock. Drugged, and enslaved. The pregnancy was a lingering reminder of that time. But she had dreams, she said. She was looking forward to the responsibility of it. She and Nadja both knew it was going to change their lives, that it was going to hurt and be hard, but Paulina was set on keeping the child.

A few hundred laps of the house later, Paula's water breaks and Daria finds a mop and follows behind the sisters, drops back and rinses it out in the tub, and then does it again, stepping around the girls each time they come through.

"We'll all be leaving soon, don't worry. I know it's a bad neighborhood, but . . . maybe we can all go to Hollywood together . . ." Nadja is saying as they go by.

Paulina's pain is increasing. She can't tolerate reclining in the bed, and even sitting hurts. When she tries, she has to get up and stalk around angrily like a pint-sized naked female sumo wrestler, calling out *". . . Haaaaaaaaahhhh!"* as she moves through the house.

Daria does everything that is required and more. Laundry begins right away. She searches for soothing music on the radio while
Paula cycles around. It is not until a contraction almost buckles her
knees that Paula allows Monica to move her back onto the bed.

"You're doing good now, honey . . ." Monica croons. Daria has
cold towels to put across Paula's forehead, has draped a scarf around
the lamp shade to reduce the room to a rosy glow.

The world has come down to a still point, a still point for Paula's birthing of her baby. This is all there is. And no interruption
from the outside world will be tolerated, for tonight Brush Creek is
in a state of grace.

Monica, her hands encased in latex gloves, begins to examine
Paula. Daria turns away, out into the hall.

Nadja squats down so she can see up between her sister's legs.
"Ohhh . . ." she murmurs, wondrous. Daria looks back in. Paula's
huge vulva is red and stretched, blood smears her thighs and the
sheets. Paula sags back against the pillows and groans while Monica's fingers explore.

"Sing a little song . . . it helps . . ."

"I don't know songs. I'm not a singer," Paula groans.

"Everybody knows some kind of song. Go ahead . . ." Monica
encourages.

Nadja looks up at her sister and smiles and then a slow loping
melody comes out of her. Something from their childhood. A song
to make children happy. Paula has her eyes closed but she smiles.
When her breath comes around again, she joins her sister. Daria sits
down in the old chair next to the lamp, and when the chorus starts
she tries to join in and learn the Russian lyrics. Nadja translates:

> *Mice are dancing in a circle,*
> *On a bench a cat is sleeping.*
> *Quiet, you mice, don't make a sound*
> *Or you'll wake up angry cat*
> *Angry cat will jump up and leap*
> *And will spoil and end your singing.*

"That's good . . ." Monica says. "That's good . . . Get me that mirror, Nadja. You want to see?" Paula gasps and nods, and they turn the lamp to get more light so that she can stare at the hand mirror's reflection of her distended genitals.

"That right there," Monica says, pointing to a gray sliver at the heart of her vulva, "that's the head right there."

There is a little ripple of laughter and Paulina sprouts tears and goes into a big contraction, and Monica just holds her hand and smiles. Nadja picks up the song again, and so it goes.

The first time Daria gets a look at the clock, it is after three in the morning.

Brutus and Zeno have come over and set up on the front porch. One by one, the women take breaks from Paula's bed and go out there to wait in the cool with the boys. They have taken up their positions outside, talking, telling stories about the shooting over on Olive Street. It's good to have them around to go and get things. Brutus has parked his Pontiac backwards in the driveway so he'll be able to get out easy. The boys sit and sip from their beers and fall silent and wince and shake their heads at Paula's noises, the lyrics to the Russian lullaby now having deteriorated to a series of trembling groans.

Monica takes a break and comes out on the porch, standing up straight, hands on hips, rolling her neck around on her shoulders, bones popping from fatigue.

"Not too much longer, I don't think," she says.

"That's good . . ."

"Everybody comes in like that, more or less . . ."

"I was a cesarean."

"Maybe that's why they called you Brutus."

"I think it might have been."

Monica takes one long look at the street and goes back in.

Daria is tired; everything is running together. That's what happens when things are too much for her, she is learning. Her mind erases things as they happen, life shifts from one flash frame to another, and she isn't quite sure of the order of events or how she's arrived wherever she is. Just a series of still pictures, she thinks. Then she rushes back inside and digs her camera out of her pack, goes back to the bedroom, and grabs pictures of the sisters smiling at the lens between contractions. Monica does another internal, pronounces everything in order . . .

Then everything moves fast.

The pain takes over the person once called Paula. She is but a passenger in her own private jumbo jet of pain. Out of her head. The nursery rhyme has become blurred rhythmic shouts, punctuated with attempts to catch her breath. They embrace her now; Daria does too, because as poisonous as her touch might be, this is a more terrible and more dangerous crisis, this making two people out of one, and she and Nadja hold the little sister on either side, her fingernails puncturing their skin as she growls and then subsides into whimpering.

Paula begins to negotiate, to plead. Please can the midwife give her a little shot? Help her out with the pain? Please? "Call the hospital," Paula begs. "Call the hospital, call the hospital . . ."

"Can't do that now. You got to have this baby right here. You're doing good . . ."

Another great low groaning.

"Now you can push? Push a little more. Can you do that, honey? Can you feel . . . when it comes again?"

And it does come again, and she groans again, the sound low and unbelievably loud coming from the tiny Paulina . . . and then she's gritting her teeth and pushing, pushing.

"*Good* . . . that's good. We're coming along. Take a big breath now, get yourself some oxygen, and do the same thing this next time coming. Just like you did before. Get ready now . . ."

Tears. Blood. As if Paula is going to explode each time it comes. "That's good, that's good. Coming out now . . . I got the head . . . this next time. Here it comes, this next time. *Big* push now . . . That's right . . . that's *good* . . ."

Suddenly, after all that time, a wet purple animal slithers from Paulina's vagina, and she groans and falls back.

"That's it, girl . . . that's it!"

"Oh . . . God . . ." Paula groans, and tries to see.

"That's everything! That's it! That's your little . . . *boy*," says Monica.

Daria begins to laugh, and so does Nadja. Monica has risen and moves quickly to the table they have set up at the end of the bed, checking the baby's eyes and airway. A tiny cry comes out of it. The little face screwed up and flattened, the skin suddenly suffused with oxygen and turning pink.

"Healthy baby boy. Got all his fingers and toes and everything else he needs. Here you go, Mama," says Monica as she puts the baby to Paulina's breast.

Daria is crying, tears streaming down her cheeks, nose running. It breaks over her, sweeping her away, the miracle of it. She has been there, a witness and participant in the impossible thing occurring. Right before her eyes!

The magnificent creature tries to twist in his mother's arms, but even with the excitement, he too is exhausted, confused, and learning that everything has changed. And with everything—the brand-new feelings, the never-felt sensations, all of it pulsing through him—he is still safe, falling asleep on his mother's breast.

Daria takes photographs until her battery dies and she has to recharge it. Digging the charger out of her pack, plugging it in with trembling hands. It's impossible. Everything is impossible. How can she go on staying here with these people? With the child now with them, the living marvel, the manifestation of . . . of everything humans are supposed to be and do—how can she stay? She walks back to the bedroom, lingers by the door. Monica is wiping her eyes. Nadja mops her sister with a warm washcloth. Paulina is smiling, exhausted, blissful.

Now the boys come to see, shuffling and nodding, embarrassed and weak-kneed, joking with Paula about how much noise she made and how she kept them all up. Brutus has hidden a bottle of champagne in the refrigerator, and they pass around coffee mugs. And Daria carefully takes the last sip and rushes to clean the glasses, fresh tears in her eyes.

Monica leaves, to hugs and applause. Paula's eyes are half

closed. They have made a crib there on the bed beside her, and she falls asleep with one hand draped over the edge of the basket, against her son's cheek. His name will be Daniel, she tells them, and Nadja smiles. A child with many fathers, named in honor of a favorite uncle. "The only nice one in the family," Nadja laughs. All that behind them now.

They let Paula sleep and Daria begins cleaning up. There is, for what has basically been an uncomplicated birth, lots of blood, bloody sheets, towels.

The boys have been shooed out of the bungalow, even Brutus, who claims not to mind on the excuse that he has business to attend to across town. He and Nadja part at the door, just a little kiss. A place marker to hold them until they can meet again.

Daria throws open the dusty curtains in the front room. Suddenly she is bone weary, staring into the yellow motes in the dawn light that slants through the room.

She has just finished making a bed for herself on the sofa when there is a knock on the door and Monica pops back in with a short man, skin black as coal, a completely shaved head, dressed nicely in tweeds with a mismatched tie. He is Dr. Durham, who will do the certificate of live birth. They go into Paula's shadowy room, and wake her gently. From the open doorway Daria can hear a series of croaking sounds from Daniel, and a few minutes later they exit. Nadja goes in and makes sure her sister has enough water, while Monica and Dr. Durham confer in the kitchen.

Dr. Durham charges nothing; his work at the Rescue is *pro bono*. There will be a fifteen-dollar fee to the Missouri Department of Health and Environment in order to register little Daniel Pravdin, and they must file within the next two weeks, the doctor explains, even though Monica knows it all already.

They all troop back out. "A new little citizen. It is a beautiful day," the doctor says, nodding to Daria as he goes down the steps.

She will leave, she will go before they invite Aunt Daria to lift the perfect baby to her toxic breast. She should have left yesterday, should have been stronger, should have never stayed. She wanted something, she wanted love. She wanted a family again. She needed to be safe too. She was weak, wounded, and sick. She let herself do the unthinkable. An ignorant fool. A killer. A pariah.

She stares at the television for a long moment there in the dusty living room. Trying to decide whether she should turn it on or not . . . reaching for the remote, holding it in her hand. She presses the power button and simultaneously the mute so the volume won't disturb them. She flicks through the silent commercials, going around the cycle until she lands on some news.

FORT DATHAN TERROR FARM!

Overnight, while little Daniel was busily fighting his way into this world, there has been a new terror attack. A group of camouflage-clad men are shown, all glaring at the camera. Mug shots. All of them dressed in identical green T-shirts. She tries to read fear or triumph in their blank faces. She taps the sound and moves closer to the screen so she can hear the fabric of America unraveling.

They are Christians, proud members of the white race who believe in their divine right to defend themselves, especially now that the end days are nigh. The federal government is their enemy, and they have sworn to destroy it, starting with the local office of the Internal Revenue Service.

The images suddenly are whisked away by the magic of television, and she finds herself watching a grainy surveillance photograph. An entire series. The images are in black and white, and the resolution is startlingly bad. What's the point of a surveillance camera if they can't see any better than that? People in a corridor, walking through glass doors. After a few jerky frames, there is a cut and another image fills the screen—

Her face.

The image is much clearer and in color. Something that has been taken automatically across the shoulder of the immigration official at JFK.

There is a noise in the hall and she flicks the channel a few times and turns off the set, manages to get one step across to the sofa and start undressing as Nadja leans in. Her eyes are half closed and she is smiling. Then she rushes into Daria's arms, presses her face into her neck and snuffles. "You're really sweet," she says. "Thank you . . ." and pulls back, wipes the tears out of her eyes, and leaves.

She hears Nadja padding down the hall to the bathroom, and she goes over to the corner of the room and grabs her pack, brings it around to the side of the sofa. Her shoes are at the end of the bed; she'll have to wait for Nadja to go to sleep before she can get the water she's stashed and slip out.

She sits there in front of the blank television for a long moment. While Nadja is in the bathroom, she looks around the back of the set.

It is despairingly simple, a cable that runs from the wall and connects into a socket in the back of the set. She unscrews it and jams the single wire against the edge of the brick fireplace until it's deformed, then screws it lightly back onto the set. There is a flush and she hears Nadja leave the bathroom, and she gets back in her bed on the sofa to wait for a chance.

"*Her*—that one right there—" Barrigar says. A red box appears around one of the people in the surveillance photographs, then enlarges until it half-fills the screen.

A young woman with strikingly white-blonde hair, cut short and spiky. Turned away from the camera so her face is not revealed.

"What you're seeing, this is raw, and this is enhanced . . ." The picture changes, clarifies. Jogs ahead a frame at a time. A backpack slung over her shoulder. A tight-fitting jacket. Jeans slung low. She turns now. She's unexpectedly very pretty; tough-looking in the way young people think tough people look.

"We assumed she had changed her appearance, so we were looking for that. We did the radius search and this blonde girl came up."

"This is in the bus station in Louisville, Kentucky," Chamai says. "Four days ago, in the afternoon. See, we're looking by radius, thinking, where is she? Where is she going to land? Radius grows larger with time . . ." Like the diagram of a spreading pandemic,

Watterman is thinking. Like those old targets from school, diagramming the blast effects of an atom bomb in five-mile increments from ground zero.

Now it's a girl at the center of the explosion.

"We're getting all our eyes on every bit of footage we can get and we start looking for the same people, then we follow them backwards from where they are to where they came from, or forwards to where they are going . . ."

"Complicated," Sam says.

"There is a lot of software that goes into this, Sam. Face recognition, *gait* recognition, all kinds of bells and whistles . . ."

"I'm sure."

"Obviously, if we can spot them, if we can locate them, then we can use satellites and surveil them like we were doing with Yaghobi. We've got drones we can put up to watch them in real time . . ."

"Domestic drones?" Sam says, not having ever really thought about such a thing. Reilly snickers at his naïveté. Sam turns to stare down the man, but when he looks, Reilly is gone. Maybe he wasn't even there.

"Do you have any coffee?" he asks. An ATF agent speeds off to get him some. He smiles his thank-you and discreetly checks to see if Reilly is there now or if it was a hallucination. Dementia. He's going senile.

"So . . . okay, we're looking, we're looking, and what we get is *her* . . . here she comes through the door to the waiting room to the café . . ."

The view has shifted. Now there is an angle right over the register. Again, Sam is struck by how pretty the terrorist is. She looks like a Nordic sea sprite with her hair like that.

"See what she's got there?"

"A bottle of water and . . . is that potato chips?"

"Yep." Watterman watches as the girl takes a billfold out of her jacket, pays with a five, and turns . . .

"Okay . . . now we follow her back . . . And now, right here—" Barrigar's finger taps on the screen. "See her sitting down?"

She sits at a table, the kind you'd find in any food court.

"So, okay, you see this right here? There? That's somebody else's feet—"

Sam watches as the smudge moves into frame. Shoes . . . or boots of some kind.

"Stop it right there—" The image shudders to a halt.

"We think that's Vermiglio." Barrigar taps the screen with his finger. "Run it forward for him slow," he says to Chamai, who is beached there in the cubicle, leaned sideways away from the screen to give the two older men a better view as he works the mouse.

All Sam can see is the sheen of the floor, the legs of the table, and the blonde's feet doing a restless dance, then she gets up to refill her coffee, comes back to the counter, vanishes off frame, comes back and buys a slice of pie. Walking back to the table, then slowing . . . Back to her companion, waiting at the table, who is doing—nothing. Just a pair of shadowed legs.

Vermiglio.

The image slows and stops. Something changes, a date/time stamp flickers on a bar at the bottom of the frame. A different angle, almost straight down over a pair of glass double doors. "Now . . . this is taken forty-five minutes later. The both of them go. See . . . she's helping someone."

Another girl. Walking stiffly.

"Her. That's her. And look—we were right. Vermiglio's changed her appearance as much as she can. Her hair is different. And you can see the way she's walking . . ." Stiffly, hobbling along.

"She's hurt."

"That's right. You can see it, she's hurtin'," says Chamai.

"And . . . there they go, off the frame."

"To catch a bus?" Sam asks.

"We're looking at all the possible routes. But the time would indicate a bus to Kansas City. It's a busy station."

"Or a cab?"

"Cabs are on the back side of the lot. No, it's a bus."

"So?"

"So . . . she's gone again."

"What do we do now?"

"Well, we're going to Kansas City, of course," Barrigar offers.

"But while we do that . . . if we can't follow forward, we follow back," says Chamai like a sideshow barker. "Time flows like an arrow in at least two directions." He clicks and a series of still images of the blonde slide across the screen. "We have walked Vermiglio's blonde friend back in time—and I have to speak up here and say that when we do this we end up with a route that doesn't exactly compute, but, hey. First . . . she arrives via Cincinnati, then before that, in Pittsburgh. And we almost missed her there because—you see what she's doing?"

"She's wearing a scarf."

"She's evading, man. She knows she's recognizable, and she's evading. Until she gets out of Pittsburgh. But all the time this blonde, you know where she was originating? Motown, gentlemen." Chamai says it triumphantly, cutting to a final image: the blonde, still covered up, walking into a different bus station, wearing sunglasses.

"Detroit," Barrigar repeats.

"So, that's a little whacked out, isn't it? To start in Detroit, go east to Pittsburgh, then make this big right turn in order to get to your real destination—which we think is probably K.C."

"So, the Canadians are looking to see if she came over the border from Windsor, which would help explain all the Vermiglio Amtrak shit . . ." says Barrigar.

"We focus on the blonde's origins in Detroit and, I'm just sayin', soon we are going to have her mama, daddy, and her granny," Chamai says, smiling.

"No police warning." Sam is not smiling. "You have to take away the suicide option . . . We can't let any of these people kill themselves like Yaghobi did." He feels his heartbeat quicken. He needs to convince them. They have to understand.

"They have had the word laid down, Sam. I talked to Roycroft this morning and he spoke to the mayor and the chief of police personally. Joe Norment says his best CDC regional people are on it. They track either one of these women down, they observe, then it's you and the negotiators. And backing you up is a full extraction team, including a medevac team—"

"Good," Sam interrupts, not really meaning it, knowing that, like all plans, this one has built into it a genetic code of potential failure. "Good," he says again, and walks away, shaking his head.

Uncomfortable. Knowing how many things can still go wrong.

So, it's not *good*. Not at all.

Noise. Someone . . . something. Knocking. She is awakened from a black sleep by the sounds. Someone running. For an instant she thinks it's a dream. Then remembers where she is, and from the sound, she knows—yes, someone running down the hall to get the front door—

—a squeal of distress—*Nadja*—

—and now she is up, fighting her way free of the blankets, standing and leaping back, all the way to the end of the big sofa, everything by reflex and not really grasping what is—

—realizing the sound was Nadja running *away* from the front door . . . Now the sound of glass breaking in the kitchen. A sudden smash against the front door, and Nadja screaming to Paulina to get up, get up, get up, and *run*!

Someone kicking open the kitchen door—

A man comes through the curtains by the recliner. He has a pistol in his hand and he stops when he sees her crouched at the end of the sofa, her feet involuntarily kicking away the pillows, trying to back away, even if it means pushing herself *through* the wall. She stands up and sends a lamp clattering to the floor.

"What's your name, sissy?" Now he's got her in the corner.

He is tall. Thin, wearing a dirty white dress shirt. He must be the one Nadja saw circling the house. And they'd all made fun of her.

The front door crashes in and a man comes falling through, catches his balance and stands there on the threshold. "Hey, little sweet one?" he calls.

He is short, only a little taller than she is. His skin is olive. His eyes dark. He is wearing a fedora and a suit in tones of black, gray, and steel blue.

"Where are you, my little sweet, sweet?" he shouts.

She can hear Nadja and Paulina screaming, furniture being slid around, and thumps on the wall where they are barricading themselves inside.

"This her?" the white man calls out. Niv-L—for she knows immediately that he is Niv-L—looks around at her for a split second and then just steps past her and down the hall.

"You don't give me any trouble now, sissy," the white man says. He reaches out and grabs her breast, then leaves, out into the hall and down to where Niv-L stands in front of Paulina's bedroom door.

"You know I need to speak with you. It's better if you help me out, you know? I don't want to hurt you. But if you don't help me out, I'm going to cap your asses . . ."

The women's screaming in Russian has not stopped all through Niv-L's presentation of his demands, and now there is a sudden shout followed by an explosion of glass from where they have tossed something through the front bedroom window. Niv-L throws his weight hard against the door and then fires two bullets into it. The white man turns and begins to run down the hall toward the porch, his gun out.

And as he gets to the front door, Daria steps into the hall and shoots him in the ear.

It knocks him sideways, and he crashes face-first into the door-jamb and falls backwards at her feet. Niv-L is running down the hall straight toward her. They both swivel their guns toward each other but she fires first, lunging toward him and pulling the trigger—the bullet going in beside his tie through his breastbone. She fires again. A second bullet into his face, pitching him back onto the hall floor, where he begins to leak a great pool of blood.

Her ears are ringing and everything sounds muffled, but she hears something behind her and she jerks around to see Nadja holding the baby in her arms, gaping at her. Behind her Paulina emerges from the porch, dressed only in a T-shirt. "Oh, God . . ." she whimpers.

There is a rumbling sound, and Daria stares past the sisters to where Brutus's car is turning into the driveway, boxing in another car . . . it can only be Niv-L's.

Now Paulina and Nadja are in the hallway, turning, trying to step away from the blood leaking out of the white man's head. Daria still holding Officer Preston's gun as Brutus runs up. He stares openmouthed at the carnage. Nadja keeps trying to shut the broken door that won't shut, and Paulina has stumbled away into the living room with the whimpering baby.

She looks down at Niv-L. His face has been warped by the bullet so that his teeth are exposed. As if he were still hungry for something.

"Hey . . ."

Niv-L's arms are curled up and his hands clutched over his chest. There is only a little spot in the shirt where her first bullet hit him, but there must be a lot of damage in the back for him to bleed out this way.

". . . we got to clean this up. Hey . . . *Daria,*" Brutus snarls, pushing her roughly. "Get your shit together, goddamn it!" He punches her, hard, on the shoulder.

"Yes . . ." she says, taking the gun and tucking it in the band of her jeans. Brutus winces, gently pulls it out by the butt and flicks the safety on, and gives it back to her. "Don't want you to hurt yourself by accident," he says.

Paula steps out of the living room and holds Daniel to her cheek, stares down at the dead white man, then over at Niv-L.

"Thank you," she says to Daria. "Thank you, very much."

They find the keys to Niv-L's Mercedes and drive it all the way around the rear of the house and park it with the trunk close to the back door, because it is Brutus's plan to get the bodies out that way.

The freshly cleaned laundry from the night before is used to sop up the blood. They pad the trunk with garbage bags, and with Paulina and the baby keeping a lookout, they wedge the two dead men into the trunk, bending their knees and fitting them in like spoons, the car sitting down on its suspension with their weight.

The shards of glass from the front window, the broken mullions, get swept off the porch. The door is shattered around the lock, but Brutus knows where he can find a new one. It is a frenzy of cleaning; Daria mops and empties the bloody water down the drain, then pours bleach all over the floor and repeats.

The day has passed and the sun is slanting low through the jungle beside 3050 when she tosses her duffel into the backseat of the Mercedes and turns to the two sisters and the baby, leaning over the porch railing.

"Seattle, remember," says Nadja, and Paula looks at her and smiles. "You will be there," she commands.

And she is not able to say a word. Nothing, not even to say that she is sorry—they wouldn't know why she would even say that—and all she can do is put her fingers to her lips, to her heart, and climb into the car. She coasts down the cracked driveway, trying to imagine seeing them all in Seattle or Portland or Honolulu in some future, but she can't. Her tears run down her face and her heart begins to flutter as she cruises behind Brutus through the still neighborhood.

The house he has picked out is only a few blocks away. She watches as he slows, flicks his turn signal, and when she looks across the street, she sees it. Made of tawny brick, with a plywood-covered front door and windows.

She pulls up the driveway of the abandoned house and parks in the shadows behind it and waits as the darkness gathers. Sitting in the cool listening to crickets, and far across the neighborhood an owl asking its question over and over again.

A minute later Brutus comes whistling up the driveway; he has a paint bucket in his hand and a crowbar. "Okay," he says. "Let's get it opened up." He steps up onto the back steps, inserts the crowbar behind the plywood, and pops it off.

She opens the trunk and together they pry the bodies apart and roll them out onto the ground. Niv-L is too heavy. His clothes are soaked with blood, and it is impossible to carry him up the steps properly. He falls onto the dusty ground and they get him in the house by each taking a foot and pulling him up the steps.

"You know what he did to those girls?" Brutus asks as they tug him up into the house. "He'd let his friends rape them. He'd throw a party and his friends could do them as much as they want. So I'm glad this motherfucker's dead . . ."

They have worked out something to tell Monica, and Brutus will have his friends begin repairs immediately. He can move the men's guns, no problem, and the sisters can make good use of his money. The same with the white guy's van. "It's already been stolen," he laughs. She has a few days' head start, Brutus tells her, time where she can drive the Mercedes before she'll need to disable any antitheft chips that are part of its ignition and GPS system.

"You got until they identify this asshole. Then that car is going to be way too hot. You have to lose it by then."

"I'll be in Las Vegas by then."

"Most of those casinos are on quarantine, I heard."

"Well . . . I'll find a way."

"You are stone cold, Daria." He says it with admiration.

They get all the garbage bags, and shoes that have fallen off, and anything else in the trunk that looks incriminating, wipe everything down, and carry it all up into the house.

Daria closes the trunk, and finds Brutus inside the house dragging the two men deeper into what once was a dining room. The house is completely vacant. Only slivers of streetlights filter through the plywood panels covering the windows.

He comes to the kitchen door and finds the bucket, pries open the top and discards it, spinning it like a Frisbee deep into the dark innards of the house. There is a chemical smell.

"What is that?" she asks.

"This here is floor sealer. It'll work fine."

He pours a pool of the sealer around the men, then makes a long thick river away from them. It smells like when they fix roofs on a hot summer day.

He finishes his river at the top of the steps, and then tosses the bucket back inside the dark house.

"You going to stick around and watch?" he asks, looking up at her. "Maybe not. If people see that car around . . ."

He lights a cigarette, takes a draw, then takes the book of matches, tucks the flap closed over it, and stands it edge up in the sealer to burn down.

"It's time," he says after he has prepared the fuse. "Let's get out of here, girl."

He gets in the Mercedes and she drives to where he's parked the Pontiac. A place where the street rises and they can get out and see. Together they wait until the fire takes hold in the abandoned house. It is just smoke at first, then they can see red light coming from the back. When the flames break through the roof, she cannot escape Brutus hugging her, lifting her off the ground and twisting her side to side, like a rag doll. "I love you. You are stone cold, Daria, stone cold . . ." he says, over and over, finally putting her down, still laughing.

There are still no sirens.

"You better get on the road," he says.

"I guess so. *Yes*." She turns and climbs in the Mercedes before he can see her crying. She looks up anyway and waves at him when she starts the engine. The duffel bag is on the seat beside her, the pistol tucked under the zipper, right on top. "Bon voyage," Brutus says, leaning on the door of his car, holding up one hand as if he were taking an oath.

She starts off down the street, past the burning house that has lit everything orange, one hand in the smoky air to let Brutus know how much she loves him.

How much she loves them all.

"Doc, Doc . . . Wake up. Time to go . . ."

Someone, somewhere, has made a decision, it seems. Dr. Samuel Watterman, the distinguished biowarfare and bioterrorism consultant, sits up and tries to shake off his profound depression. Chamai tells him that he's being loaned to the Kansas City field office as tech backup to the senior FBI negotiator who will be orchestrating the dialogue with Vermiglio when they find her.

"It's all going down as we speak. Leaving the complex in ten."

He has no possessions, so there is nothing to pack. He spends what little time is left on the phone to the hospital.

Nakamura tells him they are trying to determine if it is possible to do an operation, but because of Maggie's general health, the doctor holds out very little hope. Irene says she hasn't woken up again.

A thirty-second shower, an electric shave.

It's the decision process that takes up most of the time, he thinks. FBI Special Agent Grimaldi's coming along, it's been decreed, to be his nurse.

And then—everything goes swiftly. Over a span of minutes: a blacked-out panel truck up the state highway to the helipad, maybe another half hour to a deserted airstrip where a business jet waits. From there to Kansas City it is supposed to be only two hours.

But it feels much longer.

Almost as soon as he takes his seat in the Department of Homeland Security jet, Grimaldi links him up via super-secure laptop to a National Response Plan crisis-update teleconference.

There are twelve thumbnail windows rimming the screen, and a larger image in the center to display the sleep-deprived face of whoever is talking. Right now it's Major General "Gordo" Walthaer.

"... *on the analysis of DNA we have sampled, conclusively demonstrate that the Berlin variola strain—itself a derivative of India-1—has been further modified...*."

"Oh, God ..." Grimaldi says beside him. "Is this what you were talking about, Sam?"

"Yeah, I'm afraid so ..."

"... *the new strain has the human gene for IL-4 combined into it. This has produced extraordinary lethality, the effects of which are becoming rapidly apparent...*."

With his finger, Sam can enlarge the faces of all those at the meeting. Deputy Secretary of Homeland Security Elaine Ordoñez is in the chair. Roycroft is absent. He's sick, it turns out.

"... *and the CIA has told us that it's their belief that a terrorist subcell, one of the smaller groups who were part of the so-called coalition—*"

"That's Khan's cell ..." he says, unable to not interrupt.

"*Yes, Dr. Watterman. Khan. Just as you predicted, his smallpox is a true 'superpox' and its release is part of what we can only suppose is a greater strategy.*" Walthaer pauses, straightens the papers in front of him.

"*If you've got something to say, Sam, now's the time,*" Joe Norment says, but for once he's not being sarcastic.

"It's a betrayal. On the surface, Khan's going along with his coalition's plan, but in reality he probably has a grudge, or a list of grievances. He might not like his allies or even think they're competent; nevertheless, he's played along. He helped them launch their India-1 attacks, maybe loaned his expertise to help produce the anthrax. But from the beginning he was careful to hold back the tweaked pox. And he's the only one who has the cure."

"I'm sorry, I think it's important to add that all this is just speculation," Norment says, shaking his head.

"Khan let his pals do the heavy lifting; they released the India-1 strain—we still have no accurate idea of the number of sites. That, all by itself, is going to be effective; there will be a big die-off. But right behind it comes a second wave, Khan's superpox, designed to finish off anyone who is left. It's betrayal," Sam insists.

"I can't read the mind of a terrorist," Norment says, *"but I can tell you we had this superpox sampled in thirty-one hours, and AVI BioPharma is the lead contractor working to synthesize an antisense patch. Yes, it will take some time to rule out toxicity. We have fully implemented our experimental vaccination programs, and are fast-tracking inoculation development. . . ."*

With the slightest touch of a finger, Sam enlarges Norment's face. The CDC director is actually smiling. The final absurdity.

"And meanwhile we have Sam's serum strategy."

"Yes, meanwhile . . ." he says. It's not much and everybody knows it. The serum strategy is a stopgap. An understudy. The big money and the big push will go into developing an antisense patch—essentially a killer genetic sequence that will neuter Khan's superpox—but while they wait they can hedge their bets by following Sam's idea to clone antibodies from plasma taken from any of Khan's inoculated terrorists.

And right now there is only one terrorist alive who may carry a cure in her bloodstream—Vermiglio.

"You think they stopped with smallpox? Don't be so fricking naïve. You liberals, you just pull the rose-colored glasses down and imagine everyone is rational. These people are the exterminators of the American Dream. They unleashed the anthrax—that was their shock troops. The smallpox is their tanks. The stem rot is their infantry. Hello to you, Charlotte, North Carolina . . ."

"Hello?"

"You're on, Charlotte—"

"I just wanted to know about the possibility of ship-borne bioterroristic activity. I was in the Navy and there's an awful lot of places to hide things on a boat—"

"Yes, there are, Popeye, and we have been screaming day and night about the criminal laxity of the U.S. Customs Service in our ports."

"They have scanners . . ."

"Indeed they do. They have scanners that scan for radioactivity, but have you ever heard of lead?"

"That's my point."

"And mine too. Go ahead, Newton, Nebraska. Are you an agriculturalist, Newton?"

"Yes I am, Ray. Proud of it."

"Go ahead."

"They told us to plant all these seeds, all these seeds that they had engineered. Then last night the Agriculture Department made the announcement that there's this rust—"

"Stem rust—It's a fungus that gets on the wheat. The spores eat into the stem and take over. Vampires, that's what these spores are. They take over the plant and it turns into a zombie. The zombie takes up all the nutrients. Ug99 that's what it's called."

"And this was developed in South Africa . . ."

"That's right, and you know what happened there, remember? They had their own arms industry, they had some very sophisticated technology for sale. And their Best Friend Forever was the Israeli government of the day. Don't forget. Lotta arms deals and police training going back and forth. Righteous act? Feel free to judge, my friends. . . ."

"You know, we had a meeting this morning with one of the USDA scientists they sent out. They say we might lose seventy percent of our wheat this next harvest."

*"Seventy percent, ladies and gentlemen. My God . . .
you poor folks. I hope you can pull through. This is a crime.
I've said it. It's a crime—"*

"That's right, Ray, it is."

*"If it wasn't for you, Newton, there wouldn't be any
daily bread to break. Go ahead, Seattle, Washington. Some
great Washingtonians down through the years. I'm a George
Washingtonian myself. Go ahead, Seattle . . ."*

Staring into the velvet night, she drives. Most of the time she's
the only car on the road. Kansas City fading into a memory with
each mile she racks up in Niv-L's lush Mercedes.

The wind has come up and in the distance there is a thunderstorm and lightning flashing down. It's not hard to push this car up
to autobahn speeds, and for long stretches the highway is smooth.
All of the roads in this part of the country extend to eternity, as wide
open as you can get. A spray of rain comes and she has to touch the
wipers a time or two to get the bugs off, but that's it.

Her only idea is to put as much space and time between her and
the people at Fifty-second Street as possible. She'd had it all set up
to leave earlier, but she fell asleep. She'd been too tired, and just
crashed, that's all.

So, was it written? After all, she *was* there to save them from
Niv-L and his partner. That was a blessing, wasn't it? The girls and
the infant would surely have been caught, tortured, and killed if she
had been able to keep herself awake. So . . . she was there, there with
a gun at the right time, and no one was going to hurt that child, no
one. . . .

Was it a sign?

No. No, she does not believe in signs anymore. All she believes
in is getting down the road, speeding across the gut of the great
American beast. Two days and she'll set Niv-L's car on fire . . . or
just abandon it for someone else to steal.

Then . . .

She'll walk. And keep on walking.

". . . a total of 124 anthrax fatalities in the United States. Smallpox cases for the entire nation are reported to be greater than twelve thousand, but the incubation rate pushes this much higher."

Revealed to her by the radio, the statistics of what she has been part of change hourly. She drives. She listens. Peering through her windshield, she sees only a sliver of a world gone mad. At Topeka all exits from the interstate are barricaded. Gas stations are open, but deeper entry into the city is only through ramps guarded by Kansas state troopers.

She had played her part as Pestilence, and now others are playing theirs. Now there is talk about Famine in the winter. Now there is War.

So . . . even though she can't see much evidence of victory, as she blazes across the rolling Kansas countryside, once again they are telling her that she has won.

It gives her no pleasure. It doesn't feel like winning. It's true insanity to call this winning. The hell that she has helped unleash is busily destroying its perpetrators along with their targets.

"More worrisome, at least two different varieties of the variola virus have been analyzed by laboratories including the Army's USAMRIID facilities in Frederick, Maryland, whose staff stayed on the job despite suffering a direct biological attack. Their discovery, that one varietal of the pox has a higher resistance to existing vaccinations, is being taken as evidence that at least one strain has been genetically engineered. . . ."

Armageddon—look how fast they embrace it! This, finally, is the long-promised death-wish fulfillment. Scales are falling from the eyes of Americans with every undulation of the road. The first roadblocks, set up with automated signs and flashers, warning her away if she was even thinking about turning . . .

ENTERING NEWBERVILLE
QUARANTINE
RESIDENTS ONLY

. . . a lone patrol car at the top of the ramp.

Scanning and seeking, she lands at *All Things Considered* on KPR, which is reporting that American municipalities are interpreting quarantine regulations differently. It's a lawyers' paradise; there are federal, state, and municipal laws, regulations, punishments, penalties, and appeals administered by a forest of government agencies. Jurisdictional disputes have already sparked challenges expected to hit the Supreme Court within hours. Taken all together it's a net gain for Chaos.

She drives, and listens . . .

Martial law is to be extended in the District of Columbia, after the president meets with a delegation of both houses urging him to completely quarantine the capital.

Two men have been killed in Springfield, Illinois, where they had been surprised in a cornfield and, instead of surrendering, had run.

Tété has died. Succumbing in a "hot ward" of the special military hospital where he had been quarantined.

Thirty-seven people have died from anthrax inhalation in the Emory University neighborhood near the Centers for Disease Control and Prevention in Atlanta.

Most frightening is the breaking news of the food attacks. Fear of fear itself. It comes out in the jittery voices of the newscasters and in those who are being interviewed.

It is chilly when she fills up outside of Wichita. It's a city she has never heard of and struggles to pronounce, thinking that *Whycheetah* sounds best. She purchases half a dozen cans of soda from a vending machine.

The bathroom is locked, and the interior of the station closed. The attendant in her booth looks to be in her late forties, brown skinned, but with the mask she's wearing Daria can't begin to guess her race. She wears sanitary gloves and the money goes through the microwave before she makes change.

By dawn every state has mobilized their National Guard Units to assist with quarantine and triage. Three times she passes through agricultural checkpoints where the highway is funneled down to one lane and men in rubber suits wash down everyone's tires before they are allowed to proceed.

A few miles later she passes a group of obvious refugees—a laden-down camper van, followed by a pickup truck. Both vehicles are crammed with possessions. Leaving the rest behind and getting out of the . . . out of the *Rust Bowl*.

That's what they are calling it. She punches her way across the radio bands and listens to the sounds.

The arrows have struck home and now the beast is dying.

". . . the FBI is investigating more than two hundred and fifty people who may have had some connection to the attacks. . . . Omar Sofiane, Abu Yassin Ismail, Daria Vermiglio, Marina Koslova, along with Prana Gil and Delmos Gil, are still being sought. Angela Motosi and her son were apprehended on Wednesday at the border outpost of Del Rio, Texas.

"Rioting has broken out in Mexico City. For the latest, here is Janine Cathcart of the BBC. . . ."

Daria slows the car and takes refuge under an overpass, opens the door and squats down and pees. A dozen semis rumble by along the interstate. Then nothing. She stands for a moment looking down the endless highway. It's so quiet she can hear birds singing.

She turns and surveys the length of the highway. What is she doing here? What chain of logic brought her to this horribly artificial landscape? She is as out of place here as she would be on Mars.

Lost and alone.

All she wants, all she really wants, is to be home. Even with all its squalor and its poverty, it would be better than this dying high-

way. She remembers stoned conversations with schoolmates in Florence. Some said there were different dimensions, that everyone had
an infinite number of alternative lives, that the rules of physics did
not apply universally. There are realities in which she is still back in
her house, realities where her family is alive and happy. In such
variations maybe she could teach her mother how to laugh again.
She suddenly tears up and grinds her fists into her eyes until she can
see.

The wind has risen, and she decides that she will just stay under
the overpass. She knows that's what they do in this part of the world
when the storms come. How she knows it, she can't remember.
Something from a movie probably.

She will wait. Until tomorrow sometime, until she is dying, and
then she'll surrender. Surrender and then . . . die. Hopefully faster
than Tété did, so they can't torture her and trace her back to the
sisters. To little Daniel.

She knows what the prosecutors would say: Nadja took care of
her, Nadja had harbored her. There would be no getting around it,
because she had.

It would fall on Monica too. And Brutus, who would have loved
her if she only had let him.

No, she can't stay here, regardless of how tired she is. Some
well-meaning trooper will come along, and then it will be all over
too soon. Tormented, she climbs in the car and pumps up the volume.

It is a howl, the sound that comes out of her.

It conflates and expands, from a sob to a shriek, as she lets her
voice climb over the early-morning Wichita country-rock radio,
which is when she learns how to say the name.

It's the West she's heading for, and she blows along the interstate, rejecting the turnoff for Oklahoma, putting the rising sun over
her shoulder; and she keens along with the steel guitars and violins.
Singing to the commercials, and even with the backup singers as
they do their lead-in station identifications.

Probably lots of people have been crazy in Niv-L's car and she's
not the first.

She pounds the leather steering wheel and sings: a list of her friends' names, all the people she will never see again, a cry from the heart for little Daniel, who only deserves happiness, a long hymn for Tété, an angry rant for Ali, whom she loved, or at least thought she loved. But he used her, didn't he? So why should he escape? The announcer on the radio says something and she yells back, correcting the news, refuting their points. Mocking their accents and intonations, debating, and crooning to the radio, to the car itself, to the people who built it, to Niv-L . . . She's her own private DJ and she's broadcasting to everyone in Kansas, to the solitary birds, the distant water tanks, the phone poles, and road signs and billboards that warn her what to expect ahead. . . .

When she comes to her senses, she has lost herself down some broken and patched state highway, way out in the amber waves of stubble, and it's been more than an hour since she has seen another human being. She can't stop thinking about Daniel, that beautiful new child. His face is like a knot in her chest that turns tighter, tighter . . .

She's running. She has to run. Running away is all she knows and she races down the cracked pavement, accelerating to insanely criminal speeds, wanting to let everything go, to breathe and let all of it wash away in the wind—herself, her past, every stupid decision, every foolish dream, all her second-guessed delusions, her very being—and wash it all away behind.

But at the edge of Calista she runs over a brown dog, and when she gets to Pratt she's still screaming.

DAY 14

Upon arrival in Kansas City Sam Watterman had been locked down in a specially quarantined FBI "hotel"—for his own protection. Since then, nothing.

Chamai has vanished. Grimaldi, on whom he now realizes he has developed a sort of senior crush, is all the way across town doing something more important.

He calls Alice at the hospital but there is no answer.

He sits in his room, stares at the furniture. There is no one to talk to. Barrigar and all his homies are still back there in chicken land.

His driver knocks at the door. A plastic bag with new clothes—a blue FBI jumpsuit and stiff black cap in a plastic bag. They're supposed to be downtown in ten.

They drive through a tawny city of endless horizons and sparkling skyscrapers. He tries another call to Atlanta and gets Irene. He can tell from her voice how much she has been dreading his call. *"I'm so sorry for you, Dr. Watterman,"* is how she begins the conversation.

"How is she doing?" Somehow he is able to manufacture his I-am-in-control voice once again.

"She's slipping away, she's slipping away on us. I'm so sorry—"

and here he can hear Irene starting to cry, a snort, and then a little murmur.

"Ahh . . ." For a long moment they both stay there, breathing on the line. "Is she in any . . . pain, do you think?" he asks gently.

"No . . . no, she's just . . . starting to breathe irregularly and, you know . . . her heart is wanting to shut down. She'll be resting soon, Doctor."

There is a constriction in his throat, his breathing stops. He swallows.

"I'm so sorry; she is such a beautiful woman," Irene says, careful not to use the past tense.

"Can you ask Nakamura for morphine? If she is in pain or discomfort, well then . . ." He says everything he needs to without actually saying it. Let her rest, he is thinking. Just let the poor girl rest.

"Oh, yes. I asked and he said he would check on her at lunch and decide, and go over it with you."

"So . . ." Remembering to calculate the time zones, he checks his wristwatch, only to discover it has been taken off him at some point in the process. Probably for his own protection. He cranes over the seat and peers at the clock on the dashboard of the FBI Humvee. "I'll phone later, okay?"

"Yes, sir. Of course. I'll be right here with her. I won't leave her, not for a second. Do you want to say something to her? I can hold the phone up . . ."

For a moment there is silence. Then Irene's voice, a little distant. *"There you go . . ."*

"Hi . . . Maggie," he says. "Hi, hon . . ." It feels incredibly awkward. He imagines Irene at the bedside holding the cell phone up to Maggie's ear. He can hear her ragged breathing. For a long moment he falls silent. "I love you," he says because it's all there is, finally. There are no real words that matter anymore.

The raid on the house where Vermiglio is hiding is nothing like on television.

Nor is it a car chase. Indeed there is no panic at all. Just cops being cops, driving easy and fast, big V8 horsepower whisking him down broad thoroughfares, the streets cleared by the flashers and an occasional screech from the siren of the car that takes him into Brush Creek.

Sam rides in the backseat alone, dressed in a biohazard suit, already sweaty, the hood pulled back. What he can hear from the radio is only cryptic phrases; numbers, abbreviations. At first he finds the constant chatter to be an intrusion, then he ceases to listen.

Out the window of the squad car: dogs on chains barking, a cat streaking out of the way, policemen going house to house evacuating everyone, old people looking out their windows, a man with a hose trying to keep his garden alive, another sanding the fender of a car beneath a portable white plastic tent. One by one their day is being ruined. Mothers hurrying away with children in their arms. Nobody wants the bug. Still, one angry old man yells at the cops from his back steps that no matter what happens he'll never leave.

The car slows, accelerates, then slows again as they pass through a series of checkpoints. The Kansas City PD and local FBI have blocked off a six-block perimeter around the Vermiglio house. Ahead are ambulances. Everybody in masks. Then a brand-new orange truck and a cluster of people wearing biohazard suits with self-contained air. The house looks like it has already been through a siege. Plywood tacked up over one of the front windows. A mismatched front door painted lime green.

It's early. It's quiet. Inside they won't know what's coming.

Black-clad emergency-response cops whisk him behind the ring of trucks to meet senior FBI negotiator Kandyce Schumacher. She's in her fifties and relentlessly cheerful. Sam almost expects her to hand him a tray of cookies. She's seen it all, she says with a smile, and has no plans to treat the Vermiglio suspect any differently. It's showtime, she says, and they walk toward the driveway of the house.

"This is Ms. Morton, she's going to help us," Schumacher tells him, turning toward a large woman dressed in a pink pantsuit and sturdy industrial shoes. Sam starts to put out his hand, but he is wearing biohazard gloves, so the two of them only nod at each other.

"Can I speak to them?" Morton asks, plainly upset.

"The people in the house? Yes, ma'am, we want you to help us speak with them; we want you to come with us and help keep things as calm as possible."

"I certainly will—there's a baby in there. *Paulina?*" she suddenly shouts, and steps forward, toward the driveway. Schumacher reaches out to restrain her, but Sam stops her. It doesn't matter. Everybody in that house has been exposed. Another five minutes isn't going to change things.

"Paulina?" the woman shouts again. From inside there are noises. Someone standing behind a door. Ms. Morton climbs the front stairs laboriously. "Everybody just chill out!" she says to the lime-green door, frowning as she takes in the patched-over windows.

Sam and Schumacher wait at the bottom of the steps. Through the hazmat suit he can barely hear the conversation that is going on at the front door. After a time, Morton turns back to them, motions, and he and Schumacher go up the steps. A young woman holding a baby backs away and erupts in terrified tears when she sees them in their orange suits. The baby wails and she retreats into the bedroom. In the gloom of the hallway, Sam can see the girl—the blonde, the one from Detroit—her face pale and stricken. A young man, black, barefoot, skin slashed with tattoos, comes out of the bedroom, holding his hands high where they can be seen.

"Please . . . we don't want to go back . . ." the girl says through her tears.

He calls Nakamura at noon to authorize the morphine. Since its use is risky, the doctor is careful to explain to Sam all the dangers. The man has a rich baritone voice, like a preacher or a psychiatrist. It's more what he doesn't say than the actual words he uses. Everything between the lines. It is a kind of dance, almost formal. They are both educated men, professionals. Realists. Both of them know what in-creasing Maggie's dose will mean. When Sam gives the necessary permission, he adds his thanks.

So . . .

Sitting there on the stainless steel back bumper of one of the hazmat trucks, staring at the pavement, lost in memories of his forty-year marriage to the beautiful girl he knew as Margaret Leah Klausner—his Maggie.

It was a good marriage. Often very good. Exquisite. Wonderful times. Laughs, epic fights. She was smart, incisive. Sassy. They were a pair of survivors through all kinds of shit, tragedy, sadness, sick-ness. Amy had died before them, and they had somehow—he would never have believed it at the time—but somehow they'd got through it. Hideous, crushing, terrible grief. But even with all the reversals, the setbacks and defeats, honestly, hadn't their lives been good? They had been blessed in so many ways.

His day-old FBI cop shoes are planted upon the worn pavement of Fifty-second Street. Asphalt and gravel. Cracks and patches. Oil stains and ellipses of chewing gum. Tiny rocks polished smooth by the tires of automobiles. What had lived there in those rocks? Tiny fossils. His poor girl. She is gone by now, he thinks, watching the rising sun slice shafts through the trees.

Gone.

"Dr. Watterman, the IC asked if you'd interpret some issues for the pool?"

He looks up at the boy. A soldier or a cop—it's increasingly hard to tell—barely in his twenties. Moving easy in his Kevlar and Gore-Tex, ready to give his life for . . . his IC.

"Sure." Replace grief with work, Sam tells himself. It's what he's always done. It's how he's stayed alive. He's always been a stoic.

While the Brush Creek suspects are being quarantined and inter-rogated, he is prepped for an interview with the local news. The FBI needs a face on the ground in Kansas City who knows what they are talking about, and he's it. A camera crew is standing by, and as he waits another two arrive. In minutes there are five cameras, and a couple of radio reporters pointing microphones at him. The cameras are amazingly small, not like the heavy, spine-bending minicams of his youth. Delicate-looking carbon-fiber tripods are spread out on the pavement; microphones are aligned. They are setting a fill light. He stands in the driveway. Surely by now, he thinks.

Someone gently conceals a speaker in his ear. A young woman comes by and combs his ratty hair, another puts powder on his stubbly cheeks. He stands in front of the now-quarantined house on Fifty-second Street. It could be anywhere in America. It could be next door. Someone's voice comes through his earpiece.

"Hello? Hello, Dr. Watterman?"

"Yes. I'm here."

"Brilliant. Connie is going to ask you some questions. Just look directly at the cameras and try to keep your answers short. Just wait for Connie, Doctor. . . ." The feed changes and he can hear "Connie," wherever she is, getting ready to start her questions.

". . . Dr. Watterman, this is all terribly technical and I'm sure our listeners would appreciate a layman's version."

"I'll try. What we're talking about are the interleukin genes. 'IL-4' refers to interleukin-4, which is part of our mammalian immune system; it's a cytokine which stimulates the production of antibodies in a mouse, or a dog, or a human, and helps fight off an infection."

"That's a class of chemical that is released by the cells?"

"That's right. It's a substance released by the cells into your bloodstream. Its job is to accelerate or retard your immune system. If the Berlin smallpox virus has been altered in a way similar to the Australian mouse experiments—"

"By adding this little gene—"

"Yes, simply by the addition of this gene, what would happen is, your immune system would malfunction, and overproduce IL-4. Basically, the immune system goes into overdrive and your body can't sustain that for very long."

"This sounds similar to HIV."

"The AIDS virus also destroys a critical part of the immune system. But a genetically modified smallpox virus using the IL-4 gene can collapse the system much more rapidly . . ."

"So, just by splicing this one gene, we get a dramatic change."

"Oh, yes. By engineering IL-4 or even a different interleukin gene into a natural smallpox virus, it's possible to confer on the new virus a resistance to existing vaccinations."

"Rendering the new virus super-lethal."

"Correct."

"You say this virus was first developed on mice?"

"Yes, in Canberra. Your audience might not know it, but there are many other pox viruses—mousepox, cowpox, lots of them. What the Australians did was to introduce the IL-4 mouse gene into mousepox. The result was one hundred percent lethal to mice."

"So, if this is true—"

"It's true."

"—then all of our emergency stockpiles we've been using to immunize our doctors and nurses, our military, our political leaders . . . are they any good?"

"For all us Boomers who had vaccinations as children— which was standard right through the seventies—we've lost just about all our protection anyway. For those who have received emergency vaccinations over the last few days . . . it's unknown how much protection shots will provide against this new strain."

"Can't we just make a new vaccine?"

"We can. We are. But there's a time factor. So until we have a new vaccine, we can take the serum from that small percentage of people who have been blessed with increased immunity, and use it to grow antibodies. But this is only a stopgap. It relies totally on an extremely limited number of individual donors."

"The magnitude of this is . . . well, it's staggering. You're saying this truly is a superpox."
"In a word, yes."

Daria is stunned, and then begins to tremble. This must be what Saleem Khan meant when he said the virus was on steroids. This is what he meant when he said she should be proud. The enormity of it. *Oh . . .*

This was the supreme achievement of God's scientists. A terror disease for which there was no cure. None of the shots that Monica gave them would be doing any good. . . . *Oh . . . oh . . .*

Sobbing, shaking, she forgets to drive and the car coasts to a stop on the dusty shoulder. She had no idea, she wants to scream . . . But it's no good. There is no excuse. Nothing she can do. Her tears come, and then stop, and finally it does not take long for her to realize that she should not have been surprised. Even after all she has lived through, she has still been innocent of the horrors men can do.

They will tear her apart when they capture her. Her name and face are everywhere. Brutus would kill her in a heartbeat, for what she's done to Nadja and Paulina and Daniel. She has condemned them all to death.

She will go . . . into the mountains. Hide. Suicide herself like the boy from Nigeria. Burn herself. It's what she deserves, after all.

The gun is there on the seat.

And she will use it.

Exhausted, she hallucinates driving through different borders. Or is she sleeping as she drives? No matter which direction she picks, it all looks the same. America is huge. Getting lost is very easy to do; traffic is light until it isn't. The semis travel in caravans. Plenty of official vehicles buzz by her. Ambulances and military vehicles. Refugees. People retreating home along the back roads of Oklahoma, then Texas, then Oklahoma again, and finally New Mexico.

As the news of the genetically engineered strain of smallpox is transmitted around the country, she notices that more people than she would have imagined are behaving in a contrarian way. She has to slow as she drives through the town of Clayton. There is a big dance—the men in white straw hats, the early October weather still warm enough to linger at the picnic tables spread out around the park. Breaking every quarantine rule in the book. Not a mask in sight.

What is that? Defiance? Stupidity? Denial? Faith?

Running the gauntlet is not hard. Masked and driving a very nice set of wheels, she is waved right through. Americans are not going to give up their freedom to drive, no matter what.

She pulls into a truck stop. Her side is throbbing and she hasn't eaten. Not very sane, really.

Inside, you'd never know that the world was ending. There is country music in the background. People talk, pull their masks down to eat, sip their coffee, then put them back up. Sometimes they stay down until a waitress comes along with a wink, or a cop gestures from across the room. Partly it's the natural tendency of people to demonstrate their courage. It's normal, she thinks. It's even charming.

There is a television, but she cannot bring herself to watch and is shown to a booth, buys a hamburger and fries with a big iced tea, and sits there staring at the placemats, which are decorated with a tourist map of New Mexico surrounded by cartoon characters, vistas of cliff dwellings, rattlesnakes with silly forked tongues. The kind of thing that you'd give to children with crayons.

When the waitress comes over, Daria sees that she is wearing latex gloves.

Over the waitress's shoulder the television shows her—Daria's—face. It is a new picture, one she has never seen before. Then she recognizes it as a happy moment from their little NASDAQ party in New York City. There's Burke.

And there she is. Smiling, a little drunk, lifting a glass to the lens. A girl gone wild.

"You see that?" she says to the waitress. The woman looks around. "That's me."

"Maybe . . ." the waitress says, looking back at her to compare.

"It is me. It could be me. I look like her, don't I?" With one finger she pulls down her mask.

The waitress frowns and squints back at the television. "Maybe . . ."

"It is me. I was her. I was that girl."

"You better cover up now, honey . . ." the woman says and moves on.

The burger, when it comes, is exquisite. The fries are a rich concoction of salt, fat, and starch. The iced tea is like drinking nectar. Halfway through the meal, she begins to shake and her nose starts running inside her mask. She can't finish the meal, and crawls out of the booth, takes a twenty up to the register, and leaves it beneath the cleansing light.

She is bloated and her stomach is cramping by the time she reaches the Mercedes. When she tries to get in, she is racked by a sudden wave of nausea and vomits across the asphalt. Retches another two or three times and then stands there coughing until the spell passes. The strain of her heaving has adjusted her rib yet again into some new position. It doesn't hurt any more or less, it's just different.

She falls into the car and drives. South, she thinks.

The road is crowned, cracked and bumpy with sudden potholes. Relentlessly straight across the desert. Dull and stupid, she steers with one hand on the wheel, staring out at the great expanse, careening over the bumps. It turns into an even crappier road, and she goes slower and slower until she realizes she is stopped dead. It takes someone blowing by in a pickup truck and honking the horn to wake her up.

She goes. West, maybe.

The next time she wakes, she does not know who she is.

Her memory is shuffled or missing. She is dazed. Going mad, but very slowly. She looks around at the interior of the car . . . How do they make these things? All the edges so carefully fitted together. Luxurious curves. Strong. Safe. Fast. Expensive.

Once again the steering wheel is before her. There is a pad at its center where the air bag nests. The covering is leather. Soft and resilient. The kind of thing you wouldn't mind having explode in your face.

She is chilled and groggy. She has no idea where she is. Apparently she's parked on some farm road. Everything is flat as a pancake, a horizon of brown fields. It reminds her of that old movie where the innocent man has to run away from the airplane.

Miraculously, nobody has bothered her, no cop has come along to render aid and assistance and seen the gun she left in plain sight on the seat.

On the windshield a solitary bee wanders among the remains of the dead insects smeared across the glass. There are no flowers there, no nectar for you, she wants to tell the bee. It buzzes and then stops, crawls a few more steps, and then starts the whole dance over again. It's sick, she decides. It's dying, too.

She pushes the door open with her foot, and tries to slide out under the steering wheel. It's the only way to move, because it hurts so much to twist. She can't get her breath, and waits for the broken rib to puncture her lung so she will die, drowning in her own blood.

Well. It would solve one problem.

She clings to the sculpted fender of the Mercedes and squats beside the rear tire and pees into the parched soil. Getting back up makes her groan and gasp. She takes off her T-shirt and inspects the wound by looking at the reflections in the windows and in the side mirror. It is all soft and yellow, spreading across the skin above and below the band of dirty white tape. Her skin is clouded with a red rash. Maybe she is getting the killer pox, after all. Maybe whatever antidote they gave her in Berlin is no good. If so, nothing can stop it.

No, she will never be a grandmother.

She pulls up her tights and walks a few paces, her legs and knees stiff. While sleeping she has kicked off her shoes and left them on the floor of the car. There are ancient cigarette butts and broken glass in the dirt of the road. But she picks her way, birdlike, everything rough beneath her bare feet.

Her breath comes in a fog, she runs her tongue around her lips and gums, spits into the dust. Her eyes are crusty and she stretches her face and tries to blink her way into wakefulness.

Nothing. Not a pickup truck, or a tow truck, or a paramedic, or a highway trooper. Were it not for the road, the plowed-to-death fields, and an infinite strand of electric wires, she could be in a primal state.

She stretches experimentally, trying to assess the hole in her side. It's acting up again. Something about the way the seats are not quite flat when they recline, but whatever position she slept in, the ribs popped apart.

Her mind floats back to 3050 and what everyone is doing. They will have found out by now. They will be cursing her. They will be in tears, crushed, terrified. They will have to give up or die, and if they decide to go to the hospital, they will be streamed wherever the authorities decree. Right from the beginning they will be manipulated into betraying each other. Paulina having to go through all that with poor beautiful Daniel. It's too much.

Maybe she can keep going. She has to keep going. They'll try to run too, and maybe she can keep going until they're safely gone from Monica's. It will only be a matter of days. She can give them a head start. They won't rush to the hospital—after all, they've all had the shots—but they will abandon the infected house as fast as they can.

She was careful there. She was clean. Maybe the smallpox, or the anthrax, or whatever it was had worn off her hands by then.

Yes, they will get away. They will find freedom and new identities in Seattle and no one will ever get sick again.

And that is her evening prayer.

Driving, she passes by a ruined building that someone has festooned with partially burned effigies of Arabs. Hanging from tree branches are the remains of bedsheet puppets meant to represent generic Bedouins—straw beards, an old fez, and something that is supposed to be a turban. Graffiti painted on the tawny brick walls:

Death to Islam Death

The Great Satan is Alive and Well!

Moslams eat shit

There are lights on in distant houses, dimmed by shades, and lit only in the back rooms. On the radio—the constantly breaking news, and afterwards some mournful jazz, or classic rock to help the listener forget.

DAY 15

The Mercedes has come to a stop on a gravel road beneath the only tree for miles. On a rise behind her is a low rock wall that runs along the side of the road for a few dozen yards, and behind that is a cemetery. There are a few tombstones, but mostly the graves are marked with wooden crosses. Several are decorated with feathers, miniature U.S. flags, cacti, and plastic flowers anchored in the stony ground.

She climbs out, gets to her feet and tries to stand straight. Takes the roll of toilet paper and goes behind the tree to urinate.

When she wipes herself there is blood, and she realizes that she has lived long enough to be cursed one last time. She wads up more toilet paper inside her panties and stands there for a while looking at the morning, and the graves, and the dried-out plants. It is remarkably like the hills around her village.

She had almost forgotten. The way the light fell in the dusty evening, the children shouting, radio broadcasts leaking out of windows, the smells of cooking, of trash burning. The face of her mother, never changing regardless of what fresh tragedy engulfed her. Her village. She misses it terribly.

She walks up the rise and into the cemetery. It is surprisingly large, and as she goes, she tries to pick up clues to who is buried there.

She knows nothing of these people, only what she's seen in movies. Is she on a reservation? Are these dead Apaches? Are they Comanches or Mescaleros? Navajos? Hopi? Zuni? There is not much of a clue. Many are proud veterans, judging from the flags and military mementos that have been left behind to ornament the homegrown monuments. The mixture of last names tells her nothing. They are the original Americans writing with someone else's alphabet, and now she is walking on their graves.

In the distance she hears a truck and for a moment she tenses, thinking she might have to run away, but it is only a man driving down the gravel road, and when he sees her he raises his hand in salute.

And then he's obscured by his own dust cloud and there is silence once more. The smell of sagebrush, and something on fire, far away on the wind.

Getting through the triage station at the next town is simple enough. She just pulls her mask up and drives through the traffic cones, routed through a pool that has been improvised from hay bales and tarpaulins and filled to hubcap depth with a blue fluid that smells like bleach. Cops and barriers keep her detoured around the town, past a large football field, behind a storage facility, and back to the main road.

There are too many cops eyeing her too-expensive car. She is nervous and turns off on a yet smaller road. She is in a desert landscape now. The fields are long behind her. Rocks and what looks like broken lava. The kind of terrain that only a reptile or an insect could love.

She's still looking to see if there are any pursuers in the rearview mirror when the pavement tees onto a wide gravel road. She brakes too late, swerving in the middle of the turn, the Mercedes skidding into a ditch and scraping on the rocks, but she keeps her foot on the gas and powers out of it, gets back up on the road pointed the right way. Now there is no one, it's just her and the cactus and the cows, and she's back on cruise control.

She turns the radio on and gets about fifteen minutes of tempestuous classical music—cathartic kettle drums like great waves crashing on the shore again and again until the composer is spent. It sounds insignificant against everything around her.

"Madame Secretary, all last night and today there has been angry rhetoric in Iran and troops are massing at the border. We don't know if they have nuclear capabilities, but we do know they are dedicated to the destruction of Israel. Obviously, there is the imminent possibility of a preemptive strike against Iran. If that happens it seems certain that we may find ourselves in the long-feared conflict in which weapons of mass destruction really do come out of the closet, or the laboratory."

"In this case the laboratory, certainly."

"This morning the Department of Homeland Security said the biological attacks were ongoing?"

"That's a reference to the agricultural attacks which are just now coming to light, but in the larger picture what's really happening is that there is a global cycle of discontrol. These are desperate, opportunistic, rapidly oscillating forces—"

"And the center might not be able to hold?"

The producers of the movie would save the shot for magic hour.

Natalie Portman would coast to a stop. Ahead of her, on the outskirts of a town called Coyote, there is a troika of concrete dividers skidded across the blacktop to form a barricade. Extending from the road on either side are palisades of junked cars and trucks. Someone has cut down the brush along part of the wall, and then stopped.

Silence.

They have left a way through wide enough for the trucks, and behind that a cutoff that leads into the gas station. This safe passage has been marked with reflective neon-orange plastic barrels. Down the centerline is a chicane made up of oil drums and dirt-filled garbage bags. From her angle she sees what she will have to do—drive up and slowly navigate through the walls, all the time under the guns of . . . the coyotes, presumably.

She slows to a crawl. If they are looking at her through a sniper's scope they can see her now. In the trees, off the road, there are broken-down houses. A black patch where a car has been burned.

She parks the Mercedes in the middle of a half turn, broadside, so she can get out of there if she has to. Waits.

This is finally it . . .

She gets out, holds her hands up above her head. "Hello . . ." she calls.

Silence. She has left the automatic on the seat, and is standing in front of the car where they can see her. Go ahead, she thinks, shoot . . .

She calls again. Nothing.

She raises the hem of her hoodie, spins around.

Leans against the fender and waits with her hands up. "I surrender," she says to the barricaded gas station.

Absolute quiet except for the wind.

Waits.

Nothing. All right, then. Besides, she needs water.

She gets back in, turns the car toward the fortress and drives a couple of dozen yards closer. Taps the horn two or three times. Drives on, right up to the opening. Ahead, at the entrance to the gas station, an improvised barbed-wire gate has broken and is propped up to one side.

She still has half a tank. The smart thing would be to keep on going. She idles past the pumps and parks again, leaves the car door open, and walks toward the station, still with her hands up.

"Hello . . ." From here she can see behind the barricade—past the chicane, a rusted container has its doors open. An office or guardhouse. A white plastic picnic table beside it with a Löwenbräu umbrella speared through its middle. A lonely turquoise-green portable toilet farther back on the other side of the road. Beyond it, more cars dragged up to block the side streets and force traffic down the gauntlet.

"Hello . . ." she calls again, louder.

Inside the station a light is on, but at the front door she sees the glass is broken. Some kind of cooking smell leaking out beneath the garage doors. Maybe from a barbecue. A dog begins barking when she pushes on the door, and she stops.

"Hold on just right there—"

There is a movement. At the corner of the garage, where the service bay door is partly raised. He has a rifle and he's dressed in what he must assume is camouflage: a military-style jacket, baggy pants, and what looks like rags wrapped around his face and head. He looks like one of the mummies from Michael Jackson's "Thriller" video.

She stops, raises her hands a few more inches, watches him.

"What kind of money you got?" the man says after a good ten seconds. Still lurking back there at his position at the side of the building. The rifle still aimed right at her.

"Money? Not much. Some. Maybe a hundred," she answers. The strange thing is that she is not frightened at all, and she waits calmly through a lengthy pause, as if the man were thinking through a math problem.

"Turn yourself around," he finally says.

She does, keeping her hands aloft. This would be best, she decides. A bullet in the back. It's the logical thing that should happen. It's over now, and she knows it, but she keeps on turning, and when she gets all the way around he's still waiting behind the walls of a little pillbox he's built from tires and sand-filled paint cans.

"What kind of food you got?"

"Not much. Crackers. A box of rations that they handed me when I got back on the highway. It's all in the car."

Once again he waits, making up his mind about something.

"I can kill you," he says. The voice is not exactly high-pitched, but thin. A sharp voice. It reminds her of crows. "If you want gas, you'll have to pay me with something."

"I don't need any gas. I was just looking for water," she says.

"Are you infected?"

From somewhere behind her, it's another voice. Someone using a bullhorn, one of those things police use to shout warnings to rioters. It is a woman's voice, sharp and to the point.

"I want to surrender," Daria replies, looking along the barricade, trying to figure out where the sound is coming from. She turns, takes a step away from the man.

"Are you infected?" the voice demands again.

"Yes."

There is a pause. Daria stands there, hands up. The sky is red with thick ropy purple clouds that look like they are boiling out of the distant mountains.

"My name is Daria Vermiglio. I am one of the wanted terrorists. I surrender," she says. And a few seconds later, when there is still no reply: "There is a warrant out for me. I want to surrender."

Maybe her voice is too quiet, maybe it doesn't carry across the expanse. She walks another five or six paces closer down the faded white lines and still there is nothing. She is tired; the fatigue makes her hands relax of their own accord down to her side.

There is a slight burble of static as the bullhorn is toggled back on: *"How do you know you're infected?"*

"I have a fever and . . . rashes all over my body . . ."

"I'm sorry. We don't have room for you, ma'am."

Even though it's getting dark, the heat is still radiating off the road; she can feel it wafting over her.

"Can I get some water?"

"Do you see the shed right over to your right?"

"Yes . . ."

"There's a hose there. Do you have a container?"

"Yes."

"Do not drink from the hose, and make sure you turn the faucet all the way off and put the nozzle back in the bleach when you're done."

"Thank you."

"When you leave, use the turnoff to the right and drive out on

the road heading west. You can't come through on this road. Go west. Do you understand?"

"Yes . . ."

"We give you the water, you gotta let me have something," the man says. He has risen up from his blind.

"All right," she says. Quietly. Submissively. That's what men like. Men like to bargain, they like to think they are making a clever deal. "We can do that, if you want," she says.

"You don't have to drive away so fast. You can stay for little bit."

"Good. I'll get the food for you." She goes back to the Mercedes, opens the passenger door, and gets the ration box. With one hand she gathers the automatic and holds it flat beneath the cardboard box as she turns, closes the door with her hip, and begins carrying it across the concrete toward the man at the blind.

"You want the food, here it is," she says. He edges out to see her more clearly. The rifle comes down. She is closer now . . . perhaps within thirty feet of him. This is what they mean when they say women are devils, tricksters who use their wiles to lure men to their destruction. This is why women cannot truly enter Paradise.

"Do you live here, in the garage? Is that your wife out there?" She sees her shadow lengthen across the pavement. The sun is low now . . . he probably can't see her face, but she still tries to smile, slows down her walking. She doesn't need to go so fast.

"Stop and put it down."

He's certainly no bigger than her. He is living inside the garage, she decides. She waits before complying with his demand, puts her weight on one hip. The gun is tight in her hand now, still masked beneath the box.

"Here," she says. "I'll put this down and go get the money . . ." She takes a step forward, slowly bending to set the cardboard box down on the pavement before him—

And then comes up, only a few feet away now, firing—and her second or third bullet hits him, she can't see where, but it knocks him backwards behind the tires, and she veers away, into the garage. She can see the end of the rifle, his leg struggling, hear his groans.

The dog inside barks frantically. Behind her is an explosion and a rattling of shotgun pellets and breaking glass. She ducks into the station. Out by the container she sees the woman. She is older. Slow when she runs, the shotgun heavy in her hands, she vanishes around the corner of the container.

On the front counter is a plastic case of rebottled water. Caps have been scavenged and sealed with cling wrap and rubber bands.

She takes a bottle and goes out the front door. Down the road, the woman is driving away in a Jeep, heading toward the second wall. As she passes through it, the bullhorn squawks, and the brake lights come on as she skids through the second chicane.

Daria drinks. A full bottle, right away. Then she gets another to take along, goes to the car, and gingerly lowers herself onto the seat.

Now she can see someone moving on the second wall, and she puts the Mercedes in gear and drives, veering off the shoulder, completely off the pavement into the brush, through what once was someone's yard. In the distance, a siren starts up. Another explosion. Gunshots.

She slews down the deserted streets of what must have once been a water hole, then a country store, then a town, now finally evolved into a tourist trap with razor wire. There is a hard snapping sound, then another, as their bullets smack into the Mercedes. She zigzags and stirs up the dust behind her, jerks the steering wheel and cuts up someone's driveway, through the backyard, crashing through a rusted swing set, flattening a chain-link fence, then fishtails out onto a wide dirt street.

Then straight ahead and it is only a few seconds until Niv-L's fine car is beyond their range. Gone, with the red sun low.

Out in the scrub, dust devils spring up and then die away. In the far distance there is a row of electric power lines, leaning at crazy angles as if elbowed by the winds.

She falls asleep and runs off the road, jerks awake, slewing the Mercedes the wrong way. The car slides and almost rolls over— bumping hard over the stones, not slowing down at all, crunching right over a metal fence post and snagging a single strand of barbed wire that claws frantically beneath the floor of the car until she skids back onto the pavement, drawing a loud blat from an approaching semi.

She wrenches the car over into the darkness as the truck blows by her, then she gets back on the road and follows him. It is a tanker with an immaculate paint job and a chromium tank and numbers and warnings emblazoned all over its rump. Minimum weights, maximum weights. Several different hazmat warnings, and the legend:

DANGER
FLAMMABLE CONTENTS

She becomes mesmerized by the huge chromium tank as they drive along together. One bullet is all it takes, at least in the movies. She has learned, she thinks, how to sleep and drive at the same time. It is very clever, something she could impress the other students in Italy with.

There is a loud bleating of the semi's air horn and she realizes that she has driven right up under the rear of truck, and she wrenches the wheel and accelerates around him, pushing the Mercedes down the blacktop. Waves to the trucker as she rushes past him.

She is awake again. She knows who she is. She knows why and how she got this way. She's sorry about it all, but what good will that do? The music lands on something that is supposed to be a tango, all elongated yelps from an accordion and complaining violins.

Foolish. The trucker will be on his radio. There is only a little of her water left, and she looks at it, wobbling there on the seat next to the automatic. Stupid.

A few miles later she bumps back onto another highway, turns again toward what she thinks is west, opens the sunroof, slows to a crawl and looks up for the North Star. When she finds it, it's almost in line with the road.

Directions . . . it doesn't matter much anyway. The engine of the

Mercedes is sounding a little ragged. The endless dust and grit might have something to do with it. Or maybe it's the little red light flashing on the fuel gauge.

And as she runs out of gas, the last thing she sees is a huge sign. It is a painting of a gray bulbous head with two black teardrop eyes, a tiny mouth, and an anorexic body, with one long three-fingered hand raised to the viewer and the slogan . . .

ALIENS AMONG US
12 miles

With the lights off and the windows up, Niv-L's car could be a quiet and comfortable camp there in the chilly desert. But they are onto her now.

She swivels her legs out of the car, gets the rucksack out of the back, digs through it for things she might need. The gun. Water, and something she can use for a hat against tomorrow's sun. She decides on a T-shirt that she can wrap over her head. The mask is useless now, and she pulls it off her face and lets it fall.

She puts the pack over her shoulder and begins to walk.

Across the pavement, just ahead, is a three-strand barbed-wire fence. Someone's property. Meaningless, she thinks, the idea of owning a place like this. She pokes the rucksack through and then slowly and awkwardly bends her way between strands.

The ground is a mixture of sand with rocks strewn through it. All the plants, all the animals, everything is greedy for water. She's got the remains of the bottle she killed for back at Coyote . . . it will have to take her to the end. There is a blurry moon rising. She aims for a low hill that rises out of the desert floor. There will be a view from up there, she assumes. Somewhere to die in peace.

She goes. One foot in front of the other. Not caring, not minding what happens. Her legs encounter thorns. The thorns pierce the flesh. What does that matter? She is at the end of her own mission now. Gone far beyond what she has been trained to do, or even what she agreed to do. All that is gone. All those decisions. All those mistakes, those obligations and allegiances. All of it. She can no longer see herself as she was a month ago. That girl . . . she is so . . . irrelevant. She's gone.

All that is real now is her next step through the briars.

She is too tired to look around very much. Watching her feet in the moon shadow as they strike the ground. She heads toward the hill—a low circular pyramid, something left behind by glaciers, mauled by the wind into a flattened cone that is barely a couple of hundred feet above everything else.

Walking along, she has glimpsed but now really begins to notice the shards of iron that are spread around the landscape. At first she takes them for rusty meteorites, until she gets across the flats to the base of the cone, where she discovers her first crater.

The bottom contains a pool of dust-covered water. Nothing grows around the rim. On the opposite side is the twisted remainder of a school bus. She walks around the rim and investigates the wreckage. Now she sees other craters all around. Bits and pieces of machinery scattered everywhere; she can look at each torn fragment and reconstruct the whole in her mind. This was once the chassis of a truck. That is not a rock, it's an engine.

Ahead of her is more wreckage. A big block of cast steel with milled surfaces gone rusty, and flaking paint. A twisted artillery tube, half buried in the soil; a length of tank tread.

She starts walking toward the crest, where she has decided to kill herself while she still can. She can look east and try to pray. Once she climbs a little she can see the craters stretching away to infinity. Behind her is the highway but the view is different as she works her way around the hill—it seems much farther away.

And now that she's gone around the slope, she sees that she's really ascending the toe of a long ridge. The whole thing climbs higher than she imagined. There is no sense of scale and distances are deceiving. From this height she can see lights down at the end of the valley. There must be something there. A wide spot in the road. A gas station, or a store. More likely a water tank. The sound of the dogs, alarmed by something, their barking floats to her on the wind.

There is a ledge, a long shard of layered rock that has yet to erode under the eternal winds that sweep down the valley, and she decides to rest for a time. Once hunkered down, she realizes how much better it feels to be out of the wind. And how quiet it is.

She pulls the pack around to use as a pillow. Her fingers are sore and cracked. She finds her digital camera, takes it out and flips through the photographs.

An archive from some other planet. Happy young people lifting glasses in a bar, Burke, one of the advertising copywriters, smiling firefighters, a blurry exterior out the window of the train, a portrait of the soldier she met on the bus, his name forgotten.

She fiddles with the settings, holds the camera at arm's length and watches the little red light blink until there is a blinding flash.

When her vision clears she looks at the result—some sort of wild Medusa, with great yellow and black circles under her eyes. A last testament. She puts the camera back in its case and holds it in her lap like a doll.

Out of the wind she will sleep now, and in the morning she will be stronger and go farther. She will lose herself out here and they will never find her, and she will hide herself away and then do it.

It's a little too much like Afghanistan, Acting Deputy Sheriff Lucinda Suárez thinks. Too much like places she's in the process of trying to forget. Somewhere out in the hills beyond Kandahar district maybe. Dry country. Rocky. Why would people fight so hard for something like this? Well, when it's all you have . . .

She is tired from working all day yesterday up on the interstate. Inoculations, arguing with truckers about their paperwork. People pissed once they got into rush hour from Albuquerque and Santa Fe. Having to work backup overtime because everybody—civilian, military, public health, and police—everybody is on edge. The masks only make it worse. You can't read anyone's expression.

The news? She doesn't even listen anymore. Instead she hears the buffeting of the wind, the hum of the tires, her heart's beat, and her lungs learning how to breathe. How to not think about what could be buried just beside the road, how not to flinch at any loud sound. She is learning how to be a woman safely home from a war.

For the first time in weeks, Luci Suárez's mother is happy. Well, there will be money coming in. She tells Luci not to worry about the long hours, or shopping, or doing anything around the house. There will be food waiting when she gets home, and even if she has to stay over down in Socorro, or somewhere else, to go ahead. And besides, maybe she'll meet someone, her mother says. Always pushing.

This road she's on, tonight 380 heading east past White Sands Missile Range, is almost completely deserted. Occasionally a pair of semis blow by. They've given her a magnetized flasher to put on the roof of her truck, which works by plugging it into the cigarette lighter; the radio has enough range to reach back to the office; she has a shotgun that she has put down on the floor, water, some sandwiches, and two new blue bags full of vaccine that might or might not do any good. Still, you have to inject anyone who wants to come across the county line. The law is the law. It's just another kind of army.

This is what two tours gets you, Luci thinks. Another four weeks of emergency duty and she can qualify for the Forest Service. Get outside. Get on with the adjustment. Move into the city. Put a little something aside.

New to the department, not much more than an intern, Suárez is on the night shift and is driving out to relieve another deputy at the entrance to the rec area. It's closed off, of course. Everything public is being closed off. Theaters, schools. Anywhere crowds of people are liable to congregate. The idea behind quarantine is to hunker down. Wait this thing out. That's the big strategy that's going to defeat the germs, that's the master plan the powers-that-be have come up with. Nobody really knows if it's going to work, she knows that. But nobody talks about that part.

And then she sees the car.

She takes her foot off the gas and slows, thinking at first that it's a wreck.

No movement.

A nice car. Expensive. A white Mercedes. Recent model, beat up, scratched and scraped up like it's been run off the road.

It's the plates that wake her up. From Michigan, vanity plates—

PLEH-AHH. And then she remembers something about it from the briefing.

She stops there in the middle of 380 and reaches into the blue bag and takes out the clipboard full of bulletins, riffles through the pages and . . . yeah, there it is.

She's heard the name, she's seen the face on television. Terrorist. One of the ones who started this whole mess. The car stolen in . . . Kansas City, it says.

Armed. Dangerous.

She slips down in the seat behind the door, unsnaps her automatic. Sniper, she is thinking. And then realizes where she is . . . well, there could be snipers in New Mexico. Sure. Maybe there could be, especially now, with everything coming apart at the seams.

She puts one in the chamber and angles the truck so her bright lights are right on the car. Walks out, keeping back, keeping the gun up. This is the kind of thing they'd do. Wait for you to check it out, wait for you to call for backup, wait for the medics to come. Wait, and then they'd pop it off. Looking for wires, sweat running down the small of her back. But she's not there anymore. No. She's back. She's home.

She circles and then goes right up to the Mercedes. No one. Nothing. Trash, empty water bottles. Clothes. Door left ajar and the battery dead.

In the dust, footprints and tracks all across the shoulder and up the little bank, scuffed up there where she climbed through the barbed-wire fence.

She's out there somewhere.

She toggles on the radio, and calls it in.

"Roger, seven-six. What you got?"

"Abandoned automobile, Michigan plates, Papa-Lima-Echo-Hotel-hyphen-Alpha-Hotel-Hotel on three-eight-zero before Valley of the Fires. APB suspect Vermiglio, D. H., shows tracks walking south into range at White Sands. Am in pursuit . . ."

DAY 16

Now he rushes. To board an FBI jet that will take him to New Mexico from Kansas City. Another sixteen-seater. There are rows of seats in the front, all first-class-sized. No frills, but nice. In the back is a meeting area where passengers sit facing each other railroad-style. He digs out his secure cell phone and gets Chamai, another nighthawk. He does the time zones: almost four a.m. back at the chicken factory.

"I don't know if you're in the right place at the right time or not, Doc."

"None of us are in the right place," he says to the young agent.

"As far as people who matter goes, there's a significant contingent who want to put most of the development bucks on building an antisense patch. I don't think serum immunity has the votes, Doc. You think you can win this one?"

"I don't know. I'm not God." The lights go off and they begin to take off. "I'll call you back." He closes up the cell as they move down the runway. His mouth is furry, he needs a shower. He's constipated from all the travel. His best friend in life is gone, his mind is exhausted, and his entire life has boiled down to toiletries and a cell phone crammed into an indestructible U.S. Customs Service backpack he snatched at the K.C. field office.

He slumps against the jet window. Below, the suburbs give way to the endless fields of Kansas as the FBI jets him into the darkness. He's not surprised at the news from Chamai, not really. It's only natural to want a magic bullet, and there's lots of money on the table if you can tweak a gene here and there and save the world. He digs out the cell phone and calls Chamai back.

"Okay, so what do you think is happening?"

"*I don't know, Doc, I don't get the political gamesmanship thing. It's psycho. It's sexy, but if you're looking for minimum friction, not much grows on it.*"

"Right. Okay, Aldo, sometimes when you talk, I just don't quite, uh . . . dig it."

"*Sure, sure, Doc. Sorry. Conventional wisdom says the CDC's the big dog. They are not just going to bail on their whole vaccination plan because you say so.*"

"Actually I never said drop it, and Joe will do whatever he wants, I'm sure."

"*But the new puppy in the window is Serum Security.*"

"What do you mean?" Sam is too tired to pick up the subtle stuff. Chamai can do mental loop-de-loops all day long that go right by him.

"*Okay, Doc, follow my logic. When you get Vermiglio you'll be starting from just one sample. Growing cell lines from that is going to take time . . . we're talking months at least, right? And people are freaked that things are going to collapse before any solution can get up and running. I'm sorry, Doc. I know you want to get some sleep.*"

"I don't sleep much these days."

"*Yeah, Doc. I'm sorry. Okay, well, FYI, they're working up a range of options for new triage guidelines as soon as serum becomes available. The slow growth rate is going to make them go very restrictive. At first it's going to be POTUS—Congress, the Supreme Court—*"

"Look, that's continuity-of-government stuff. Completely out of my control, Aldo . . ."

"*I know that, Doc. I'm just filling you in. Whoever has first dibs on the antidote and by how much, that's what I'm talking about.*"

There's going to be a list, and getting to the top of it is worth a whole lot. And when those names come out it's going to go viral immediately. There's going to be a heap of perceived inequities that pushes up the security issue. When you told me these blood products were worth something, I believed you, Doc, but nothing like this, man . . ."

"Right. That's realistic. Not pretty, but realistic."

"Exactly. The value of Vermiglio's blood products on the black market is going to go through the roof, Doc."

"We don't even have it yet, Aldo."

"Sure, but if you do, and when you do, you can see where I'm going, as far as security, I mean?"

"Weren't we going to give all this away? I thought that the policy was to share technology. Hasn't anybody said to Joe or Gordo that this is a *global* public health threat? We need to have four thousand labs working on it all over the world instead of whatever it is, seventy-five, a hundred? Or you could wait for things to completely collapse and then decide to do something, right?"

"Take a deep breath, Sam." It's Barrigar who has come on the line.

"I am, I am . . ."

"I was in the neighborhood and I caught the last part of that . . ."

"It's okay. I would never accuse a special agent of improper eavesdropping."

"Good man. So, what you're saying is . . . ?"

"I'm saying a lot of things. But what they should be worried about is flu season. People who have been getting flu shots or smallpox inoculations, anything that would trigger your immune system to go into gear—those people may well be vulnerable to a modified smallpox virus that uses a spliced-in immune system regulator. Paradoxically, all the fast-track vaccination programs might be actually *priming* people for the Berlin Pox."

"Well, they don't want to hear that, Sam . . ." Barrigar says, and there is a long pause.

"Oh . . . right. I know," Sam says, bitterly. The world is full of people who wish they were deaf.

"But look, I'm going to contact some people and get back to you, okay? We're taking off right behind you. . . ."

Sam flips the phone closed and looks out the window.

More of the same. Kansas, Oklahoma, Texas . . . all those places with straight-line borders. Agribusiness and oversalinization. Hormones and antibiotics. Every grazing animal tagged to prevent an outbreak of Creutzfeldt-Jakob disease. Perfectly circular lakes, holding ponds, water holes, and then the rebellious curve of a river, flickering silver in the moonlight.

The world is growing hotter. From now on, all through the development phase of a superpox vaccine, there will be increasing public health issues. The most likely cataclysm would follow an early spring. Warm, wet weather would lead to an epidemic of a vector-borne disease like West Nile virus, dengue fever, or malaria. If and when something like that should occur, it would stress the CDC past the breaking point.

Everything breaking. All over the world. Natural outbreaks combining with multiple biowarfare events. All occurring at more or less the same time, all that hell coming at once. *All-in.*

"All-in" was a joke, a category of simulation that had been branded as implausible, unlikely to occur, and too expensive to practice. You had to budget for time on the computers back in his day. So, why tie everything up and allocate megabucks to rehearse for something almost infinitely catastrophic? He remembered they'd done it once, to scare the shit out of everybody and help justify the funding, and then moved on to more plausible scenarios. After all, the damage in a typical Chemical, Biological, Radiological, and Nuclear drill was so huge that when you started adding multiple threats, the chaos grew exponentially.

All-in.

Too destructive to prepare for.

Asleep in the lee of the rock ledge, she alternates between bouts of unconsciousness and dreams of running down Florentine streets. Haunted faces peering from the arched doorways. She sees her mother, and someone who must be her father, but when she looks again, he's vanished.

She follows him—in and out of houses, beneath stairs, into tiny crawlspaces dank as tombs. Long after the man-who-must-be-her-father disappears, she's still being impelled down the streets, only now it's Manhattan and she is dodging traffic. Her father is laughing at her, turning around in the taxi and laughing at her . . . The dreams shift and churn. She does not really surface, but only slides deeper, dying a little more with each breath.

It's the helicopter that wakes her.

She feels it first as an earth tremor, then a great roar crashing over her so quickly that even with a bullet wound in her side she still jerks into a sitting position. The sky is a rim of blue above the mountains, and the distant police flashers throw spastic shadows out into the desert.

She is much too far away to see Niv-L's car. The helicopter has buzzed over at a low level, wheeled, and now curves away across the valley. A thin white searchlight stabs the desert floor.

And more distant, miles across the desert, she can see vehicles approaching, jittering lights—red, blue, and yellow, a chorus of sirens faint as an insect's whine.

Behind the ridge the sky is beginning to lighten and she lifts the rucksack. The camera is there in the dirt. She leaves it for the archaeologists and begins walking, trying to put some distance between her and the forces gathering at the highway.

She lets gravity take her down the slope toward the wide valley. She's too exposed up on the slope. Below there are blasted hulks, shell craters full of noxious water. Somewhere she will find a place to hide.

She is walking hard, almost running, but she hasn't eaten since . . . It doesn't matter. She's tired almost immediately and can only keep up the pace for a short spell. But it's still dark in this wide valley, and she keeps trying to push, now, when she can hide in the shadows.

She takes the water in little sips, roiling it about her mouth, letting it trickle down, wetting her T-shirt and clamping it over her nose and mouth . . . just the vapor will keep her cooler. Wouldn't the fierce Wahhabists be proud of her now? She could star in an adventure epic . . . wounded, dying. *Desert Girl—Terror Queen of the Tuareg* . . . She has become a true nomad, her head sheltered from the sun . . . her face and hair covered and no longer giving offense to God.

What can she learn in this silence? Written in the sky: a wide contrail . . . that she realizes is a formation flight of six fighter jets, scratching a yellow scar in the sky.

The wind picks up. Her knees are shaky and her side is either on fire or numb. She can feel her heartbeat pulsing in her throat. She needs more water but she also needs to make it last. She's not running anymore, she's barely staggering. Only halfway across the valley and now she can go no further.

A helicopter is cutting across the desert floor. Pointed straight at her, coming at a tremendous rate of speed. She slumps to the ground, and takes a long drink. Her face is dry and she has pushed herself too hard. There is no food. She is shivering.

The helicopter slams over her, the wind scours the desert around her, the fine alkaline sand stinging her eyes.

Then she hears a radio. Someone talking on a radio.

Someone close by.

She digs the gun out of the pocket of the rucksack, and aims it behind her. Nothing. No one. Or, no one she can see. The helicopter is making a wide circle over the valley and is angling back toward her.

Ahead of her is a blown-apart hulk—what was once a tank, or an armored personnel carrier. A ghost from some past war.

Too tired to run any longer, she crouches in its shadow as the helicopter passes, and once it's gone, she finds a stick and uses it to poke around and scatter the snakes she imagines are nesting in there. There are hatches and holes punched through the armor and she crawls in, waving her stick ahead of her like a blind woman, smooths out a place, and collapses. She will wait out the helicopters here, hide from the radios.

Keep the gun ready and wait.

* * *

The landing wakes him, and a moment later comes the vibration of his cell. He digs it out and puts it between his ear and the cool window of the jet.

"*Hey, Sam.*" It's Marty Grimaldi.

"Hey, kid . . . We just landed. I can see the helicopters . . ."

"*How are you? Did you get some sleep?*"

"I got some . . . daze, is what I would call it."

"*Agent Schumacher wants to patch you in to the deputy sheriff who is on the ground at Vermiglio's location.*"

"Sure. Okay."

"*She does not have any gear beyond her medical kit.*"

"Okay. Who'm I talking to?"

"*It's a deputy sheriff and she's first on scene. She's the one who found the car and is tracking Vermiglio. She's a veteran and is described as very capable. She's had emergency medical training.*"

"Okay."

"*Good . . . I'm going to put you through. Just hold on, Sam.*"

". . . *be advised that you will be receiving special instructions, do you copy?*"

"Copy that."

"*Stand by.*"

Acting Deputy Suárez walks cautiously through the low light of early morning. Blue shadows and a certain thickness to the air. When the helicopter buzzes her side of the ridge, she has to put her finger in her ear to hear. The radios that have been passed out back at the Socorro County HQ are crap, not like the ones they had in Afghanistan with earbuds that would fit under your balaclava, little microphone wands that could pick up a whisper and leave your hands free. No, these are outdated police bricks that you wear on your belt and drop everything you're doing just to use them. Awkward. They slow you down. They endanger you.

The helicopter makes another pass, banking toward the valley, following the slope and raising dust and grit. She turns away, holds her breath, closes her eyes, and keys the microphone.

"This is seven-six. Request copy heli units that friendly is in the area," she shouts into the radio, but there is no response. Those guys tend toward the trigger-happy at the best of times, and in the early light one blur looks like any other.

She has been following Vermiglio's tracks up the side of a low ridge, and down again. She has found the camp where the girl was hiding under a rock shelf, and she has found her camera. Her flashlight is getting dimmer so she snaps it off to save the battery.

The radio has been on constantly, directions and then redirections. Orders and then counterorders. Everybody is squabbling over the jurisdictional turf, and finally she ends up patched in to the White Sands base commander. He's sending out a team of MPs; they'll be there within the hour, he assures her. Less than a minute later someone phones to counter that. The MPs aren't coming at all, stand by to ground-assist a heli-assault unit that's spinning up. Luci is informed, in case she didn't know it, that Vermiglio is a terror suspect and the effort to find her is a Homeland Security matter. She is hot with Berlin. Suárez's mission is to locate Vermiglio, then wait for units to come to her assistance. She turns on her cell phone so they can try to GPS her that way, and switches on the flashlight and waves it until one of the choppers picks her up and drops a box of flares.

"*Seven-six?*"

"Seven-six."

"*Stand by . . .*"

I'm already standing by, she wants to scream. This is the worst she's ever seen it. All these different levels of government. Confusion and then more confusion. Somebody's learning curve caught up in someone else's pissing contest. The radio is a sea of static, and floating in it may be the one crucial message that you'll probably miss if the helicopters are too close.

"*Hello, Deputy?*" It's a different voice. Not the dispatcher, but a man. It sounds like he's been patched in through a new line. She stops and wedges her finger into her free ear. *"Hello?"* says the strange voice. Civilian.

"Roger. I copy."

"Is this Deputy Suárez?"

"Roger that."

"Oh, good. Great. You know about the special instructions?"

"No, sir. Negative on special instructions," she adds, just to prod the voice back to proper procedure.

"This is Watterman here."

"Roger. Are you the negotiator?"

"No, that's me," says a female voice. *"Go ahead, Sam. You're speaking with Deputy Suárez."*

"Okay, thanks. Look, this girl needs to be apprehended alive. It's absolutely crucial." The voice has risen in pitch. Luci can hear the man starting to lose it. *"Whatever you do, don't hurt her."*

"Roger. I copy that," she says.

"We will be evacuating her to a Level 4 quarantined hospital. Uh . . . do you copy?" the man says.

"Roger. I copy."

"Great. Good. Fantastic. Thank you. Alive. Whatever happens, okay, Deputy? We're on our way . . ."

"Sure . . . I got it," she says. "I thought she was armed and dangerous?" she says, but there is no answer.

"Seven-six?" The dispatcher comes on again.

"Seven-six."

"Stand by . . ." the voice says again.

The negotiator comes on the line. Schumacher. She's in another chopper. Watterman is a doctor. He's from CDC, Schumacher says. They're all less than five minutes away, she promises.

Then Watterman again. *"The important thing is not to panic,"* he tells her. Even with a crappy radio she can hear the fear in his voice.

"Stand by . . ."

She follows the girl's path where it skids down the side of the ridge. It looks like Vermiglio is running, trying to get out ahead, not even thinking about somebody following her. It's like she doesn't care, Suárez thinks.

Shapes loom in the darkness. Broken construction equipment, rusted school buses, ancient cars and pickup trucks. Corroding strips of aluminum blasted out of the side of some USAF station wagon. She hears dogs barking. There's probably a canine unit out there somewhere.

In high school, to prepare the class for their visit to the Trinity nuclear test site, they showed a film. A shock film. Like the ones of traffic accidents to warn them about drinking and driving. But in this there was footage of entire houses being blown away by a not-so-divine wind. Trees burnt instantaneously and bent over like straw. A typical living room from the fifties, re-created with all details correct. Department store mannequins standing in for the family. Then the blinding light from the picture window. Even in slow motion it was quick. The shattered glass, the burning skin, and then the shock wave. Everything blown away . . . Down there somewhere, Luci thinks, peering into the shadows of the mountains.

Back at Socorro headquarters the sheriff comes on to ask how she's doing. "Good. I'm good," Luci says. But to be honest, she doesn't know how she's doing. Basically she is in pursuit of an armed and dangerous suicide terrorist who has nothing to lose.

There is a popping over her head and she instinctively goes into a squat. A line of pink flares fall; off-target, bisecting her route. All it does is add to the crazy shadows, and fill the mountainside with hissing that makes it hard to listen for whatever she is approaching.

Someone from the FBI gets patched in. She stops to take it. Ahead of her in the shifting light, she can see several large lumps; the scuff marks from Vermiglio's shoes.

The FBI man is easy. His voice reminds her of the one that pilots use when you're about to take off. Settle back, everything's cool and cowboy. But she's the one on point, so she says as little as possible, and sticks to procedure.

"We're going to redefine the mission," the FBI man says.

"Copy that."

"The important thing is to interrogate her." They will provide the questions. *"Keep her awake, keep her talking. Let her know she can exchange information for her life. . . . You got all that?"*

"Copy," Suárez says.

Another helicopter has joined the team; this one has a spotlight that plays across the scrub below her.

One of the dark lumps is a vehicle, blasted upside down. Squashed against the rocky edge of a crater. It's not a tank, or at least not a modern one she can recognize. It's something else— maybe a fifty-year-old self-propelled howitzer left over from the Vietnam era. Something dragged out there and left for the observers and bombardiers to aim at. The tracks are rusted steel with rubber treads that have split and crumbled. The hatches have been blown out and there are jagged holes gouged through the armor plate.

That's where Vermiglio's tracks go.

"Contact . . ." Luci whispers into the radio.

They land in a great cloud of dust and Sam is pushed out of the helicopter by two Evacs on either side. Both have toy-sized automatic weapons and are wearing the latest in biohazard suits. He hadn't even seen them, these little ninjas, in the shadows when he was loaded into the helicopter. Their faces are sheathed like insects, and they wear tight suits that make them look like lightly armored motorcyclists. There are microphones and cameras built into a ridge atop their armored skullcaps. You can't even see eyes behind their lenses.

They wait while he kneels in the dust and gets on his suit, a typical hazmat bunny suit that has come out of a locker somewhere at White Sands. This is the worst place in the world, he thinks, for a hazmat suit. Thorns, every kind of cacti under the sun. Shards of exploded metal and glass strewn underfoot. He gets his hood latched on, turns on his air, and they all get going again.

Two other helicopters converge on their location. One is the medical chopper that will take the girl to the hospital once they capture her. Farther out he can see a different series of helicopters.

They touch down like mosquitoes to the surface of a puddle, then roar away, and he realizes that they are landing Special Forces out there.

"Tell them to stay back, right? We don't want to scare her. Does everybody copy that?" he says. His voice booms in the hood.

"*Roger,*" Schumacher says, backing him up. "*All personnel are reminded this is a Level 4 biohazard area. Full restriction on that, and full Q and T. Copy?*"

There begins a series of confirmations that are interrupted by a sharp crack. The sound is somewhat dulled by his hood, and Sam blunders ahead a half dozen steps before one of the Evacs yanks him down. "*Gunfire. One shot,*" a voice hisses in his ear.

Ahead he can see the deputy sheriff spring up and move away into the brush.

"We have to take her alive if possible, remember that! Alive!"

He hears a snap. Immediately, welling up through the brush, comes a cloud of red smoke. Another flare fizzes through the air, thrown like a high fly ball to land near the overturned tank.

"*. . . she's up, she's up!*" someone says.

He begins to run, and the Evacs follow him; they cut through the brush, weave around the broken metal obstacles that litter the area. The ground is uneven and cratered. Now that he is past the tank, he can see that the girl has got ahead of them and is running, staggering into the desert.

"No!" he shouts, waving his arms, but she can't hear him. Not with the hood on. He opens it and pushes it back over his head. "No!" he manages to scream, and begins to run toward her.

But she is too far out ahead of them. Maybe fifty yards away. He can see her plainly; she stops and whirls and points a pistol up at the helicopter and squeezes off a shot. A half second later a smaller helicopter, flat-black, hovering behind, spits out a single answering burst of machine-gun fire.

The girl is consumed by dust.

Sam is running, the hard metal seal of the hazmat suit slapping against the back of his skull.

The ground slopes down and he realizes they are heading into a wide riverbed. There is no real water at all, only slightly denser plant life at the bottom of the slope. In his ear, Schumacher is urging, "... *Maintain ... Maintain ...*" over and over.

He gets to the place where they shot her. The dust still hangs in the air. There is what looks like a splotch of something, fluid—blood. Just ahead of him there is a torn-up car, a rusted hulk with a shredded roof. He can see she has fallen inside, splayed out on the floor where the steering wheel ought to be. More blood, a smear down her leg.

"Can you hear me?" he calls.

Thirsty, Daria reaches for her water, but it is gone now.

Everything is new; she looks around the burned-out car, she stares out into the desert. There are animals out there. Birds fleeing. Larger animals too. She can see them moving through the brush.

The wind blows dust and bits of dry desert plants into the side of the car, flat little metallic chimes. The wind swirls and the grit is blown inside, stinging her face.

The world seems to be rocking, as if in a slow-motion earthquake. Smoke drifts by and there is a red fire burning somewhere around her. She can see the many holes that have been slashed through the roof of the car. Hell—she is here. There is no need to go farther.

Now is the time, she decides. In the distance there is thunder. Or maybe it is an explosion, or bullets being spewed from another helicopter. A fog of yellow smoke envelops her. Out there, things are moving in the dirt.

She breathes as deeply as she can, scratches her fingers against the flaking rust of the floor of the car, tries to connect with the nerve endings and get her fingers working. It's like relearning how to walk, but she wills her hand to move until it rests against the grip of the gun.

"*Can you hear me?*" comes a man's voice.

* * *

From inside there is a groan. A rasping sound.

"Can you hear me?" Watterman says again, louder.

"*Is she alive?*" It's Schumacher's voice. "*Seven-six, is the target viable?*" someone asks. The voices are small, like bees buzzing in Sam's ear.

"Daria . . . I've got some water. Do you want some water? I just want to help you, that's all. Just want to make it a little easier, okay?" he says. He needs to get in there, get a look to see how badly she's wounded. He can do this, he tells himself.

Nothing. Just that raspy breathing. He takes a step forward, and then another, moving until he can see her better—slumped down in the shot-up derelict, leaning against the firewall, with her hand on an automatic. The weapon is resting on her stomach and she is breathing.

He holds the water bottle out to her. "I've got some water with me. Can I just leave it right here?"

There is no answer. He can see her plainly now. A great brown stain on her side. She's filthy, her clothes are torn, bloody. Her hair is matted and her skin is yellow and scratched. Somehow, incredibly, she's only been hit by a fragment, maybe a stone or maybe steel splinters. Surely if one of the high-caliber rounds from the helicopter had hit her, she would be jelly. Still . . . something has punctured her skin, little punctures in at least three places that he can see. They have antipersonnel rounds they can fire—little flechettes for crowd control—is that what they used? Is she still breathing? She's hot. Level 4, with Khan's superpox. Too late, now. Get in, get a line into her, he remembers.

"Okay, I'm just going to bring this to you, okay? No strings at-tached. Don't shoot me. I'm not going to hurt you." He reaches into the door of the car and places the water on the broken rusted floor where the seat ought to be.

"*Watch yourself, Sam . . .*" he hears Schumacher say.

"This is just water. Here, look, I'll drink some too. It doesn't have anything in it. You have to keep up your fluids, Daria. Here you go . . ." He swallows, reaches across the transmission tunnel and places the bottle on the floor beside her. "Okay?"

Now that he's closer he sees that she's cut—once across her stomach, and a slash on her thigh—an ugly cut right down to the muscle that is seeping blood. It's not enough, somehow. There has to be more after a burst of gunfire like that. He tries to see behind her, but can't find any pool of blood, no arterial blood spurting. She stares at him as he cranes his neck and tries to inspect all around her.

"You're bleeding, okay? You're in shock and we need to get you some first aid. Right away," he promises. There is another flurry of buzzing in his earbud, and he realizes what he has just said has been interpreted as some kind of permission.

"*Sam, back out of there, give it some time,*" Schumacher murmurs in his ear. But he can't do that. She's hurt. And he doesn't want to lose her. He *can't* lose her. So far, he hasn't had to touch her. Maybe it will be all right. The girl is shaking her head slowly from side to side. Words gurgle out of her mouth. Maybe she can't speak English.

"We're going to take care of you." He tries to be like Schumacher, supercasual, and even sits back on the rusted floor across the car from her. Behind her, the two Evacs have crept up. One of them holds a black nylon bag with a red cross prominently displayed on its side.

"I know Saleem Khan. I know what he did. I know what he gave you, Daria. I think I know how to cure it, or at least slow it down. But for that we need you."

The girl's face collapses, and she coughs.

"Didn't you get a shot in Berlin? Or an . . . inoculation, where they scrape a place, a little place on your shoulder? Or maybe Khan gave you an injection?" he says, miming the action in his biceps like an addict. It sounds like Mr. Rogers trying to explain a morality tale to a small child. He waits to see if she will nod. She only looks up at him, eyes like a dog to its master.

"Well, the shot had something in it. A . . . an antidote. Do you know what I mean when I say 'antidote'? It's a cure. It gives you an immunity . . ." And as her eyes roll back, "No, no . . . please don't," he pleads. "*Please.* There's a medical team for you right here."

For a moment he falls silent and they study each other. He stares into the dark eyes of this mass murderer. A monster. She looks nothing like the pictures, and he is suddenly aware of how small she is. A waif. Now she is going to die and cheat them all. Couldn't he just leap over the rusting transmission tunnel and grab the gun before she could use it? He feels his muscles tensing. Why not? What does he have to live for anymore? Everything that's any good has been ripped out of his life. He should have stayed at home with Maggie. Maybe if he had said no . . . He should have told Roycroft on the conference call that he'd been warning them about this for a quarter century and was, yes, retired, goddamn it. . . .

"You know what you've done, don't you? You do understand it all? Don't you?"

She lifts her head, stares into his eyes.

"And . . . you know what's going to happen, that perhaps millions of people are going to die. You know that." She begins to tremble and her eyes are full of tears. But there could be a million reasons for that.

"In Berlin, did Khan tell you? Did you know?" he says. His jaw is so tight it hurts.

"*Deep breath, Sam . . . stay positive . . . tell her we can help her.*"

"Even . . . if you did, still . . . we can help you. Instead of . . . well, starting now you can save lives. You can repay for what you've done. Just . . . put the gun down. Please. Then the medics can have a look at you . . . ?"

But the girl doesn't put the gun down.

By now they have had plenty of time to set up, Suárez knows. By now they have tagged her, at least two of them from different angles. If the girl puts down the gun, she lives. Anything else, well . . . maybe the "special instructions" or whatever the fuck it is will prevail in a case like this, but . . . anything else, the terrorist bitch is meat.

The second negotiator comes up to kneel behind Watterman. They are both talking to the girl now. Bribes. Guarantees. Whatever they can dream up to disarm her.

From where Suárez hovers by the rear fender of the vehicle, she can see the girl, see her hand on the automatic. It rests across her stomach; she will have to raise her arm to point it at the negotiators. If there're two snipers that have tagged her, even if the guy with the shot can't see her gun hand, and the other can, they can work it off a voice command.

This is where they have to have patience, Suárez is thinking. This is where all the testosterone and adrenaline start to become a liability. The smart thing to do is for everyone to fuck off out of there, drop back a hundred yards and wait it out. Sooner or later she'll want a pizza. Suárez turns and looks around to see if she can see where they've set up. If she edges up the fender any closer, she'll probably mess up their angle, so she duckwalks back a couple of steps and crouches by the blown-off rear axle.

There's more crap on the radio. Unnecessary crap. They're all lucky to be alive. And the girl's a Berlin carrier. Fantastic timing, Suárez. To have come all this way. Fought, just about been killed more than once. Had a double helping of shit and got through it and adjusting fine and now something like this.

"You know there is no choice, don't you?" she hears the doctor say.

Burning.

The fire is all around her. She can feel her cells bursting open, exploding. She loses and regains consciousness with each shallow breath.

"Can you hear me?"

Does she make a beautiful picture? Will she leave a splendid corpse? Will teenage girls cry when they get to this part in the movie?

In death, as told in Islamic tradition, does her rotting flesh have the fragrance of musk?

She has murdered. Murdered *children*. Innocent children. She has ruined families and destroyed everything around her. And now she is destroyed herself. There is a sound. A low cry that comes and goes, a dark animal sound. Over and over it comes to her, until she realizes that the sound is coming from her mouth.

The world begins to move again.

A face is there, a devil staring at her. They are going to ferry her down to hell. They are calling to her. Yes, yes, she can hear them. She tries to trick the devil, tries to lift the gun, tries to fight back and kill it, if only to demonstrate that she hates them, hates the demons, hates being one herself . . . hates the long road that has led her into their company.

She tries to get up. To do it she has to use the barrel of the gun to raise herself up and get to her knees and get out. She has no breath. Light-headed. Dizzy.

Daria twists away, tries to get her legs to work. The man reaches to help her. He manages to grab her wrist but she yanks away, and he overreaches and falls across the rusted floor of the car, as she struggles to a standing position.

She can read the frustration and pain on his face. He wants to play the part of her ally. It seems that he is another of the damned. Just like her, a citizen of the underworld. Poor man, she thinks. Poor old man. Watching him scrabble around at her ankles. If there were more time, she would help him.

Whatever the helicopter did to her, she can hardly breathe. There is a rumbling in her lungs. For a moment she sees spots on the desert floor, and lurches back against the jagged metal of the fender.

She can never relive her life, no matter what her schoolmates told her. She can never unmake this path. Choices, decisions, even accidents, are like a tree's roots in time, one branching into two, two into five . . . on and on. The old man wants to save her life, but . . . her *life* . . . is nothing really. Not nearly as valuable as little Daniel's . . .

Right in front of her there are two devils. They are pretending to be from the Red Cross, but any fool can easily see that in actuality they are insects, gargoyles. They crouch at her feet. She can see their mouths moving, hear their insect voices.

Well, she will not let them have her. She will deny them the pleasure. In the end they are just perverts, torturers, and hired thugs. They assume now that she's wounded they'll have an easy time of it. Why even waste firing a shot? Instead they are trying to lure her into giving up her last sting.

And the old man, offering her forgiveness. Who is he? A friend of Khan's? This qualifies him to forgive?

"It's not possible," she says. It comes out like a groan and she coughs and there is blood, flecks of it flying out of her and down onto the dust.

"We're going to take care of you."

"Pull it back," she hears the other negotiator say. *"Pull it back, Sam—"*

But as she struggles to stand, he decides to jump her, to leap straight toward the gun. But there is no spring to his legs anymore and he knows he'll fail. Still, he is up on one knee, almost ready, and after all, he's closest to her. But there's that voice ordering him to back out. Slowly. Everything is under control.

"Pull it back, Sam . . ."

"Is there a surgeon? Is he prepped? Is he ready to go? Does anybody copy that?" he says. "Please . . ." Across her chest a red dot hovers. If she dies, they need her blood and they need her spleen. They've been told that. They'll have to do it right here, or at best in the helicopter.

"Back out, Sam . . ." Schumacher is saying, her voice implacable.

There is a great heaving in her chest, and the world grows dark . . .

She hears their voices again. A helicopter is near. The crackle of sand and gravel being blown against the metal of the car.

There is no victory.

There is no triumph.

There is no redemption. No omens, incantations, or magic spells that can heal these wounds.

There is no paradise.

There is no prophet. No messiah, no virgin. No adequate revenge, no sufficient penance. No vessel large enough to hold the tears.

There is no love.

No grace or blessing. No burning bush. Only men striding through blowing sand. They grab and they spend and they go about the world spreading their seed and justifying every dream that comes into their minds. Win or lose, they will laugh and celebrate and pretend to pray.

Noise. All noise, like sand in the wind. She can hear their feet against the earth. The old man grovels below her, her only mourner. Thank you, she wants to say. She can see his face—torn with a fear unimaginable. She can hear the chorus of their excited, synthetic voices. She raises the dead trooper's pistol.

There is no God.

The time is now and she already has her mouth open to receive the bullet.

The gunshot shatters the bones of her shoulder, and the destroyed arm is flung back uselessly as she spins backwards, slapping into the rough metal of the door. And now there is the spurting of arterial blood, and the medics pounce on her.

Sam clambers through the broken car, too late to catch her as she crumples, and then tries to cover her with his body, they must not fire again . . . but immediately the medics have pushed him away. "Get a line into her," he screams.

He moves to her head, tries to lift her so that the medics can do their work. All around on the ground, her blood. To lift her he has to reach around her, has to hold her, has to *cradle her in his arms* . . .

She is light as a feather. Warm. Only bones. Dust-covered, smelling of infection, and swarming with ants. She groans as they move her, a great stain of pus and blood spreading across her T-shirt. Wounded when she killed the cop, he remembers.

She opens her mouth, trying to talk. Fragments of words . . . groans . . .

". . . *surrender* . . ." he hears her say. ". . . *surrender* . . ." Staring up at him, her eyes trying to focus—too late for that. Too late.

They have a line in. Everything rushing. No time at all.

Watterman presses the water bottle to the girl's lips; the eyes slowly begin to roll up. Dying. Dead. Shaking her. No breathing, no pulse.

Later he will look back and think that he must have made some kind of a decision, but as it happens in the actual moment, he doesn't think at all. A heartbeat—not even that—and he bends down, arches the girl's neck, and begins breathing into her. Two breaths and compressing, *one-two-three*. And again. Breathing for her.

The Evacs are rushing around and it's like every grade-B movie ever scripted, like an overeager, out-of-control rehearsal. Oh, God . . . *fool*. Yes, he thinks, smallpox. Now it's done. Now it's over, breathing for her, pounding on her heart. Someone is shouting—Schumacher shoves her way in and helps to hold the girl up. "Don't go, don't go . . ." she is saying.

Breathing for her, breathing for her. Feeling the girl's shoulders heave, her heart fluttering, the barest clutch of her fingers, reaching for the bottle to give her the promised reward of water. The girl's eyes flicker, rolling back into life, struggling to focus.

"Don't go. Stay with us. Stay with us, Daria . . ."

Black-clad medics all around. Everyone is suited up and breathing bottled oxygen. Whoever is in charge has decided she has to be dragged out of there, right away, so they load her onto a stretcher.

Breathing for her.

Khan's superpox.

They are carrying Vermiglio out and he goes along, clinging to the stretcher. They have the precious line in her now.

It's not far . . . only a dozen yards to the helicopters, but they don't even get that far before she goes into cardiac arrest. They have to stop, put her down, clear, and defibrillate her. Sam stands back, shivering, shaking. They do it again and she comes back, and they hoist her up and begin to run toward the medical chopper.

"We need her blood. We need as much of her blood as we can get," he shouts to the medic running alongside him. They know that. They know that already, he reminds himself. The girl is back from the dead, staring up at him. "Who's the surgeon?" he asks the man beside him. "Did they brief you?"

One of the Evacs comes forward as they get to the helicopter.

"I'm briefed. We can recover from her whenever we need to," the Evac says. There is a pause as they get a second line into her and begin to lift her, almost tenderly, into the machine.

"Can you do it in here?" Watterman demands. They are harnessing the gurney to the floor.

"Yes, sir, we can do it as we go."

Strong hands pull him inside with her. He is dizzy from the exertion of running up the slope. Her eyes try to focus and follow him. Her lips are moving. There is a whirl of smoke and dust as the pilot throttles up. Outside he sees the deputy—Suárez—crouching in the dust, one arm raised, thumb up.

". . . *Target is viable,*" someone is saying on the radio.

"*Roger that, Tango.*"

"*Excellent . . . fantastic . . .*" a voice says.

"Do it," Sam says.

The surgeon looks up at him.

"Do it," he repeats. "Do it now."

"She's still alive."

"Not for long. Get ready." They've got the second line into her. How much can they take before she dies? There are already two bags and one of the medics has started on a third. It won't be long. They are readying the cold packs.

The third bag is done, a moment later a fourth. No, it will not be long, he thinks.

They roar upward; radio traffic, the helicopter's engine screaming, the dust storm falling away behind them. Watterman is beside her on the floor. "It's over now," he tells her. "It's over. You can rest . . ."

Five.

In one of the pouches of the first-aid bag, there is a plastic bottle of rubbing alcohol, and Watterman claws it out, uncaps it, takes a big swig and washes his mouth out, spits, and then does it again and again. When he gets down to the bottom, he pours what's left of the alcohol over his face, inhales some in his nose, and rubs and rubs it into his skin.

Another bag is done and he sees her watching him rub the stinging alcohol over his face.

He pulls himself closer. The girl's face is slack; she blinks slowly, staring up at him. Her skin is pale . . . almost yellow. Her mouth hangs open as if she were starving.

"I'm sorry," Sam says.

Across the barriers of race and nations, of cultures and religions clashing, they face each other. What does she see, he wonders? An old man, a balding, big-nosed Jew, a scientist, an infidel, a vampire?

And what does he see? A filthy terrorist, a murderer of innocents. A deluded, fanatical Islamist dupe. In the end, just a young woman dying. Just a girl. A young woman dying needlessly. Needlessly.

Seven.

They have her blood now. Yes, the quarantine laws will melt away. Somehow order will be restored. The best scientists in the world will collaborate and eventually there will be a cure. The Khans of this world will be hunted down and made to atone. The genie will be frightened back into its flask, and there will be an end to the killing. Children will laugh again. People will take off their masks and go back to work.

He leans against the throbbing wall of the helicopter. They are flying over the broken mountains, the blasted desert.

"We have to isolate you, sir," one of the medics says.

Yes, he thinks. You do. The girl turns, is he going away? Her face is open, and for a moment he stares into her eyes. He is trembling, why? He does not know, it is beyond . . . He can only grasp her hand and feel her fingers flutter.

The helicopter banks above the spinning lights of the airfield at White Sands. One of the Evacs is checking her now, searching for a final heartbeat.

He can feel her fingers relax as she dies. The surgeon begins his first cut, and Watterman looks until he has to look away.

They slowly descend to the concrete. There are emergency vehicles waiting and a medical jet that will be taking them to a hot ward in Albuquerque. Everything is flashing. At least a dozen ambulances and biohazard vehicles are pulled up below them. Faces turned up, expectant behind their masks. The pilot has been told to stop the hotdogging and take it slow. Surgeon's orders.

A splenectomy doesn't take long if you don't have to worry about anesthesia or blood loss, and they are finished with her now. Almost. They might get something from her liver and there is maybe another unit they can recover by pumping her system.

The spleen will be full of B cells. Priceless. It won't take that long to clone from it. If they can get into gear soon, they'll be able to mass-manufacture plasma. You can clone those B cells in cows, milk their blood, and grow them in vats until the antisense is ready.

He climbs down from the helicopter, staggers. He is exhausted, sweating, and his stomach, normally strong, is woozy from the flying.

". . . good job, everybody. Great job, Sam . . ." Schumacher calls to him. She is still hooded. And they wait together while what's left of Daria Vermiglio's body is slid into a biohazard bag and packed into a sealed ambulance. Beyond the cordon of emergency vehicles, he can see Barrigar and Grimaldi. There are camera crews hastily setting up behind the barriers manned by a line of military police.

There is something wrong with his hearing.

His hands and feet are spray-washed by a two-person decontamination team. He holds his arms out and dutifully spins around as they work around him. Shakes his head.

Still . . . all his hearing is gone. It's all just reduced to a distant blur.

Now he is being led to the ambulance by one of the masked Evacs. The spleen and the bags of blood are in coolers. It's okay. It's over. Everything is done. In the end, it was him. He was the chosen one, the only one who could do what he did. It was his fate. Fate put him in that situation and . . . and at least he tried. He tried. And now it's over and his part is done, and for now all is right with the world, then.

He walks across the concrete loose-ankled, as if treading on slow-motion pillows. His skin stings and there is salt in his eyes. Above him, the heavens are shaking, and everyone stops to look up as an elite team of fighter jets overfly them. A tsunami of sound crashes over the crowd as the pilots break apart into the newly risen sun.

He can hear now. It's all coming back. Ahead the maw of the darkened ambulance awaits. From behind the barricades there are cheers—citizens and soldiers shouting encouragement, blessings, applause, reminders, battle cries, short angry chants, laughter and declarations of love and rage, and promises always to remember.

We have won.

SOURCES AND ACKNOWLEDGMENTS

The Messenger is fiction but it is not fantasy. Bioterror is not only possible, it is cheap, technologically feasible, and, in its opening stages, almost undetectable. That a large-scale bioterror attack has not yet occurred in North America is simply good luck. Billions have been spent in the United States alone, but the threat shows no signs of easing. To make matters worse, the "solution" in this book—serum therapy—might well be ineffective against genetically engineered pathogens.

The most popular English-language source for those wanting more on biological hazards is the work of Richard Preston. Preston became famous for his excellent *The Hot Zone* (New York: Anchor Books, 1995), which concerns the Ebola virus. More relevant for me was his equally excellent *The Demon in the Freezer* (New York: Ballantine Books, 2002), for the production and history of smallpox and anthrax, as well as a discussion of IL-4 gene manipulation and the Ramshaw-Jackson mousepox experiments. For readers looking for a good bioterror thriller I recommend Preston's *The Cobra Event* (New York: Ballantine Books, 1997).

Regarding smallpox:

For the harrowing dimensions of U.S. and Soviet biowarfare efforts, and the likelihood that both technology and samples could migrate, see *Biohazard: The Chilling True Story of the Largest Covert Biological Weapons Program in the World—Told from the Inside by the Man Who Ran It,* by Ken Alibek, with Stephen Handelman (New York: Random House, 1999). An essential.

Other recommendations:

Guillemin, Jeanne. *Biological Weapons: From the Invention of State-Sponsored Programs to Contemporary Bioterrorism.* New York: Columbia University Press, 2005.

Koblentz, Gregory D. *Living Weapons: Biological Warfare and International Security.* Ithaca, NY: Cornell University Press, 2009. Comprehensive.

Miller, Judith, Stephen Engelberg, and William Broad. *Germs: Biological Weapons and America's Secret War.* New York: Simon & Schuster, 2001. The team who first broke the story of Project Bacchus.

Regis, Ed. *The Biology of Doom: The History of America's Secret Germ Warfare Project.* New York: Henry Holt and Co., 1999.

For historical antecedents:

Barenblatt, Daniel. *A Plague upon Humanity: The Secret Genocide of Axis Japan's Germ Warfare Operation.* New York: HarperCollins, 2004.

Coen, Bob, and Eric Nadler. *Dead Silence: Fear and Terror on the Anthrax Trail.* New York: Counterpoint, 2009. For more on Project Coast.

Koenig, Robert. *The Fourth Horseman: One Man's Secret Campaign to Fight the Great War in America.* New York: Public Affairs, 2006.

On terror and terrorists:

Carr, Caleb. *The Lessons of Terror: A History of Warfare Against Civilians.* New York: Random House, 2003.

Cohen, Jared. *Children of Jihad: A Young American's Travels among the Youth of the Middle East.* New York: Gotham, 2007.

Fidler, David P., and Lawrence O. Gostin. *Biosecurity in the Global Age: Biological Weapons, Public Health and the Rule of Law.* Stanford, CA: Stanford University Press, 2008.

LoCicero, Alice, and Samuel J. Sinclair. *Creating Young Martyrs: Conditions That Make Dying in a Terrorist Attack Seem Like a Good Idea.* Westport, CT: Praeger, 2008.

Even an old map can help get you where you want to go; mine was *American Map Road Atlas 2005* (Maspeth, NY: American Map Corporation). Cartography copyright by MapQuest, Inc. Plus thanks to Google Earth's street view.

For more about the Ug99 fungus, see Brendan I. Koerner's "Red Menace: Stop the Ug99 Fungus Before Its Spores Bring Starvation," in *Wired,* March 2010. For more on antisense, see David E. Hoffman's "Going Viral: The Pentagon Takes on a New Enemy: Swine Flu," in *The New Yorker,* January 31, 2011, p. 26.

My portrait of Brush Creek has been adjusted for dramatic effect, and everything about 3050 is fictional. Tony Rizzo's series in the *Kansas City Star* was very helpful: "Murder Factory, Part 1: 64130, the ZIP Code of Notoriety in Missouri," January 24, 2009; "Part 2: Decades of Blight Leave ZIP Code 64130 Reeling in Violence," January 25, 2009; "Part 3: KC Needs to Fight Back and 'Close' the Factory," January 26, 2009.

Sayyid Qutb did much of his writing in prison. His revulsion of North American culture includes lawn care, haircuts, greed, and narcissism, and he insisted that most of the world is in *jaljilla,* a pre-Islamic state of mind—so deluded you don't know you're deluded. *Milestones* (often titled *Signposts on the Way*) is considered his greatest work. Qutb is the subject of the BBC documentary *The*

Power of Nightmares: The Rise of the Politics of Fear, which discusses the philosophical mirror between Qutb and Leo Strauss, mentor of Irving Kristol and his son, William, Paul Wolfowitz, Donald Rumsfeld, et al.

My description of White Sands Missile Range was inspired by the eerie photographs by Richard Misrach in *Bravo 20: The Bombing of the American West* (with Myriam Weisang Misrach; Baltimore: Johns Hopkins University Press, 1990). The Bravo 20 site is in Nevada.

Everything in this book is fictional, and all mistakes are my fault or the fault of my characters. Many institutions, television programs, celebrities, political personalities, nations, businesses, networks, and locations are mentioned, but none should be confused with their real counterparts. *Klic!* magazine does not exist, and there is no business named Seyylol AG. Niv-L is fictional and so is his license plate. The shelter in Louisville is a fantasy. Daria is a fictional composite of attitudes and experiences, and her origins have been deliberately obscured so that she should not be perceived as representing any specific group or nationality.

While Sam Watterman's career debacle is similar to that of Stephen Hatfill's—the USAMRIID scientist who successfully sued the FBI after he was wrongly named as a person of interest in the Amerithrax investigations—Watterman is an entirely fictional character. For a good summary of the FBI's anthrax investigation, see another *Wired* article, "The Strain," by Noah Shachtman, April 2011, pp. 122–36.

A debt of thanks with accrued interest is owed my partner, Suzie Payne, for her support and insight all through the entire process. To my brother, the endlessly creative Richard Miller; to Kate Miciak, my astute editor at Random House; and to Denise Bukowski for being my lifeline to the business. I owe a great debt to my friend, filmmaker Daniel Conrad, for his close readings and advice regarding Sam Watterman, plus a free cram course in microbiology 101.

To my son, for helping me see many things that should be obvious, but aren't. To Jason Rody, Noel Neeb, Lesleh Donaldson, and Denise Bukowski, for their help with New York locations.

Edda Onesti is captain of the ever-growing Italian squad: Francesco Belardetti, Alessandra Bava, Gina Bastone, Albarosa Simonetti, and Nina Vdb, with ambassadors B. J. Clayden, Jane Stokes, and Lesleh Donaldson. Many thanks to Susanne Schwager for ongoing German lessons.

Thanks to the staff of *Calhoun's,* to the librarians at the University of British Columbia, and to a few people who may prefer not to be named. Also many thanks to Jim Prier, Suzanne and Miles Walker, Brenda Leadlay, Elaine Avila, David Petersen, Ty Haller, John and Carolyn Carter, the Drinking Club, and Andy Toth, for readings, references, corrections, ideas, coffee, opinions, inspiration, and encouragement.

A complete list of sources consulted for *The Messenger* is posted on stephenmillerwriter.com

Finally . . . I have logged thousands of miles on Amtrak and consider myself a dedicated fan. I've had some wonderful continental voyages, and while I have sometimes been late, I have only had a few experiences with bored, snarky, or overworked staff in all those trips. It seems a small price to avoid flying.

ABOUT THE AUTHOR

North Carolina born and raised, STEPHEN MILLER is an actor on stage, film, and television as well as the author of plays, screenplays, and novels. Unforgettable moments in his acting career include swimming with Hume Cronyn, improvising for a day with Robert De Niro, carrying Bette Davis down a flight of concrete stairs, stunt-driving with Burt Reynolds, and delivering Laura Dern's child, as well as three appearances on *The X-Files*. The author of five previous novels, Miller is currently at work on his next novel.

www.stephenmillerwriter.com

ABOUT THE TYPE

This book was set in Sabon, a typeface designed by the well-known German typographer Jan Tschichold (1902–74). Sabon's design is based upon the orginial letter forms of Claude Garamond and was created specifically to be used for three sources: foundry type for hand composition, Linotype, and Monotype. Tschichold named his typeface for the famous Frankfurt typefounder Jacques Sabon, who died in 1580.